In the Hall of the Mountain King

"Liar. Foreigner. Priestess' bastard. Ianon groans at the thought of such a king," said Prince Moranden, facing his rival, the Sun-priest Mirain.

"Ianon," said Prince Mirain, "no. Only Moranden, whose soul gnaws itself in rage that he cannot have a throne."

Moranden fell upon him, mad-enraged, possessed, it did not matter. Mirain went down, and then darkness swept between scarlet and fallen white, severing them. The deep voice of the king spoke with softness more devastating than any bellow of rage. "Get out!"

Moranden staggered, face slack with shock, and crumpled to his knees. The king met his son's eyes; the younger man flinched. "Moranden of Ianon is dead. Begone, nameless one, or die like the hound you are."

Moranden looked around. Every back was turned to him. Laughter escaped him. "Such is the justice of Ianon. So I am condemned. Without defense, without recourse."

The king stood still. Mirain and Moranden between them had forced him to choose. It was bitter, bitter. But Moranden knew only what he had always known: that he was not the one his father loved. A black rage swept over him.

"A curse upon you all!" He spun in a flare of scarlet. A torch caught a last blood-red gleam, and he was gone, into the outer darkness.

Also by Judith Tarr
published by Tor Books

JUDITH TARR

THE HALL OF THE
VOLUME
ONE OF
AVARYAN RISING
MOUNTAIN
KING

TOR®

A TOM DOHERTY ASSOCIATES BOOK
NEW YORK

THE HALL OF THE MOUNTAIN KING

Copyright © 1986 by Judith Tarr

A TOR Book

Published by Tom Doherty Associates, Inc.
49 West 24 Street
New York, NY 10010

Cover art by Robert Gould

ISBN: 0-812-55607-0   Can. ISBN: 0-812-55608-9

First edition: November 1986
First mass market printing: September 1988

Printed in the United States of America

0 9 8 7 6 5 4 3 2 1

**For
Meredith**

A Note on Pronunciation

With regard to the pronunciation of the names herein, the most useful rule is that of medieval Latin, with the addition of English *J* and *Y*. To be precise:

•Consonants are essentially as in English. *C* and *G* are always hard, as in *can* and *gold*, never soft as in *cent* and *gem*. *S* is always as in *hiss*, never as in *his*.

•Vowels are somewhat different from the English. *A* as in *father:* Vadin is VAH-deen. *E* as in French *fée:* Elian as AY-lee-ahn; Han-Gilen is hahn-gee-LAYN. *I* is much as the English *Y:* consider *hymn* and the suffix *-ly*, and the consonantal *yawn;* hence, Ianon is YAH-non, Mirain is mee-RAYN, Alidan is ah-LEE-dahn. *O* as in *oh*, never as in *toss*. *U* as in Latin, comparable to English *oo (look, loom):* Uveryen is oo-VER-yen, Umijan is OO-mee-jahn.

•*Y* can be either vowel or consonant, as in English; before a vowel is it is a consonant (Avaryan is ah-VAHR-yan, Odiya is OH-dee-yah), but before a consonant it is a vowel (Ymin is EE-min, Yrios is EE-ree-ohss).

•*Ei* is pronounced as in *reign* (Geitan is GAY-tahn); *ai*, except in the archaic and anomalous *Mirain* (see above), is comparable to the English *bye:* Abaidan is ah-BYE-dahn. Otherwise, paired vowels are pronounced separately: Amilien is ah-MEE-lee-en.

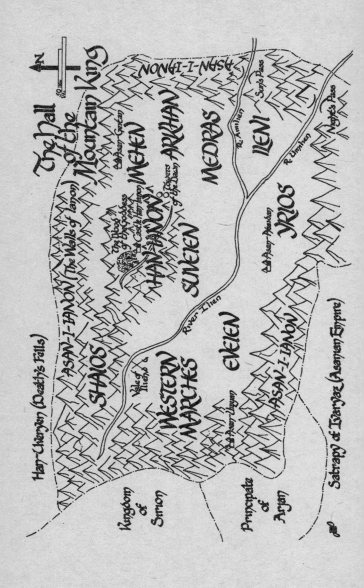

One

THE OLD KING STOOD UPON THE BATTLEMENTS, GAZING southward. The wind whipped back his long white hair and boomed in his heavy cloak. But his eyes never blinked, his face never flinched, as stern and immovable as an image carved in obsidian.

The walls fell sheer below him, stone set on stone, castle and crag set in the green Vale, field and forest rolling into the mountain bastions of his kingdom. North and west and south, the wall of lofty peaks was unbroken. In the east lay the Gate of Han-Ianon, the pass which was the only entrance to the heart of his realm. On either side of it rose the Towers of the Dawn. Gods had built them long ages ago, or so it was said; built them and departed, leaving them as a monument, the wonders of the north. They were tall and they were unassailable, and they were beautiful, wrought of stone as rare as it was wonderful. Silver-grey under stars or moons, silver-white in the sun, in the dawn it glowed with all the colors of the waking sky: white and silver and rose, blood-red and palest emerald. That same stone glimmered still under his feet although it was full morning, the sun poised above the distant Towers. An omen, the priests would say, that the dawnstone had kept its radiance so long. Against all reason, against all the years of hopeless hope, he yearned to believe in it.

*   *   *

FROM HIS POST AT THE SOUTHERN GATE VADIN COULD SEE
the lone still figure dwarfed by height and distance. Every
morning it stood there between sunrise and the second
hour, in every weather, even in the dead of winter; it had
stood so for years, people said, more years than Vadin
had been alive.

He swallowed a yawn. Although sentry duty was the
least strenuous office of a royal squire, it was also the least
engrossing. And he was short on sleep; he had been at
liberty last night, he and two more of the younger squires,
and they had drunk and diced and drunk some more,
and he had had a run of luck. In the end he had won first
go at the girl. This time, at the thought of her, it was a
smile that he swallowed.

Swallowed hard and as close to invisibly as he could.
Old Adjan the arms master asked very little of the young
hellions in his charge. Merely absolute obedience to his
every command, absolute perfection in hall and on the
practice field, and absolute stillness while on guard. One's
eyes might move within the sheltering helmet; one might,
at regular intervals, pace from portal to portal of the gate,
which was when one could glance upward at the flutter of
black that was the king. For the rest, one made oneself an
image of black stone and lacquered bronze, and made
certain that one observed every flicker of movement about
one's post. It had been excruciating at first, that stillness.
Raw boy that he had been, brought up wild in his father's
castle in the hills of Imehen, he had imagined no torture
greater than that of standing in armor with his spear at
one precise angle and no other, hour upon hour, while
the sun beat down upon his head or the rain lashed his
face or the wind bit him to the bone. Now it was merely
dull. He had learned to take his ease while seeming to
stand at rigid attention, and to set his eyes to their task of
observation while letting his mind wander as it would.
Now and then it would wander back to his eyes' labor,
contemplating the people who passed to and fro in the
town below. Some approached the castle, urchins staring
at the great tall guards in their splendid livery, one at

each of the lesser gates and half a company at the Gate of Gods that faced the east; at servants and sightseers and the odd nobleman passing within or going out. At the very beginning of Vadin's watch, the Prince Moranden himself had ridden out with a goodly company of lords and attendants, armed and accoutered for the hunt. The king's son had had a glance for the lanky lad on guard, a flicker of recognition, a quick smile. A proud man, the prince, but never too proud to take notice of a squire.

Vadin glanced at the sun. Not long now before Kav came to relieve him. Then an hour of mounted drill and an hour at swordplay, and he was to wait on the king tonight. A signal honor, that last, rarely granted to any squire in his first year of service. Adjan had been sour when he announced it, but Adjan was always sour; more to the point, the old soldier had appended no biting sarcasm. He had only growled, "Pick up your jawbone, boy, and stop dawdling. It's almost sunup." Which meant that he was pleased with his newest and most callow recruit, gods alone knew why; but Vadin had learned not to argue with fortune.

While his mind reflected, his eye had been recording on its own, independent of his will. The Lady Odiya's elderly maid scuttling on an errand; an elder of the council with his followers; a gaggle of farmfolk come to market, taking time to gape at the glowing wonder of the castle. As they wandered back down toward the town, they left one behind, a man who stood still in the road's center and stared up at the battlements.

No, not a man. A boy perhaps Vadin's own age, perhaps a year or two younger for his beard was just beginning, very erect and very proud and patently no rustic. He could not but be Ianyn, blackwood-dark as he was, yet he was got up like a southerner in coat and trousers, with a southern shortsword at his side. Vadin would have called him a paradox but for the flame of gold at his throat, the torque of a priest of the Sun, and the broad white browband that marked him an initiate on his seven years' Journey. This one was young for it, but not overly

so; and it explained the Ianyn face atop the dress of the
Hundred Realms. No doubt the trousers were a penance
for some infraction.

The priest left off his staring and began to walk, drawing closer to the gate. Vadin blinked. The world had gone
out of focus. Or else—

If Vadin's training had been beaten into him even a
little less thoroughly, he would have laughed. This boy
with the face of a mountain lord, who carried himself as if
he had been as high as all Han-Ianon, was hardly bigger
than a child. The closer he came, the smaller he seemed.
Then he raised his eyes, and Vadin's breath caught. They
were full of—they blazed with—

They flicked away. He was only a ragged priest in
trousers, standing not even shoulder-high to Vadin. And
Vadin was flogging himself awake. The boy was almost
through the gate. With haste that would have won a scowl
from the arms master, Vadin thrust out his spear to bar
the way. The stranger halted. He was not frightened; he
was not visibly angry. If anything, he seemed amused.

Gods, but he was haughty. Vadin mustered his harshest
tone, which was also his deepest, booming out in most
satisfactory fashion. "Hold, stranger, in the king's name.
Come you out of the Hundred Realms?"

"Yes." The priest's voice was as startling as his eyes, a
full octave deeper than Vadin's but eerily clear, with the
soft vowels of the south. "I do."

"Then I must conduct you to his majesty." At once, the
order went, without exception, without regard for any
other order or duty. Beneath the stoic mask of the guard,
Vadin was beginning to enjoy himself. He had the immense satisfaction of collaring an armed warrior, a full
knight to boot, and ordering him—with all due respect—to
hold the gate until Vadin or his relief should come. "King's
business," he said, careful not to sound too cheerful.
"Standing order." The man did not need to ask which
one. The torque and the trousers made it obvious.

Their bearer looked on it all with the merest suggestion
of a smile. When Vadin would have led him he managed
to set himself in the lead, striding forward without hesita-

tion, asking no direction. He had a smooth hunter's stride, barely swaying the black braid that hung to his waist behind him, and surprisingly fast. Vadin had to stretch his long legs to keep pace.

THE KING TURNED HIS FACE TOWARD THE CRUEL SUN. AGAIN it was climbing to its zenith, again it brought him no hope. Once he would have cursed it, but time had robbed him of rage as of so much else. Even the omen of the dawnstone meant nothing. She would not return.

"My lord."

Habit and kingship brought him about slowly, with royal dignity. One of his squires stood before him in the armor of a gate guard. The newest one, the lordling from Imehen, for whom Adjan had such unwontedly high hopes. He was standing straight and soldierly, a credit to his master. "Sire," he said clearly enough, if somewhat stiffly, "a traveler has come from the Hundred Realms. I have brought him to you as you commanded."

The king saw the other then. He had been lost in his guard's shadow, a shadow himself, small and lithe and dark. But when he lifted his head, the tall squire shrank to vanishing. He had a face a man could not forget, fine-boned and eagle-proud, neither handsome nor ugly but simply and supremely itself. The eyes in it met the old man's steadily, with calm and royal confidence; almost, but not quite, he smiled.

Almost, but not quite, the king returned his smile. Hope was rising once more. Swelling; quivering on the edge of fear.

The boy stepped away from his guard, one pace only, as if to shake off the intruding presence. Something in the movement betrayed the tension beneath his calm. Yet when he spoke his voice was steady, and unlike his face, incontestably beautiful. "I greet you, my lord, and I commend your liege man's courtesy."

The king glanced at Vadin, who was careful to wear no expression at all. "Did you resist him?" the king asked the stranger.

"Not at all, my lord. But," the boy added, again with his almost-smile, "I was somewhat haughty."

From the glitter in the squire's eyes, that was no less than the truth. The king swallowed laughter, found it echoed in the clear bright eyes, and lost it in a dart of memory and of old, old grief. He had not laughed so, nor met such utter, joyous fearlessness, since—

His voice came hard and harsh. "From the Hundred Realms, are you, boy?"

"Han-Gilen, sire."

The king drew a slow breath. His face had neither changed nor softened. Yet his heart was hammering against his ribs. "Han-Gilen," he said. "Tell me, boy. Have you heard aught of my daughter?"

"Your daughter, my lord?" The voice was cool, but the eyes had shifted, gazing over the southward sweep of Han-Ianon.

The king turned, following them. "Once on a time, I had a daughter. When she was born I made her my heir. When she was still a young maid I consecrated her to the Sun. And when she reached the time of her womanhood she went away as all the Sun's children must do, on the seven years' wandering of her priestess-Journey. At the end of it she should have returned, full priestess and full wise, with wondrous tales to tell. But the seven years passed, and seven again, and she did not come. And now it is thrice the time appointed, and still no man has seen her, nor has she sent me word. I have heard only rumors, travelers' tales out of the south. A priestess from the north, Journeying in the Hundred Realms, abandoned her vows and her heritage to wed a ruling prince; but nay, she spurned the prince to rule as high priestess in the Temple of the Sun in Han-Gilen; she went mad and turned seer and proclaimed that the god had spoken to her in visions; she . . . died."

There was a silence. Abruptly the king spun about, swirling his black cloak. "Mad, they call me. Mad, because I stand here day upon day, year upon year, praying for my daughter's return. Though I grow old and soon will die, I name no heir, while yonder in my hall my son leads my younger warriors in a round of gaming, or sleeps deep beside his latest woman. A strong man is the Prince Moranden of Ianon, a great warrior, a leader of men. He is more than fit to hold the high seat." The king bared his teeth, more snarl than smile. "No man should grieve so for a daughter when such a son has grown to grace his hall. So men say. They do not know him as I know him." His fists clenched, hard and knotted, thin as an eagle's claws. "Boy! Know you aught of my daughter?"

The young priest had listened without expression. He reached now into his scrip and brought forth a glitter of metal, a torque of gold twisted with mountain copper.

The king reeled. Strong young hands caught him, helped him to a seat upon the parapet. Dimly he saw the face close above his own, calm and still; but the eyes were dark with old sorrow.

"Dead," he said. "She is dead." He took the torque in hands that could not still their trembling. "How long?"

"Five winters since."

Anger kindled. "And you waited until now?"

The boy's chin came up; his nostrils flared. "I would have come, my lord. But there was war, and I was forbidden, and no one else could be spared. Do not fault me for what I could not help."

There had been a time when a boy, or even a man grown, would have been whipped for such insolence. But the king swallowed his wrath lest it destroy his grief. "What was she to you?"

The boy met his gaze squarely. "She was my mother."

He had gone beyond shock, beyond even surprise. For that tale too had come to him, that she had borne a son. And for a priestess wedded to the god to conceive a child by any mortal man, the penalty was death. Death for herself, for her lover, and for their progeny.

"No," said this young stranger whose face in its every line spoke poignantly of her. "She never died for me."

"Then how?"

The boy closed his eyes upon a grief as stark and as terrible as the king's own; his voice came soft, as if he did not trust it. "Sanelin Amalin was a very great lady. She came to Han-Gilen at the end of its war upon the Nine Cities, when all its people mourned the death of the prince's prophet, who had also been his beloved brother. She stood up in the midst of the funeral rites and foretold the fate of the princedom, and the Red Prince accepted her as his seer. Soon thereafter, for her great sanctity, she was taken into the temple in Han-Gilen. Within a year she was its high priestess. There was no one more holy or more deeply venerated. Yet there were those who hated her for that very sanctity, among them she who had been high priestess before Sanelin's coming, a proud woman and a hard one, who had treated the stranger cruelly and been deposed for it. In the dark of the moons, five winters past, this woman and certain of her followers lured the lady from the temple with a tale of sickness only she could heal. I think . . . I know she saw the truth. Yet she went. I followed her with the prince hard upon my heels. We were just too late. They threw me down and stunned me and wounded my lord most cruelly, struck my mother to the heart, and fled." His breath shuddered as he drew it in. "Her last words were of you. She wished you to know of her glory, of her death. She said, 'My father would have had me be both queen and priestess. Yet I have been more than either. He will grieve, but I think he will understand.' "

The wind sighed upon the stones. Vadin shifted in a creaking of leather and bronze. In the world below, children shouted and a stallion screamed and a tuneless voice bawled a snatch of a drinking song. Very quietly the king said, "You tell a noble tale, stranger who calls himself my kin. Yet, though I may be mad, I am not yet a dotard. How came a high priestess to bear a son? Did she then lay aside her vows? Did she wed the Red Prince of Han-Gilen?"

"She broke no vows, nor was she ever aught but Avaryan's bride."

"You speak in riddles, stranger."

"I speak the truth, my lord grandsire."

The king's eyes glittered. "You are proud for one who by his words is no man's son."

"Both of which," said the other, "I am."

The king rose. He was very tall even for one of his people; he towered over the boy, who nevertheless betrayed no hint of fear. That too had been Sanelin, small as her western mother had been small, yet utterly indomitable. "You are the very image of her. How then?" His hand gripped the boy's shoulder with cruel strength. *"How?"*

"She was the Bride of the Sun."

So bright, those eyes were, so bright and so terrible. The king threw up all his shields against them. "That is a title. A symbol. The gods do not walk in the world as once they did. They do not lie with the daughters of men. Not even with the holy ones, their own priestesses. Not in these days."

The boy said nothing, only raised his hands. The left had bled where the nails had driven into flesh. The right could not. Gold flamed there, the disk of the Sun with its manifold rays, filling the hollow of his palm.

The king slitted his eyes against the brightness. A deep and holy terror had risen to engulf him. But he was strong and he was king; he reckoned his lineage back to the sons of the lesser gods.

"He came," said this child of the great one, "while she kept vigil in the Temple of Han-Gilen where is his most sacred image. He came, and he loved her. Of that union I was conceived; for it she suffered and came in time to glory. You could say that she died of it, by the envy of those who reckoned themselves holy but could not endure true sanctity."

"And you? Why did they let you live?"

"My father defended me."

"Yet he let her die."

"He took her to himself. She was glad, my lord. If you could have seen—dying, she shone, and she laughed with purest delight. She had her lover at last, wholly and forever." He shone himself in speaking of it, a radiance touched only lightly now with sorrow.

The king could not partake of it. Nor, for long, could the stranger. He let his hands fall, veiling the brilliance of the god's sign. Without it he seemed no more than any other traveler, ragged and footsore, armored with pride that was half defiance. It kept his chin up and his eyes level, but his fists were clenched at his sides. "My lord," he said, "I make no claim upon you. If you bid me go, I will go."

"And if I bid you stay?"

The dark eyes kindled. Sanelin's eyes, set with the sun's fire. "If you bid me stay, I will stay, for that is the path which the god has marked for me."

"Not the god alone," said the king. He raised a hand as if to touch the boy's shoulder, but the gesture ended before it was well begun. "Go now. Bathe; you need it sorely. Eat. Rest. My squire will see that you have all you desire. I shall speak with you again." And as they moved to obey: "How are you called, grandchild?"

"Mirain, my lord."

"Mirain." The king tested it upon his tongue. "Mirain. She named you well." He drew himself erect. "What keeps you? Go!"

Two

THEY CALLED HER THE QUEEN WHO WAS NOT. IN LAW she was the king's concubine, captive daughter of a rebel from the Western Marches, mother of his sole acknowledged son. In her own country that would have sufficed to make her his wife, and her child heir to throne and castle; here where they had cast aside the old gods and the great goddess to become slaves of the Sun, a concubine was only that, her son always and inescapably a bastard.

She did not stoop to bitterness. She held the highest title these apostates allowed, that of First Lady of the Palace; she had a realm of her own, the women's quarters of the castle with their halls and their courts, barred and protected in proper fashion, with her own eunuchs to stand guard. Though those were aging, alas, and his majesty would permit her to buy no more; when she had been so unwise as to suggest that he send her young slaves of his own choosing and a surgeon to render them fit for her service, his rage had come close to frightening her.

They were turning barbarian here. They had few slaves, and no eunuchs. In a little while, no doubt, they would put on trousers and shave their beards and affect the dainty accents of the south.

She contemplated her reflection in the great oval mirror. It had been her father's shield; she had had it silvered and polished at extravagant expense, that she might never forget whence she had come. The lovely maiden it had once reflected was long gone, she of the wild lynxeyes and the headlong temper. The eyes were quiet now, as the lynx is quiet before it springs. The face was beautiful still, a goddess-mask, flawless and implacable.

She waved away the servant with the paints and brushes, snatched the veil from the other's hands and draped it herself. Doliya tarried overlong in the market; damn the old gabbler, could she never perform a simple errand without dallying in every wineshop along the way? Not but that the woman's delays had often proven profitable; secrets had a way of escaping when wine loosened men's tongues, and Doliya's ears were wickedly keen.

"Great lady." The voice of her chief eunuch, thin with age. As was he, a gangling spider-limbed grotesque of a creature, who had never learned to creep and cringe and act the proper servant. His father had been her father's enemy; it had amused the old monster to slaughter all that line save the youngest son, and to have the child cut and trained and given to his daughter as a slave. It was a crooked comfort to see how old he was and how much younger she seemed, and to know that she was a full year the elder.

He was accustomed to her brooding stares, and unafraid of them. "Great lady," he repeated, "there is that which you should know."

His level tone, his expressionless face, told her much. Whatever tidings he bore, he rejoiced to bear them; which meant that she would not be pleased to hear them. Such games he played, he her bitter enemy, he the perfect faithful servant. Impeccable service, he had told her once when he was still young enough to blurt out secrets, could be a potent revenge. She would never dare to trust him completely; she would never dare not to. She had laughed and taken up his gauntlet and made him the chief of her servants.

"Tell me," she bade him at last, coolly, sipping iced wine from a goblet of tourmaline and silver.

He smiled. This was bitter news indeed, then, and he was in no haste to reveal it. He sat in a chair the twin of her own, commanded wine and received it, drank more slowly even than she. At last he set down the cup; laced his long withered fingers; allowed himself a second smile. "A stranger has come into the king's presence, great lady. A stranger from the south, a priest of the burning god." For all her control, she tensed; his amusement deepened. "He brings word of the king's heir, of her who departed so long ago; some would say by your connivance, although that surely is a falsehood. You may rejoice, great lady. Sanelin Amalin is dead."

The lady raised a brow. "I am to be surprised? Vain hope, my old friend. I have known it for long and long."

He continued to smile. "Of course you have, great lady. Have you also known that she delivered herself of a son? A son of her god, bearing the Sun in his hand, wrapped in divinity as in a cloak. With my own eyes I saw him. He has spoken with the king; the king's folk serve him; he lodges, great lady, in the chambers of the king's heir."

She sat very, very still. Her heart had stopped, and burst into life again, hammering upon the walls of her flesh. Ginan smiled. She thought of flesh flayed living from bone, shaped the thought with great care, and thrust it behind those glittering eyes. They dimmed; he greyed, his smile died. But his satisfaction could not so easily be vanquished. All her care and all her plotting—all the women who came to the king, who could conceive no children to supplant her son; the one whose spells sufficed to conceive a son but not to bear him alive, who died herself in the bearing—all for naught. Because she had not gone so far as to dispose of the heir herself, trusting to the Journey and, if that failed, to the priestess' vows. Sanelin would never know man, never bear a child. If she returned, if she took the throne, how easy then to cast a spell, to distill a poison, to assure that Moranden son of Odiya of Umijan became king by right of all Ianon.

Almost, almost, the lady could admire her. Insufferable little saint that she had been, still she had found a way both to thwart her enemy and to keep her name for sanctity. It seemed that the barbarians had believed the lie; the whelp had been suffered to live. Unless . . .

Ginan knew her well enough to read the flicker of her eyes. His smile returned undaunted. "No, great lady, he is no impostor. He is the very image and likeness of his mother."

"Dwarfish and unlovely? Ah, the poor child."

"As tall as he needs to be, and well above any need of beauty. He is a striking young man, great lady; he carries himself like a king."

"Yet," she mused, "a priest."

"A priest who is a king, great lady, may marry and beget sons. As indeed some had speculated that the princess might do if she were ruling queen, for the kingdom's sake. As it seems that she did."

"He is not king yet." Odiya said it with great care. She refilled her cup and raised it. "Nor shall he be while I have power in this kingdom. May the goddess be my witness."

VADIN DID PRECISELY AS HE WAS BIDDEN. IT KEPT HIM FROM having to think. He did not understand half of what he had heard on the battlements; he was not certain that he believed the rest. That this foreigner should be the son of the king's daughter, of a woman so long mourned that she seemed as dim as a legend, yes, perhaps he could credit that. But that the boy should have been sired by a god . . .

Mirain bathed, which truly he had needed, and he let the king's servants carry away his ragged trousers and bring him a proper kilt. But he raised an uproar by calling for a razor. First they had to find one; then he insisted on shaving his face as smooth as a woman's. Vadin's own twitched as he watched. The servants were appalled, and the eldest of them ventured to remonstrate, but Mirain would hear none of it. "It's hot," he said in his mincing accent. "It's unlovely. It itches." He grinned at their shocked faces, shocking them even further, and sat to the repast which they had spread for him. Perched on a chair that had been carved to Ianyn measure, devouring honeycakes and laughing still at the servants' outraged propriety, he looked even younger than he was. He did not look like the son of the Sun.

He finished the last drippingly sweet cake, licked his fingers, and sighed. "I haven't eaten so well since I left Han-Gilen." The eldest servant bowed a degree. Mirain bowed half a degree in return, but lightly, smiling. "I commend your service, sirs."

It was a dismissal. They obeyed it, all but Vadin. He kept his post by the door and said nothing, and won his reward: Mirain let him be.

As soon as the men had gone, Mirain's face stilled. He no longer had the likeness of a child. Slowly he turned about, his right hand clenching and unclenching, his brows drawing together until he was the very likeness of the king his grandsire. His nose wrinkled very slightly. Vadin could guess why. Although the rooms to which the king's men had brought him were rich, clean and well swept, they breathed an air of long disuse. No feet but servants' feet had trod that splendid carpet out of Asanion in time out of mind; no one had leaned upon the windowframe as now he leaned, looking down into a sheltered garden or up over the luminous battlements to the mountains of Ianon.

He turned his hand palm up upon the casement. Flecks of blinding gold played over his face, over the walls and ceiling, into Vadin's eyes. They vanished as his fingers closed; he turned his eyes to the sun which had begotten them. "So, my lord," he said to it, "you led me here. Drove me, rather. What now? The king grieves, but he begins to rejoice, seeing in me the rebirth of his daughter. Shall I heed my fates and prophecies and his own command, and stay and be his death? Or shall I take flight while yet there is time? For you see, my lord, I think that I could love him."

Perhaps he gained an answer. If so it did not comfort him. He drew a long breath that caught sharply upon a wordless sound. A cry, a gasp of bitter laughter. "Oh aye, I could have refused. Han-Gilen would have kept me. I was no foreigner there for all my foreign face, eagle's shadow that it was amid all the red and brown and gold; I was the prince's fosterling, the priestess' child, the holy one, venerated and protected. Protected!" That was certainly laughter, and certainly bitter. "They were protecting me to death. At least if I die here, I die of my own folly and naught else."

He turned from the sun. His eyes were full of it, but it had no power to blind them. As they caught Vadin he started, as if he had forgotten the squire's presence. Probably, Vadin thought, he had hardly been aware of it at all, no more than he was aware of the floor under his feet.

Unless, of course, it rose and tripped him. His scrutiny was both leisurely and thorough, taking in the squire as if he had been a bullock at market. Noting with due interest the narrow beaky face with its uncertain young beard; the long awkward body in the king's livery; the spear grounded beside one foot, gripped with force enough to grey the prominent knuckles.

Mirain's eyes glinted. In scorn, Vadin knew. *His* body was hardly awkward at all, and he acted as if he knew it. He had a way of tilting his head that was both arrogant and seeming friendly, and a lift of the brows that a courtesan should have studied, it was so perfectly disarming. "My name is Mirain," he said, "as you've heard. What may I call you?"

Dismissed, Vadin wanted to snap. But training held. "Vadin, my lord. Vadin alVadin of Asan-Geitan."

Mirain leaned against the casement. "Geitan? That's in Imehen, is it not? Your father must be alVadin too; my mother told me that Geitan's lord is always Vadin, just as Ianon's king is always Raban like my grandfather, or Mirain."

Like this interloper. Vadin drew himself up the last possible fraction. "It is so, my lord."

"My mother also taught me to speak Ianyn. Not remarkably well, I fear; I've been too long in the south. Will you be my teacher, Vadin? I'm a disgrace as I am, with a face like mine and a Gileni princeling lisping out of it."

"You're not staying!" Vadin bit his tongue, too late. Adjan would see him flogged for this, even if the foreigner did not.

The foreigner did not even flinch. He took off the band of his Journey and turned it in his hands, and sighed faintly. "Maybe I should not. I'm an outlander here; my Journey is hardly a year old. But," he said, and his eyes flashed up, catching Vadin unawares, "there is still the geas that my mother laid upon me. To tell her father of her glory and her death; to comfort him as best I could. Those I have done. But then she commanded me to take her place, the place her vows and her fate had compelled her to abandon, for which she bore and trained me."

"She placed great trust in blood and in fate," a new voice said. Its owner came forward in the silence. A woman, tall and very slender, robed all in grey with silver at her throat, the garb of a sacred singer. Her face was as beautiful as her voice, and as cool, and as unreadable.

"So she did," said Mirain as coolly as she. "Was she not a seer?"

"Some would say that she was mad."

"As mad as her father, no doubt. As mad as I."

The woman stood before him. She was tall for a woman, even a woman of Ianon; his head came just to her chin. "My lord gave you her rooms. His own son has never had so much."

"You know who I am." It was not a question.

"By now most of the castle knows it. The servants have ears and tongues, and you have her face."

"But she was beautiful. Not even charity could call me that."

"All her beauty was in her eyes and in the way she moved. No carved or painted likeness could ever capture it."

"Nor any in flesh." He shook off the complaint with its air of long use, and regarded her, loosing a rare and splendid smile. "You would be Ymin."

Strong though she was, she was still a woman, and that smile held a mighty magic. Her eyes warmed; her face softened a very little. "She told you of me?"

"Often and often. How could she forget her foster sister? She hoped you would win your torque. The loveliest woman and the sweetest singer in Ianon, she said you would be. She was a true prophet."

Almost Ymin smiled. "Your own torque, my young lord, could as easily be silver as gold. Was it our blunt-spoken Sanelin who taught you such courtesy?"

"She taught me to speak the truth."

"Then the sweetness must be the legacy of Han-Gilen, which we singers call the Land of Honey."

"Sweet speech is certainly an art much valued there, although they value honor more. The worst of all sins, say they, is the Lie, and they raise their children to abhor it."

"Wise people. Strength is greatest here, of the body most often, of the will but little less. There is no place in the north for the gentle man or for the weakling."

"Hard as the stones of the north, they say in Han-Gilen."

Mirain turned back to the window. Ymin set herself beside him. He did not glance at her. "Why did you depart?" she asked him.

"It was time and past time, though my lord prince would have had me wait longer, till I had my growth and an army to ride with me. But the god has no care for manhood, or for the lack of it. I left in secret; I walked in secret until I had passed the borders of Han-Gilen. It was a very long way to go afoot, with winter coming and a long cruel war but lately ended." His voice changed, took on a hint of pride. "I fought in it; well, my lord said. I was his squire, with his son, the Prince-Heir Halenan. He made us both knights and armed us alike. I was sorry to leave them. And the princess, Halenan's sister . . . she helped me to slip away."

"Was she very beautiful?"

He stared at her, briefly speechless. "Elian? She was all of eight years old!"

Ymin's laughter was sudden and heart-deep, a ripple of pure notes. He frowned; unwillingly his lips twitched. "Maybe," he admitted, "someday she will be lovely. When I saw her last, she was dressed like a boy in ancient tattered breeches and a shirt of mine—much too large for her—and her hair never would stay in its braids. Still, that was splendid, like her father's and her brother's and no one else's in the world: red as fire. She was trying to look like a bold bad conspirator, but her eyes were all bleared with crying, and her nose was red, and she could hardly say a word." He sighed. "She was a living terror. When we rode off to war, we found her among our baggage. 'If Mirain can go,' she said, 'why can't I?' She was six years old. Her father gave her a royal tongue-lashing and sent her home in disgrace. But he gave his steward orders to have her taught weaponry. She had won, in her way, and she knew it."

"You loved, it seems," she said, "and were well loved."

"I have been fortunate."

She looked at him for a long moment. Her face had changed, grown cool again. "My lord, what will you do here?"

His hands rested on the casement, the fingers tightening until the knuckles greyed. "I will remain. When the time comes I will be king. The king who drives back the shadows, the son of the Sun."

"Your will is firm for one so young."

"My will has nothing to do with what must be." His tone was faintly bitter, faintly weary.

"The gods' love," she said slowly, "is a torment of fire."

"And a curse on all one cares for. Hold to your coldness against me, singer, if you would be wise."

She laid her hand upon his arm. Her eyes were clear again and steady upon him, as steady as her voice. "My lord, do you know truly what you are doing? Can you? Your mother raised you and trained you and commanded you to be what her fate had forbidden her to be, high ruler in Ianon. But the place for which she shaped you is twenty years gone."

"It is known even in far Han-Gilen that the King of Ianon has no chosen successor. That he awaits the return of his daughter."

"Is it also known that he keeps his vigil all but alone?" She spoke more rapidly, less calmly. "Kingdoms can rise and fall in a score of years. Babes then unborn have since borne children of their own. None of whom has any memory of a priestess who set forth on her Journey and never came back.

"But they do know, they do remember those who remained here. Your mother had a brother, my lord. He was a child when she left. Now he is a man and a prince, and his father has never let him forget that he is not judged worthy of the name of heir; that he is bastard seed, acknowledged, endured, even loved, but never equal to the one who is gone. Whereas to the people, who have no care for the passions of kings except as they breed war or peace, he is their sole and rightful prince. He has dwelt among them all his life; he is one of their own, and he is strong and fair, and he wields his lordship well enough. They love him."

"And I," said Mirain, "am a foreigner and an interloper, an upstart, a presumptuous stranger."

Vadin's thoughts to a word; the squire knew a stab of superstitious dread. And another of annoyance. All of it should be obvious to the merest child, which Mirain most certainly was not. He seemed undismayed by it. He was not stupid, Vadin was certain; very probably he was mad. It was in his blood.

He prowled the room, not precisely as if he were restless; it seemed to help him think. He was doing it again, that witch's trick of his, filling the wide space, towering over the two who watched him. When he halted and turned, he shrank a little. "Suppose I leave quietly, singer. Have you considered what that might do to the king? It could very easily kill him."

"It will kill him to have you here."

"One way or another." Mirain's head tilted. "You could be speaking for my enemies."

"If so," she said unruffled, "they have moved upon you with supernatural speed."

"It has happened to me before."

"Were you ever a child, my lord?"

He stood back on his heels, eyes wide and ingenuous. "Why, lady, what am I now but a babe scarce weaned?"

She dropped her mask and laughed aloud. It was not all mockery. Much of it was honest merriment. When it passed, her eyes danced still; she said, "You are a match for me, I think. You may even be a match for the whole of Ianon." She sobered fully. "When you are king, my lord, and more than king, will you let me make songs for you?"

"If I forbade it, would that prevent you?"

Ymin looked down, then up, a swift bright glance. "No, my lord."

He laughed half in pain. "You see what kingship I can claim, when not even a singer will obey me."

"When it comes to singing," she said, "I obey only the god."

"And your own will."

"That most certainly." She stepped away from the window. "The god calls me now to sing his office. Will you come?"

Mirain paused, a breath only. Then: "No. Not . . . quite yet."

She bowed her head slightly. "Then may he prosper you. Good day, my lord."

WHEN SHE WAS GONE, MIRAIN SENT VADIN AWAY. NONE too soon for the squire's peace of mind. He was soul-glad to be back among his own, comfortable, sane and human kind, driving his body until it was all one mindless ache. He drove himself so far that when Adjan called him out of the baths, he could only think that he had earned a reprimand somewhere on the practice field. That was terror enough, but he had survived the old soldier's discipline before. It was only pain; it passed, and everyone forgot it.

Adjan inspected his damply naked person with no expression that he could discern. In spite of himself he began to be afraid. When Adjan roared in rage, all was well. But when he was silent, then it was wisest to run.

Vadin could not be wise. He could not even cover his shriveling privates.

After an eternity the arms master said, "Dry yourself and report to me. Full livery. Without," he added acidly, "your spear."

Vadin dried himself and dressed with all the care his shaking hands could muster. He was beginning to think again, after a fashion. He kept seeing Mirain's face. Damn it, the foreigner had sent him away. Ordered him on no uncertain terms, and barred the door behind him. What had the little bastard done, brewed up a mess of sorceries over the bedroom hearth?

He braided his hair so tightly it hurt, flung the scarlet cloak over his shoulders, and went to face his master.

Adjan was standing in the cubicle that served him as both workroom and bedchamber. On the battered stool that the squires called the throne of judgment sat the king.

Vadin came very close to disgracing himself and all his house. Came within a twitch of turning and bolting, and if he had, he would not have stopped until he came to Imehen. Pride alone held him back, pride and Adjan's black grim stare. His body snapped itself to full attention, and stayed there while the king examined him. He was raw with all the scrutiny, and growing angry. Was he a prize stud-colt, that all these people should memorize his every line?

His majesty raised a brow—gods, precisely like Mirain—and said to Adjan, "He has promise, I grant you. But this demands performance."

"He can perform," the arms master said, no more smoothly or politely than he ever did. "Are you questioning my judgment?"

"I am pointing out that this task would challenge a seasoned soldier, let alone a boy in his first year of service."

"And I say that's to his advantage. He'll keep up his training; he'll simply be assigned to a different duty."

"Day and night, Captain. Whatever befalls."

"Maybe nothing."

"Maybe death. Or worse."

"He's young; he's brighter than he looks; and he's resilient. Where an older man would break, he'll bend and spring back stronger than before. I say he's the best choice, sire. You won't find a better in the time you're allowing."

The king stroked his beard, frowning at Vadin, hardly seeing him except as a tool for the task. Whatever it was. Vadin's heart was pounding. Something high and perilous; some great and glorious deed, as in the songs. For that his father had sent him here. For that he had prayed. He was no longer afraid; he was ready to sing.

"Vadin of Geitan," the king said at last, his voice like drums beating, "your commander has persuaded me. You shall continue to train among my squires, but you are no longer in my service. Henceforth you are the liege man of the Prince Mirain."

Vadin was not hearing properly. No longer serving the king—serving the prince—Moranden? There was only one prince in the castle. There could not be—

"Mirain," said the king relentlessly, "stands in need of a good and loyal man. He has come late and all unlooked for; he is godly wise, but I do not think that he knows truly what he faces here. I call on you to be his guide and his guard."

High. Honorable. Perilous. Vadin wanted to laugh. Nursemaid to a priestess' bastard. He would dare death, oh yes, death by stoning or poison when Ianon turned against the upstart.

The king was not asking him to choose. He was a thing; a servant. A half-trained hound, mute and helpless while his master handed his lead to a new owner.

No, he thought. *No.* He would speak. He would stalk away. Go home, no, he could not do that to his father or his poor proud mother, but maybe the prince would take

him. The true prince, the man who had time to smile at a
guard or to speak to a squire in the market or to greet a
boy coming new and homesick and scared into a city
greater than he had ever dreamed of. Moranden had
taken the edge off his terror, made him feel like a lord
and a kinsman, and better yet, remembered him thereafter. Moranden would be glad of his service.

"Go now," the king said. "Guard my grandson."

Vadin gathered himself to cry out. Found himself bowing low, mute, obedient. Went as, and where, he was
commanded.

THE FOREIGNER WAS GONE. FOR A BLISSFUL INSTANT VADIN
knew that he had changed his mind; he had escaped
while he could. Then Vadin thought to go to the window
Mirain had seemed so fond of, and there were the braid
and the torque and the girl-smooth face, exploring the
garden. Vadin took a long moment to steel himself. At
last he went down.

Mirain had folded himself on the grass, bent over his
cupped hands. When Vadin's shadow blocked the sun he
looked up. "See," he said, raising his hands a little, carefully. Something fluttered in them, small and vividly blue,
with a flash of scarlet at the throat and on the iridescent
wings. The dragonel scaled the pinnacle of Mirain's fore-
finger and coiled there, wings beating gently for balance.
Mirain laughed softly. The creature echoed him four oc-
taves higher. With blurring suddenness it took wing, dart-
ing away into a tangle of fruitthorn.

Mirain stretched and sighed and smiled his sudden
smile. "I never thought northerners were a folk for
gardens."

"We're not." Vadin tried an insolence; he dropped beside the other, full livery and all. Mirain chose to pay no
attention. "The king had it made for the yellow woman—
for the queen. She pined amid all our bare stone.
Herdfields weren't enough, and the women's courts were
too severe with their herbs and such. She had to have
flowers." His lip curled a little as he said it.

"The yellow woman," Mirain repeated. "Poor lady, she died before my mother could know her. I understand that she was very beautiful but very fragile, like a flower herself."

"So the singers say."

Mirain plucked a scarlet blossom. He had small hands for a man, but the fingers were long and tapering, with a touch as delicate as a girl's. They closed over the flower. When they opened they cupped a hard green fruit. It ripened swiftly, darkening and swelling and speckling with gold.

He held the thornfruit under Vadin's nose. Thornfruit in spring, real as his own staring eyes, with its sweet potent scent, its suggestion of a blush. "Yes," said Mirain, "I am a mage, a born master; I need no spells to work my magics, only a firm will."

A sun kindled in his hand. The fruit vanished. Mirain clasped his knees and rocked, and regarded Vadin, and waited. For what? Abject submission? Cowering terror?

"Plain acceptance," the mage said, dry as old leaves.

Vadin gave him red rage. "Get out of my mind!"

Mirian raised a cheer. "Bravo, Vadin! Obey my grandfather, endure me, but keep your rebellion alive. I do detest a servile servant."

"Why?" demanded Vadin. "One word of power and I'm your ensorceled slave."

"Why?" Mirain echoed him. "By the king's orders you're mine already." He sat erect, suddenly grim. "Vadin alVadin, I do not accept unwilling service. For one thing, it hurts my head. For another, it's an invitation to assassination. But I will not stoop to win your willingness with my power. If your loyalties lie elsewhere, go to them. I can settle matters with the king."

Vadin's anger changed as Mirain spoke. He had been close to hate. He was still, but to a different side of it, a side much closer to his pride. Instead of roaring or howling or striking out, he heard himself say coldly, "You're a supercilious little bastard, do you know that?"

"I can afford to be," Mirain answered.

Vadin laughed in spite of himself. "Sure you can. You're planning to be king of the world." He stood and planted his hands on his hips. "What makes you think you can get rid of me? I'm a good squire, my lord. I served my master loyally; my master gave me to you. Now I'm your man. Your loyal man, my lord."

Mirain's eyes widened and fixed; his chin came up. "I refuse your service, sir."

"I refuse your refusal, my lord." *I am an idiot, my very unwelcome lord.*

"You most certainly are." That stopped Vadin short; Mirain grinned like a direwolf. "Very well, sir defiance. You are my man, and may the god have mercy on your soul."

Three

THE KING'S SUMMONS CAME AT EVENING, AND WITH IT A robe of honor, royal white embroidered with scarlet and gold. Someone had been cutting and stitching: it fit Mirain admirably. He preened in it, vain as a sunbird; and he did look well. He had his hair braided differently, Ianyn prince's braid, although he had not let the servant add the twist that marked the royal heir. "I'm not that yet," he said, "and I may never be."

Vadin restrained a snort, which Mirain pretended not to hear. The servant struggled with the heavy black mane. Freed, it was as outrageous as its bearer's moods; it curled with abandon, and it had a life of its own, a will to escape the grimly patient fingers and run wild down Mirain's back. A brand of his Asanian blood, like his smallness, like his dancer's grace.

At last the servant won his battle. Mirain applauded him; young man that he was, he broke into a smile, swiftly controlled. It was almost amusing to see how easily these bondmen fell into Mirain's hand. His glittering golden hand.

THE KING SAT ENTHRONED IN THE GREAT HALL WITH BEFORE and below him the lords and chieftains of his court, gathered for the evening feast. He rose as Mirain entered; the rest rose perforce, a royal greeting.

Mirain stood straight in the face of it and met the old king's gaze, that was dark and keen and quietly exultant, filled with a welcome as fierce as it was joyous. "Mirain of Han-Gilen," he said in a ringing voice, "son of my daughter. Come, sit by me; share the honor of the feast."

Mirain bowed and advanced down the long hall through a spreading silence. His back was erect, his chin up. Unconsciously Vadin, following in his wake, matched his bearing and his steadiness.

The king's hand clasped Mirain's and set him to the right of the throne, in a seat but little lower. The heir's place. Eyes glittered; voices murmured. Not in thrice seven years had that chair been filled.

Mirain sat very still in it, as if the slightest movement might send him leaping into flight. Vadin could almost taste his tension. Surely he had planned for this. But now that he had it, it seemed he was human enough to have a doubt or two. His fist had clenched in his lap. A muscle had knotted in his jaw. He raised his chin another degree, to imperial hauteur, and held it there.

The king sat beside him. A sigh ran through the hall as the court returned to their seats. Their lord raised a hand.

The door of the hall flew open. Figures filled it. Prince Moranden strode through them, resplendent in scarlet and in mountain copper. Tall even for a northerner and broad with it, he towered above the seated nobles. The men with him, lords, warriors, servants, passed insubstantial as shadows. But their eyes gleamed.

He stalked to the dais and halted before the king. "Your pardon for my lateness, sire. The hunt kept me away longer than I had looked for."

The king sat too still, spoke too gently. "Sit then, and let the feast begin."

"Ah, Father," Moranden said, "you waited for me. It was courteous, but you had no need."

"Indeed, sir, we did not. Will you sit?"

Still the prince lingered. As if for the first time, his eyes found Mirain. Stopped; widened. They were all innocent surprise, and yet Vadin's blood ran cold from heart to clenched fists. "What, Father! A guest? You do him great honor." His eyes narrowed; his lips thinned. "Nay, nay, I had forgotten. The boy who came this morning, the little priest from the south with the news we've all dreaded for so long. Shouldn't we be mourning instead of feasting?"

"One does not mourn a priestess whom the god has taken to himself." Mirain's voice was soft and steady, but higher than it should have been, the voice of a boy just come to manhood. It was well feigned. A stranger would have heard the youthful tenor with its hint of uncertainty, as if it would break on the next word, and seen the clear-skinned beardless face, and taken it all for what it seemed.

It seemed that Moranden did. His tension eased. The fire of wrath sank to an ember, swiftly banked in ash. He walked easily around the dais to settle beside the heir's place. It was not his wonted seat. Even in the lower chair he dwarfed his sister-son. "Well, lad," he said with hearty good humor, "are you pleased with the hospitality of Han-Ianon?"

"I am well content," Mirain answered him, as ingenuous as he, "and pleased to greet you at last, uncle."

"Uncle?" asked Moranden. "Are we kin?"

"Through my mother. Your sister Sanelin. Is it not her place I sit in?"

Moranden had taken half a loaf of bread and begun to break it. It crumbled in his tensed fingers, falling unheeded to his plate. "So," he said, "that's what kept her. Who was her lover? A prince? A beggar? Some fellow pilgrim?"

"No mortal man."

"I suppose everyone believed that. At least until she died. Or did they kill her?"

"They did not." Mirain turned slightly, with an effort Vadin could just see; he took up a bit of meat and began slowly to eat it.

"She left you alone then," Moranden said, "and you came to us. Not much welcome anywhere for a priestess' bastard, is there?"

"I am not a bastard." Mirain's voice was as calm as ever, but it had dropped an octave.

The king stirred at his left hand. "Enough," he said, low and harsh. "I will not have you coming to blows in my hall."

Moranden lounged in his seat. "Blows, Father? I was only exchanging courtesies with my sister's son. If so he is. Ianon is a rich prize for an ambitious wanderer."

"I do not lie," Mirain said in his proper tone at last. His nostrils were pinched tight below the haughty arch of his nose.

"Enough!" rapped the king. Suddenly he smote his hands together.

Although Ymin had sat among the court, she had not been eating with them. She rose now with fluid grace and went to a low seat which the servants had set before the dais. As she sat, one handed her an instrument, a small harp of golden wood with strings of silver.

It was common enough that she should sing so in hall. But this was a new song. It began softly as a hymn of praise to the rising sun. Then, as the court quieted, caught by the melody, she changed to a stronger mode, that half-chant which told the deeds of gods and heroes. A god tonight, the high god, Avaryan whose face was the sun; and a priestess, royal born; and the son who came forth from their loving, born at the rising of the daystar, god's child, prince, Lord of the Sun.

Mirain forsook even his feeble efforts to eat. His fists clenched upon the table in front of him; his face set, expressionless.

Silence was strange after the long singing. The king's voice broke it, concealing no longer his deep joy. "As Avaryan is my witness," he said, "it is so. Behold the prince, Mirain alAvaryan, son of my daughter, son of the Sun. Behold the heir of Ianon!"

Hardly had the echoes died when a young lord leaped up: Hagan, who would embrace any cause if only it were new enough to catch his fancy. And this cause was the king's own. "Mirain!" he cried. "Avaryan's son, heir of Ianon. Mirain!"

One by one, then all together, the court joined in his cry. The hall rang with their homage. Mirain rose to meet it, raising the fire of his hand, loosing his sudden, fierce elation. The old king smiled. But Moranden scowled blackly into his wine, as all his hopes vanished, shattered in that great wave of sound.

Four

VADIN OPENED HIS EYES AT THE STROKE OF THE DAWN bell. For a moment he could not imagine where he was. It was too quiet. None of the muted clamor of the squires' barracks, growing not so muted as the more vigorous pummeled the sluggards out of bed. Nor ever the warm nest of his brothers in Geitan, with Kerin's arm thrown over him, and Cuthan burrowed into his side like an overgrown pup, and a hound or four doing service for the blankets that the baby, Silan, had a way of stealing for himself. Vadin was very much alone, cold where his blanket had slipped, and surrounded by unfamiliar walls. Walls that glowed like clouds over Brightmoon. He peered at them.

A figure barred them. Memory flooded. Mirain stared down at him as he lay abed in his new room, a fold of the wall between the prince's bedchamber and the outer door. He scowled back. His liege lord was dressed in kilt and short cloak, girded with his southern sword, with no jewel but the torque he wore even to sleep. Much as he had drunk, late as he had feasted, he seemed as fresh as if he had slept from sunset to sunrise. "Come," he said, "up. Would you sleep the sun to his nooning?"

Vadin sprang erect, scouring the sleep out of his eyes. Mirain held up a kilt, the king's scarlet livery. He snatched it. "You are not to do that!"

Mirain let him wrap it and belt it, but when he looked up again he saw a comb in the prince's hand and a gleam in the prince's eye. He leaped; Mirain eluded him with animal ease, then startled him speechless by setting the comb in his hand and saying, "Be quick, or I'll keep no breakfast for you."

A squire did not eat with his lord, still less share a plate and a cup. "The servants have a thing or two to learn," Mirain observed as he passed the latter.

"My lord, you are not to—"

The bright eyes flashed up. "Do you command me, Vadin of Geitan?"

Vadin stiffened. "I am a squire. You," he said, "are Throne Prince of Ianon."

"So." Mirain's head tilted. "Formality is easier, is it not? A servant need have no feeling for the man he serves. Only for the title."

"I am loyal to my lord. He need have no fear of treachery."

"And no hope of binding you with friendship."

Vadin swallowed past the stone in his throat. "Friendship must be earned," he said. "My lord."

The prince rose slowly. He had no excess of inches to make him awkward. His body fit itself; he moved with the grace and economy of an Ishandri dancer. A little tight now, like his face, like his voice. "I would explore my grandsire's castle. May the throne prince take that liberty?"

"The throne prince may do as he pleases."

Mirain's brows went up. With no more warning than that, he strode to the door. Vadin had to scramble for cloak and sword and dagger, and don them at a run.

At this hour only squires and servants were awake. The high ones liked their sleep after a hard night's feasting, and the king never left his rooms until the last bell before sunrise, when he mounted to the battlements. Save that this morning he had no need to stand watch; Vadin wondered if he would, by sheer force of custom.

Han-Ianon's fortress was very large and very intricate, a labyrinth of courts and passages, halls and chambers and gardens and outbuildings, towers and dungeons, barracks and kitchens and the eunuch-guarded stronghold of the women. Only the last eluded Mirain's scrutiny, and that, Vadin suspected, only for the moment. Mirain approached the guard, a creature less epicene than most of Odiya's monsters, who might almost have been a man but for the too-smooth face; but the prince did not either speak or attempt to pass. He simply looked at the eunuch, who retreated with infinite slowness until he could retreat no more, for the door was at his back. The prince's face wore no expression at all.

Still without a word, Mirain turned on his heel. Afar atop the tower of the priests, a single piercing voice hymned the sunrise.

Mirain descended through the Chain of Courts to the outer ward and the stables of the castle. There at last the tension began to leave him. He brightened as he wandered down the long lines of stalls, among the grooms whose high calling left no time for gaping at princes, past broodmares and colts in training, hunters and racing mares and chariot teams, and, set apart, the great fierce battle-stallions each in his armored stall. Here and there he paused. He had a good eye for senel-flesh, Vadin granted him that. He ignored the haughty spotted mare for the drab little dun stalled beside her, making much of that least prepossessing and most swift of all the king's mares. He stood his ground when Prince Moranden's stallion menaced him with sharpened horns, and the tall striped dun retreated in confusion. He persuaded the whitehorn bay to take a tidbit from his hand.

As he turned from the bay to Vadin, he was close to smiling. "Show me yours," he said.

Vadin had not known how disarmed he was, and how easily, until he found himself standing in the lesser aisle among the squires' mounts. His own grey Rami lazed hipshot midway down the line. Her rump was only a little less bony than his own; but the tassel of her tail was full and silken, and her legs were long and fine, and her neck was serpent-supple as it curved about, the long ears pricked, the silver eyes mild. Vadin melted under that limpid regard.

"She is beautiful," Mirain said.

Vadin congealed into temper. "Her ears are too long. She's ribby. She toes out behind."

"But her gaits are silk and her heart is gold." Mirain was beside her, and she was suffering him to touch her. Even her head. Even her quivering ears. She blew gently into the foreigner's shoulder; and Vadin knew his heart would burst with jealousy.

"She is mine!" he almost shouted. "I raised her from a foal. No one else has ever sat on her back. Last year she won the Great Race in Imehen, from Anhei to Morajan between sunrise and noon, and straight into the melee after, where all the boys vied to become men. She never faltered. Never once. Even against horned stallions."

Mirain's hand had found one of the scars, the worst one, that furrowed her neck from poll to shoulder. "And what was the price of that?" he asked.

"She tore out the beast's throat." Vadin shivered, remembering: the blood, and the stallion's dying scream, and gentle Rami wilder with war than with pain. She had carried him to the victory, and he had hardly noticed. He had been too desperate with fear for her.

"Ianon's seneldi are famous even in the Hundred Realms," Mirain said, "for their beauty and their strength, and for their great valor."

"I've seen southern stock." Vadin did not dignify them with a sneer. "A trader from Poros used to haunt Geitan. Every year he'd come. Every year he'd pay emeralds for our culls. Geldings, and now and then a stallion the gelders hadn't got to. One year he tried to steal a mare. After that we made sure he didn't come back."

"My mother said a Ianyn lord could forgive the murder of his firstborn son, if properly persuaded. But never the theft of a senel."

"Firstborn sons are much less rare than good seneldi."

"True enough," said Mirain. Vadin could not tell if he was jesting. He bade Rami a courteous farewell, left the stall, looked about. The aisle led into waxing morning, the stableyard and a paddock or two, and the training rings. One or two colts were out, but Mirain did not tarry to watch them. He had heard what the squires called the morning hymn: the belling of a stallion and the hammering of hoofs on wood and stone, and piercing through it at intervals, a shrill scream of seneldi rage.

Mirain advanced unerringly to the source: in a corner of the wall a high fence, and within that a small stone hut. Its windows were barred. Triple bolts warded the door, trembling under the ceaseless crashing blows.

"The Mad One," Vadin said before Mirain could ask. "The stable used to belong to the king stallion when he came up from the fields to cover the king's own mares. But the old herdlord died in the spring, and there'll not be another till the last of this year's foals is born. Meanwhile the Mad One has a prison to himself. He's the king's own, bred from the best of the herds, and my lord had high hopes for him: he's as fast as a mare, but he has a stallion's strength, and his horns are an ell long already. But he's proven to be a rogue. He killed a stablehand before they locked him up. If he's not tamed by High Summer, he'll be given to the goddess."

"Sacrificed." Mirain's voice was thick with revulsion. The Sun's priests did not worship their god with blood. He leaned on the gate. Within the prison the Mad One shrilled his wrath.

Before Vadin could move, the prince was over the fence, running toward the hut.

Vadin flung himself in pursuit. And struck a wall he could not see. It held fast against him, rage though he would, and left him powerless to do more than watch.

Mirain had shot the threefold bolts. As the door burst open, he sprang aside. The Mad One hurtled out, foaming, tossing his splendid mane. He was more than beautiful. He was breathtaking: an emperor of seneldi, long and slender of leg, deep of chest, with the arched neck and the lean small-muzzled head of the Ianyn breed. His horns were straight and keen as twin swords; his hoofs were honed obsidian, his coat a black fire. His great flaw was Mirain's own. He was not tall for one of his kind. But he was tall enough, and he was wonderful to see. Wonderful and deadly.

He halted a scant handspan from the fence and wheeled snorting. His eye rolled, red as blood, red as madness. It fixed upon the one who stood by the open door. His lean ears flattened. His head lowered, horns armed for battle. He charged.

One moment Mirain stood full in his path. The next, the prince was gone, the senel eluding the wall with speed more of cat than of herd-creature. Mirain's laughter was sharp and wild. The Mad One spun toward it. The prince advanced slowly, with no sign of fear. He was smiling; grinning, daring the stallion to touch him. The horns missed him by a hair's breadth. The sharp cloven hoofs slashed only air.

The Mad One stood still. His nostrils flared, scarlet as his eyes. He tossed his head and stamped, as if to demand, *How dare you be unafraid of me?*

"How dare I indeed?" Mirain shot back. "You are no madder than I, and far less royal. For you are the son of the dawn wind, but I am the son of the Sun."

Black lightning struck where he stood. He was not there. He stood with hand on hip, breathing easily, unshaken. "Do you threaten me, sir? Are you so bold? Come now, be sensible. You may have been stolen away from your old kingdom, but that was only to set you in a greater one. Would you not be my king of stallions?"

A stamp; a snort; a feint.

Mirain did not move, save that his head came up. "*I* should come to *you* with a hundred mares behind me? Does an emperor bear tribute to a vassal king?" He stepped forward well within reach of hoof and horn. The Mad One had only to rear and strike, to cut him down. "I should not trouble myself with you. There are seneldi in the barns yonder who would give their souls to bear me on their backs. But you are a king. Royalty, even in exile, demands its share of respect."

The Mad One surveyed him in something close to bafflement. He touched the velvet muzzle. The stallion quivered, but neither nipped nor pulled away. His hand traveled upward to the roots of the horns, resting lightly

upon the whorl of hair between them. "Well, my lord?
Shall we be kings together?"

Slowly the proud head bowed, sniffed at the golden
hand, blew upon it.

Mirain drew closer still. Suddenly he was astride. The
Mad One stood frozen, then reared, belling. The prince
laughed. He was still laughing as the senel came down
running, leaped the high fence, and hurtled through the
stableyard. Men and animals scattered before them. "The
Mad One!" a deep voice bellowed. "The Mad One is
loose!"

"Which one?" muttered Vadin. Sourly; but with a
touch—a very reluctant touch—of admiration.

THEY MET THE KING COMING DOWN FROM THE HALL, WHILE
behind them eddied a turbulent crowd. The Mad One
came to a dancing halt; Mirain bowed to his grandsire.
"I've found a friend, my lord," he said.

Vadin was as close as anyone dared to go: just out of
reach of the stallion's heels. He would almost rather have
been closer still than face the king's cold accusing eye. But
that was fixed on Mirain, and on the senel who, untaught,
bore his rider with ease and grace; whose mien had lost
not a whit of either its pride or its wildness.

The coldness warmed. The thin lips twitched just per-
ceptibly. "A friend indeed, grandson, and a great lord of
seneldi. But I fear you will have to look after him yourself. No man will come near him."

"No longer," Mirain said, "if only none ventures to ride
him. For after all, he is a king."

"After all," the king agreed with a touch of irony, "he
is."

"We go now into the Vale. Will you come with us, sire?"

The king's smile won free, startling as the sun at midnight, and more miraculous. "Certainly I shall. Hian,
saddle my charger. I ride forth with the prince."

FROM A TOWER OF THE CASTLE MORANDEN SAW THEM: THE
boy on the black stallion without bridle or saddle, and
the old king on the red destrier, and a tangle of lords and

servants and hangers-on. His knuckles greyed as he gripped the window ledge. "Priestess' bastard," he gritted through clenched teeth.

"That is most unkind."

He whirled upon Ymin. "Unkind? *Unkind?* You have all you can ask for. All your prophecies fulfilled, new songs to sing, and a pretty lad to pleasure your eye. But I—I have had a kingdom snatched from my hands."

"You never had it," she pointed out serenely, sitting cross-legged on his bed.

"I did when that whelp bewitched my father."

"Your father never named you his heir."

"And who else would there have been?"

She spread her hands. "Who knows? But Mirain has come. He is the god's son, Moranden. Of that I am certain."

"So you've come to gloat over me."

"No. To make you see sense. That boy can tame the Mad One. What could he not do to you?"

"No beggar's by-blow can snare me with spells."

"Moranden," she said with sudden, passionate urgency, "he is the one. The king foretold. Accept him. Yield to him."

He stood over her and seized her roughly, shaking her. "I yield to no one. Not to you, and not ever to a bastard boy."

"He is your sister's son."

"My sister!" he spat. "Sanelin, Sanelin, always Sanelin. Look, Moranden, look at your sister, how proud, how queenly, how very, very holy. Come, lad, be strong; when your sister comes back, would you have her be ashamed of you? Ah, Sanelin, dear lady, where has she gone? So long, so far, and never a true word." He spat again, as if to rid his tongue of a foulness. "Who ever took any notice of me? I was only Moranden, the afterthought, begotten on a captive. She was the loved one. She was the heir. She—woman and half-breed and priestess that she was— *she* would have Ianon. And for me, nothing. No throne, no kingdom. Nothing at all."

"Except honor and lordship and all the wealth you could wish for."

"*Nothing,*" he repeated with vicious softness.

Ymin was silent. He laughed, a hideous, strangled sound. "Then she died. I heard the news; I went away in secret and danced the fiercest joy-dance I knew; I dreamed of my kingdom. And now he comes, that puny child, claiming all she had. All. With such utter, absolute, unshakable certainty that he has the right—" Moranden broke off, flinging up his head. "Shall I bow to that interloper? Shall I endure what I have endured for all the years of my manhood? By all the gods and the powers below, I will not!"

"You are a fool." Ymin's voice was soft, edged with contempt. "Your mother on the other hand, whose words you parrot so faithfully—she is mad. In Han-Ianon even we women cut our leading-strings when our breasts begin to bud. No doubt it is different in the Marches." She broke free and rose. "I go to serve my prince. If you assail him, expect no mercy from me. He is my lord as you have never been, nor ever will be."

Five

IN HAN-GILEN AND IN THE LANDS OF THE SOUTH RULED
but one high god, the Lord of Light. But in the north
the old ways held firm, the cult not of the One but of
the Two, the Light coeval and coequal with his sister the
Dark: Avaryan and Uveryen, Sun and Shadow, bound and
battling for all eternity. Each had his priests and each
his sacrifices. For Avaryan, the holy fire and the chants
of praise; but for his sister, darkness and silence and the
blood of chosen victims.

Avaryan's worship centered in his temples about his
gold-torqued priesthood. Uveryen suffered no walls or
images. Her realm was the realm of air and darkness, her
priests chosen and consecrated in secret, masked and
cowled and eternally nameless. In her holy groves and in
the deep places of the earth they practiced her mysteries;
nor ever did they suffer a stranger's presence.

Vadin crouched behind a stone, willing even his heart
to be silent. It was a long cruel way from the castle to the
place of the goddess, the wood upon the mountain spur
where no axe had ever fallen. A long way, the last and
worst of it on foot with all the stealth of his hunter's
training, and before him one who was a better hunter
than he. But Prince Moranden had not been looking for
pursuit. He had ridden out quietly with a hawk on his

wrist, as if for a solitary hunt; none but Vadin had seen him go, or dared to follow.

Whatever Moranden's thoughts of the one who had supplanted him, before men's faces he smiled and did proper obeisance. And stayed away as often as he might on one pretext or another. Hunting most often, or hawking, or governing his domains, for he was Lord of the Western Marches.

Vadin had neither right nor duty to creep after him like a spy or an assassin. But Mirain had gone where Vadin could not follow, into Avaryan's temple. It was a day of fasting for the Sun's priests, the dark of Brightmoon, when the god's power grew weak before the might of the Dark; they would chant and pray from sunrise to sunrise, bolstering their god's strength with their own. Mirain, who had gone on his second day in the castle to chant the sunset hymn, had found himself more welcome there than anywhere else in Ianon, except perhaps in his grandfather's presence; thereafter he had sought the temple as often as he might. And he had made it clear that Vadin was not to dog his heels there, even in the outer chambers which were open to any who came.

Thus Vadin was at liberty, and by hell's own contriving he could take no joy in it. Mirain was already gone when he woke in the dawn; woke from a nightmare that haunted him long past waking. He rose, pulled on what garments came to hand, eyed with utterly unwonted disfavor the breakfast that Mirain's servants had left for him. He abandoned it untouched, wandering he cared not where, until he found himself in the stables; and saw Moranden saddling the black-barred dun.

Without thought for what he did, Vadin flung bridle and saddle on Rami and sent her in pursuit. If he had been thinking, he might have acknowledged some deep urge to accost this prince who had been kind to him. To be kind in return, somehow. To explain a betrayal that, doubtless, Moranden had never noticed among so many others.

Moranden had ridden easily but swiftly, without undue stealth, almost straight to the wood. No one hunted there if he valued his life and his soul, nor did anyone ride for pleasure beneath those dim trees. The prince had not loosed his falcon, and he had not turned back even from the guardians of the goddess' grove, the black birds which seemed to infest every branch. The air was full of their cries, the ground of their foul droppings.

Vadin shuddered in his place of concealment. Whether Moranden's intrusion had obscured his own, or whether he had moved more skillfully than he knew, the birds paid him no heed. Yet the wood itself seemed to tremble in outrage. Outlander that he was, bound by the king's command to the son of the Sun, still he dared to trespass in the domain of the Dark. The sky was black with thunder, casting deep twilight under the trees, where one by one the goddess' birds had settled to their rest.

Moranden stood a short spearcast from him, near the edge of a clearing. Open though it was, the darkness seemed no less there. The ground was bare, without grass or flower, save in the center where lay a slab of stone. Rough, hewn by no man's hands, it rose out of the barren earth; a great mound of flowers lay upon it, deep red like heart's blood. A mockery, it may have been, of the blossoms which adorned Avaryan's temple at this season of his waxing power.

Or was Avaryan's altar the mockery?

Again Vadin shivered. This was no place and no worship of his. Northern born, he feared the goddess and accorded her due respect, but he had never been able to love her. Love before Uveryen was a weakness. She fed on fear and on the bitterness of hate.

Moranden stood as if frozen, his falcon motionless upon his wrist, his stallion tethered at the wood's edge far from swift escape. Vadin could not see his face. His shoulders were braced, the muscles taut between them; his free hand was a fist.

The dim air stirred and thickened. Vadin swallowed a cry. Where had been only emptiness stood a half circle of figures. Black robes, black cowls, no face, no hand, no glimpse of brightness. Nor did they speak, these priests of the goddess. Or priestesses? There was no way to tell.

One glided forward. Moranden trembled, a sudden spasm, but held his ground. Perhaps he could not do otherwise.

Wings clapped. The falcon erupted from his hand, jesses broken. Blackness swept over it. A single feather fell, wintry gold, spiraling to Moranden's feet.

The birds of the goddess withdrew. Neither blood nor bone remained of the hawk, not even the bells upon its jesses.

"A pleasant morsel."

The voice was harsh and toneless. Vadin, glancing startled at the robed figure, saw upon its shoulder a black bird. Its beak opened. "A sufficient sacrifice," it said, "for the moment. What do you look for in return?"

Moranden's hand was raised as if the falcon perched even yet upon it. Very slowly he lowered it. "What—" His speech was thick; he shook his head hard and lifted it, drawing a long breath. "I look for nothing. I came as I was summoned. Is there to be no rite? Have I lost my best falcon for nothing?"

"There will be a rite." A mortal voice, this one, and not born within the circle. One stood beyond it, beyond the altar itself, robed as the rest. But her cowl was cast back from a face neither young nor gentle, beautiful and terrible as the flowers on the stone. "There will be a rite," she repeated, coming forward, "and you shall be the Young God once more. But only once. Hereafter we will have done with pretense, and with the blood of mere mute beasts."

The black bird left its perch to settle upon her shoulder. She smoothed its feathers with a finger, crooning to it.

Moranden stood taut, but it was a different tautness, with less of fear, less of awe, and more of impatience. "Pretense? What do you mean, pretense? That *is* the rite: the dance, the coupling. The sacrifice."

"The sacrifice," she said, "yes."

His breath hissed between his teeth. "You don't—" Her hand raised infinitesimally, sketching a flick of assent. "That is forbidden."

"By whom?" She stood full before him now, the bird motionless, eyes glittering. "By whom, Moranden? By the priests of burning Avaryan, and by the king who is their puppet. He gave his daughter to the Sun, who by long custom should have gone to the Dark. But in the end the goddess had her blood."

"Then the goddess should be content."

"Gods are never content."

Moranden's back was stiff. "So then. Once more I act the Young God; but it will be no act. I would have preferred that you had warned me."

Surely this woman was the Lady Odiya, and she was more terribly splendid even than rumor made her. She seemed torn between rage and bitter laughter. "You are a fine figure of a man, my child, and much to the Lady's taste. But you are also a fool. Once more, I have said, you act the god's part. Then do you abdicate in another's favor. Another will undergo the full and ancient rite."

"And die in it," Moranden said harshly. "I don't like it, Mother. Time was when every ninth year a young man died for the good of the tribe; and maybe the tribe was the better for it. Myself, I doubt it. Waste is waste, even in the gods' name."

"Fool," said the Lady Odiya. Once again the black bird shifted. Its talons gripped Moranden's shoulder. Its beak clacked beside his ear as he stood frozen, robbed of breath and arrogance alike. "Sacrifice is never wasted. Not when it can purchase the goddess' favor."

"It is murder."

"Murder," echoed the bird, mocking him. "Man," it said, "would you be king?"

"I would be king," Moranden answered; and that was not the least courageous thing he had ever done, to speak in a steady voice with such a horror on his shoulder. "But what does that have to do with—"

The bird pecked him very, very lightly a hair's breadth from his eye. His head jerked; his hand flew up. "Man," said the bird, arresting the hand in midflight, "you would be king. What would you give to gain the throne?"

"Anything," gritted Moranden. "Anything at all. Except—"

The beak poised like a dagger. "*Except*, man?"

"Except my honor. My soul," he said, "you may have. My life even, if you must."

"The goddess asks none of these. Yet. She asks only this. Give her your sister's son."

Moranden must have known what the creature would ask. Yet he stood as if stunned, bereft of speech.

His mother spoke softly, almost gently. "Give her the boy. Give her the being you hate most in this world, the one who has snatched your throne and your kingdom and given you naught but his scorn. Let him usurp your place but once more; let him die for you. Then you shall be king."

Moranden's eyes clenched shut; his mouth opened, half gasp, half cry. "No!"

The bird tightened its claws until blood welled, vivid upon the bare shoulder. He paid no heed to the pain. "I will have the throne, and very likely I'll have to kill the little bastard to get it. But not this way. Not creeping about in the dark."

Odiya had drawn herself to her full height. "Creeping, Moranden? Is it so you see me? Is it so you have looked on all your life of worship? Have I borne an apostate to destroy us all?"

"I'm a warrior, not a woman or a priest. I do my killing in the daylight where men can see it."

"*He* is a priest!" cried the queen who was not. "He is a sorcerer, a mage born. While you prate of honor and of war, he will witch you into the shadows you despise, and destroy you."

But Moranden was not to be swayed. "So be it. At least I'll die with my honor intact."

"Honor, Moranden? Is it honor to bow to him? Will you die his slave, you who are the only son of Ianon's king? Will you let him set his foot upon your neck?"

"I cannot—" Moranden's breath caught, almost a sob. "It's infamy. To sell—even—that—to betray my own blood."

"Even," the bird said, "to be king?"

"I was meant to be king! I was born—"

"So too was he."

Moranden's lips clamped upon wrath.

"He is mightier than you," said the bird. "He is the one foretold: the Sunborn, the god-king who shall bring all the world beneath his sway and turn all men to the worship of Avaryan. Beside him you are but a shadow, an empty posturer who dares to fancy himself worthy of a throne."

"He is a bastard child," Moranden spat with sudden venom.

"He is the son of the Sun."

Moranden ground his teeth.

"Foreigner and interloper though he is, all Ianon pays him homage. Its people are learning to love him; its beasts fawn before him; its very stones bow beneath his feet. *Lord*, they call him; *king* and *emperor*, god-begotten, prince of the morning."

"I hate him," grated Moranden. "I—hate—"

The bird's beak clashed; its wings stretched. "When we have him," it said, "you shall be king."

Moranden raised his fists. "No. You want him, you fetch him yourself. But be quick, or I'll have him. My way. None other. Or die. And be damned to all your treacheries!"

Sharply, viciously, the bird stabbed his cheek, driving deep through flesh into bone. Moranden's head snapped back. The bird sprang into the air. "Damned!" it shrieked. "Lost and damned!"

The wood was a tumult of wings and voices, sharp talons and cold mocking eyes. And beneath it, a sound as beautiful as it was horrible: the ripple of a woman's laughter.

VADIN STAGGERED ERECT. VAST SHAPES LOOMED ABOUT HIM, trees both immense and ancient, cloaked in the presence of the goddess. Branches clawed at him, roots surged up against his feet; twigs thrust into his face, beating him back. He struck against them, wildly yet with a fixed, half-mad purpose.

His arms flailed at nothing. He stumbled painfully against stone. Flower-sweetness filled his brain, stronger than wine, stronger than dreamsmoke. He flung himself away.

By slow degrees his mind cleared. The space about the altar was empty of birds, of robed priests, of the goddess embodied in the mortal woman. Close by him, almost at his feet, lay what they had discarded. Its face was a mask of blood.

He dropped to his knees beside Moranden. With the hem of his cloak he wiped away the blood. Moranden neither moved nor uttered a sound. One eye stared blindly at the sky; the other was lost in a rush of scarlet.

Vadin might have wept had there been time, or had this been the place for it. Setting his jaw, he stooped and drew the slack arm around his shoulders. With all his half-grown strength, with curses and prayers, he dragged Moranden up. Grimly, step by step, he began to walk.

The wood was deathly silent. The only sound was the rasp of his breath and the hiss of Moranden's in his ear; the shuffling of their feet in the mould; and the hammering of his heart. There were eyes upon him. They watched; they waited. He could taste their hatred, cold and cruel, like blood and iron.

He shut it out with all his will, flooding the levels of his mind with every frivolity he could remember. Love songs, lovemaking, wine and mirth and bawdy jests. And he walked, dragging his senseless burden. Slowly, carefully, to the tune of a drunkard's dirge, while the wood closed in about him. In stillness was death, in surrender destruction; in terror, damnation.

Light glimmered. Surely it was illusion. This wood had no end. He was trapped within it until hé went mad or died.

The light grew. And suddenly it was all about him, the clear light of day upon a long slope, and Rami tethered at a safe distance from Moranden's stallion, and the Vale below him. With a long sigh he let Moranden slide to the ground. His own body followed, suddenly boneless. A red mist thickened about him.

A shadow loomed in it, darkness edged with fire. It

stooped over him, spreading vast wings, crying out in words of power and terror. He cried back and fought, drawing strength from the depths of his will. The shadow gripped him. A hand lifted, all dark, but in its center a sun.

Vadin gasped and went slack. The shadow was Mirain with the Mad One behind him, the hands Mirain's, holding Vadin up with ease that belied his body's smallness. There was blood on his face, on his kilt.

"Not mine," he said in his own familiar voice. "It covers you." He shifted Vadin's weight to his shoulder, raised his hand again. Involuntarily Vadin flinched. The god's brand flamed even yet, like molten gold.

It was warm, not hot; flesh-warm. It eased him down, drew forth a cloth from he knew not where, began gently to cleanse his face. He struck it aside. "Let me be. I need nothing. Help me look after the prince."

Mirain's expression had been grave, intent. Now it darkened. "You should have left him where he lay."

Vadin was as weak as a child, yet he dragged himself up, away from Mirain, toward Moranden. The elder prince lay slack and somehow shrunken, as if the goddess had taken life with his blood, draining away his soul. As he had done by the altar, Vadin strove to stanch the flood. He could not see Moranden's eye. It was all blood. If it was pierced—

"It is no more than he deserves."

Vadin whirled in a white rage. Mirain, even proud Mirain, fell back a step. But he came forward again and looked down at his mother's brother and said in that calm, young, royal voice, "He plots treason. He deserves to lose much more than an eye."

"He is your kin."

"He is my enemy."

Vadin struck him. But the blow was feeble. Worse were the words he flung without measure or mercy. "Who are you to judge this man? You, you haughty prince, so firm in your righteousness, with the god's blood in your veins and your empire in front of you, what do you know of right or of power or of deserving?" His wrath had brought him to his feet; it held him there, towering over Mirain. "From the moment of your birth you were destined to be king. So you say. So the songs say. So even I was beginning to believe, in spite of all I could do.

"But now." His voice lowered almost to a whisper. "Now I see you for what you are. Go back to your grandfather and leave me to remember who is truly my lord!"

He was far beyond any care for his own safety. But when his voice had stilled, his heart beat hard, and not only with anger. All expression had vanished from Mirain's face, but the black eyes were blazing. He could strike Vadin down with the merest flick of his hand, blind him as he had blinded his mother's betrayer, turn all his high words to the croaking of carrion birds.

Vadin raised his chin and made himself meet that unmeetable gaze. "Or," he said quite calmly, "you can help me. He needs a healer, and quickly. Will your lordship deign to fetch one?"

Mirain's fist clenched. Vadin waited for him to strike. He said, "It would take too long to bring anyone from the castle."

Vadin turned his back on him. Moranden had changed even while they spoke. His face was grey beneath the lurid scarlet of the wound; his eyes were glazed, his breath rattling in his throat. "But," Vadin said to the heedless air, "his hurt is so small, and he so strong."

"The goddess is stronger than he."

Mirain knelt on the other side of Moranden's body. Vadin regarded him with a flat, empty stare. He was neither prince nor enemy now, only a weary annoyance. "Yes," Vadin said without inflection, "she is strong. Will you kill him now? He's at your mercy."

Mirain looked at Vadin in something close to horror. Later, maybe, he would find some small comfort in that. "You are strong," Vadin went on. He cradled Moranden's head in his lap. "Now, god's son. Destroy this priest of the Dark."

Mirain tossed his head from side to side as if in pain. "I cannot. Not this way. Not . . ."

"Then," Vadin said, "heal him."

Mirain stared. He had never looked younger or less royal. "Heal him," Vadin repeated without compunction. "You're a mage, you told me yourself. You're full to bursting with your father's power. It can destroy this man, or it can save him. Choose!"

"And if I choose neither?" Mirain could hardly speak; his voice cracked on the final word, to his bitter and visible shame.

"If you won't choose, you're no king. Now or ever."

Mirain moved convulsively, flinging up his hand: defense, protest, royal outrage. Vadin held fast, although he averted his eyes from the flame of gold. "Choose," he said again.

Mirain's hand lowered. Slowly it settled upon Moranden's cheek. The elder prince trembled under it, and twisted as if in pain.

Death, Vadin thought dully. *He chooses death*. As in his own way Moranden had chosen, for the sake of the kingship. They were kin indeed, these two, closer than either could bear to know.

Mirain's eyes closed. His face tightened with strain; his breath came harsh. Someone cried out—Moranden, Mirain, Vadin, perhaps all three.

Mirain sank back upon his heels. Vadin looked down; his eyes stretched wide. Moranden lay still, eyes closed as if in sleep, breathing easily. Where the wound had been, on the high arch of cheekbone at the very edge of his eye, was a scar in the shape of a spearhead. It faded even as Vadin watched, and greyed as if with age.

A stir drew his glance upward again. Mirain stood erect, cradling his golden hand. "I am mad," he said. "Someday I may be king. But I am not a murderer. Not even when I can see—" A shudder racked him. "May the god preserve us all."

Six

VADIN STOOD ONCE MORE IN THE SHADOWS. CLEAN shadows, fire-cast, dancing about the edges of the king's chamber, seeming to keep time to the music of Ymin's harp. She played no melody that he could discern, simply a pattern of single notes, random and beautiful as rain upon a pool.

The king sat at a table near the fire. A lamp shed a steady yellow glow upon the book before him. He was a great rarity in a Ianyn lord: he could read. And did so as often as he could, and savored it enough to want to learn the intricate letters of Han-Gilen. Or maybe that was only an excuse to keep his grandson near him, standing as he stood now with his arm about the old man's shoulders, reading in a low clear voice. By all accounts the king had never been a man for touching, walking apart in the armor of his royalty; but Mirain had pierced those strong defenses. Strangely enough, the king seemed to accept that, even to take pleasure in it, although any other who dared such familiarity would have paid in pain.

They laughed, the old man and the young one, at a sudden turn of wit. So close together in the lamp's light, their faces were strikingly alike: proud, high-nosed, deep-eyed. When Mirain was old he would look just so, like a carven king.

Vadin shivered in a sudden chill. Mirain's face, gaining

years in his mind's eye, blurred suddenly and faded. As if Mirain would never grow old. As if—

The squire shook himself hard. This whole hideous day had bereft him of his wits. Moondark fancies to begin it, and the horror in the wood, and the rest lost in a fog. When he tried to think he could not, or else saw night-mare visions. And Mirain had said no word to him since they left Moranden to recover his senses in the sunlight with words of guard upon him; since they rode back to the castle together, the prince half a length ahead and the squire behind as was eminently proper. With each of Rami's long smooth strides, Vadin had sunk deeper into silence. But Mirain had conducted himself as if nothing had happened, except that he made no effort to pierce his servant's new-forged armor.

The book was rolled and bound, the music stilled. Mirain sat at the king's feet with his arm across the scarred and age-hardened knees. "Yes," he said with the hint of a smile, "I walked up from Han-Gilen. At first because I would have been too conspicuous astride, with the prince scouring the land for me; and afterward because I found it pleasant. Outside of Han-Gilen, no one knew my face, and I kept my hand out of sight. I was only a vagabond like any other." His smile widened. "Sometimes I was wet or cold or hungry; but I was free, and it was splendid. I could go where I chose, stop where I pleased. I tarried a whole cycle of Greatmoon in a village that had lost its priest."

"A village?" The king's voice was a low rumble. "Among common folk?"

"Farmfolk and hunters," Mirain answered him. "They were good people, on the whole. And not one knew who or what I was. No one called me king or prince. No one bowed to me for my father's sake. One"—he laughed a little—"one even brawled with me. One of the girls had taken to following me about, and she was promised to a wealthy man as folk are reckoned there. His house had a door of wood, and his father had a bull and nine cows. He would not suffer such a rival as I, a spindling lad with a braid like a woman's. He challenged me. I accepted, of course; the lady was watching."

"And you promptly struck the peasant down for his insolence."

Mirain laughed again, freely. "I was trying to be careful, because I was war-trained by masters and he was but a plowboy. And he came round with a great sweeping blow and flattened me."

The king bridled. But Mirain was grinning. He smiled at last, wryly. "What said the lady to that?"

"She shrieked and ran to my aid, which was rather gratifying. But in the end she decided she would rather have a bull and nine cows and a wooden door, than a lover whose body was vowed to the god. I said the marriage-words for them the day I left. By then their new priestess had come, but both of them insisted: None but I must see them wedded. I foretold for them a dozen children and a lifetime of prosperity, and they were well content."

"Were you?" Ymin asked, abandoning her harp for the fire's warmth.

Mirain turned to her, half grave, half smiling. "I was free again. I understand now why the law enjoins a Journey upon the young initiate, though mine perforce was shortened. But I made a year do for seven."

"You may yet have your full Journey," said the king.

Mirain clasped the gaunt gnarled hand in his young strong one. "No, my lord. My mother Journeyed for both of us while you waited with no word of her. You will not have to wait again."

The king's free hand passed over Mirain's thick waving hair, a rare caress. "I would wait for you though it were a hundred years."

"One and twenty are quite enough." Mirain raised his head. "Grandfather. Do I trouble you too much? Would you rather I had never come?"

Ymin drew her breath in sharply, but the king smiled. "You know I would not."

"Yes," Mirain admitted, "I do know. Nor would I be aught but here."

"Even to be free upon the world's road?"

"Even so," he said.

WHEN MIRAIN LEFT THE KING HE DID NOT GO DIRECTLY to bed, but remained for a time at his window. This had become a custom of his, a moment of silence with the garden's night scents rising to sweeten his chamber. It had been early spring when first he came, the passes but newly opened after winter's snows. Now it was full spring. Brightmoon was dark, but Greatmoon was rising, waxing to the full. The battlements glowed blue-white before him. "Father," Mirain said, "when you begot me, did you bethink yourself that I might not be equal to your task?"

The silence was absolute. Mirain sighed a little; when he spoke again it might have been Vadin he addressed, however obliquely. "Ah well. It's not as if he were a mortal man, or one of the thousand tamed gods of the west, to come at any creature's bidding. Even his own son." He rested his cheek against the edge of the window. The stone was luminous with somewhat more than moon-light, although it was far yet from dawn. It knew him, the king had said more than once. Where he was, the castle responded as to the sun's coming.

He turned, his right hand a fist at his side. It could not clench as tightly as it might, stiffened by gold where gold had no right to be. "It hurts," he said, soft yet taut. "It burns. It fills my hand like a great golden coin, a coin heated in fire, that I can never let go. Sometimes it's greater, sometimes less; sometimes it seems no worse than metal warmed too much by the sun, sometimes it takes all my poor strength to endure in silence. I'm proud of that, Vadin. I've never wept or cried out, or even spoken of it, since I was a young child. No one ever knew what pain was mine, except my mother, and the Prince of Han-Gilen. And certainly—certainly my sister." He paused; his brows knit, eased. He almost smiled. "Odd that I should think of her tonight. It must be my mood. Rampant self-pity. Little good it does, either, to put a name to it. Shall I conjure it away? Look."

Vadin had no choice, no time to choose. Mirain's eyes

had seized him, enspelled him, sucked him in. He was within them. He *was* Mirain. A body of no great beauty or consequence, centered about a white agony. But the agony retreated, held at bay by a will as strong as forged iron. He saw a face: a child's thin solemn countenance with skin the color of amber and hair as red as new copper. From the time she could walk she had appointed herself Mirain's shadow; which often made the wits laugh, for he was the dark one, all blackwood and raven, and she was honey and fire. But she was unshakable, even for ridicule, even for outright cruelty.

"You shame me!" he had cried once. She had escaped her nurse and scorned the placid mount deemed proper for a maidchild of barely seven summers, and stolen his own outgrown pony, and set out after him as he rode upon a hunt. She had mastered the black devil of a pony, which surprised him not at all; but her intrusion on the chase, among a round dozen of the prince's squires, put him out of all charity.

"You shame me," he repeated in his coldest voice. "You drag at me like shackles. I don't want you here, I don't want you dangling at my tail, I don't—"

She looked at him. The pony was too large for her, the saddlecloth awry, her hair tangled with twigs and straggling over her eyes, but her stare set all the rest at naught. It was not the stare of a young child. "You're not ashamed," she said. "You don't hate me either."

He opened his mouth and shut it again. The hunt was long gone, hot on a scent and unmindful of his absence. He could hear the baying of the hounds growing faint even as he tarried.

The pony tossed its wicked head and threatened his stallion with its horns. It was all she could do to hold it back, but she did it without any lessening of her intensity. "I let you alone when you really need it. You know that."

"I must need it very seldom indeed, then."

"When you wanted to play with Kieri in the hayloft—"

His cheeks flamed; his head throbbed. He flung himself at her. They tumbled to the ground together, their mounts shying over and past them; he beneath, she flailing on top of him. She was a negligible weight, but her elbows were wickedly sharp.

He lay winded, trying to curse her. She sat on him and laughed. "Hal says you have to play all you can now before you win your torque, because after that—"

He clapped his marked hand over her mouth. The sight of it alone was enough for most, but Elian feared neither god nor man. She sank her teeth into it.

By design or by fortune, she bypassed the brand and bit flesh. Pain on top of spiraling pain emptied him of all wrath or shame and cast him howling on the edge of darkness.

The lesser pain faded. The greater swelled without cause, without end, beyond all hope of bearing. Yet he bore it, fully and horribly aware of it, even as the pit gaped before his feet. It would not swallow him into merciful oblivion. It would—not—

The pain was gone.

Not wholly. It had shrunk to its least dimensions, the closest to painlessness he could ever know, but after that blinding agony it was relief so perfect that he could have wept. His eyes, clearing, saw Elian kneeling by him, clutching his hand to her heart. Her face was grey-green, her voice a croak. "Mirain. Oh, Mirain!"

He had no strength to pull his hand away. He could barely speak. "What—what did you—"

"I took it away." Her face twisted. "It hurt. How can anything hurt so much?"

"You took it away," he repeated stupidly. "You . . . took it . . . Elian. Witch-baby. Do you know what you've done?"

"It *hurt*." She cradled it as tenderly as if it had been her own. "It always hurts. Why, Mirain?"

"You can heal it. Elian, little firemane, you have your father's magic."

She disregarded that. Of course she had the power; she had always had it; and being what he was, he should have known. "Why does it hurt, Mirain?"

"Because my father makes it hurt."

Her brows met. Her jaw thrust forward. "Tell him to stop."

Even in his weakness he could laugh. "But, infant, he's the god. No one can tell him what to do."

"*I* can. He hurts you. He shouldn't. Especially there, where it hurts most. It's not right."

"It makes me remember who I am; what I'm for. It keeps me from growing too proud."

She scowled, stubborn. "There's no need for it."

"No?" he asked. "I was being cruel to you. You see how I paid."

"I have good strong teeth. Even if half of them aren't grown in yet." She patted his hand, which showed no marks of her passing. "You won't hurt again while I have anything to say about it."

"NOR DID I," SAID MIRAIN. "MUCH. BUT I LEFT HER, TO follow where my father led. No one here can cool the fire."

Vadin had no voice to speak. It was all lost in horror. Sorcery—soul-slavery—

"My father wrought me," Mirain said. "He shaped me for his purposes. The Sword of the Sun, his mightiest weapon against the Dark. But he made me in mortal likeness, flesh and blood and bone, and worst of all, a mind that can think and be afraid. I may not be strong enough. I may fail him. And if I fail—"

"Stop it!" Vadin's shout was raw with the twofold effort. Of speaking; of keeping his hands from that gold-circled throat. "My body is yours to do with as you will. My service is yours for as long as my body lasts. But if you touch my mind again, by all the gods that ever were, I'll kill you."

"I didn't touch your mind," Mirain said, low and still.

"You didn't, did you? No. You raped it."

For all the heed Mirain paid him, he might never have spoken. "I didn't touch you. I opened my own mind, and you plunged headlong into it."

"Wizard's logic. You led me into a trap. You violated me."

"I showed you the truth."

"Yes. That under the upstart prince is a trembling coward."

Mirain laughed. It sounded like honest mirth, with no great measure of mockery. But priests were good liars, and princes better, and royal pretenders best of all. "I'll lay you a wager, Vadin. Before this year is out, you'll call me friend. You'll do it willingly, and you'll do it gladly, and you'll do it without the least regret."

"I'll see you in hell first."

"That's possible," Mirain said, lightly but not in jest. "What will you lay on it?"

"My soul."

Mirain's breath hissed sharply. His teeth were sharper still, bared in a grin. "I warn you, Vadin. I can take it."

"I know you can." This was blackly wonderful, like racing the lightning, or dancing on blades. "And you? What stakes can you offer?"

"A place at my right hand, and the highest lordship, save only mine alone, in my empire that will be."

"I can claim that, Mirain of Han-Gilen."

"I know you can," said Mirain. His hand cast darts of light into Vadin's eyes. Its clasp that sealed the wager was startling for more than mere strength: it did not sear Vadin's own hand to ash. All the fire burned within.

They drew apart in the same instant, with the same feral wariness. Half of one another, half of the one who had come into the room behind them. Someone large, with a long stride, but light on his feet. They turned slowly, as if at ease, but their bodies tensed.

Prince Moranden stood in his accustomed stance, legs well apart, shoulders back. The goddess' brand had done nothing to mar his beauty, and he held his head as if he knew it. His eyes flicked from one to the other. With a quiver of the lids he dismissed the squire, focusing full and burning-cold upon his sister's son.

Mirain let the silence stretch until it broke. "Uncle," he said lightly, coolly, "you honor me. How may I serve you?"

The southern formality curled Moranden's lip. He sat without asking leave, stretching out at his ease. Vadin thought of the black lion of the mountains, that was most deadly when it seemed most quiet. "You, my lord?" asked the elder prince. "Serve me? That's an honor too great for this humble mortal to claim."

Mirain left the window and approached another chair, but he did not sit in it. While he stood, he was a little taller than his unwelcome guest. He leaned against the carven back. "We are inundated with honor tonight. I honor you with my service, you honor me with your presence. Is it courtesy that brings you here at last? Or need? Or simple goodwill?"

Moranden laughed sincerely, but with an edge of bitterness. "Your manners are prettier than mine, prince. Shall we leave off playing? Courtesy's a word I don't know the meaning of, northern savage that I am. Need . . . the day I need the likes of you, my young kinsman, you can be sure I'm in dire straits."

"Then," said Mirain levelly, "it must be goodwill."

The elder prince hooked a knee over the arm of his chair. "Very good, sister-son! So good I'll even tell you a truth. I'd give my soul to be rid of you. I think I already have."

"Given your soul," Mirain asked, "or got rid of me?"

"Both." Moranden rubbed his cheek as if the scar pained him. But he smiled a white wolf-smile. "O beloved of my father, if you were given the chance and an ample reward, would you go back where you came from?"

"What sort of reward?"

"Why, anything. Anything at all, short of the throne."

"Which you would take for yourself."

"Of course. I've waited long enough for it. Considerably longer than you, and considerably closer quarters."

"My mother," Mirain said softly, "was the king's heir."

"Much it meant to her, that she never bothered to come and prove it. But she was half a foreigner herself. I've heard the tales of her mother, the yellow woman; the Asanian emperor, having got her on a slave, thought it a fine jest to toss her to an outsize barbarian. Who fancied he was getting a princess, and strutted with it. She proved a poor bargain. One daughter as undersized as herself: that was all she could give to her lord and master."

"But the daughter had a child, who if equally undersized, at least was comfortably male."

Moranden looked him up and down. "Are you?"

"Shall I strip and let you see?"

Moranden laughed. He was laughing too much and too freely. Yes, Vadin thought; there was a scent of wine on him, and something else, sharp, acrid. Hate? Fear? He laughed, and his eyes glittered beneath the lowered lids. "Yes, by the gods! Strip and show me."

Mirain's own eyes were bitter-bright. With a swift movement he stripped off his kilt. "Well, sir?"

Moranden took his time about it. He rose for it, walking completely around the motionless prince like a buyer in a slave market. When he faced Mirain again, he set his hands on his hips and his head to one side. "Maybe," he said. One hand flashed out to Mirain's cheek, catching on the soft young stubble. "You don't try overly hard to prove it. Why do you make yourself like a eunuch? Are you someone's fancy-boy?"

Mirain sat where Moranden had sat, lolling where Moranden had lolled, smiling through set teeth. "Even if I were so bent, my vows would forbid it."

"Convenient, those vows of yours."

"They bind me. Until I come to the throne; then I'm free of them."

"No doubt you can hardly wait."

"I can wait as long as I must."

Again Moranden's hand went to his face. He brought it down sharply and clasped it behind him, scowling down the proud arch of his nose. Abruptly he said, "I remember. What you did."

"Under compulsion."

"You did it." Moranden's shoulders flexed. They did not take well to humility, even such haughty humility as this. "I owe you for that. My life, maybe. I was close to the edge when you brought me back."

"In my father's name. That should comfort you; for if

the Dark One had your soul, you could not have answered that call."

"I owe you," Moranden repeated. The words were coming hard, as if around bile. "I'll give you this in return. Go now, and take what I offered you. Take all you can carry. You can conquer the world better from the Hundred Realms than you ever could from the wilds of the north."

"But Ianon is mine by blood-right and heir-right. What better place to begin?"

"If we let you."

It was a lion's growl. Mirain laughed at it. He looked feverish; his words came as if of their own accord, demon-words, light and mocking. "Let, say you? Let? When it took half a cask of wine to bring you here tonight?" He leaned back in his chair, foot swinging idly; but he cradled his hand as if it had been a wounded creature. "If your gratitude comes so hard, need I fear your enmity?"

Moranden seemed to swell in the firelight. With no memory of movement, Vadin found himself beside his liege lord, sword drawn and on guard. Above its glitter he met Moranden's eyes and found there a black and naked hate. "Child," said the elder prince deep in his throat. "Kingling. I won't offer again. Thanks or reward. Or anything else."

"That is well. You spare me the effort of refusal."

"You think yourself clever. Think on, little fool. But don't expect me to lick your feet."

"That," said Mirain, "I would not dream of." He yawned. "It grows late, and no doubt you are weary. You may go to your bed."

Moranden stood speechless. Abruptly he spun away.

For a long while prince and squire stared at the empty air, the closed door. Moranden had shut it with softness more potent than any violence.

Mirain raised his burning hand, turned it, clenched it: defying him, denying him, rejecting him utterly. "He cannot touch me. He has not the power. For he is a mortal man, and I am the king who will be. I . . . will . . . be king."

Seven

"THERE SLINKS THE FOREIGNER'S DOG."
Vadin had been offending no one. He was
free for the first time since Moranden's wounding, standing in the market contemplating a bit of frip-
pery and the girl to whom he would give it, with Kav's
comfortable bulk and still more comfortable silence for
companions. It was Kav who kept him from lunging blindly
toward the voice, who wrapped a broad hand around his
narrow arm and simply stood, firm as the earth beneath
their feet.

The voice was young and lordly and pitched to mad-
den, sneering just behind Vadin's right ear. "Ah, look! He
buys bangles and beads for his dainty master. How do
they serve one another, do you think? Does the boy become a man when the lamps are out?"

"Let me go!" Vadin snarled at his captor.

Kav did not shift his grip. The clear eyes in the heavy
sullen face flicked once toward the voice, and then away.

Again it pricked, with laughter in it. "They go well
together, longshanks and shortshanks, cowards of a feather.
Did you hear what his highness will do when the throne
comes to him? He'll dress all the lords in trousers, command them to shave their beards, and make them swear
to serve him as slaves serve their masters."

Kav moved steadily and inexorably away from the voice

and toward the wineshop. One or two squires were there already and well in their cups. Vadin fought; he could as easily have fought the castle wall. His hand fell to his dagger.

"Don't," Kav said in his deep growl of a voice.

Vadin cursed him. He grunted, which was his way of laughing. They were under the awning; he set Vadin firmly on the bench between Olvan and Ayan and thrust a cup into the clenching fist. Vadin gulped the sour ale, crying through it, "He spoke treason! He said—he said I—"

"Words," said Kav.

"Words breed blows, damn you!"

"Did he say anything you haven't thought yourself?"

"I don't *say* it." Vadin stopped, straightened. All three were looking at him. His mouth tasted of sickness. He lashed out. "Yes. Stare. You worship the ground he walks on. You'd kiss his foot if he asked."

"Except that he wouldn't," Ayan said, refilling Vadin's cup, "and that's why we worship him. Doesn't he take weapons practice with the rest of us? And didn't he insist on it, and dare the king's displeasure? And he a knight in Han-Gilen and ten times as good as most of us will ever be."

"Five times," Vadin judged sourly. "You know what people say about that. He won't take on anyone who'll come close to him; he knows he'll lose. So he makes fools of us, and witches us into loving him for it."

Olvan snorted. "Jealous nonsense. He learns from Adjan, who's the best teacher in Ianon. He teaches us when we insist. He likes us."

"Gods don't learn or like. They rule."

"Prince Mirain is only half a god," Ayan pointed out. But his tongue caressed the name, and he sighed; then he frowned. "We know that. We know him. But it's true, people are saying things, and not in whispers anymore, either. I was on watch last night; I broke up a fight, and people on both sides were howling that they were loyal to the true prince. They were breaking heads over it."

"Who won?" Kav inquired.

"No one," said Vadin before Ayan could speak. "No one at all." His cup was empty again. He could not remember draining it. He poured another, and another. He was going to have someone's neck. He was not certain whose. But lovely Ledi was there to divert him, even without the bauble he had meant to buy her. And another cup of ale, and a song or two, and a warm tangle in Ledi's bed, all four and she, and when he was done he would remember rage.

"Because," he said once or a dozen times, "no one—no one—calls Vadin alVadin a coward."

WITH THE SUN'S COMING, LEDI LEFT THE TANGLE TO SORT itself: Olvan and Ayan coiled about one another, and Kav solid and sufficient unto himself, and Vadin hunting blindly for the soft woman-body. He found something, and its skin was velvet, but steel-hard beneath; and it was much too narrow and supple to be Ledi. His eyes dragged themselves open. He had his arm crooked lovingly about Mirain's waist; the prince regarded him with wry amusement. He recoiled.

The wryness deepened. Vadin opened his mouth; Mirain's hand covered it. His other, golden, beckoned.

Out in the courtyard, with the sun beating down on his tortured skull, Vadin let it free. "What in the thrice nine hells are you doing here?"

Mirain's glance was pointed. Vadin fumbled into kilt and belt and cloak, and plunged his head into the vat of rainwater beside the gate. He came up a little clearer of mind, if in no less pain. "I thought I had the whole night to myself."

"You did." Mirain tilted his head. "Your Ledi is a woman of great wit and wisdom."

Vadin fought down his rising temper. "My lord," he said with great care, "I would thank you not to—"

"I'm not mocking her. She served me new bread and honey, and she talked with me. She wasn't afraid of me."

"And why should she be?"

Mirain looked at him. Down at him. With all the pride of a crowned king and all the puissance of a god. Then he

was Mirain again, shoulder-high to Vadin, saying, "I see.
I'm small, and therefore harmless. Who in Ianon can say
differently?"

"All the king's squires, and one of your own, and a
certain prince." Vadin shook himself before he turned
into a poet. "Why are you here? Is something wrong?"

Mirain shrugged. He was looking very young and very
guileless and therefore, to Vadin's mind, very suspicious.
"I missed your presence."

"You had Pathan. Pathan the prince, who's heir to two
fiefs and a princedom, and who's fought his way to captain of squires, and who'll make knight this High Summer. More than that; he'll be Younger Champion, and in
a year or two he'll give the elder good reason to fear for
his title. He should have been your squire from the first.
He's worthy of you."

"Do you think that, Vadin?"

Vadin was not to be trapped, even by his own runaway
tongue. "The king should think so. You're the light of his
fading eyes."

"Pathan is pleasant enough," Mirain said. "Handsome.
Brilliant. Not remarkably larger than I, and undisturbed
by it. He plays a wicked game of kings-and-cities."

Vadin, who was none of those things, smote his hands
together. "*So!* Ask your grandfather for him. He'd be
hugely honored."

"Unfortunately," Mirain went on undeterred, "he bores
me to tears. All that relentless perfection. And such utterly unshakable loyalty to his king's chosen heir. When
he woke me—impeccably attired at the ungodly hour a
Sun-priest has to wake, and waiting on me with flawless
effacement—it was all I could do not to scream. I did
order him out. I think I was acceptably polite."

Vadin could see it. Pathan, the epitome of the squire,
the vision toward which Adjan struggled ceaselessly to
drive all the rest, waking Mirain with the exact courteous
touch, bathing and dressing and serving him without the
slightest slip of mind or body, and being dismissed with
Mirain's inimitable, acid, southern-bred politeness. After,

no doubt, a strong dose of that prince's resistance to any service which he preferred to perform himself.

Vadin's lips kept twitching. He bit them; they escaped. The laughter burst out of him all at once.

Mirain's grin was utterly wicked. Vadin fought for a scowl, managed only a dying gasp. "You—Pathan—you're as mad as I am."

"One could say I have deplorable taste. In seneldi, in causes, and in friends."

The last word drove Vadin back into himself. "I'm your servant. My lord."

The black eyes narrowed a fraction. The proud head bowed once, conceding nothing. "Ledi will feed you. Then I require your service."

Which was to trail behind him through every square and alley of the town in the market-day crowd, testing the currents of speech and, no doubt, of mind; tarrying to overhear a round of gossip, to down a cup of wine, to watch a sword-dancer. Like any proper wizard, Mirain could make himself invisible when he chose. Else surely people would not have been so free with their scandal-mongering, and they had much to say of the two princes, the new and the old.

"I'm for the man I know," said a buyer at the senel fair. "And what do we know about this Mirain? He comes all unlooked for, he wears a torque and a braid like a Sun-priest, he claims to be the gods know what. He could be out to slaughter us all."

"Prince Moranden is a hard man," opined a copper-smith's wife as she sat on her doorstep spinning wool into thread. "He looks fine and fair; he has a smile or a word for everyone; but he has a cold eye. I saw it happen when I was a girl in Shaios. Sweet as honey, Lord Keian was, till the day his father died; and people said afterward that maybe the old man had had help on his way. And when the heir came to the high seat, he went stark bitter. Killed all his kin, even to the women and babes, and taxed us till we starved, and went to war against Suveien. And won, thank the gods, but he died winning, and his lady ruled us well till the little lord Tien was old enough to take his place."

The elders sighed over their gaming in the sun, and the eldest said, "It's an ill day when there are two high princes and only one throne to be had, and the elder's not likely to step down for the upstart younger, chosen heir or not. They've drawn their lines; and mark my words, they won't take long now to come to blows."

"I hear they have already," the youngest of them observed, casting dice for his move in kings-and-cities. "I hear the young one came at the elder with a catsclaw dagger and laid his face open, and called on magic to heal it up again."

"For regret?" an onlooker wondered.

"For contempt. And the elder prince has a scar to remind him of the insult."

"Foreigners," muttered the eldest. "Both of them. Now if the king had had the sense to take a wife at home—"

The onlooker leaned across the board. "I hear they're neither of them his kin. The young one's an enchanter from the Nine Cities, painted up like one of us and enspelled to look like the princess who's dead; the elder belongs to one of the Marcher rebels. I remember when the king brought that woman here, and I remember how soon he got the whelp on her. Who's to say she wasn't carrying it when he took her?"

MIRIAN PULLED VADIN AWAY, AND NONE TO SOON. HE himself seemed no more than amused. "An enchanter," he said. "From the Nine Cities." He laughed. "O that I were! What would I do to this poor kingdom, do you think?"

"Turn it into a land of the walking dead."

Mirain sobered abruptly. "Don't say such things!" Vadin stared, startled at the change in him. His lips were touched with grey, his eyes wide and wild.

Little by little he calmed. Very quietly he said, "Never speak of what could be. Would you be heard and heeded?"

"Would you do what I said you would?"

"The goddess is my father's sister. She would give all her power to have me for her own, for that would wound

him to the heart. And it would be—not impossible—
perhaps not even difficult. Perhaps . . . perhaps . . . almost easy. To let her—to be—"

Vadin hauled Mirain up by the shoulders and shook
him hard. And when he could walk, after a fashion, saw
him into a stall and plied him with wine until the darkness began to fade. He caught at the cup and drank
deep enough to drown, and came up gasping; but his
eyes were clear. "My thanks," he said at last.

Vadin lifted his hand, let it fall. One did one's duty.

Mirain sighed and drained the wine. If he might have
spoken again, another voice forestalled him, a clear trained
voice embarked upon a tale.

"Indeed, sirs, it was a prodigy: a woman white as a
bone, with eyes the color of blood." It was a talespinner in
the motley rags of his calling, with a cup in one hand and
a girl on his knee. Fine dark wine and a fine dark girl. He
paused to savor both. She giggled; he kissed her soundly
and drank deep. "Aye, white she was, which was a wonder
and a horror. She belonged to the goddess, people said.
Her kinsmen kept her in a cage built like a temple and
fed her with sacrifices—taking the best portions for themselves, of course. She would writhe and babble; they
would call it prophecy, and interpret it for whatever price
the market would bear. Whole suns of gold, even, when
the local chieftains came to ask about their wars. They
were always pleased, because they were always promised
victory."

"And did they get it?"

The man turned to Mirain with no hint of surprise to
find him there. "Some did, prince. Some didn't; but they
never came back to gainsay her. Till one fine day a young
man came striding into the shrine. He gave her his sacrifice: a bit of journey-bread and a handful of berries. Her
keepers would have whipped him out then, but they were
curious to see what he would do. Very little, in fact. He
sat down in front of the cage, and the sibyl ate what he
had brought, untidily enough to be sure, with her unholy
eyes upon him all the while. He stared straight back; he
even smiled.

"He was mad, the keepers decided. He looked like a poor wayfarer, but they thought they glimpsed gold on him under the rags. Maybe, after all, he was a prince in disguise. 'Put your question,' they commanded him at length when he showed no sign of beginning.

"He paid them no heed at all. By then the sibyl had come to the bars of her cage, reaching through it. Her hands were as thin and sharp-taloned as a white eagle's. She was filthy; she stank. Yet our young hero took her hand and smiled and said, 'I shall set you free.'

"Her kinsmen reached for their daggers. But they found that they could not move. They were caged as securely as their prisoner, bound with chains no eye could see.

" 'Only name my name,' the stranger said, 'and you shall be free.'

"They had proclaimed themselves the mouthpieces of prophecy; yet not one could utter a word. But the madwoman, the idiot, the wordless seeress, bowed as low as the stranger would let her, and said clearly, 'Avaryan. Your name is Avaryan.' " The talespinner paused. The silence had spread from the wineseller's stall to the street without. His hearers waited, hardly breathing. He struck his hands together with a sound like a thunderclap. "And behold! Fire fell from heaven and shattered the cage, and smote to the ground all that false and venal priesthood; and their victim stood forth free and sane. But she wept. For the stranger who was the god—the stranger had vanished away."

The stall erupted into applause; a shower of coins fell into the girl's cupped hands. Mirain added his own, a silver solidus of Han-Gilen. For every patron the girl had a kiss or a curtsey, but she won the talespinner's own low bow. "My tale was pleasing to my prince?"

"It was well told," said Mirain, "though I pity the poor sibyl. Does she live yet?"

"Ah, my lord, that is another story."

Mirain smiled. "And you, of course, will tell it if we beg you."

"If my prince commands," said the talespinner.

"Well?" Mirain asked of the others. "Shall I?"

"Aye!" they called back.

Mirain turned to the talespinner. "Tell on then, with this bit of copper to sweeten your labor."

"WELL NOW, THAT'S BLISS, TO HAVE TIME TO SPARE FOR market tales."

Vadin had seen him come. Mirain must have sensed it; he turned slowly, with perfect calm. Moranden stood directly behind him. He smiled with a very slight edge. "What, uncle! Back already from the hunt?"

If that struck the mark, Moranden showed no sign of it. "No hunting for me today. But then, you wouldn't know, would you? Our troubles haven't yet come into the talespinners' repertoires."

People were watching and listening, distracted from the tale by the prospect of a royal quarrel. But Moranden blocked the only clear path of escape. "There's more to be had in the market than old legends," Mirain said. "Is it true, uncle, that the mountain folk have been raiding on the Western Marches?"

"A tribe or three," replied Moranden.

"And others have taken advantage of the opportunity, have they not? Have settled the tribes to be sure, but finding themselves armed and armored, have declared themselves free of their lord. A dire thing, that, and worse yet when the lord is royal and my uncle. Surely people lie when they accuse you of over-harshness."

Moranden's eyes narrowed and began to glitter. The scar was livid beneath them; his face twisted a little as if he knew pain. But wrath was stronger, tempered with hate. "Not all of us can rule under the sun of loving kindness, or take our ease among the rabble. Some must fight to keep that rabble in hand."

"As you will be doing, my lord?"

"As I must do. I leave at dawn to settle your borders, Throne Prince of Ianon. Do I merit your highness' blessing?"

Mirain was silent, tight-lipped. Moranden smiled. "Remember, my prince, as you sleep safe within these walls.

No enemy has ever walked here, or so they say; nor shall he while I live to defend you."

Mirain's head came up. "You need not trouble yourself to protect me."

"Indeed?" Moranden looked down at him, measuring him with unveiled scorn. "Then who will?"

"I guard myself," gritted Mirain. "I am no ill warrior."

"You are not," his uncle conceded. "Certainly you hold your own among the younger lads."

Vadin should have moved then. He should have moved long since. But even breath was frozen out of him, or enspelled into stillness. He could only stand and watch, and know what this mad master of his would say. Said with great care, with the precision of icy rage. "I am a knight of Han-Gilen and a man in any reckoning; and I fight my own battles. Look for me at dawn, mine uncle. I ride at your right hand."

"YOU ARE INSANE." THEY HAD ALL SAID IT, VADIN LOUDEST and longest and to no effect at all. Ymin said it now, facing Mirain without fear although he rode still on a red tide of wrath. "You are quite mad. Moranden is a danger to you even in the castle under the king's protection. If you ride to war with him, he will have what he longs for."

"I can protect myself."

"Can you?" She thrust back her sleeves, gripping her forearms until the long nails, hardened from years of plucking the strings of her harp, seemed to pierce through flesh and muscle into bone. But her voice betrayed only impatience with his folly. "You are behaving like a spoiled child. And well he knows it. He sought you for just this purpose, to set you precisely where he wants you: in his hands, and too wild with rage and rivalry to care what befalls you."

He rounded upon her. "He has challenged me openly. If I refuse him, I have no right or power to claim kingship."

"If you refuse him, you prove that you are man enough, and king enough, to ignore an insult."

His face was closed, his will implacable. "I ride at dawn."

She reached for him. "Mirain," she said, not quite pleading. "If not for your own sake, for your grandsire's. Forsake this folly."

"No." He eluded her hands, and left them there in his chamber, the singer alone and hopeless, Vadin forgotten by the wall. The door thudded shut behind him.

Eight

VADIN SHIVERED, STRUGGLING TO STAY AWAKE. IT WAS an unholy hour to be out of bed: the black watch of the night when men most often died, and demons walked, and Uveryen defied her bright brother to overcome her power. He was ghastly cold, sitting in the king's antechamber, waiting on the royal pleasure. With the sublime illogic of the half-asleep, he did not fear for life or limb. He fretted over his baggage. Should he have packed one more warm cloak? Or one less? Had he forgotten something vital? Mirain's armor—was it—

"My lord will see you now."

The quiet words brought him lurching to his feet. They tangled. He sorted them with vicious patience, under the servant's cool eye. In some semblance of good order, he entered the lion's den.

The king was as the king always was, broad awake, fully clad, and somehow not quite human. Like a man in armor, warded against the world; but this one's armor was his own flesh and bone. Vadin, bowing at his feet, wondered if he had always been like that. An iron king, ruling with an iron will, loving nothing that lived.

Except Mirain. Vadin rose at the king's command, roused at last, beginning to be afraid. Princes did not often pay for their insanities. Their servants often did, bitterly.

The king stood close enough to touch. Vadin swallowed. Part of him was surprised. He did not have to look up by much. Two fingers' breadth. Three. He had never been so close before. He could see a scar on the king's cheek, a knife scar it must have been, thin and all but invisible, running into the braided beard. There were few lines on the king's face. It was all pared clean, skin stretched taut over haughty bones. Mirain's bones.

But not Mirain's eyes. These were hooded, deep but not bottomless, studying Vadin as he studied the king. No god flamed in them. No madness, either. But of magecraft, something. A flicker, low yet steady, strong enough to see a man's soul, too weak to walk in his mind.

"Sit," the king said.

Vadin obeyed without thinking. The chair was the king's own, high and ornate. The king would not let him find another. His tired body made the best of its cushions; his mind waited, alert for escape.

The king revived the dying fire, squatting on his haunches, tending the fragile new flames with great care. Vadin counted scars on the bare and corded back. Every man had scars; they were his pride, the badge of his manhood. The king had a royal throng of them.

The old man's voice seemed to come out of the fire, his words born in Vadin's own thoughts. "I fought many battles. To gain the eye of the king my father. To earn the name of prince. To become prince-heir, and to become king, and to hold my kingship. By the god's mercy, I had no need to wrest it from my father. A seneldi stallion killed him for me: a stallion and his own arrogance, that would suffer no creature to be greater than he. Of that beast's line I bred the Mad One. It was revenge, of a sort. The sons of the regicide would serve the sons of the king. The stallion himself I took and tamed and rode into every battle, until he died under me. Shot, I think. I do not remember. There have been so many. It has been so long."

He sounded ineffably old, ineffably weary. Vadin said nothing. It seemed to be his curse that kings confided in him. Or else and more likely, he was not going to live long enough for his knowledge to matter.

The king sat on his heels with ease that belied both voice and words. "It perturbs you, does it not? To know that I was young once. That I was born and not cast up armed and crowned from the earth; that I was a child and a youth and a young man. And yet I was all of them. I even had a mother. She died while I was still among the women. She had enemies; they said she had lovers. 'And why not?' she cried when they came for her. 'One night a year my lord and master grants me of his charity. All the rest belong to his wives and his concubines. He casts his seed where he pleases. Am I not a queen? May I not do the same?' She paid the price of her presumption. My father made me watch as they flayed her alive and bathed her in salt and hanged her from the battlements. I was royal. I must know how kings disposed of their betrayers. I was not seven summers old.

"I learned my father's lesson. A king must endure no threat to his rule. Not even where he loves, if that love turns against him. The throne is a dead thing, but its power is all-encompassing. It knows no human tenderness. It suffers no compassion.

"And on that day of my mother's death, with the screams of her dying ringing in my brain, I swore that I would be king; because for me to take the throne, my father must die. I know now that he was a hard man, cold and often cruel, but he was not evil. He was merely king. Then and for a long time after, I knew only that he had murdered my mother."

Vadin choked back a yawn. He kept waiting for the blow to fall. It was all very sad, and it explained a little of the king's madness, but Vadin could not see what it had to do with Mirain. Or with dragging Mirain's squire out of his warm blankets in the deeps of the night.

"Alas for me," said the king, "I learned to hate my father; I learned to cast aside mercy, to be most royally implacable. But I never learned not to love. For the kingdom's sake I took an Asanian queen. She would hold back the Golden Empire; she would enrich us with her splendid dowry. Herself I did not consider, save as a price to be paid: a pallid dwarfish creature, bred like a beast to ornament a western palace. And when she came, indeed she was small, as small as a maid of ten summers, but her heart was mighty; and in the arts of the bedchamber she had no equal.

"They say this land was too harsh for her. Yet she was learning to endure it, even perhaps to love it. She was growing strong; she was beginning to accept our ways. And I killed her. I set my child in her, knowing what I did, knowing what I must do, although she was too small by far to bear an heir of Ianyn kings. She kindled, and for a little while I dared to hope. The child was not large; she was bearing well, without pain. Yet when her time came, all went awry. The child was twisted in the womb, fighting its birth. Fighting with the strength of the mageborn, which taxed the full power of priests and birthing-women and, in desperation, of the shamans whom even then I had in mind to banish from my kingdom. They prevailed. My queen did not. She lingered a little. She saw her daughter. She heard me give the little one the name of heir. Then, content, she died.

"I mourned her. I still mourn her. But she had left my Sanelin, who had all her mother's valor and all her sweetness, but who was strong with the strength of our people.

"Yes," the king said, meeting Vadin's eyes with a shock like two blades clashing, "I loved my daughter too much. I loved her for herself, and I loved her for her mother who was lost. But I did not love her blindly. Nor was it merely the grieving lover who made his lady's child his heir. I knew what we had made together, my queen and I. In the body of a maidchild, slender and Asanian-small, dwelt the soul of an emperor."

"It was unfortunate," Vadin ventured, "that she was a woman."

The king rose. For all his age and his height and the weight of his bones, he moved like Mirain: like a panther springing. Vadin steeled himself for the killing stroke.

It never came. "Aye and aye," the king said heavily, "it was unfortunate. More unfortunate still that I had no

sons. She was my only child, and she was pure gold; and
the Sun took her. It was no choice of mine. From her
infancy she knew who must be her lord and her lover. He
had made her for himself. At last he took her from me.
Rightly, after all; a daughter passes from her lord father
to her lord husband, and she was Avaryan's bride. But
she was also Ianon's heir."

Sometimes one gambled. Vadin made a reckless cast.
"The Prince Moranden—"

The panther roused, snarling. It was laughter, harsh
with disuse, ragged with pain. "You love him, do you not?
Many love him. He is lordly; he is proud; he has his
mother's beauty. But she is goddess-wise. He is not even
clever."

"Why do you hate him?" Vadin asked. "What has he
done to you?"

"He was born." The king said it quietly, without rancor.
"Of all the errors of my life, the greatest was my taking
captive the daughter of Umijan. She was suckled on hate;
she came to me in hate. But her beauty struck me to the
heart. I thought that I could tame her; I dreamed that
she would come, if not to love me, at least to esteem me
as her consort. I was a fool. The lynx does not lie down
on the hunter's hearth."

"You should have killed her before she got her claws
into your son."

"He was hers from the moment of his conception."

"Did you try to change it? You never let him forget
who was your favorite. You made it obvious who would
have the throne. Sanelin, or no one. It's a wonder he
didn't slit your throat as soon as he knew how."

"He tried. Several times. I forgave him. I love him. I
will not give my throne to him."

"What if Mirain had never come?"

"I knew that he would. Not only was it foretold. Not
only had the god promised me in dreams that the great
one would come. I knew that my daughter would be no
more willing than I, to let her heritage fall into the hands
of Odiya of Umijan."

Vadin marveled that he was here, sitting while the king

stood, talking to him as if he were—why, as if he were
Mirain. "I don't understand. I've known men who were
never properly weaned. Prince Moranden is nothing like
them. He's strong. He's Ianon's champion. He has no
equal on the field, and few enough off it."

"There is more to the world than the wielding of a
sword." The king turned his hands, much calloused with
it, and half smiled. "Moranden is his mother's creature.
When she commands, he obeys. Where she hates, he
detests. She is the shape and he the shadow. Were he
king on the throne of Ianon, she would rule. She rules
already wherever he is lord."

"But—" Vadin began. He stopped. What use? The king
knew what he knew. No Imeheni yokel could teach him
otherwise.

If there was anything to teach him. Vadin shifted un-
comfortably. Moranden was no monster. He had been
kind to a lad from the outlands who was no threat to his
power. He could be charming if it suited his purposes.
But he was honorable even when it did not serve him. He
was a mortal man; of course he was flawed. Even Mirain
was far from perfect.

The servants fought to wait on Mirain. Moranden's
name met with a shrug, a sigh, an acceptance of one's
duty. Sometimes, they conceded, it was pleasant to serve
him. Sometimes it was perilous. He was a lord. What
could one expect?

He was not cruel. He was no more capricious than any
other prince. Mirain was infinitely less predictable.

Mirain was Mirain. Even Vadin could not envision him
as anything but what he was; nor was it conceivable that
he would let anyone command him, let alone do his
ruling for him. Moranden—yes, Moranden was a bit of a
weathercock. Everyone knew it. A man could win his
favor, not with copper, nothing so venal, but his friends
were often the ones who flattered him most cleverly. He
had no patience with the drudgeries of kingship: councils,
audiences, endless and innumerable ceremonies. He had
sunk low in the market, when he accused Mirain of shirk-
ing those duties, and let people think that he himself had

been laboring long hours over them. Probably he had been dicing with his lordlings until the king called him to defend the Marches.

Vadin snorted softly to himself. Next he would be exonerating Mirain for idling in the market while the kingdom went to war. Mirain had not been idling, after all. Not exactly. He had been acquainting himself with his people.

"If Moranden is Odiya's puppet," Vadin said at last, "why did you give him a princedom?"

"I gave his mother a princedom, for a price. She would not set her son on me; I would leave them free to govern as they chose. Within the limits of the law."

"Which you had made."

"Just so," said the king.

Vadin sat back. "What are you telling me, my lord? What am I supposed to do?"

"Keep them from killing one another."

"Keep—" Vadin laughed. His voice came within a hair of cracking. "My lord, I don't know what Adjan told you about me, but I'm only human. I can't come between the thunder and the lightning."

The king seized him as if he had been a weanling pup, dragging him to his feet, shaking him until his eyes blurred. "You will do it. You will stand between them. You will not let them die at one another's hands."

"This time."

The king wound his fingers in Vadin's braids, wrenching his head back. "Never while I live. Swear it, Vadin alVadin."

"I can't," Vadin gasped. "Moranden—maybe—but Mirain—" The king's grip tightened to agony. He was mad. Stark mad. "My lord, I—"

The old man let him go. He fell to all fours. His head throbbed; he choked on bile. Trembling, hating himself for it, he peered up. The king knelt beside him. Not madness, he saw with bitter clarity. Love. The king gave tears to them; both of them. His voice was thick, but it yielded nothing. Even his pleading was proud. "You must try. You are all I have. The only one whom both are fond of. The only one whom I can trust."

It was too much. Mirain, and the king too. Vadin crouched and shook. The king touched him. He started like a deer. "It is the price you pay," the king said, "for your quality."

Little by little Vadin stilled. He drew himself up. Half his braids were down, the rest working loose. He shook them out of his eyes, and looked at the king. "My lord, I will do all I can, even if it kills me."

"It may kill us all." The king raised him, holding him with only a shadow of strength. "Go. Defend your lord. From himself, if need be."

THE COLD LIGHT OF DAWN FOUND MIRAIN'S TEMPER CALMED but his will unshaken. Vadin looked at him and did not know whether to rage or to despair. "By the gods," he muttered under his breath, "if the king breaks his heart for that lunatic's sake, I'll—I'll—" Rami shifted under him, troubled. He bit back the hot swift tears and glared at the madman. Mirain bore no mark of his royalty, went armed like all the rest with sword and spear and shield, light plain armor and plain tunic beneath it and plain helmet on his head. And yet he was impossible to mistake, riding his wild black demon without bit or bridle, laughing as the beast lashed out at a soldier's gelding.

A tall figure approached him on foot. The Mad One stood suddenly still, ears pricked, eyes gleaming ember-bright in the torchlight. Mirain bowed in the saddle. "Good morning, Grandfather."

"You will go," the king said. It was not a question. A little of the old, cold madness had returned to his face. "Fight well for me, young Mirain. But not so well that you die of it."

"I do not intend to die," said Mirain. He leaned out of his saddle and kissed the king's brow. "Look for me when Brightmoon waxes again."

"And every day until then." Abruptly the king turned away from him to confront Moranden. The elder prince, intent upon the mustering of his troops, had not yet mounted; a groom held the bridle of his charger. He met his father's stare with one as level, and as cold, and as unreadable. "Come back to me," the king said. "Both of you. Alive and whole."

Moranden said no word, but bowed and sprang astride. The gates swung back; a horn sounded, fierce and high. With a shout the company leaped forth.

THEY PASSED THE TOWERS OF THE DAWN IN THE FULL MORN- ing, riding steadily from the Vale to the height of the pass, winding down the steep ways into the outer fiefdoms of Ianon. The long riding lulled Vadin into a sort of peace. The king had been fiercely alive when they left him, and Mirain was far from dead, and Vadin knew certainly that at least a tithe of the men about him were the king's own. This might even prove to be no more than it seemed: a quelling of rebellion, a first testing of Ianon's heir in battle. Moranden was an honorable man; he would not do a murder that was certain to kill his father.

Vadin would let grief come when it came. Meanwhile he tried to be wise; he opened himself to the clean bright air and the company of men about him and the strong beast-body beneath him. Green Arkhan unfurled beneath Rami's feet; Avaryan wheeled to his zenith and sank west- ward behind the mountain walls.

Mirain was an exemplary soldier. He kept his place in the line beside Vadin, just ahead of the squires with the remounts; he held his Mad One to a quiet pace with no outbursts of stallion-temper; when the company was silent he was silent, and when they sang he always seemed to know the songs. His accent, Vadin began to notice, had changed. His Ianyn was as good as Vadin's own, if not better: he had no Imeheni burr but the lilt of a lord of Han-Ianon, clear and melodious yet pitched to carry through field or hall. And he was working the magic of his presence. The men near him had fallen under his spell; Vadin watched it spread. They were not falling at his feet. Not yet. But they were warming to him. They were forgetting to hate him; as for shunning him, that battle was long lost.

Moranden knew it. He did not show it, but Vadin could

sense a growing darkness in him. A set to his shoulders; a sharpening of the dun stallion's temper.

"IT CAN'T WORK, YOU KNOW."

They were camped on the borders of Medras, sacrificing comfort in a lord's hall for the sake of speed and sobriety. Fine clear night that it was, Mirain had elected to bivouac with his mount, with a small fire and a warm blanket and the Mad One for wall and guard. The stallion admitted Vadin on sufferance, as much for Rami's sake as for Mirain's; he had taken an interest in the mare, chaste enough for it was not her season, and she was not inclined to discourage him. But no one else ventured near, or appeared to wish to.

"It can't work," Vadin repeated. "You can bedazzle people when they're near you, but when their eyes clear they turn straight back to your uncle."

Mirain fed the fire with deadwood from the thicket in which they camped. The flames, leaping, made his face strange: sharpened the curve of his nose, carved deep hollows beneath his cheekbones, glittered in his eyes. "Bedazzle people, Vadin? How am I doing that?"

Impatience flung Vadin's hand up and out, made him snap, "Don't play the innocent with me. You're subverting my lord's men under his very nose. And he can see it as well as I can."

"I am not—" Mirain rose abruptly. The Mad One snorted and threw up his head; the prince gentled him, centering himself on it, shutting Vadin out.

Vadin hammered at his gates. "Sure you aren't. You talk to them like a northerner born. Me you lisp at as sweetly and southernly as you ever did. Who's being played for a fool?"

Mirain's back was obdurately silent. One ruby eye glowed beyond and just above it, beneath a fire-honed blade of horn. Rami grazed peacefully on the edge of the firelight, oblivious to two-legged troubles. Not for the first time, Vadin cursed all mages and their intransigence. How could a mere man beat sense into the likes of them?

Mirain spun. "Sense? What sense? You accuse me of

machinations I never meant. You fault me for trying my tongue in good Ianyn, and again for easing it with you who know and occasionally forget to despise me. What should I do, refuse to have anything to do with these men I have to fight beside?"

"Pack up and ride straight back to Han-Ianon where you belong."

"Ah no," said Mirain. "You won't turn me back now. It was too late for that when I faced Moranden in the market."

"You two should be brothers. You hate each other too absolutely to be anything less."

"I don't hate him." Mirain said it as if he believed it. Perhaps he did. Perhaps even Vadin did. "He lusts after what is mine. He'll never have it. Maybe one day I can teach him, if not to love me, at least to accept the truth."

"Are you really as arrogant as that, or are you simple? Men like him don't back down."

"They can be persuaded to step sidewise."

Vadin spat into the fire. "And the moons will dance the sword-dance, and the sun will shine all night."

To his great surprise, except that he was learning to be amazed by nothing Mirain said or did, the prince dropped down beside him and grinned. "Another wager, O doubter?"

"I won't rob you this time, O madman."

Mirain laughed. His teeth were very white. He lay with his head pillowed on his saddle, wrapping his blanket about him, eyes bright upon Vadin. "I won't kill him. That's too easy. I'll win him instead. Of his own free will, without magery."

"What am I, then? Your practice stroke?"

"My friend." Mirain was a shadow on shadow, even his eyes briefly hooded. They flashed open, silencing the snap of protest. "I'll do it, Vadin."

Vadin could understand how Mirain looked on Moranden. One could not hate a man afflicted with insanity. One pitied him; one had a hopeless compulsion to cure him. They were both mad, these princes. They were going to die for it. Then what would Ianon do for a king?

Mirain was asleep. He could do that: will himself into

oblivion between breath and breath, and leave the fretting to lesser mortals. Vadin inched toward him. He did not move. Nor did the Mad One, which was more to the point. The squire peered down at him. The fire, dying, only deepened the shadow of him, but his face was clear enough to memory. A face one could not forget. Someone had said that—Ymin, the king. It was in a song. Mirain had laughed when he heard it. Aye, he said, he was ugly enough to be remarkable.

He was stone blind and stark mad. With a sound between a growl and a groan, Vadin rolled himself into his own blanket. The gods looked after the afflicted, said all the priests. Let them do it, then, and give this poor mortal peace.

PERHAPS, AFTER ALL, THE GODS DID THEIR DUTY. NO ONE tried to slip poison into Mirain's field rations or a dagger into his back. Moranden paid him no more heed than he paid any other trooper, and no less; and Vadin heard no such words as he had heard in Han-Ianon's market. The elder prince was ruling himself and he was ruling his men.

On the third day the bright weather faded. The dawn was dim, the sunrise scarlet and grey; by noon the rain fell in torrents. The company wrapped their weapons in oiled leather and themselves in heavy hooded cloaks and pressed on without pausing.

Early summer though it was, the rain was northern rain, mountain bred; it chilled to the bone. Men grumbled under their breaths, laying wagers on whether the prince would command them to harden themselves yet further by camping in the storm. Mirain took up one such. "He won't," he said. "We'll lodge warm and dry tonight."

He won a silver-hafted dagger. For as the grey light dimmed to dark, Moranden led his company up a long twisting track to a castle. It was smaller even than Asan-Geitan, and poorer, but it had a roof to keep out the rain. The men cheered as its gate creaked open to admit them.

Mirain would have been content to lodge in the guardroom with the rest. But as he moved toward the corner

Vadin had claimed for him, Moranden's voice brought them both about. "Lord prince!"

Moranden was easy, affable, even smiling. The lord of the castle, a thin elderly man, looked ready to faint. As Vadin made his way behind Mirain through the crowding of men, he strangled laughter. The poor man was terrified enough to be playing host to the greatest lord in Ianon; now that lord presented him with the throne prince himself. Who looked like a child, drenched and shivering; who raised his head and stood suddenly towering, full of the god; who spoke to the baron in his own rough patois and won his soul.

Vadin trailed the three of them in a sort of stupor. Much of it was wet and misery; some was fascination. He had never seen Mirain's magic worked so near, or to such devastating effect. Except that it was not magic, not exactly; not a thing of spells and cantrips. It was his whole self. His face, his bearing, his presence. His infallible knowledge of what to say, and when, and how. And his incomparable eyes.

They had the best the lord could offer, Moranden the room given over to guests, Mirain the lord's own chamber. The lord's own slaves built up the fire in the hearth, which smoked, but which was warm; even the squire had a warm robe, almost clean, and a cup of wine heated to scalding, and the slaves would not let him wait on his lord. He was a lord himself here. They were pitiably inept, but less so with him than with Mirain, who awed them into immobility. Until the prince loosed a smile and a word; then they fell over one another to please him.

Warm and dry and with the wine rising from his stomach to his brain, Vadin woke somewhat from his bemusement. After Han-Ianon this castle was shabby and unkempt and not remarkably clean, but it had an air of comfort; it felt like home. The slaves were ill-washed but well enough fed; the wine was good; the coverlet of the bed was beautiful. He remarked on the last, and Mirain smiled. "Your lady's weaving?" he asked the man who tended the fire, persuading it by degrees to smoke upward and not outward.

The slave bowed too low and too often, but he answered clearly enough. "Oh, yes, my lord, the Lady Gitani did it. It's poor stuff, I fear, as you great ones reckon it, but it's warm; the wool came from our own flocks."

"It's not poor at all; it's splendid. Look, Vadin, how pure a blue, like the sky in winter. Where ever did the lady find the dyes?"

"You must speak to her, great lord," the slave said, bowing. "She can tell you. It's a woman's art, my lord, but you a prince—she can tell you." He bowed yet again and took flight.

Mirain stood stroking the coverlet, smiling a little still, with the familiar wry twist. "How differently they look on a prince. When I was only a priest, I lodged in the stable or, if the family were pious, with the servants; no one ever stammered when I spoke to him. But I was Mirain then as I am now. Why should it matter?"

"You didn't have power then. You couldn't order one of them put to death, and be obeyed."

Mirain turned his eyes on Vadin. "Is that what makes a prince? The power to kill without penalty?"

"That's one way of putting it."

"No," Mirain said. "It has to be more than that."

"Not if you're a scullion in a hill fort."

The prince folded himself onto the splendid weaving, brows knit, chin on fist. Without the slaves to interfere, Vadin busied himself with their belongings, spreading wet garments to dry, inspecting the arms and armor in their wrappings. When he looked up again Mirain said, "I will be more than an exalted executioner. I will teach folk to see what a king can be. A guide, a guard. A protector of the weak against the strong."

Vadin rolled his eyes heavenward and squinted at Mirain's sword. The blade was beginning to dull. He reached for the whetstone.

"You scoff," Mirain said more in sorrow than in anger. "Is that all you know? Fear and force, and all power to the strongest?"

"What else is there?"

"Peace. Fearlessness. Law that rules every man, from the lowest to the highest."

"What odd dreams you have, my lord. Are they a southern sickness?"

"Now you're laughing at me." Mirain sighed deeply. "I know. If a king hopes to rule, he has to rule by force or he'll be struck from his throne. But if the force could be tempered with mercy—if he could teach another way, a gentler way, to those who were able to learn; if he could keep to his resolve and not surrender to the seductions of power—imagine it, Vadin. Imagine what he could do."

"He wouldn't last long in Ianon, my lord. We're howling barbarians here."

Mirain snorted. "You're no more a barbarian than the Prince of Han-Gilen."

"Not likely," said Vadin. "You won't catch me dead in trousers."

"Prince Orsan would shudder at the thought of a kilt. How ghastly to ride in. How utterly immodest."

"He must be as soft as a woman."

"No more than I."

Vadin eyed Mirain askance. "Have you been walking a shade gingerly for the past day or two?" He dodged the headrest from the bed, flung with alarming force. "What were you saying about mercy, my lord?"

"I had mercy. I took care to miss."

"See?" said Vadin. "Superior force. That's what makes you the prince and me the squire."

"Dear heaven, a philosopher. One of the new logicians, yet. I'll teach you to read, and you'll be a great master in the Nine Cities."

"Gods forbid," said Vadin with feeling.

VADIN DINED IN HALL, SEATED PERFORCE WITH THE PRINCES while the lesser folk took their ease below. At least he was allowed to set himself beside Mirain; no one had the wits or the courage to forbid him. He kept a wary eye on Moranden and a warier one on his own wild charge, who was enrapturing the lord's family as utterly as he had their kinsman. The women in particular were falling in

love with him, although one doe-eyed youth—the youngest son, Vadin supposed—was long lost already. He waited
on Mirain with something approaching grace, melting at
a word or a glance, trembling if chance or duty brought
him close enough to touch.

"Pretty," Vadin observed when the boy had retreated to
fill the wine jar.

Mirain lifted a brow. "He's going to beg me to take him
when I go. Shall I?"

"Why not? He looks as if he might be trainable."

The brow lifted another degree, but Mirain turned to
answer a question, and did not turn back again.

Left to himself, Vadin watched the boy out of the
corner of his eye. His amusement was going sour. Mirain
did not mean it, of course. He already had more servants
than he could bear. But the lad was extraordinarily pretty.
Beautiful, in truth. Slender, graceful, with those great
liquid eyes; his beard was only a sheen of down on his
soft skin, and although his hair had grown long from the
shaven head of childhood, he had not yet confined it in
the braids of a man. Wrapped in soft wool and hung with
jewels, he would make an exquisite girl. He was acting
like one, swooning over Mirain.

Vadin's forehead ached. He realized that he was scowling. And who was he to disapprove? He had had a fling
or two himself, though he much preferred to bed a woman.

Mirain smiled at the boy. What was his name? Ithan,
Istan, something of the sort. It was one of Mirain's
courtesan-smiles, not quite warm enough to burn. The
boy swayed toward him. Caught himself, drew back in
charming confusion. His glance crossed Vadin's; he flinched
visibly and all but fled.

Amid all the sighing and swooning, Vadin could still
observe that Mirain left the hall sober and without inci-
dent, and moreover without lingering overmuch. Maybe
he had grown as heartily sick of young love as Vadin had.

He slept at once and deeply, as always. Vadin, sharing
the overlarge bed, lay awake as always. Not thinking of
much; aware of the warm body near him, wishing it were

Ledi's. One or two of the slaves had cast him glances;
maybe, if he could slip out . . .

Mirain turned in his sleep. He came to Vadin as a pup
to its dam, burrowed into the long bony body, sighed
once and was still. Vadin's sigh was much deeper. Mirain
did not feel anything like a woman, except for his skin.
And his hair; it put Ithan's—Istan's—to shame. He had
shaken it out of its braid; by morning it would be a
hideous tangle. Without thinking, Vadin smoothed the
mass of it. And kept smoothing it, stroking, keeping his
hand light lest he wake Mirain. It was soothing, like
petting a favorite hound.

Ianon would rise up in arms if it knew he thought such
a thing. Mirain would laugh. He loved to look splendid
and he knew when he did, but he was convinced of his
own ugliness. Not that he was handsome, and he was
anything but pretty. But beautiful, maybe. An odd, striking, inescapable beauty.

Vadin's hand stilled. He listened to the slow strong
breathing, contemplated the arm that had settled itself
across his chest. Suddenly he wanted to break free and
bolt. Just as suddenly, he wanted to clutch at Mirain and
babble an endless stream of nonsense. Waking him thereby
and chancing his new-roused temper. Vadin lay very still
and very quiet and made himself remember how to breathe.
In, out. In, out. So. Out. In—

He had not lost his wager yet. That turned on friendship. There was nothing in it about falling in love.

Damn him, thought Vadin, still counting breaths. *Damn
him, damn him, damn him.*

Nine

JSTAN BEGGED AS MIRAIN HAD FORETOLD, AND MIRAIN was kind to him, but firm. "I ride to battle; and I have a squire of the king's own choosing. Stay, grow strong, learn well all that your masters can teach. And when your hair is braided, if you can and will, come to Han-Ianon and I will welcome you."

The boy's great eyes swam with tears, but he held them back. He looked less like a boy then, and not at all like a girl. When Mirain rode away he was on the tower over the gate, watching. Vadin knew he would not move until they were long out of sight.

Mirain had not forgotten him; that was not his way. But he was focused ahead upon the loom of peaks that was the Marches, and the blue coverlet, given him as a gift, was folded away among the baggage.

Vadin was calm, riding beside him. Waking had been agony, not least for that he had lain immobile and sleepless for most of the night; and it was Mirain's rousing that had startled him into consciousness. The prince disentangled himself with no sign of shame, cross-grained as he always was on first waking but trying to train himself out of it, and oblivious to the wave of heat that laid Vadin low. Vadin looked at him and remembered, and considered hating himself, and froze in sudden horror. Mirain of all people, mage and god's son, walker in minds, could never be deceived. Vadin could feign the most perfect indifference, or be wise and conduct himself exactly as he always had, and Mirain would know. Would see. And if he cared, Vadin knew he would die of it; but if he did not, that would be infinitely worse.

He had brought wine to Vadin still helpless under the coverlet, and he was the same as always. The god did not flame out of his eyes; they were clouded with sleep, but clearing, seeing nothing untoward. Vadin gulped the warm sweet wine, and it steadied him. Maybe, after all, he had nothing to fear. He did not have the kind of eyes that swooned, and Mirain would not invade a mind that resisted; and Avaryan's child or no, he was at his worst in the morning. By the time Mirain's wits were fully gathered, Vadin had himself well in hand.

With the wind in his face, fresh and cold with unmelted snows, he knew that he could master this. He was not like Istan. It was not Mirain's body he wanted; or not so much that he was weak with it. He would have something else. Maybe something unheard of.

"Look!" cried Mirain, flinging up his arm. Great wings boomed; an eagle dropped from the sky to settle like a falcon trained to jesses: a white eagle of the mountains, the royal bird of Ianon, companion of kings. Eye met eye, sun-fire to Sun-fire. With a high fierce cry the eagle cast itself sunward. It carried Mirain's soul with it, the body riding empty, easy in the tall war-saddle.

Vadin bent his stinging eyes upon Rami's ears. Gods and demons, he was lost indeed; jealous of a bird. And all for a wanderwit sorcerer who wanted to be a king. Who would probably die for wanting it. His eyes brimmed and overflowed; he swore at the whip of the wind.

THE MARCHES CAME ON SLOWLY, IN HILLS THAT SWELLED and rose and broke into mountains; in a spreading bleakness, green overwhelmed by the power of stone, trees stunted and twisted in the merciless wind. Summer had gained no foothold here. Where green could go, it was spring still, the snows but lately gone; the peaks were white with it, daring the sun to conquer them. But far away below was green and warmth and quiet, and as they rose higher Vadin could see the walls of Ianon's Vale across the rolling land, though not either Towers or castle. The former looked away from him toward the sunrise; the latter lay too well protected within its circling mountains.

They rode more cautiously now in a net of scouts and spies, feeling out this country that had risen against its lord. Yet they did not creep about like thieves. Moranden would have it known that he was in the Marches, but never precisely where. He would ride openly through a village, a cluster of huts beneath a crag; wind swiftly along hidden paths to a hold far distant; and take his rest there for a day, a night, or perhaps but an hour.

"Confusion," Mirain said to Vadin. "It makes the rebels uneasy. They're not as powerful here as they'd like to be; and the waverers are being reminded, often by their lord's own presence, that they swore oaths of fealty unto death."

A petty chieftain remembered, and tried to appease both sides. He housed and feasted a ringleader, arrested him in his bed and sent word of the capture to the Prince Moranden. Moranden came, smiled, saw the rebel executed. And as the executioner brought him the head gaping and bleeding, raised his hand. His men seized the chieftain; the executioner, under Moranden's cold eye, did his duty yet again.

Vadin was no stranger to summary justice. He had grown up with it. But it was Mirain, raised in the gentle south, who watched unflinching, and Vadin who needed his head held afterward while he was thoroughly and shamefully sick. "I can kill," he gasped. "I can kill in battle. I know I can. But I can't—can't ever— Gods, his eyes when they took him. His *eyes*."

Mirain did not insult him with either pity or sympathy. "He knew what he risked, but he refused to believe it. Traitors never do."

They had the garderobe to themselves, for a little while. Vadin turned in the doorway, his back to the curtain of leather that opened on the stair. "Would you have done what your uncle did?"

Mirain took time to relieve himself. It was dim, the cresset flickering above his bent head, but Vadin saw the thinning of his lips. At last he said, "I don't know. I . . . don't know." He straightened his kilt. "I've never been betrayed."

Yet. The word, unspoken, hung in the heavy air.

MORANDEN HAD MADE HIS POINT. HIS VASSALS SENT HIM numerous protestations of loyalty. But the leaders, the begetters of the uprising, knew that they could expect no mercy. Gathering what forces they could, they fled in search of safety.

"Umijan," said the chief of Moranden's scouts, who had foundered a senel to reach his lord on the road between Shuan and Kerath. Vadin heard; Mirain, driven perhaps by prescience, had worked his way to the head of the line, and the elder prince's guards had made no effort to stop him.

"Yes," the scout repeated between gasps, accepting Moranden's own flask, drinking deep. "They hid a man in Kerath, nigh dead with fever, but not nigh enough. He babbled before he died. Umijan will shelter the rebels if they get there soon enough, and if they swear the proper oaths."

Moranden's face was rigid. Umijan was the heart of the Marches, its lord his close kinsman. Half-brother, whispered some who whispered also that he was no son of Raban the king. Save only for the giant-builded keep of Han-Ianon, it was the strongest holding in the kingdom, nor had it ever been taken. Once barricaded within, the fugitives could hold fast for as long as they chose. Or as Baron Ustaren chose, and he would not yield lightly; for he came of a long line of rebels against any lordship but their own.

"What if we come there first?" Mirain's voice brought them all about; at least one blade bared against him. He stared it down. "What if we come to Umijan before them?" he repeated. "What will Ustaren do then?"

"Impossible," rasped the captain nearest Moranden. "If they passed Kerath a full day and more ago, riding as fast as they should have been, they'll be inside the walls by tomorrow's sunset. We'll never catch them, let alone pass them."

"If we do," Mirain persisted, "will the lord hold to his treason? Or is he only playing a game he was bred to play? A race; to the winner his aid, to the loser his enmity."

The scout grinned. "That's it, my prince; there you have it. The Great Game, and he's a master of it, is my lord of Umijan. But the lead's too great. We can't close it in the time we have."

Moranden's charger fretted, ears flat, eye rolling at the Mad One. The elder prince forestalled a lunge, staining the foam with blood beneath the bit, but his mind was not on it. His eyes lay on Mirain. Vadin could not read them. They hated, yes, always, but not to blindness; they measured the mount and the rider, and narrowed. "Well, sister-son," he said, and that was a great concession before the army, "since your lordship chooses not to keep the place you were assigned to, tell us what you know that we're still ignorant of."

"I know nothing, lord commander," Mirain said without perceptible mockery, "but I don't believe we've lost the race. Give me ten men on the swiftest seneldi we have; provision us with what we can consume in the saddle; and I'll greet the traitors in your name from Umijan's gate."

"Why you? Why risk the throne prince on a venture that could kill him?"

"Because," Mirain answered, "the Mad One is the swiftest senel in Ianon, and he will suffer no rider but myself. He can win the race if no other can."

They watched, all the men who were close enough, and passed the tale in a murmur through the ranks. Mirain was challenging Moranden, whose commands hitherto he had not questioned; and Moranden was all too well aware of it. But there was no enmity in the challenge, on either side. Not this time, not with a common enemy before them.

"If I send you," said Moranden, "and you fall afoul of the enemy, or fail to convince Ustaren that you're a king and not a pawn in this game of his, I'll have more than Umijan raised against me."

"No. By my father I swear it. This venture is on my head alone. If you give me leave, my lord commander."

"And if I don't, my lord soldier?"

"I submit to your will. And," said Mirain, "we lose Umijan."

The dun stallion lowered its horns, snorting in outrage. Moranden's fist hammered it into submission. Suddenly he laughed, a deep free sound untainted with bitterness. "You have gall, boy. You may even have a chance. Pick your men, if you haven't already; Rakan, see to their provisioning."

Vadin did not ask to go. He assumed it. Rami could outrun anything on feet, perhaps even the Mad One himself. When he went to fill his saddlebags with journeybread and presscakes and a double ration of water, Rakan the quartermaster gave him hardly a glance. He was part of Mirain, like the Mad One. He added all unnecessary burdens to the pile at Rakan's feet, even to shield and armor, even to his helmet, so light would they have to travel; but he kept sword and dagger, for no nobleman would go abroad without them. He regretted the sacrifice of his armor, although he would get it back when the army came to Umijan. Kilt and cloak were poor protection against edged bronze.

But they were not riding to a fight; they were riding to win a Marcher lord to Moranden's side in the game.

Mirain chose his men quickly enough to prove his uncle right. He chose well, Vadin judged and Moranden conceded. They were all young, but seasoned and strong; lightly built, most of them, long and light like Vadin or small and light like Mirain, and superbly mounted. They gathered ahead of the company, their seneldi fretting with eagerness, while Mirain faced Moranden once more and said, "Wish us well, my lord."

Moranden bowed his head. His eyes held Mirain's for a long moment. He did not smile, nor did he frown. Only

Vadin was close enough to hear what he said. "For the king, priestess' bastard. For the kingdom one of us will rule. Ride hard and ride straight, and may the gods bring you there before the enemy."

Mirain smiled. "I'll see you in Umijan, my uncle." The Mad One wheeled on his haunches, belling. With a flash of his golden hand, Mirain flung them all into a gallop.

Afterward, when Vadin tried to remember that wild ride, he could call up most clearly the blur of wind and thunder, and Rami's mane whipping his hands, her long ears now flat with speed, now pricked as the riders slowed to breathe and eat and, far too briefly, to rest. They kept to the rhythm of the Great Race, grueling but not quite killing if senel and rider both were of the best. Rami was; Vadin was determined to be. She strode forth tirelessly, matching the Mad One pace for pace, even showing him her heels when once he faltered. A stone had caught him in a moment of carelessness; he surged up beside her on the narrow track, aimed a nip at her shoulder for her presumption. She scorned to notice him. Behind his flattened ears shone Mirain's sudden grin. Vadin bared his own teeth in reply, less grin than grimace.

They lost a man on the ridge called the Blade, sliding down its sheer side into a long level valley. His tall roan mare, taking the descent too suddenly, overbalanced; scrambled; hung suspended, and somersaulted screaming into air. The snap of her neck breaking was abrupt and hideous, but more hideous yet was the stillness of her rider. The three men behind could not stop, could only swerve and pray; of those ahead, one nearly died himself as his mount shied away from the plummeting bodies.

The last man slid to a halt on grass, trembling, the senel gasping, the soldier cursing in a steady drone. Mirain's voice cut across both. "The gods have taken their tribute. The army will tend the bodies when it passes. On now, for the love of Ianon. On!"

They lost the second man on a road of stones and scree. The spotted gelding stumbled and fell and came up lame; although his young rider wept on his neck, they left both to limp on as best they could. Avaryan was sinking and the country worsening, and they had lost their first bright edge of speed. And two gone already, with the night before them and the worst still far away.

But at last it seemed that the gods of this cruel country were sated. The company settled into a steady ground-devouring pace, close but not crowding, shifting as one or another dropped back to rest a little. Only the Mad One never relinquished his place; he ran before them all, untiring, with only the merest sheen of sweat to brighten his flanks.

Avaryan set in a torrent of fire. The stars bloomed one by one. Brightmoon would rise late and half full; Greatmoon climbed the sky at their backs, huge and ghostly pale. The Mad One ran as one with the shadows, but Mirain kept about him a last shimmer of sunset. It crowned him, faint yet clear; it glowed in the scarlet of his cloak.

"Sunborn," someone said, far back behind Vadin. "Avaryan-lord. An-Sh'Endor." He had a fine voice; he made a chant of it, though no one else could spare breath for aught but living. Vadin found it echoing in his brain, set to the beat of Rami's hoofs. It was strong; there was power in it, the magic of true names. It bound them all to the one who led them, who found the way for them through the crowding dark. *Sunborn, Avaryan-lord, An-Sh'Endor.*

Just before the first glimmer of dawn, Mirain bade them halt. He had found a stream among the stones, and a patch or two of winter-blasted grass. They cooled their gasping mounts, watered and fed them, rubbed them down and dropped, falling into a sleep like death.

Vadin fought it. He had to see—he had to be sure—Mirain—

He opened his eyes on sunlight. They were strewn over the slope like the aftermath of battle, save only that no carrion birds had come to torment them. Those were circling, hopeful but not yet bold.

Mirain stood near him, face turned toward the sun as if he drank its sustenance. Vadin remembered part of his dream that might have been real: a dark sweet voice singing Avaryan into the sky. The prince turned, smiling slightly. Although Vadin knew beyond questioning that he had not slept, no weariness scarred him. His smile widened a fraction. "Priesthood," he said. "It thrives on long vigils." He bent, set something near Vadin's hand. "Eat. Drink. It's growing late."

Vadin groaned, but he obeyed. Mirain went round from man to man with a word and a touch for each, a cake, a bit of fruit, a gesture toward the stream. No one else voiced a complaint. In very little time by the sun, they were up and saddled and astride. Their water bottles were full, their mounts refreshed, although they rode with care at first to limber stiffened muscles. The sun warmed them; the wind was clean and keen. They stretched into racing pace.

The Black Peaks rose before them, curved about the high vale of Umijan. Somewhere in that tumble of ridge and valley, crag and tarn, ran the enemy. Sunset would find him at Umijan's gates. Sunset must find them within, with Baron Ustaren their sworn ally.

"Pray gods we get to the Gullet before the traitors," said Jeran, who was Marcher born, "or they'll swallow us while Ustaren watches."

The Gullet: the last stretch of the race, the long narrow way between walls of stone, rising slowly and then more steeply to the crag of the castle. Eight troopers and a prince, armed only with swords, mounted on spent seneldi, could find neither cover nor defense there.

Vadin was not afraid. He was far too intent on keeping the pace. Thus when they started up yet another of a thousand nameless slopes, he stopped without thinking, and only wondered when he saw the Mad One's saddle empty, Mirain running low to the crest. Still unthinking, he half fell to the ground, pursuing as stealthily as his exhausted body would allow, coming up beside the prince. The ridge looked down on a river meadow walled with crags and swarming with an army. Mounted men, men afoot, even a few chariots, advancing as the tide advances, steady and inexorable.

"The Gullet?" Vadin whispered, although he could see nothing that resembled a castle.

"Not yet," answered Mirain. "But this is the way, and there is no other, only a tangle of blind valleys."

Vadin peered at the walls. They were not precisely sheer to his hillman's eye, but a senel could not climb or traverse them. And the valley was full of rebels. With no wood or copse to conceal a passing company, only grass and stones and the bright path of the stream.

Jeran was beside them, greatly daring, whistling softly when he saw what there was to see. "They're slower than I thought: still an hour's gallop from the Gullet." He was haggard, caked with dust as they all were, trembling with weariness, but he grinned. "We'll make it yet, Sunborn."

Mirain did not react to his new title. He was intent on the army. "Arrogant," he muttered. "No scouts. No vanguard. Rearguard— No. They're all in the valley. We've come at them sidewise, that's luck, but not luck enough. Unless . . ." He paused, eyes narrowing. "Look; they're in good order, but not as good as they should be. They don't expect trouble."

"Will we give them some, my lord?" Jeran asked quickly, with a ghost of eagerness.

Mirain's eye glinted upon him. If Vadin had not known better, he would have sworn that Mirain was as fresh as a lordling newly risen from his bed. But his steadiness had to be an act of will: the strong face of a king before his people. Better that than the other choice, that he was much less human than he liked to appear. He touched the Marcher's shoulder, and the man glowed, waking to new vigor. "Tell the men to rest a little. If any dares not trust his mount or himself, let him be truthful. We must reach Umijan before yonder army."

No one would admit to weakness. No one flinched under Mirain's stare, although he did not spare the power of it, searching each hollowed face. At last his head bowed. He breathed deep, as if he had come to a decision. Slowly he raised his hands. "We are all at the edge of our endurance. But we must ride as we have never ridden before, and we must ride straight through the enemy. Else we are all lost." The unmarked hand spread toward the seneldi. Even the Mad One's proud neck drooped, although he

tried to arch it under his lord's eye; his sides were matted
with sweat and foam, his breath coming with effort. And
he was the best of them all. Mirain turned his golden
palm to catch the sun. "I have no strength to give you all,
but what I have, I would give to our seneldi. Have I your
leave?"

They stared at him, dulled minds struggling to understand. Vadin had an advantage: he had seen what Mirain
could do. "Magic," he said sharply, to wake them. "God-
power. He's asking leave to put a spell of endurance on
your beasts."

One by one, raggedly together, they assented. They
were Mirain's now, heart and soul. They watched him
with awe and—yes—love, as he laid his hand on each
broad brow beneath the horns of the lone gelding, between the eyes of the mares. And life flowed back into the
spent bodies. Light kindled in dimmed eyes; nostrils flared,
testing the wind. Last of all Mirain came to the Mad One.
That one hardly needed his touch to swell and preen and
stamp, but Mirain stood long by the strengthened shoulder, both hands on it, cheek against the tangled mane.
With a sudden, almost convulsive movement he turned.
Not Vadin alone caught his breath. In so little time,
Mirain's face had aged years. But he sprang into the
saddle, straight as ever, and the Mad One moved forward. "Come," Mirain commanded. "Follow me."

They rode openly over the crest, down the long slope
toward the mass of the army. Whether by some trick of
Mirain's power, or because they had not looked to be
overtaken, the rebels made no move against them. Perhaps, with the sun in their eyes and the dust rising to
cloud their advance, men judged the swift newcomers to
be stragglers of their own force. No banner taught them
otherwise, and no armor glinted warning. Filthy, worn to
rags, mounted on lathered and gasping seneldi, the strangers might as easily have been fugitives in search of
sanctuary.

There was space to skirt the left flank, a stretch like a
road between army and cliff, and Mirain claimed it, with
his men pounding after. Vadin heard a voice, a call that

sounded like a question, growing peremptory. He crouched
over Rami's neck. "Run," he prayed. "Longears, Rack-of-
bones, love of my life, *run*." His right eye was full of the
glitter of weapons. His back crawled, yearning for its lost
armor. He fixed his whole being on the flying tassel of
the Mad One's tail. It would carry him out of this. It
would bring him safely home.

The voice begot echoes, not all born of air and mountain-
side. "Hold, I say! In whose name do you ride?"

"My own!" Mirain bellowed back. "Behind you—Moranden
of the Vale—a day's ride—"

The Mad One veered. Mirain's arm swept the rest onward, but he sat his stallion well within bowshot of the
captain who had hailed him. Vadin was bone-weary but
he was not yet dead; he knew what Mirain was trying to
do, and he had strength left to be appalled. He caught at
the reins. But Rami with her velvet mouth, Rami whose
obedience had never been less than perfect, Rami had the
bit in her teeth and would not turn aside. He heard
Mirain's voice, indistinct with distance. The lunatic was
telling them where Moranden was, and how many men
he had, and what his spies had said; but not what Mirain
himself had said. And the army had slowed to hear him.
The ranks behind were straggling. Some were cheering.

"But you," called a captain with a voice of brass. "How
do you know this? Why are your men—" He broke off.
He spurred his senel closer to the Mad One, who danced
away, horns lowered. "Who are you?"

Mirain laughed and bared the torque at his throat and
spun the stallion about. "Mirain," he called over his shoulder. "Mirain Prince of Ianon!"

The Mad One seemed to take wing, so swift was his
escape. Behind him the army milled in disorder. But
some of its men were quick of wit. Something sang, sweet
and high and deadly. The Mad One came level with
Rami.

A senel shrieked. Down—one was down before them
with an arrow in its heart. Rami swerved; the Mad One
leaped over the struggling body.

The rebels were beginning to move. It struck Vadin

then, purest truth. If Mirain could hold them with his voice, could not one man hold them with his sword, tangle them further, gain more precious moments? Rami was free again, light in his hands. He gathered the reins to turn her about.

A band of unseen steel imprisoned his wrists. The mare strained forward. The Mad One's eye burned briefly upon Vadin's. Mad himself and raging, helpless as a man in chains, Vadin craned over his shoulder. Six. They were only six. Knots of men and beasts marked the fallen.

One of the six was free, or set free, stealing the glory Vadin had chosen. Riding in that swooping arc, singing a wicked satire, whirling his bright sword. Arrows could not touch him. Spears fell spent about him. Singing, he plunged into the foremost rank, and men howled and died. "Mirain!" Vadin stormed at a rider of stone. *"Mirain!"*

The vale narrowed before them. There at last beyond doubting was the black gorge and the loom of Umijan against the setting sun. Behind them the army had loosed its most deadly weapon: a company of mounted archers.

"Ride!" cried Mirain. "Trust to the god and ride! Umijan is before us."

Aye, like the very keep of hell, black Gullet, black crag, black castle. And the last of the Gullet was the Tongue, and that was a path against one sheer wall, for the other dropped away to a precipice and far below a cold gleam of water; and this eagles' track reared steeply to the frown of the gate. Truly Umijan could never be taken, for there was not even space for three men abreast to assail its walls, and the cliff that edged the path melted into the very crag of the castle.

If Vadin had had a grain of strength left, he would have laughed. He knew the gods did. Of all that terrible race, this must be the worst, with arrows raining and life pouring away and one misstep the road to certain death. With every stride he knew Rami's great heart would burst. The air beckoned, the emptiness beyond the narrow polished path, singing of rest. He clung to the pale mane, straining as Rami strained, willing her to run swift, run straight, run steady. "Only a little way now. Only a little. Up, my love. Up to the gate. Up!"

She heard him. The archers or the road had taken Vian. There was only Jeran behind him, and little Tuan, and Mirain—Mirain mad to the last, herding them, defying death to take him. Tuan's staggering roan went down, barring the narrow way. The Mad One swayed on the very edge of the precipice. Tuan shouted, shrill as a child, and howled as Mirain swept him headfirst across the saddle. The stallion gathered and hurtled over the dying mare. The foremost archer spurred upon his heels. The mare, thrashing, caught the foreleg of the rebel's mount. It screamed and toppled and spun slowly over the rim.

The Mad One hurled himself up the steep ledge. Jeran lagged, his lovely golden mare dying as she ran, he weeping and cursing and beseeching her forgiveness as he lashed her on. But it was the Mad One who gave her strength, who gored her flank with cruel horns, driving her upward.

Vadin burst into quiet, and for an eternal instant he knew that it was death. Until he saw walls and a paved court and people thronging, and the Mad One plunging through the gates with Jeran's mare before him, and the gates swinging shut. Slowly, slowly, the golden mare crumpled to the stones. Jeran lay beside her and wept.

The race was won. They had come to Umijan.

Ten

VADIN WAS ON THE GROUND. IT WAS COLD, AND HE DID not remember falling. He dragged himself up, inch by tortured inch, knowing all the while that when he was on his feet he would go mad. He must tend Rami, or she would die; he must tend Mirain, or his honor as a squire would die.

They had Rami, people who insisted that they knew how to care for her. More gathered about Jeran's mare, and a valiant few tended the Mad One. Mirain—

Mirain stood in a circle of giants, eye to eye with the tallest of them all, who stood to Vadin as Vadin stood to Mirain. Even in his fog of exhaustion Vadin knew who this must be; the likeness to Moranden was uncanny.

Mirain's voice came clear and proud and indomitable. "Good day, lord baron, and greetings in the name of the Prince Moranden. He bids you make ready for his coming; he requests that his resting place be free of vermin."

Vadin sucked in his breath. The people about looked as shocked as he felt, and some were stiff with outrage. But Baron Ustaren looked at his kinsman's ambassador and laughed. "What! Shall I leave no rats for my cousin to hunt at his leisure?"

"Only if you are prepared to be counted among the quarry."

Vadin edged toward Mirain. Not that he had much

hope of being useful; some of the onloookers had throwing spears and some had strung bows. And men in Umijan were large even for northerners. He was the merest stripling here, with barely strength to stand, let alone to fight.

They let him stand at his lord's back, which proved the sublimity of their contempt. Mirain was oblivious to him. The prince was staring the baron down, and succeeding in it. Ustaren had less pride than Moranden had, or more guile; he yielded with all appearance of goodwill. "The rats shall be disposed of. How may I name the bearer of his lordship's command?"

"As Prince Moranden himself names me," Mirain answered. "Messenger."

"So then, sir messenger, shall I house you among the warriors? Or would I be wiser to treat you as my guest? or as a priest? or perhaps as the heir of Ianon?"

"Wherever I am placed, I remain myself." Mirain's chin lifted a degree. "Lord baron, you have vermin to hunt, and my companions stand in sore need of tending. Have I your leave?"

Ustaren bowed low and shaped a sign that Vadin almost knew. Others repeated it as he said, "All shall be done as the Sun's son commands." His voice raised to a roar. "Ho, Umijan! We ride to fight."

VADIN LAY IN A BED THAT SHOULD HAVE BEEN CELESTIALLY soft, and ached in each separate muscle and bone. He had slept as much as he was going to, but his body could not heal itself as quickly as that. Even his ears throbbed dully. Someone was snoring, or more likely some two, Jeran and Tuan abed in the guard's niche of Umijan's great chamber. Mirain, who never snored, held the other half of that vast bed, long enough and broad enough to dwarf even the Lord of Umijan.

Someone must have laid them all in their places, undressed them and cleaned them. Vadin remembered coming here, and knowing whose chamber it was, but no more than that. The two soldiers had been carried unconscious. Vadin had walked, and been inordinately proud of it. Mirain had not only walked, he had been giving orders. He would have put himself to bed, simply to prove that he could do it.

With some effort and no little pain, Vadin raised himself on his elbow. Mirain slept like a child, lying on his stomach with his face turned toward Vadin and his hand fisted beside it. Maybe, had he been younger, his thumb would have been in his mouth. But the face was no child's. Even in sleep it was furrowed with exhaustion.

Vadin's teeth clicked together. Mirain did not sleep on his face. He slept sprawled on his back or curled neatly on his side. And not weariness alone had graven that deep line between his brows.

Very carefully Vadin folded back the blankets. Mirain's back was clear, smooth, unhurt. No arrow had found its way there. He was wearing a kilt, clearly not his own; it was overlong and wrapped twice about him. As if that could have deceived Vadin, who knew that Mirain slept as bare as any other man in Ianon.

The kilt, pathetic subterfuge that it was, had slipped upward as he slept, baring what it was meant to hide. Vadin wanted to howl like a beast. Soft, Mirain was not, he had proven it beyond all questioning, but he had not ridden all his life in the poor protection of kilt or battle tunic. And he had ridden the greatest of all Great Races, half a day and a night and nigh a full day again, and never once, never for an instant, had he let slip that he was being flayed alive.

Vadin should have known. He should have thought. He should have—

"Nonsense." Mirain was awake. He looked no less haggard, but his eyes were clear. "You will say no word of this."

Vadin understood. Not that anyone would think the less of Mirain for it, but that damnable pride of his—

"That has nothing to do with it!" Mirain snapped. "Can't you taste the danger here? If it's known that I'm hurt, they'll hover over us day and night, not merely keep a watch on the door."

The part about danger was true enough. Vadin started

to unwind the kilt; Mirain glared but did not try to stop him.

It was not as bad as he had feared. The wounds were clean, though not pleasant to see. They had not festered. Vadin covered them with care, and rose. Not till he reached the door did he realize that he had forgotten how much he hurt. He drew the bolt and called out, "Redroot salve and the softest bandages you can find, and something to eat. Be quick!" He was slow in closing the door, and he was careful to move stiffly.

The salve came in a covered jar, and it was redroot indeed; its pungency made his eyes water. The bandages were fine and soft, the food substantial and steaming, and there was a pitcher of ale. They were sparing no trouble here. For Mirain's sake, Vadin wondered briefly, or for Moranden's? He bolted the door in curious faces and advanced on Mirain.

The prince was sitting up, which was admirable for appearances but appalling for his hurts. "Lie down," Vadin ordered him.

For a miracle he obeyed. Once he was flat again, he loosed a faint sigh and closed his eyes. Vadin's own were wide and burning dry. He remembered his mother the day the brindled stallion had gored his father; she had looked the way he felt now. Stiff and quiet, and very, very angry. The anger tainted his voice, made the words cruel. "Brace yourself. This will sting."

Vadin's hands were gentler than his tongue. Mirain was quiet, all but unflinching. But of course; he lived with a fire in his hand to which this was a mere flush of warmth. Not that the pain itself was any less, or the shame. Vadin said, "You're an initiate now. You've blooded your saddle; you've been anointed with redroot."

"What makes you think I need the reassurance?"

"So you don't," said Vadin, beginning the slow task of covering salved flesh with bandages. "So you're snapping at me because it amuses you. How do you think I got this leathered hide? Days in the saddle and nights on my face with redroot burning me to the bone, and half a dozen stints of wearing bandages wrapped like trousers."

"You should wear trousers to start with, and spare yourself suffering."

"That would be too easy. Or you'd have done it yourself."

Mirain stood for Vadin to finish, moving with care, looking as grim as his grandfather. "Easy. That's the heart of it. Trousers reek of ease and comfort and southern effeminacy. I can't wear them here and be looked on as either a man or a prince. Whereas my shaven face, now that is scandalous, but it's endurable: it's difficult, it's troublesome, it often draws blood. Men in Ianon will sacrifice their beards gladly for a fashion or a flattery, but they'll die before they wrap their legs in trousers."

"I'll die before I do either." Vadin bound off the last bandage, but he remained on his knees. It was strange to look up at Mirain and to know that it had nothing to do with wizardry. He sat on his heels. "I've earned my comfort in a kilt; I'm not about to atone for it with a razor."

"You *are* a philosopher." Mirain grinned so suddenly that Vadin blinked, and ran a finger down the squire's cheek. It was a gesture just short of insult, and just short of a caress. "Also much handsomer than I, and charmingly blind to the fact. It's not only your fine character that endears you to Ledi."

"Of course not. She loves my fine copper, and my occasional silver."

"Not to mention your splendid smile. And that cleft in your chin . . . ah!"

Vadin locked his hands together before they hit something. "You had better dress," he said, "my lord. Before the others wake and see."

"They won't." But Mirain went in search of clothing and found a tunic that made him a rather handsome robe, and Vadin found his temper again. As the prince approached the food, he was able to follow suit, even to keep from glowering. Even, in time, to muster a smile, albeit with a touch of a snarl.

WHEN MORANDEN RODE IN AT LAST, MIRAIN WAS THERE IN his own kilt and cloak, now clean and mended. The elder prince had for escort his kinsman of Umijan; and every

Umijeni behind them carried on his spear the head of a rebel. So too did a number of Ianyn, and they were singing as they came.

The women of Umijan raised their own shrill paean, the chant that was half of exultation for the victory, half of grief for the fallen. Amid the tumult Mirain stood alone with the three who were left of his companions, and there was a circle of stillness about them, a flicker of fingers in the sign Vadin had seen before. Again its familiarity pricked, again he had no time to remember. They were all coming toward Mirain, Moranden leading, handing the reins to one who reached for them, facing his sister's son. He was full of victory, magnanimous with it; he embraced his rival, and Mirain grinned at him as if they had never been aught but friends. Vadin could not understand why he was so little minded to join in the cheer that went up. It was not a feeble cheer. The army clashed spear on shield, roaring their names. *Mirain! Moranden! Moranden! Mirain!*

When some semblance of quiet had fallen, Moranden said, "Well done, kinsman. Splendidly done. If you weren't a knight of Han-Gilen, I'd make you one of Ianon."

Mirain smiled up into the glad and lordly face, so amiable to see, and responded with all sweetness, "I take your words as they are meant, my uncle."

Moranden laughed and clapped him on the back, staggering him, and turned to the baron. "I trust you've housed and looked after my kinsman as he deserves. He's no less than Ianon's heir."

"I've set him in my own chamber," Ustaren said, "and given him my own slaves to command as he wills."

"With which," said Mirain, "I am well content."

Such a love-feast. It was making Vadin ill. Mercifully they cut it short; there were wounded to see to, and trophies to hang, and women to be bedded in the rites of triumph. Mirain was encouraged to rest, with much solicitude for the toll his ride must have taken. Not that they knew the truth of it, or could guess; he refused to walk lame, and two days out of the saddle had smoothed the furrows of exhaustion from his face. He was being pampered like a royal maiden, nor could he help but know it, yet he left the courtyard with good grace.

Jeran went to see his mare, who was expected to live; Mirain had had something to do with that. Tuan followed with an eye on the hayloft and one of the serving maids. Mirain trailed at some distance.

They had had to set the Mad One apart in a stable of his own. He endured strange hands upon him, provided that they presumed only to tend him, but he would not suffer the stallion who ruled as king here. The beast, a splendid young bay, would bear the scars until he died, although the Mad One had forborne to slay him. For scorn, Vadin suspected. The black demon seemed content in his exile, with Rami near him and Jeran's mare coming slowly back to life within his sight. He accepted the delicacies Mirain had saved for him, submitted to the prince's scrutiny, snorted when Vadin observed, "Not a mark on him. You'd think he'd done nothing more strenuous than march on parade."

Mirain fondled Rami's head. The gap in the wall through which it had appeared had not been there before the Mad One came. "This beauty too," he said; "already she frets to be idle."

"You can talk to her," Vadin said more sullenly than he had meant.

"Seneldi don't use words." Mirain inspected the Mad One's hoof, bending with care, speaking as to it. "To Rami I'm a great one who shines in the night, a master of magic. I can speak clearly to her and know what she wishes me to know, and maybe she thinks well of me. But you are the one she loves."

Vadin barely heard. The words were only words, sound obscuring the thoughts behind, and memory had smitten him with such force that he nearly fell. Men in Han-Ianon, Marcher born, and secret signs, and a flicker of fingers wherever Mirain was. "The sign," he said. "The sign they all make where you can't quite see. It's a Great Sign. It's the sign against a prince of demons."

"I know," said Mirain calmly, releasing the hoof, smoothing a tangle in the black mane.

"You know?" Vadin shook with the effort of shouting in a whisper. "You know what it means? This is the goddess' country. What she is in Han-Gilen, and what the king would make her in Ianon, Avaryan is here. Enemy. Adversary. Burning devil. And they know that you're his son. Any man in Umijan could cut you down and be counted a saint for doing it."

"None has tried yet. None tried when we were all helpless. And now Moranden is here, and his army comes from the Vale."

"How do you know Moranden won't egg the murderer on? He goaded you into coming here. This may be his very own trap, all nicely baited."

"Have you turned so completely against him?"

Bile stung Vadin's throat. He choked it down. "No. No, I haven't. I only know what I would do if I were Moranden and this were my fief. I'd challenge you and kill you, and see that the truth never found its way eastward."

"And yet," Mirain said, "you forget. The army has learned to wish me well."

"That's too easily unlearned." Vadin gripped his arm, pulling him about. "Let's run for it. Now."

Mirain looked from Vadin's hand to his face, and raised a cool brow. "Have you suddenly turned coward?"

"I don't linger in closing traps."

Slowly Mirain's free hand raised in denial. "No, Vadin. I know what my pride has brought me to, but I can't flee now. The game is too well begun. I have to play it out."

"Even to your death?"

"Or Moranden's."

"Or both." Vadin let him go. "Why am I arguing with you? Ymin herself couldn't talk sense into you; and that was before you even started. Go ahead then. Kill yourself. You'll be comfortably dead, and you won't have to face what comes after."

That stung Mirain, but not enough. "If the god wills it, so be it. But I'll do all I can to forestall it. Can that content you?"

It would have to. Mirain would yield no further than that.

*   *   *

BARON USTAREN KEPT PRINCELY STATE IN HIS HALL. HIS knights dined on white wood, his captains on copper; for himself and his highborn guests there were plates and goblets of chased silver.

Here as elsewhere in the Marches, women did not eat with their men; but maids served the high table, robed and modestly veiled, with downcast eyes. One or two, Vadin thought, might have been lovely. The one who hovered about Mirain certainly was, if a soft dark eye and a lissome figure were any guide; though she was taller than Vadin, and beside Mirain she was a giantess. Unobtrusively Vadin tried to penetrate her veil, to see whether her face matched her eyes.

Mirain watched her likewise with an intensity that came close to insult. Close, but not, it seemed, on the mark. Ustaren laid a heavy hand on his shoulder and grinned. "My sister's daughter," he said, cocking his head toward the girl. "Do you like her?"

Mirain shaped his words with visible care. "She is very beautiful; she serves me well. She honors your house."

"Would she honor yours, Prince of Ianon?"

She had frozen like a hunted doe. Her fear was palpable. Of the baron; of Moranden, who watched and listened and said no word; of Mirain. Of Mirain most of all, a fear mingled with fascination and a strange, reluctant, piercing pity.

"I am young," he said, "to think of such things."

Ustaren laughed, a great bellow of mirth. "Too young for that, prince? Your stature may be a child's, but all the tales grant you a man's years. Do they lie after all?"

The hall, Vadin noticed abruptly, was very still. Neither Tuan nor Jeran sat close by, nor any other of the men who had shown themselves loyal to Mirain. Indeed he could not find them at all. Every man whose face Vadin knew, was Moranden's, watching Mirain steadily, with palpable hostility.

Old tactics, and effective. Separate the enemy from his allies; surround him and conquer.

Mirain's cup was full of strong sweet wine. He raised it

and drank, saluting Ustaren. "A man is a man, whatever his size."

"Or maybe," said Ustaren, "he's half a god. Tell me, did he come to your mother as a man comes? Or as a spirit, or a shower of gold, or a warm rain? How would a god take his bride?"

Mirain's eyes glittered, but his voice was level. "That was, and remains, between herself and the god."

"However he came," Ustaren said unruffled, "he left his mark on you. Or so they say."

Mirain's fist clenched upon it. "He was so gracious as to leave me proof of my parentage."

"Are mere mortals permitted to look upon it?"

The tension in the hall had risen until it was all but visible. Vadin's brain throbbed with it. He struggled to speak.

"The mark!" a man cried. "Let us see the mark!"

Mirain rose suddenly, nearly oversetting his chair. One or two men laughed, thinking he had drunk his fair share. He flung up his fist. "Yes, my father marked me. Branded me for all to see. Here; look at it!"

Gold caught fire in his palm. Someone cried aloud.

Behind Vadin danger crouched. He tensed to leap. Too late. Strong arms locked about him, dragging him back.

Where Mirain's heart had been, a black blade clove the air. The maidservant spun, eyes wide and fixed.

Moranden surged to his feet. Men of Umijan were all about him. Two had Vadin, who fought with all the strength he had. But Mirain was free. People in the hall had drawn back, taking the tables with them. A wide space lay open around the central fire, and there was order in the folk who rimmed it, the order of ritual. Men outside, veiled women in a circle within, and in the center, Mirain with the baron's kinswoman. She had cast aside her veil; she was even more lovely than Vadin had suspected. And far more deadly. In each hand she held a dagger; one was black and straight, one bronze-brown and curved. She moved slowly, fluidly, as in a dance, closing in upon her prey.

Vadin bit a careless hand. Its owner struck him half senseless but did not let him go. As he gathered to renew his struggle, Moranden shouted with the roughness of rage, "No! I forbid this!"

It was Mirain who answered him, Mirain casting aside his robe of honor, never losing a step in the dance of death. His voice was frighteningly gentle. "Let be, kinsman. I'll die and give you what you long for, or I'll live to face you on the field of honor. How can you fail?" He flashed his white smile. "*I* don't intend to."

The black knife licked out. He danced away. The girl smiled. "O valiant," she said almost tenderly. "O brave boy, brought here to fight in the war we made for you. It is a pity you must die. You are so young."

"The black blade," Moranden said harshly over the fading echo of her words. "The black blade is poisoned. The other is for your heart when she has you. After it has taken your manhood."

"Gentle poison," she said. "It makes its victim long to lie down and love me. Will you come to it? You are the goddess' own, so fair to see."

"So beloved of her enemy." Mirain saluted Moranden, who could not or would not aid him, but who had given him what honor demanded. He matched the woman step for step, mirroring her, keeping a distance which she could not close. She was no swifter than he, but she was no slower.

At first Vadin thought his ears tricked him. The hall was as silent as any hall could be with half a thousand people in it, and a fire blazing, and two mad creatures stalking one another around the hearth. But under the silence and about it and through it wove a slow sweet music. Darkness shot with gold. A voice at once deep and clear. Mirain had begun to sing.

The woman—no, she was a priestess, a votary of the goddess; she could be no other—the priestess sprang, clawed with bronze and black iron. The chant broke. Resumed. It was clearly audible now, but the words were strange. They seemed to have no meaning, or a meaning beyond mere human words.

A massive form lunged into the circle. Ustaren, still-faced, still-eyed, enchanted. Mirain was gone like a shadow. The priestess wheeled, her daggers a blur in her hands. Black slashed foremost. The force of the baron's advance drove him full upon the poisoned blade. Slowly, with no more sound than a sigh, he sank down. The priestess laughed high and wild. "Blood! Blood for the goddess!"

Mirain was on her, cat-quick, cat-fluid. The black dagger lodged deep in Ustaren's body, stilling as the heart stilled. The bronze flashed so close to Mirain's cheek that surely it was shaven anew. He laughed sharp and fierce. His golden hand closed upon the woman's wrist; she wailed in agony.

The knife fell, she after it. He let her fall. The dagger he caught, wheeling about. The fire roared to the roof and collapsed into embers. He walked over it. Through it. The circle broke, shrinking from the terror of his eyes. They swept the greying faces. The god filled them, flamed in them, consumed them. "You fools," he said with terrible softness. "You brave, blind, treacherous fools."

"Hell-spawn!" howled one bolder, or madder, than the rest. It might have been a woman. It might have been a man shrill with fear.

Mirain did not answer. He faced his mother's brother and said, "I will remember that you spoke for me. Do you remember that I brought about the death of the chief of your rebels, the raiser of the Marches, the master of the tribes. He would have trapped us both, me to my death, you to be his puppet in the king's hall. I leave you his holding and his people." He hurled the dagger to the floor at Moranden's feet. It clattered in the silence. "Do with them as you will, my lord of the Western Marches. My father calls me elsewhere."

Eleven

SINCE MIRAIN LEFT, THE KING HAD TAKEN TO THE battlements again, gazing not southward now but westward. Ymin was with him through much of his vigil, still and silent, her eyes as often upon him as upon the horizon. He was old, she thought. He had always been old; yet he had been strong, like an ancient tree. Now he was brittle and like to break. When the wind blew chill from the mountains, he shivered, huddling in his cloak; when the sun beat down, he bowed under it.

On the fourth day of Brightmoon's waning, the twentieth since Mirain's leaving, the sun rose beyond a heavy curtain of cloud. A thin grey rain darkened the castle; yet the king kept his watch. Even Ymin had striven in vain to dissuade him. He stood unheeding under the canopy his servants had erected for him, with the rain in his face and the wind in his hair. Now and then a shiver would rack his body, despite a rich cloak of embroidered leather lined with fleece.

Those who came and went on the kingdom's business—for the king ruled as firmly from his battlements as from his throne—looked at one another and made signs which they thought he could not see. Surely, and at long last, he had fallen into his dotage.

He did not deign to notice them. Ymin suffered them, for having failed to entice him from his post she held her peace. Sometimes she sang to herself, old songs and new ones, rain-songs and hymns to the Sun.

Suddenly she faltered. He had stiffened and stepped forward into the full force of the wind.

The Vale of Ianon was hidden in a thin mist. Shapes moved within it, now all but invisible, now clear to see: farmfolk on errands that could not wait for a clear sky, a traveler or two trudging toward warmth and dry feet. Once there had been a post-rider, and once a lady's carriage.

This was a mounted company, drab in the rain. There were four of them. No banner floated over them; whatever badges they bore lay hidden under dark cloaks. Their mounts moved swiftly enough, but the beasts' necks were low with weariness.

The foremost was glistening black in the rain, and it alone seemed to run easily. It wore no bridle.

The king had already reached the stair to the gate.

THE RIDERS CLATTERED UNDER THE CARVEN ARCH. ONE by one, wearily, they dismounted to give reverence to the king. He ignored them. Mirain was slowest to leave his senel's back, yet he seemed less worn than the rest. He even smiled a little as he came to his grandfather's embrace, standing back when the king would let him and saying, "Why, you are as wet as I! Grandfather, have you been waiting for me?"

"Yes." The king held him at arm's length. "Where is Moranden?"

Mirain's face did not change. "Behind me. He had matters to settle."

"Such as the war?"

"The war is over." Mirain shivered and sneezed. "Grandfather, by your leave, may I dismiss my escort?"

If the king recognized the evasion, he saw the truth in it. "You also. I shall speak with you when you are dry and rested."

THERE WAS A FIRE ON THE HEARTH IN THE KING'S CHAMBER and spiced wine warming over it, and in front of it the king, with Ymin on the stool beside him. Mirain sat by them without a word, accepting the cup the singer handed him. He had bathed; his hair was clean and loose and beginning to dry, and he had on a long soft robe. His face in firelight was still, almost a mask, his mouth set in a grimmer line than perhaps he knew of.

The king stirred. "Tell me," he said simply.

For a long moment Mirain was silent, staring down at his untouched wine. At length he said, "The war is over. Not that it was much of one, in the end. It was all a trick. Ustaren of Umijan played a large part in it. He is dead. I am here. Moranden will follow when he has settled his fief."

Again there was a silence. When Mirain showed no sign of continuing, the king said, "You left him early and all but alone. Why?"

"There was nothing for me to do."

"You could have remained to rule in my name. You are my heir, and will be king."

"Moranden is Lord of the Western Marches."

The king regarded him long and deeply. "Perhaps," he said, "you fled."

Mirain flung up his head. "Are you accusing me of cowardice?"

"I am saying what others will say. Are you prepared to defend yourself?"

"In that part of Ianon," Mirain said, "my parentage is not a thing to boast of. Lacking a war to fight in, I judged it best to return here."

"How did Ustaren die?"

If the question had been meant to take Mirain off guard, it failed. "He fell at the hands of one of his kin, a priestess of the goddess. She was quite mad. She was aiming," he added, "at me."

The king's face drew taut. "No one moved to defend you?"

"My uncle tried, as did my squire. They were prevented. Ustaren died. I did not."

"And you left."

"Before any others could die for me. It is not time yet to teach the Marches the error of their religion."

The king bowed his head as if suddenly it had grown too heavy to lift. In his eyes was a horror, a vision of Mirain dead with a black dagger in his heart.

Mirain knelt in front of him and laid his hands on the gnarled knees. "Grandfather," he said with an undertone of urgency, "I am safe. See; I am here, and alive, and unhurt. I will not die and leave you alone. By my father's hand I swear it."

"Your father's hand." The king lifted Mirain's own, touching with a fingertip the sun of gold. Briefly, painfully, he smiled. "Go to bed, child. You look to be in need of it."

Mirain hesitated, then rose and kissed his brow. "Good night, Grandfather."

"Good night," the king said, almost too softly to be heard.

YMIN EASED THE DOOR SHUT BEHIND HER. THE CHAMBER was dim, the nightlamp burning with its shaded flame, flickering in a waft of air. The lad from Imehen surged up in his niche, eyes glittering, his body a shadow of alarm. She sang a Word; he subsided slowly.

Mirain was in bed but not asleep. He did not move as Ymin came to stand beside him. Nor did he glance at her, although he brought one arm up, bending it, pillowing his head on it. He was not wearing his torque. He looked odd without it, younger, strangely defenseless.

That, she knew, was an illusion. Even at his lowest ebb, Mirain never lacked for defenses. He had only to raise his hand.

He spoke softly, coolly, without greeting. "You have great skill with the Voice."

"If I did not, I would not be the king's singer."

He turned his eyes upon her then. Perhaps he was amused. Certainly he was holding something at bay. "I cannot be so enchanted. Even," he said, "when I yearn to be."

She sat on the bed beside him. "Have you proven that?"

"My initiation into the priesthood was . . . hampered. One of the priests was young and strong and impatient. He tried force." Mirain paused for a heartbeat. The thing in his eyes, the surging darkness, the sudden light, came almost near enough to name. "He lived. He healed, after a fashion."

"You won your torque."

"Avaryan's priests would not refuse it to Avaryan's son. Even though he could not submit that last fraction of his will. Even though he had come within a breath of murder. Even though he could not master the power which was a deadly danger to them all."

"Perhaps," she said, "the power has its own laws, and your soul knows them but your mind does not. The rite of the torque was made for simple mortal folk, to teach them submission, to waken them to the might of the god. As his son you have need of neither."

"I have more need than any." He was quiet still, but she was beginning to understand. The darkness was wrath, and grief, and hatred of himself. The light was Sun-fire crying to be set free.

"Tell me," she bade him gently, yet with a tang of iron. "Tell me what you are hiding from the king."

His eyes hooded. "What is there to hide?"

Suddenly she had no patience at all. "Must we play at truth-and-falsehood like a pair of children? The king suffers it; he longs to spare you pain. I have no such scruples. You left Umijan because Moranden tried to kill you. Did you not?"

"Not Moranden. Ustaren, through a kinswoman of his, a priestess of the Dark One. Moranden gave me what aid he could."

"It was not enough."

"It was more than he needed to give."

"And that galls you."

Abruptly he rolled onto his face. The coverlet slipped; he made no effort to regain it. She looked with pleasure at his smooth-skinned compact body; saw the healing scars and knew them for what they were; yielded to temptation, running a light hand down his back. He shivered under it, but his voice was clear and unshaken. "It gladdens me. Moranden may have meant betrayal; he may have meant to challenge me. But in extremity he came to my aid. He may yet become my ally."

"Why then did you abandon him? Why did you not remain to press your advantage? Now he is in the Marches among his own people; he will forget alliance and remember only enmity, until he raises the folk against you. Why did you set him free to betray you?"

He moved all at once with blurring speed, half rising, seizing her hand in a grip she could not break. She met his wide dark stare. His nostrils flared; his lips drew back. "*I* did not set him free. I had no say in the matter. For I was threatened, and the power came, and it did as it chose. It lured Ustaren to his death. It laid the priestess low. It flung the Marches in Moranden's face and drove me back to this my kennel, where I may be safe and warm and protected from all harm." As suddenly as he had seized her he let her go, drawing into a knot of rage and misery. "The power did all these things, and now it sleeps. And I wake to face what I have done. Murder, madness, cowardice—"

"Wisdom." She had silenced him. "Yes, wisdom. I spoke ill before; I did not think. You were best away once your power had revealed itself, and Moranden will not turn against you yet. Not he. He will challenge you in the open before all Ianon. So much your power knew when it sent you back to us."

"My power did more than defend me. It killed. And I—I exulted. I gave blood to the goddess, and the god flamed in me, and it was sweeter than wine, sweeter than honey, sweeter even than desire." His voice broke on the last word; he coiled tighter, rocking, face hidden in his heavy hair. "I wonder, singer. Are these vows of mine a dire mistake? Perhaps if—I—" He laughed with a catch in it. "Maybe it's all perfectly simple. I only need do what any man does when the need is on him, and the power will see how sweet it is and forget the delights of slaughter."

Her foolish brain wondered if he had had more wine than was good for him. But her nose caught no scent but his own faint, distinct, male musk; and her eyes saw that his own were clear, if troubled; and her heart knew that he was only being himself. Begotten of a god, branded with it, laden with a destiny and compelled to pursue it, yet he was also a man, a very young one, a boy half grown given powers and burdens that would stagger a man in full prime.

She felt him in her mind, drawn into it, walking the paths of her thoughts. His face was set hard against pity. She felt none, which shocked him into himself. She watched him begin to be angry, realize how ridiculous it was, try to swallow mirth. He looked his proper age then. Before he could laugh she silenced him, laying her hand upon his lips. They were very warm.

She drew back carefully. His eyes were his own again. Grief and guilt would linger, anger would return, but the great storm had passed. Now he was regarding her, and for a Sun-priest raised in Han-Gilen he was astoundingly free of shame; he did not try to hide his body's tribute. "You had better go," he said steadily, with only the faintest hint of breathlessness.

Ymin did not move. "Would you like me to sing you to sleep?"

He stiffened, stung. "Do I seem so very much a child?"

"You seem very much a man. Who has sworn oaths that only death or a throne may break; who has done deeds to sing of, and suffered for them, and begun to find peace. You are the king who will be, and I am the king's singer. Shall I sing for you?"

The moment was gone, the danger faded. He lay on his side and drew up the coverlet, not quickly, not as if he would hide anything, but with a certain finality. Then he smiled with all the sweetness in the world, and she could have killed him, for now that he had mastered himself he had robbed her of all her lofty detachment. And he did not even know what he had done. "Sing for me," he said, simple as a child.

She drew a long breath and obeyed.

Twelve

WHEN VADIN WOKE FROM A DREAM OF SONGS AND MAGIC, he could have sung himself. Mirain was up and bathing and trying not to growl at the servants, and when Vadin came into the bathing-room he greeted his squire with a mixture of glare and grin that was almost painful, so long had he been locked away with his wrath and his god. "Come in here," he said, "and give these busybodies an excuse to flutter about elsewhere."

They were not even insulted, let alone deterred. They were bursting with joy to have their wild young lord back again; to have him waging his daily battle with them, which always had the same ending. He bathed and dressed and fed himself, but they drew his water and set the cleansing-foam where he could reach it, held the towels for him, laid out his clothing and served him at table. In Vadin's mind, they won the war by a hair.

As usual, Mirain shared bath and breakfast with Vadin. As usual, Vadin protested to the last. It was all perfectly as usual. After days in the saddle and nights in a tent and never a word except for the most dire necessity, it was an honest miracle.

And yet, when the old fey look came back, Vadin was not surprised. It was less staring-mad than it had been, and it did not last long. Only long enough for Mirain to look Vadin up and down, purse his lips, and say, "Put on

your earrings. All of them. And the copper collar, I think.
And your armlets, and the belt you keep for festivals."

Vadin's brows went up. "Where am I going? Whoring?"

A smile touched the corner of Mirain's mouth. "In a
manner of speaking. I want you to look like the lord you
are."

"Then I'd better take off your livery, my lord."

"No." The refusal was absolute. "Jayan, Ashirai, I give
this victim to you. He is my squire. He is also the heir of
Geitan. Make him the epitome of both."

The young servant and the old one, free Asanian and
captive easterner, fell upon him with undisguised pleasure. He suffered it somewhat more graciously than Mirain
ever did, which he took time to be proud of. It crowded
out anxiety. Mirain's expression boded ill for someone, he
dared not think whom.

The servants took Vadin's hair out of its squire's braids,
combed it, braided it anew as befit the heir of a lord. They
trimmed the ragged edges of his beard and plaited it with
copper, and arranged his livery to perfection, and decked
him as Mirain had commanded. They even did what he
never troubled to do except for the very highest festivals:
painted the sigil of his house between his brows, the red
lion crouched to spring upon a crescent moon. And at the
last they set him in front of the tall mirror, and a stranger
stared back at him. Rather a handsome young fellow if
truth be told, and lordly enough in his finery.

Royalty came to stand beside him, and it did not dimin-
ish him. It made him look more than ever the Ianyn
nobleman; never Mirain's equal, but lofty enough in his
own right. He could hold his head the higher for knowing that there was one to whom he would gladly bow it.

Mirain's reflection grinned at his own. "You, my friend,
are frankly beautiful. Beautiful enough to call on a lady."

Vadin turned to face his prince. The anxiety was gathering into a knot in his middle. Mirain was a sworn priest;
he could not send a go-between to one he fancied as a
bride. Still less could he contemplate an alliance of plain
pleasure. Which left—

"I have a gift," Mirain said, "for a great lady. I cannot,

of course, insult her by presenting it with my own hands.
Nor can I demean her by sending a servant. Will you bear
it for me?"

Vadin's eyes narrowed. The request was so simple, so
devoid of compulsion, that it was ominous. "Who is this
lady? Or shouldn't I ask?"

"You should," Mirain said willingly. "It is the Lady
Odiya. Will you go to her, Vadin?"

Dread mounted. Outrage drove it back. "Damn it, you
don't have to play the courtesan with me! Why not give
me my orders and have done with it?"

Mirain's head tilted. "I don't want to command you.
Will you go of your own will?"

"Didn't I just tell you I would?" Now Mirain was laughing, and that was maddening, but it was better than anything that had come before. "You want—whatever it
is—given from my hand to hers?"

"Yes." Mirain set it in his hand: a small box much
longer than it was wide, carved of some fragrant southern
wood and inlaid with gold. "You are to entrust it to no
one else, and to see that no one hinders you."

That would not be easy, if the rumors were true. Vadin
traced a curve of the inlay. "Do I linger for a response?"

"See that she opens the box. Say that I am returning
what belongs to her." Mirain's teeth bared. It was not a
smile. "You'll be in no danger. I assure you of that."

Vadin could think of any number of replies. None of
them was wise with Mirain in this mood. He chose silence
and a very low bow and a swift departure.

IMEHENI WOMEN WERE RAISED TO BE MODEST, BUT THEY
were not cloistered, and they certainly were not guarded
by eunuchs. That was an affectation for barbarians and
for Marchers. Vadin, face to face with Odiya's unmanned
guard, found himself briefly bereft of words. The creature was as tall as himself and even more elongated, and
his face was too smooth and his hair was too rich and his
eyes were too deadly flat. They took in the young lord in his
festival clothes and his vaunting maleness, and gave nothing back.

Vadin drove his voice at that mask of a face. "I come in the name of the throne prince. I would speak with the Lady Odiya. Let me pass."

The eyes shifted minutely. Vadin gathered himself for a second assault. The guard raised his lowered spear and stepped aside.

Vadin's spine crawled. He was admitted. So easily. As if he were expected.

This was an alien world, this eunuch-warded fastness, full of strange scents, amurmur with high voices. Not only Odiya dwelt here. Others of the king's ladies held each a room or a suite or a whole court, and most of those were free to come and go; Vadin had seen them sometimes in hall or about the castle, elderly ladies as a rule, mingling with kindred and courtiers. There were nine of them altogether, highborn and low, beautiful and not, chosen by custom and by the king's favor, that in his union with them he should make the kingdom strong. But the tenth was First Lady of the Palace. However exalted the others might be, however noble their lineage and their titles, it was she who ruled here, and she ruled absolutely.

Vadin, let into her domain, might have wandered for a long while without guidance. But he was a hunter, and hunters learned wisdom: to stop when lost, and to wait. In a little while one came, another eunuch, very old and withered, with eyes as bright as the other's had been dull. "Come," he said, and his voice was almost deep enough to be a man's.

Vadin went. He felt as if he were caught in a dream, and yet he was intensely alert, aware of every flicker of sound or movement. The box, light in his hand, held the weight of worlds.

People passed him, coming and going. Servants, a lady or two, once a pretty page who stopped to stare. In envy, maybe. This was no place for a male, even for a child of seven summers, even one with the almond eyes and the red-brown skin of the southlands. His owner, whoever she was, was kind, or fastidious; she had replaced the iron slave-collar with a necklet of copper.

The eunuch led Vadin past the child, up a long stair.

At its summit stood another guard, a monster, a great hairless slug of a creature. But the worst of it was not its size or its smoothness; it was white, as white as the women the talespinner had told of, but its eyes were grey as iron. Vadin shuddered in his own, warm, dusk-and-velvet hide, and took great care in passing, as if the eunuch could infect him with that maggot-pallor.

His guide was smiling with an edge of malice. "What, my young lord, do you not approve of Kashi? He is very rare and very wonderful, a son of the uttermost west, where folk are the color of snow. My lady paid a great fortune for him."

Vadin did not deign to respond. Bad enough that those bitter eyes had seen his revulsion; he would not give them more to mock at. Was he not the heir of Geitan? Was he not the throne prince's envoy?

His haughtiness carried him almost to the end. The Lady Odiya sat in a chamber of broad windows, and those open to wind and sun; and after all the guards and the tales and the seclusion, she was not even wearing a veil. Her long hair was braided like a man's, its raven sheen touched only lightly with silver, and her body was clad in a gown as plain as a servant's, and she wore no jewel; and her beauty was as piercing as it had been in the Wood of the Goddess. There was no softness in it, nothing gentle, nothing he had ever thought of as womanly, yet she was woman to the core of her. Woman as the goddess was woman, female incarnate, sister to the she-wolf and the tigress, daughter of moons and tides and darkness, relentless as the earth itself.

Pain startled Vadin out of his stupor, the edges of the box sharp as blades under his clenched fingers. A spell—she was casting a spell. He looked at her, and he made himself see an aging woman in a dark gown, her body thin under it, almost sexless. Her hair was dulled, her face carved to the bone by the bitter years. But she was still beautiful.

His body, trained, had brought him to one knee and bowed his head the precise degree due a royal concubine. His limbs felt even more ungainly than usual, his ribs more prominent, his beard more ragged. How dared he inflict his unlovely self upon this great queen?

Spells. The voice in his head sounded exactly like Mirain's. *Give her the box, Vadin.*

He was doing it. He was saying the words which Mirain had given him to say. "The throne prince sends this gift, great lady; what you have lost, he has found and now returns to you."

She took the box. Her face betrayed nothing. In that, it was like Mirain's, or like the king's. Royal.

"I am to see you open it, great lady," Vadin said.

Her eyes lifted. He could not have moved if he had wished to. She took in every line of his face from brow to chin. She said, "You are . . . almost . . . beautiful. You will be fair indeed when your body grows into itself. If," she said, "you live so long."

"Open the box," said Vadin. Or Mirain wielding Vadin's tongue, or terror leaving no wits and almost no words. His mind saw a dark chamber far from help, a knife raised and glittering, a new guard at the door. A young one who could remember what it was to be a man.

The lady's eyes released him so abruptly that he swayed. Her long fingers found the catch, raised the lid. She gazed down without surprise, but her calm had broken. That was rage which glittered beneath her brows, which bared her teeth. Two were missing, unlovely gaps, breaking the last of her spell.

With sudden violence she flung the box away. Its contents gleamed dully in her hand: the black dagger of Umijan's priestess. Vadin gaped at it. He had last seen it buried to the hilt in Ustaren's heart.

"Tell your master," said Odiya, and her voice was as harsh as that of a carrion bird, "tell your mighty prince that I have received his gift. I will keep it until the time comes for it to drink his blood. For my servants have been weak, but they will grow strong; and the goddess hungers."

"I hear," said Vadin's throat and tongue and lips. "I am not afraid. Let the goddess lust after Sun-blood, but let her be warned. Its fire consumes all that comes of darkness."

"But in the end, it is the fire which is consumed."

"Who can know what the true end will be?" Vadin bowed again, again with precision. "Good day, my lady Odiya."

Thirteen

ORANDEN RODE INTO HAN-IANON IN THE LIGHT OF A blazing noon, with his men in their ranks behind him and his banners flying.

"Bold as brass," someone said as they clattered through the market.

"Hush!" another warned her fiercely. "Ears can hear."

"And so they should! Why, I've heard tell—"

Ymin edged her way through the press. She knew what the woman had heard. Everyone was hearing it.

"Tried to murder the heir, he did, or so they say."

"When they're not saying that he saved the prince's life."

"Saved it! Why, he lured the young lord away and tied him to an altar, and actually offered him up to the—"

"Be a good thing if he had. Mincing little foreigner. At least the other's proper Ianyn."

The singer pressed her lips together. That refrain would not die for all her singing and the king's proclaiming and Mirain's own great magic. With Moranden gone it had faded somewhat; now it would grow strong again, and the lines would draw themselves more firmly than ever. She shivered in the sun's heat, and cursed that clarity of her mind which could come so close to prophecy.

A sudden tumult drowned out all but itself. Ymin, crushed in the crowd, saw Moranden's company pause. A

secone troop was riding down from the keep, no banner
over it and no great order to it: a company of the king's
squires on holiday with hawks on wrists and hounds on
leads. One of the hounds had escaped and was wreaking
havoc among the stalls; two or three of the young hellions
had spurred after it, baying like hounds on a scent.

Yet in the center of pandemonium was stillness, in the
summer heat an island of cold. Mirain faced his mother's
brother, he and his Mad One motionless but for the
glitter of eyes. Moranden's weary charger fretted and
stamped and fought to lower its horns.

A whoop and a yelp heralded the hound's capture. It
was loud in the spreading silence. Ears strained; breathing quieted. The squires had drawn themselves into a line
at Mirain's back, and their eyes were bright and hard.

"Greetings, uncle." Mirain's voice was clear and cool
and proud, distinct in the stillness. "How goes the war?"

Moranden grinned, a baring of white teeth. "Well, prince.
Well indeed." He leaned upon his high pommel, the
image of lordly ease. "Better by far than it was going
when you left it."

One or two of the squires, the lad from Geitan foremost, started forward. Mirain raised a hand; they stopped
short. He smiled. "When I left," he said, "there was no
war at all. Only"—he hesitated, as if he did not wish to
say the word—"only treachery. I am glad to see that you
are free of it."

Ymin's breath caught. The eyes about her were avid.

Moranden bowed over his charger's neck. "I have always been loyal to my rightful ruler."

"I do not doubt it," Mirain said. The Mad One danced
around Moranden's dun, the point of a spear that clove a
path through the company. Moranden's men followed it
with their eyes. With a bark of command the elder prince
brought them about, spurring his stallion up the road to
the castle.

A sigh ran through the crowd. Of relief, it might have
been, that the rivals had not come to blows. Or, more
likely, of disappointment.

*   *   *

THERE WAS LITTLE ENOUGH TIME FOR ANYONE TO FEEL himself cheated. Moranden had returned a few scant days before the greater of Ianon's two highest festivals, the feast of High Summer that was consecrated to Avaryan. And this one would be more splendid than any before it; for the central and holiest day of the festival was also Mirain's birth-feast, his first in the castle and his sixteenth in the world. Every lord and chieftain in Ianon, and many a commoner, had come to look on the heir to the kingdom; most bore gifts, as rich as each could afford.

Mirain woke early on the day itself, the solstice day, first of the new year, well before dawn. Yet Vadin was up before him, and more remarkable still, the king. When his eyes opened they fell first upon his grandfather's face, that bent over him, regarding him with a steady, patient stare. He sat up, scowling slightly, shaking his hair out of his eyes. "My lord, what—"

"Gifts," the king said. All his sternness melted; he loosed his rare and splendid smile. "Gifts for the Throne Prince of Ianon."

Gifts indeed. Vadin brought them one by one, an honor he had fought for; he fought less successfully to keep the grin from his face. Full panoply, made to Mirain's measure but with room for him to grow in: armor wrought as only smiths in Asanion could make it, light and strong and washed with gold, the breastplate graven with the rayed sun of his father; a tunic of well-padded leather to wear beneath, its skirt cut for ease and comfort and strengthened with gilded bronze; and a helmet of bright and burnished gold gràven with flame-patterns and surmounted with a scarlet plume. And with these, baldric and scabbard likewise of scarlet and gold, and a sword of precious Asanian steel, its blade keen enough to draw blood from the air; and a cloak of scarlet clasped with gold, and a round Sun-shield, and a spear, and a saddle of scarlet leather inlaid with gold.

Mirain stroked the soft tooled leather and looked up at the king. Vadin had never seen him so close to speechlessness. "My lord," he said. "Grandfather. This gift is beyond price."

"Should the Sun's son defend his realm in less?" The king beckoned to the one servant Vadin had not managed to dispose of. "But that is for the time to come. This I give you for your festival."

It was a robe of honor, a royal robe of cloth of gold. The servant dressed Mirain in it, braided his hair with gold, weighted him with the treasure of the mountain kings. Mirain stood erect under it, meeting the old man's smile with one of his own.

"A fine prince you make," the king said.

"Cloth of gold," Mirain answered, "and a coronet. And," he added with a wicked glint, "a fine air of arrogance."

The king laughed aloud, so rare a thing that even Mirain stared astonished. He held out his hand. "Come, young king. Sing the sun into the sky for me."

MIRAIN SANG THE SUNRISE RITE FROM THE ALTAR OF HAN-Ianon, chief among the priests, shining with more than gold and new sunlight. Vadin was there for once, with everyone else who could crowd into the temple, and he gasped with the rest of them when Avaryan, rising, struck the crystal upon the temple's summit and cast a spear of white fire upon the altar. That was not magic but art, a wonder of the yearly festival, familiar as the dancing fires at harvest time. But Mirain stood before the shining altar, and he raised his hand, and Avaryan himself came down to fill it.

For a searing instant Vadin knew that he would be blind. Then he realized that he could see. He stood in the heart of the sun, in a world of pure light, and for all its blazing brilliance it lay cool and clean upon him. It was singing, chanting in a voice he knew, in words he had heard every High Summer since he was old enough to stand in the temple. He blinked; the brilliance faded, or melded itself into the world. Mirain went on with the rite in a cloud of priests and incense. The moment of the god's coming might never have been.

Maybe it never had. No one else remembered it. Kav stared at him when he asked, following the crowd to the hall and the morning feast there; Olvan laughed and said something about sorcerers' apprentices. At first Vadin could not get close enough to Mirain to ask, and when he pushed and cursed his way to his proper place behind the prince's chair, Mirain had taken it into his head to leave the lords to their glory and break his fast among the common folk in the market. The king smiled and let him go, and many of the high ones went with him, and Vadin's question lost itself in the tumult.

IN THE THIRD HOUR OF THE MORNING, ALL BUT THE MOST determined feasters streamed down from castle and city to the fields about it, gathering for the Summer Games: games of strength and skill, war-games and peace-games, footraces and mounted races and contests between lords in their war chariots.

This day was Mirain's, and he sat as ruler of the games, even the king set beside but slightly below him. He had stopped when he saw how it was to be, had looked as if he would protest, but the king met his eye and held it. Slowly he took the seat ordained for him. Slowly his frown lightened. When Vadin left to take his place among the squires, Mirain's unease seemed to have melted, to have turned all to joy.

The lord of the games could not compete in them. But the Lord of the Western Marches set himself to take every lordly prize. He heaped his winnings like the spoils of war, drawing the younger knights to him with the fascination of his victories.

"My lord is magnificent today."

Mirain looked down from the high seat, favoring Ymin with a slow smile. "But," he said, "he has to take his prizes from my hands."

She settled at his feet, which was the singer's privilege. On the field Moranden waited with a dozen princes and barons, the ragged line of chariots shifting as the teams fretted. His own beasts were quiet under his strong hand: matched mares, striped gold and umber. Their manes were clipped into stiff crests; their hoofs were sharpened and pointed with bronze.

Light and whippy though the racing chariot was,

Moranden stood in it with easy grace. Like the rest he wore only a loinguard and a broad studded belt; the muscles rippled across his chest and shoulders. A garland of scarlet flowers lay upon them, a lady's favor.

"He is splendid to see," Mirain observed without perceptible envy.

"My lord is magnanimous today."

Mirain met her bright mirthful gaze and laughed. "My lady is full of compliments."

"The air is bursting with them. All Ianon is in love with you, for this day at least. Does that please you?"

Mirain drew a deep, joyous breath. "It sings in me." He spread his arms, which, by more than chance, was the signal for the race to begin. The seneldi sprang forward. The crowd roared. Mirain laughed.

He was smiling still when Moranden brought his foaming team round before the dais and leaped, running along the yoke-tree, springing lightly to the ground. His body gleamed with sweat; his nostrils flared; his eyes glittered.

Mirain rose with the prize, a harness of gold. Before Moranden could ascend the dais, he came down. Younger prince faced elder, Mirain on the second step, Moranden upon the grass.

"Well won again, kinsman," Mirain said. "You do our house great honor."

"That is its due." Moranden accepted the gold trappings with a deep bow. "After all, sister-son, I'm its only defender on this field."

"Every king should have such a champion."

"Is that a southern custom?" Moranden asked. "In the north, every king is his own champion."

Mirain's eyes narrowed, but he laughed. "Why, uncle! You have almost a southern wit." He bowed, a king's bow, catching the sun's fire in all his ornaments. "May you win often again for the honor of the mountain kings."

He returned to his throne, Moranden to his chariot. Ymin, watching them, sighed a very little.

The king marked her. Leaning toward her, he said very low, "Come, child. Stallions will fight and men will strike sparks from one another, and strong men the more strongly."

"These," she said, "are altogether too strong for my heart's ease."

"Strong, and young. Age will calm them."

"If either suffers the other to live so long." She shook herself, and smiled at the king. Hope was so rare in him, and so precious. "Ah, sire," she said almost lightly, "I seem determined to cast a shadow on your sun."

He gestured negation. "You cannot. For see, my son is the greatest of the victors, and my heir"—his voice softened—"my heir is the greatest of my princes. And Ianon knows it and him."

"So," she added too softly even for him to hear, "do both my lords. Both equally, and both all too well."

VADIN WAS NO MORANDEN, BUT HE WAS HOLDING HIS OWN. He won the mounted race; he took a good second at swordplay among the young men. Then he won again twice, footrace and spearcast, and as he came for the latter prize he met Mirain's broad grin and realized with a shock that he had done it: he had put himself in the running for Younger Champion. So had Pathan the prince and quiet methodical Kav and a haughty lordling from Suveien. He thought briefly, ignobly, of running away to hide. Then Mirain said, "Win it for me, Vadin."

Vadin glared. "No tricks, Sunborn."

"No tricks," Mirain conceded, but his eyes danced. Vadin left him with a bow and a glance of deep distrust.

The Younger Champion won his crown in mounted combat, full-armed, with unblunted weapons. It was the same deadly rite as that which made a man, but easier, Vadin thought as his friends saw to his arming. He did not have to fight these battles after running the Great Race. Rami was fresh and eager, and his mood was rising to match hers. He knew he was good; he had been reckoned one of the best in Imehen. "We'll see if I'm one of the best in Ianon," he said to the mare. She rolled a molten eye and snorted, scenting battle. Lightly he vaulted onto her back. Hands passed up his weapons. Sword on its baldric, dagger at his belt, two throwing spears, the round shield with its Geitani blazon. The heralds were singing out his name. He was matched with the Suveieni. He touched heel to Rami's side; she danced forward, head up.

One mercy: the Suveieni charger was a mare likewise, a fine tall roan. No need to fear a goring from this one. Nor, on trial, was the rider so very much to be afraid of. He was good enough and he was fast, but he lost his temper easily, and with it much of his skill. Vadin let him flail and curse himself into exhaustion, and when his temper had robbed him of defenses, struck him down neatly, almost regretfully, with a flat-bladed blow.

On the other side of the field, Kav had put up a valiant fight, but Pathan had not only skill, he had brilliance. It was Pathan who remained to face Vadin when the vanquished left the battleground, Kav on his own feet and the Suveieni on his shield. As Vadin paused to breathe his mount, to lave his streaming face, to swallow a mouthful of water, he stared at the paragon of squires. The king would knight him tonight, that was an open secret. And here was Vadin alVadin, raw recruit two years at least from knighthood, daring to challenge him.

Pathan did not look as if he feared the outcome. He even smiled and saluted when he sensed Vadin's eye upon him. Hard though Kav had fought him, his armor shone unmarred, his handsome face unbloodied, his plume un-ruffled. His cream-pale stallion looked newly groomed; he sat the saddle as if he had been born there, light, easy, breathing without effort.

Rami was still fresh enough, but Vadin was dusty and his shield had a dent in it and he knew he reeked royally. He drew a deep breath. Mirain was a flame of gold on the field's edge; Vadin could have sworn he felt those eyes upon him, daring him to turn tail. As if Rami would have allowed it. He tightened his grip on spears and shield, bowed his head to the herald's glance. He was as ready as he would ever be.

The horn sang. Rami was already moving. A spear left his hand, aimed for the center of the prince's shield.

Wind gusted, struck it awry. A blow like a hammer sent Vadin reeling back. He wrenched the spear from his own shield, flung the second—fool, fool, Adjan would have raged at him, he had not aimed before he loosed. But neither had Pathan, or perhaps the wind was doubly traitor. Vadin swept out his sword. At which Pathan had defeated him before. But not mounted, not with Rami fighting with him. The stallion was trained and he was swift and he had his wicked ivory horns; but Rami had learned about stallions and their weapons.

So too had Vadin. And these were sharpened, he could see. It was allowed. His folly that he had given his heart to a bare-browed mare, his loss that he would not burden her with horns of bronze set in her headstall.

They were playing, Pathan and the stallion. Teasing, feinting, pretending that neither could land a blow. Vadin astounded himself; he landed one, and it rocked Pathan in the saddle. How could the perfect swordsman have failed to see it coming?

Maybe he was not perfect. His mount shied infinitesimally from the clash of the blade on shield or helm or blade; he did not always seem to know it, and when he did, the touch of his heel brought the senel in too close, or not close enough. Vadin could not match his speed, could not quite match his skill, but maybe—

It had to be soon. Vadin's strength was waning, his skill failing even in defense. He held Rami steady between his knees, raised his aching shield arm a degree, parried a wicked slashing blow. Pathan's blade flicked back, flicked aside in a feint, darted into the gap in Vadin's parry. By a miracle Vadin was there, and the force of the meeting nearly felled him. Nearly. The stallion veered just visibly. Pathan kicked him inward. He skittered a fraction of a step. Pathan's new assault left an opening, a breath's pause, the thickness of a good bronze blade. Vadin filled it. Evaded the shield, turned the point of his sword, and disarmed and dismounted Pathan in the same swift serpentine movement.

There was a stunned silence. Pathan lay on his back, eyes open and glazed, and for an instant Vadin knew that he was dead. Then he stirred and groaned and sat up cradling a hand that stung without mercy. Vadin knew; he had learned his trick the hard way from the arms master in Geitan. He sprang from Rami's back, reaching to help Pathan to his feet, babbling like a fool. "I'm sorry, I didn't mean to, it was only—"

"You idiot of a child," growled Pathan, striking away the hand that stretched to him, rising stiffly but without visible pain.

Vadin opened his mouth and shut it again. Gods help him, he had made a fool of this proud prince before all Ianon, ruined the day of his knighthood, turned his lofty goodwill to bitter enmity.

Pathan's laughter stopped Vadin short. "Idiot child," the prince repeated, and this time his wry amusement was clear to see, "don't you ever know when you've won?"

Vadin blinked. One of those last fierce blows must have addled his brain. He turned slowly. Rami was cropping grass like the veriest plowbeast. Beyond her the folk of Ianon were going wild.

Pathan struck him, not gently. "Mount up, infant. Go and get your prize."

The heralds were there and saying much the same, and one had Rami's reins, and now that Vadin was aware of it the roar of the crowd was deafening. He took a moment to gather himself; as lightly as he could, he mounted, gathering the reins as Rami began to dance. *She* knew what was expected of her. He straightened his weary shoulders, raised his chin, and set his eyes firmly forward.

Mirain was not on the dais. The Mad One was coming, Mirain astride bearing the crown of gold and copper that a quick eye and a clever trick had won Vadin. Rami champed the bit and bucked lightly. *"Just so,"* Vadin replied, and let her go.

They met at a gallop, black senel and silver, and wheeled about one another, manes flying, and halted in the same breath. Mirain said nothing, but his eyes said everything. Vadin's cheeks were hot, and only partly with exertion; he ducked his head like a child praised too lavishly. A cool weight settled on his brows. He looked up in mild startlement as Mirain's hands lowered, empty. "Go on," the prince said. And when he hesitated: "Rami, of your courtesy, salvage your lord's honor."

She tossed her head, clamped the bit in her teeth, and began the victor's circuit of the field. The Mad One did not follow, and for this splendidly mortifying moment no one was even aware of him or of the one who rode him. Vadin looked back once. Mirain did not mind at all. "Sweet modesty," his voice said soft and clear in Vadin's ear, with laughter in it, and pride, and deep affection.

Damn it, why did they all have to be so indulgent? Was he a braidless boy to be smiled at and clucked over and made allowances for? Demons take them, he was a man grown; and he had proven it.

Anger did what nothing yet had been able to do. Awakened him to the truth. He had won. He was Younger Champion. He was the best of the squires in Ianon. He flung his sword up and caught it to a roar of approval, and wheeled Rami full about, and sent her plunging madly round that wide and glorious field.

Fourteen

AS THE SUN BEGAN TO SINK, THE GAMES ENDED IN SPLENDOR. Moranden had won the crown that was elder brother to Vadin's, as he had done at every High Summer since he won his knighthood. By custom the two champions met upon the field in a dance of war, a crossing of blades and a matching of their mounts' paces; rode side by side to the throne and bowed; and clasped hands in the amity of brothers and warriors. Moranden was not gentle, and his dance was swift enough to strain Vadin's lesser strength and speed, and his handclasp was painfully tight; but that was the custom: amicable as the Elder Champion might be, he neither forgot nor let the other forget that one day they would contest for his title. "You fought well," Moranden said as if he meant it, and he smiled his famous smile. "That last stroke—I don't suppose you'd teach it to me? Unless"—his smile widened to a grin—"you're planning to use it on me next High Summer."

"Not next year," Vadin said, "or for a good count of years after, I don't think, my lord. I'll need more than a trick and a stroke of luck to overcome the best fighting man in Ianon."

Moranden's brows raised. "Don't be so certain, sir. The mount lacked something in training, but the rider lacked somewhat in skill; and you had the eyes to see it. That's a rare gift." He clasped Vadin's hand again. "We ride to the castle together. I for one won't be ashamed of my company."

Nor was Vadin, but he was not at ease. He could not revel in the adulation that beat upon him. His eyes were on Mirain, who rode just ahead of him with the king. The younger prince had his share of the glory back again, and he rode on it, shining with it, borne as on wings. For that hour at least his people loved him utterly; even the fear of the Mad One had no power to hold them back. They reached for him, slowing him, doing battle for the touch of his hand or the glimmer of his smile.

The king's guards thrust forward, armed for his defense. The king stopped them with a glance. See, it said; Mirain could take no hurt. Not here, not now. All Han-Ianon lay in the hollow of his hand.

The great hall lay open to the long summer dusk, ablaze with torches, filled to bursting with the people of Ianon. Those who could not crowd themselves into the hall itself filled the court without and spread into the side courts, even the lowest of them feasting like lords on the bounty of the king.

Mirain sat upon the dais under a canopy of white silk edged with gold. His hall robe was startling in its simplicity, all white but for the torque of his priesthood; his head was bare, his hair in its single braid, and no jewel glittered at brow or throat or finger. Yet he shone, as brilliant in himself as any of the gold-decked princes of Ianon.

Moranden had taken the Elder Champion's place down the table on the king's right, flanked by glittering princelings, himself in black and vivid scarlet with a ruby like a drop of blood between his brows. His companions paid Mirain little heed, drinking more than they ate, waxing hilarious as the light died from the sky. They quieted but little for the dancers or the players, little more for Pathan's solemn knighting at the king's hands, and not at all for the singers led by Ymin and chanting the praises of the god. Although Moranden roistered with them, even from his own place of honor on the king's left Vadin could perceive that the prince's cup was seldom refilled; that he watched Mirain without seeming to watch: a steady, side-long, unreadable stare.

But Mirain was far beyond notice of aught but his own elation. He was young, he was beloved, he would be king. His mood left no room for either hate or fear, let alone for simple caution. And Vadin, trapped among his own exuberant admirers, could not get close enough to beat him to his senses.

A very young singer came forth, a child with a voice like a flute, who sang of Mirain's birth at sunrise in the center of the god's great rite. The princelings paused in their revelry, caught in spite of themselves by the unnerving purity of that voice. Save one; tone-deaf or deaf with drink, he drawled, "Sunborn indeed. Prophecies, forsooth. How they do make up these tales!"

Every word was distinct, loud and dissonant against the chanting. Vadin tensed to surge up, subsided slowly. He could do nothing but make matters worse.

Mirain stirred. His eyes, that had been shining, lost in contemplation of wonders, focused slowly. Yet he was still half in his dream.

"Who knows what really happened?" growled another young lord. "He walks in here, he tells a pretty tale, he gets it all: throne, castle, and kingdom. Good work, says I, and mortal fast."

The singer did not falter, but he looked toward Ymin with frightened eyes. She did not move, perhaps could not. Mirain had roused all at once. The king's hand gripped his arm, thin and iron-hard yet trembling visibly. The prince spared him not even a glance. "Guards," he said softly and clearly, "remove these men."

A third lordling leaped up, sending his winecup flying. "Yes! Remove them, he says, before they betray too much of the truth."

He spoke to the hall, but his eyes rested on Moranden. The elder prince sat at his ease, lifting no hand as the guards seized his followers, although they strained toward him and shouted his name. He was watching Mirain.

The song ended unnoticed. The singer fled behind Ymin's skirts, too terrified for tears.

The third man fought against his captors, crying out, "Liar! He lies! He is no son of the god. His mother lay with the Prince of Han-Gilen; the high priestess of the temple would have put her to death for it; her lover cast down the priestess and set up the stranger in her place. But the priestess had her just revenge. She killed the liar with her own hand. I know it. My kinsman was there; he saw, he heard. This is no son of Avaryan. You give your worship to a lie."

A guard raised his fist as if to club the man into silence.

"No," Mirain said. His eyes were very wide and very bright. "Let him say what he has been taught to say."

For an instant the young man was nonplussed. Even his fellows were still, staring. He filled his lungs to shout, "No one taught me. This is an adventurer, a no-man's-son, sent up from the south to seize a kingdom. When he has it, the Prince of Han-Gilen will claim it and him."

Mirain laughed in genuine amusement. "There, sir, you betray yourself. What could Prince Orsan possibly want with a kingdom as remote, as barbaric, and as isolated as Ianon? Already he rules the richest of the Hundred Realms."

"No realm is too rich," the man cried. "Tell the truth now, priestess' bastard. Your mother lied to save her lover and herself. But you betrayed her. For bearing you she died. You were her death."

Mirain was on his feet. The lordling struck again, struck deep. "You are accursed, matricide, destroyer of all you touch. 'Go to Ianon,' they begged you in Han-Gilen. 'Go, take your curse with you. The king is old; he is mad; soon he will die. Ianon is yours for the taking.'" He raised his arms in a grand gesture. "One thing they forgot. Ianon is not only an aged king and a pack of coward lords. One man is strong. One man remembers his honor and the honor of the kingdom. While the Prince Moranden lives, you shall not rule in Ianon."

Mirain's head tilted. "I suppose you have consulted him." He turned his eyes upon Moranden. "Mine uncle? Does this mockingbird belong to you?"

"He speaks out of turn," Moranden replied coolly, "but as for the truth of what he says, you know better than I."

"We all know it." Ymin's trained voice cut across the growing uproar, stilling it. "I have seen it and I have sung it. This is the one foretold. This is the king who comes from the Sun. Ill befall you, Moranden of Ianon, if you dare to oppose him. For he is gentle and he is merciful, but I have no such virtues; and I will wield against you all the power of my office."

Moranden laughed. "Such power, too, milady singer! You've always been his loyal lapdog. A gleam of gold, a well-told tale, and he had your heart in his hand. Look at him now! Gasping like a fish, with all his plots laid bare."

"What could he say to such monstrous words as yours?"

"What's monstrous in the truth? He knows it. He gags at it. And hides behind the skirts of whoever has the gall to defend him." Moranden's lip curled. "Some king he'll be, who needs a woman to fight his battles for him."

"Better that than a king who needs a woman to think his thoughts for him." Moranden surged up. Mirain faced him, icy calm. "Be silent henceforth, kinsman, and perhaps I shall forgive you for what your puppet has said of my mother. But I shall never forget it."

"Liar. Foreigner. Priestess' bastard. Because my father loved you and because you have a look of my sister, whom I also loved, I suffered you. But too much is too much. Before my father and my sister, there was Ianon; and Ianon groans at the thought of such a king."

"Ianon," said Mirain, "no. Only Moranden, whose soul gnaws itself in rage that he cannot have a throne." The hall was deathly silent. Mirain met the black and burning eyes of his mother's brother. "And if you won it, my lord—if you won it, could you hope to hold it?"

"Child." Moranden's voice was different, softer, more deadly. "Not you alone are beloved of the high ones. Nor is this Han-Gilen, that casts out all gods but one and rears up in its pride and fancies itself blessed of Avaryan. The gods are shut out, but the gods remain. She remains, who alone is Avaryan's equal. *Is*, child. Is, was, and will be."

Mirain spoke as through a choking fog. Proud words, but muffled, bereft of their force. "I will chain her."

His kinsman laughed. "Will you, little man? Try it then. Try it now, Sunborn, child of the morning."

"I am—not—" Mirain reeled. His hand flew up, but its fire was dim. The laughter did not falter. Mirain cried out against it. "Moranden! Can you not see? You too are a puppet. You are being used, you are being wielded. Another voice is speaking through you."

"I am no man's toy!"

"No man's indeed, but a goddess' and a woman's."

Moranden fell upon him, mad-enraged, possessed, it did not matter. Vadin saw Mirain go down, and a wall of bodies between, and no weapon in all that hall of festival; and it was a nightmare, Umijan come again, with Mirain beaten before he began.

Darkness swept between scarlet and fallen white, severing them, hurling the scarlet against the wall. A deep voice spoke with softness more devastating than any bellow of rage. "Get out."

Moranden staggered, face slack with shock, and crumpled to his knees. The king looked down at him. Old and strong and terrible, he met his son's eyes; the younger man flinched visibly. "Get out," he said again.

Moranden's mouth worked. Words rent themselves from him. "Father! I—"

Hands like iron smote him to the ground. Stronger than they and more cruel, the harsh voice held him pinioned where he lay. "If the sun's rising finds you within reach of my castle, I will hunt you like a beast. Exile, accursed, let no man raise a hand to aid you. Let no woman take you into her house. Let no dweller in Ianon feed you or clothe you or give you to drink, lest' by so doing he share your fate." The king turned away from him. "Moranden of Ianon is dead. Begone, nameless one, or die like the hound you are."

Moranden looked about. Every back was turned to him. Even his boldest followers had turned with the rest, sealing his exile.

Laughter escaped him. It was sharp, wild, edged like

blades. "Such is the justice of Ianon. So am I condemned, without defense, without recourse. Alas for our kingdom!"

No one turned. The king stood most still and most implacable. Mirain and Moranden between them had forced him to choose. He had chosen. It was bitter, bitter. But Moranden saw only the motionless back, knew only what he had always known: that he was not the one his father loved.

A black rage swept over him, mastered him. He whirled to his feet. "A curse!" he cried. "A curse upon you all!"

Mirain stood once more, disarrayed but uncowed; he alone would meet Moranden's eyes. The light the elder prince saw there was bitter. "You," he said, almost purring. "You have Ianon now. I wish you joy of it." He bowed deeply, mockingly, and spun in a flare of scarlet. Past the king, past Mirain, past the lords and commons of Ianon he strode ever more swiftly. A torch caught a last blood-red gleam, and he was gone, into the outer darkness.

"GRANDFATHER." MIRAIN'S VOICE WAS LOUD IN THE SILENCE. "Grandfather, call him back."

The king wheeled upon him. He gasped. The old lord's face was like a skull. Yet, "Call him back," Mirain repeated.

"He sought your throne and your life."

Mirain did what he had never done to anyone but his father: knelt at the king's feet and bowed his head. "Sire, I beg you."

Within the skull, puzzlement mingled with wrath. "Why?"

"It is not finished. It must be finished, or Ianon will be rent asunder."

"No," the king said, flat and hard.

Mirain's eyes glittered. "He must come back. We must fight now, while the battle is new, and the god must choose between us."

"I choose," grated the king. "You shall not fight."

"That is not for you to ordain, my lord of Ianon."

The king was immovable even before the enormity of that insolence. "I will not call him back."

Mirain looked up at the great and royal height of him. "Then I too must leave you."

A tremor racked the king's body. "Leave?" he repeated, as if the word had no meaning.

"It is war now between my kinsman and myself. A war which you, my lord, have made certain. Whatever befalls, whether battle or, by some mighty chance, reconcilement, I will not shatter this kingdom with the force of our enmity." Mirain's chin lifted still higher. "Since Moranden has gone into exile, so too must I."

In the hall and in the courtyards beyond, no one breathed. The king had the look of a man who has suffered a mortal blow. His daughter was dead. His son had turned openly upon his chosen heir. His daughter's son stood before him and cast his kingdom in his face.

"But," he demanded harshly, "when I am dead, who will rule in Ianon?"

"There are lords and princes enough. And every one knows his father." Mirain bowed low, even to the floor. "Farewell, my lord. May the god keep you."

He turned as Moranden had, white to the other's scarlet. Yet as he strode forth, the king seized his arm. He halted, eyes blazing. "Mirain," the king said. His fingers tightened. "Sunborn. By your father's hand—"

Mirain tensed to pull free, and froze. The king swayed. Mirain caught at a body turned all to bone and thin skin, yet massive still, overwhelming his slightness. Slowly he sank beneath the weight of it.

Death unfolded in the king's face, death held at bay and now let in for the kill. "No!" Mirain cried, clutching his grandfather's body as if his hands alone could hold it to life. "Not now. Not for me!"

"For you," the king whispered, "no." All his life and strength gathered in his eyes, that opened wide, fixed upon Mirain's face. "Summon my servants. I will not lie on the floor of my hall like one of the hounds."

LAMPS GUTTERED IN THE KING'S CHAMBER, CASTING LONG shadows upon the great bed. The healers' chants had faded; the priests were silent. Alone in a corner, Ymin sat with her harp. Her fingers had fallen from the strings, her voice sunk to a murmur and died. Tears glistened upon her cheeks.

Mirain knelt beside the bed. He had not moved since the king was laid there, not for Vadin, not for the healers or the priests, not ever for those high lords whose rank had won them past the guards. One hand gripped the king's; the other, the right, lay upon the still brow.

The king had slid from waking into a dim dream, and into light again. Even closed, his eyes turned toward Mirain.

Far away a cock crowed, calling forth the dawn. The king stirred. His eyes opened; his fingers tightened. His lips softened, almost a smile. "Yes," he said very low. "Curse me. Curse the oath you swore me."

"I swore not to die and leave you alone."

"You cannot abandon me now."

"No," Mirain said, yet wearily, without anger. "You have seen to it that I cannot."

"I? Not entirely, child. I had aid. Call it fate. Call it—"

"Poison. Subtle, sorcerous, and beyond my power to heal." The weariness was gone, the wrath returned. Although no spoken word had passed between them since they left the hall, it seemed that this battle of wills had been waging for long hours. Mirain bent forward. "She will pay for it."

"She will not." This too had an air of use, of resistance that would not be shaken.

"She has always been your weakness. She has been your death."

"That has been my great gift. To choose my death, and to choose its instrument; and to know that she was beautiful. But she has won no victory. My heir and not hers shall hold my throne." A breath, a cough: all the laughter he could muster. "Admit it, Sunborn. Beneath all the seemly and filial grief, you are glad of it."

"No. Never."

"Liar," the king said, amused still, almost tender. "I leave you no sage advice; even if your courtesy would bid you listen, you would not heed it. This only I command you: Rule in joy."

Mirain's eyes were hot and dry, his voice rough. "I shall see you to your pyre. What then if I simply walk away?"

"You will not."

"I can call Moranden back."

"Will you?" With the last of his strength the king drew Mirain's hand to his heart. "From the moment I saw you, I knew you. Avaryan's son . . . you are worthy of your father."

"You believe that?"

"I know." The king's eyelids drooped; his heart labored. With a deep sigh he loosed his will's hold upon it. Beat by beat it slowed. Mirain snatched at it with a cry, calling forth all the power he had from his father. The king's heart throbbed, briefly strong; slipped free; quivered; stilled.

Ianon's king was dead.

Ianon's king rose and settled the still hands upon the still breast, and turned. At the sight of his face, lords and healers and priests sank down, bowing to the floor.

"He willed this," Mirain said to them in a tight still voice. "Even unto death, to bind me here. He willed it!"

"Hail, king." Ymin's voice, silencing him; and Vadin's hoarse with weeping, and the rest in ragged chorus: "Hail, Mirain, king in Ianon."

Vadin, watching him even through the tears, saw the change begin in his eyes. Grief, anger, reluctance, none grew less. Yet at the name of king a light kindled. There was nothing of triumph in it. Only, and purely, acceptance.

And yet, accepting, at last he could weep.

Fifteen

"**P**RECIPITOUS FOOL." ODIYA HAD NO PATIENCE TO spare for the son she had borne. "If you had curbed your hounds, if you had seen fit to rest upon your victories—"

Moranden whirled upon her. "Curb my hounds? They were not mine!"

"They followed you. You made no effort to silence them."

"And who encouraged them to speak?" He stood over her. "No masks now, Mother. No pretenses. I know whose mind conceived that web of deception in Umijan. I know who stands behind tonight's madness. And so, madam, does the king."

"So did the king."

His hand gripped her throat. "What have you done? What have you done to him?"

"I," she said, "nothing. He wished to die. That gift was given him. When she chooses, the goddess can be merciful."

"The goddess!" He spat. "And who asked her? Who danced the spells? Who brewed the poison? It was poison, wasn't it? My lordlings, my anger, my exile—diversions, no more. The little bastard was right. You were using me!"

"Of course I used you," she said coolly. "You are an apt tool. Attractive, malleable, only intermittently clever. Yon interloper is a hundredfold the king that you will ever be."

"You are no mother to me, you daughter of tigers."

"I am giving you the throne you lust after."

His eyes narrowed. His grief was deep and rending, but his mind was clear, doing its cold duty. In that much he was his mother's son; and perhaps his father's. "The throne," he muttered. "It's empty now. And the boy—I heard him plead for me. He'll revoke my sentence. I'll challenge him; he'll fall. By tomorrow's dawn I'll be king."

"By tomorrow's dawn you will be riding to the Marches."

"Are you mad? I should leave now that you've thrown all Ianon in my face?"

"You shall go into exile as the lord your father has commanded. You grieve, you are justly angered, but you are a man of honor; you do as your king has bidden. If the new king calls you back, why then, is he any king of yours? You have sworn no oaths to him, nor will you, slayer of your father that he is."

"*You* slew my—"

She slapped him. He stood with his mouth open, staring. "Fool," she said to him. "Idiot child. It is no man you face. It is a mage, the son of a god. All Ianon's Vale lies under his spell. Every man he meets learns swiftly to worship him. Remember the ride to the west; remember how he was, effacing himself among your men, subverting them with a look or a smile, winning their souls with his magic. And he was the great victor in the war that never was. He conceived the race to Umijan, he ran it and won it while you tarried for dull duty. You were but the lord commander; he was the great hero.

"And you would stand up in hall before the king's body and dare to contend with him for the throne." Her lip curled. "Think! You were loved by some, respected by all, looked on as king to be. Outside of the Vale in great measure you are still. Go there; show yourself; keep yourself before the people while the foreigner learns that a throne can bind its claimant to it as with chains. And when at last he has gained the strength to break them, when he comes forth from the Vale to claim the whole of his kingdom, let him find that he is king only of the inmost lands. The rest shall be yours, an army at your back,

sworn to you as rightful king. Then may you challenge
the usurper. Then shall you rule in Ianon."

Moranden had stilled as she spoke, had gathered his
wits, had mastered his temper. He heard her out almost
calmly, toying with the copper-woven braids of his beard.
When she ended, he paced from end to end of the long bare
chamber, paused, turned to face her. "Wait—I can wait.
I've waited a score of years already. But even my poor wit
can see the flaw in your plotting. If the little bastard is a
mage—and I don't doubt it's possible; I saw him in
Umijan—if he's a master of magic, how can I ever challenge him? I'm a warrior, not a sorcerer."

"He fancies himself a man of war. Challenged as he will
be challenged if you heed me, he will lay aside his power
to come against you. And I can see to it that he holds to
his vow."

"You. Always you."

"And where would you be if it were not for me?" She
held out her hand. "Bid me farewell, my son. Your mount
and your baggage are ready; your escort waits. Be swift,
or the dawn will catch you."

He came as if he could not help it, but his bow was stiff
and his lips did not touch her palm. "You'll stay here?
After what you've done?"

"I will see my old enemy laid upon his pyre." She
gestured imperiously. "Go. I will send word to you in the
Marches."

With a last sharp inclination of the head, he turned on
his heel and left her.

SHE WAS STILL THERE AS THE SUN ROSE, ALONE BY THE
eastward window, her mantle wrapped about her and
her veil drawn over her head.

The light step upon her threshold, the presence at her
back, did not at once bring her about. "Strangers do not
often come here," she said to the flaming sky.

"I do not think," said a dark soft voice, "that we are
strangers to one another."

She turned then. For all her wisdom and all her spies,
he surprised her a little. He was so small, and yet he stood

so far above her. And he looked so very much like his
mother's father.

With a swift gesture she averted his spell. He dwindled.
Somewhat. He was still in his white robe, rumpled now
and stained, and his face was drawn with exhaustion. But
he was calm; she could find no anger in him. "The king is
dead," he said.

She astounded herself. She sank down under the weight
of those simple words; she lay on her face, and she wept
like a woman whose dearest love has been slain. And the
pain was real. It tore at her vitals.

"Hate," Mirain said, "is womb-kin to love. Uveryen and
Avaryan were born at one birthing."

She raised herself upon her hands. He knelt by her, not
touching her, watching her as one would watch a beast
engaged in some strange rite of its kind. But it was not a
cold regard. It burned with subtle fire.

He shifted slightly, sitting on his heels, setting his fists
upon his thighs. The right hand could not close fully; the
tension in it was the tautness of pain. "You belong to me
now," he said, "you and all my grandfather's chattels.
Did you consider that when you dared to linger here?"

She came erect all in a motion, like the lynx she was
named for. "I belong to no one. His death loosed my
bonds; I am free."

His gesture of denial flashed sudden gold. "If you had
been a slave, that would have been so; so likewise if you
had been but a concubine. But he took you in clan-
marriage, and clan-wives pass to the heir. To be used by
him, or bestowed by him, as he sees fit."

"No," she said. "He never—"

"It is written in the book of his reign. It is recorded in
the annals of his singer. Surely you knew."

Odiya's arms locked about her throbbing middle. Her
grief was gone. Her hate was a crimson fire. Lies, black
lies. She knew the form of clan-marriage, which in the
west they called the mating of the sword. She had never
undergone it. She had been taken from her chamber, she
had been thrown down in her father's hall before his high
seat, she had been—

"He never raped you in front of his men, nor ever in your father's blood." The voice was neither young nor gentle. It smote her with its likeness to the old king's. "He passed the sword over you. He spoke the words that mated you. He gave his name to the child you carried."

"Moranden is his son!" So far had she fallen; she fought her way back to the heart of this battle. "We were not sword-mated. We were *not*."

"Because you would not say the words? That matters nothing under the blade." Mirain stood, head tilted back, regarding her down the long curve of his nose. It was a feat, that; she should have laughed at him, to break his spell again, to restore her strength. But she could only stare, raging within, and know that he was stronger than ever she had dreamed of.

She knew now. She would not underrate him again. She let her head bow, her body droop as if in defeat. "What will you do with me?"

"What should I do?" He said it so lightly that she nearly betrayed herself. "I don't want you for my bed. I don't trust you in my castle, and I don't trust you outside of it. I'm not even sure I trust you dead."

Her dread ran only as deep as her face. "Would you slay a helpless woman?"

He laughed in purest mirth. "Why, lady! Have you forgotten your daily hour with the sword? Or the potion you distilled yourself, which so sweetened my grandsire's wine?" His laughter vanished; he went cold. "Enough. You tempt me; you lure me into your darkness. Living or dead you are my enemy, living or dead you will strive to cast me down."

She waited in grim patience. She was not so strong in power, perhaps, but she was older and her hate was purer, unalloyed by childish fancies of compassion. For he was dreaming of that, even through his cruel words. If he had meant to kill her, he would not have tarried so long.

He spread his hands, the dark and the golden. "You may see the king to his pyre. But if you do that, be aware that you have chosen, that you must follow him into the fire. If you would live, depart this day from the castle and swear never again to raise your hand against the throne or its lord. Though if it is life you choose, I do not think your goddess will be long in taking it."

"That is a choice?"

"It is all you will have."

She was silent. Not debating her choice; that was not worth so much. Considering him. Letting her hate run cold and clear. "I could wish," she said through it, "that you had been my child."

"You can thank all your gods that I am not."

She smiled. "I choose life. As you knew I would. That is the great beauty in being a woman: one need not stand on honor, nor fear the shame of cowardice."

He bowed low as to a queen, and returned her smile without strain. "Ah, lady," he said, "well I know it, who am a king and the son of a god. Honor binds me, and shame, and my given word. But what they all mean . . . why, that is the great beauty in what I am. I can make them in my own image."

She went down lower still, even to the floor, and only half of it was mockery. When she rose again, he had gone. Even with the sunlight blazing through the broad window, the chamber seemed dark and dull, drained of the splendor that was his presence.

Sixteen

THEY BUILT THE PYRE OF RABAN, KING IN IANON, IN the great court of his castle, and raised it high up to heaven: all of rare woods, well seasoned and steeped in oil, scented with the gods' own incense. At his feet they laid his best-loved hound to guard and guide his way into the god-country; his head lay upon the flank of his red charger, his mount upon the road. He himself was clad in a plain hooded mantle to deceive the demons who might lie in wait for a king but not for a simple wayfarer, yet lest he be so mistaken before the gods' gate, beneath the cloak he wore all the jeweled splendor of his kingship.

Mirain stood alone before the pyre. His kilt was plain to starkness, belted with a strap of leather and dyed the dull ocher of mourning; he had neither bound nor braided his hair nor put on any jewel. Barefoot and bareheaded, with no kin to stand at his back, he looked far too frail for the burden the old king had left him.

The rite of death was long, the sun seeming to hang motionless in a sky like hammered brass. More than one of Ianon's gathered people gave way to Avaryan's power, or retreated into what shade there was, or did as Vadin did: made their own shade with their ocher mantles. Yet Mirain, in the courtyard's center, sought no relief and received none. His voice in the responses was as firm at the end as when he began.

At last a priestess of Avaryan came forth with the vessel of the sacred fire. All bowed before it. Reverently she laid it upon the altar which stood between Mirain and the pyre. An acolyte, following her, knelt in front of her with an unlit torch. She blessed it; he turned to Mirain.

The young king did not move. The acolyte blinked and began to frown, not daring to prompt him but all too well aware of the waiting priestess.

Slowly Mirain reached for the torch. His fingers closed upon the wooden haft, raised it. The fire flickered in its basin; the pyre loomed above him. *Kindle it*, the watchers willed him. *For the gods' love, kindle the fire!*

Somewhere within the too-still body, strangeness stirred. Mirain flung the torch spinning up and up into the sun. His arms, freed, spread wide; his head fell back, his eyes opened wide to the sun's fire. It flooded into him, filled him. Out of the towering flame that had been his mortal body, a single dart sprang forth. Straight into the heart of the pyre it flew, and the oiled wood roared into flame.

The priests fled from that great eruption of light and heat. But Mirain stood full in front of it, oblivious to his peril. His body was his own again; he sang a hymn of grief and triumph mingled, sacred to the Sun.

THE EARTH WAS DULL AND COLD, A DARK RAIN FALLING with the evening, quenching the fire. Mirain shivered, blinking, staring without comprehension at the charred and smoldering heap which had been his grandfather's pyre.

How often Vadin had spoken to him since his song faded, the squire himself did not know. Yet Vadin tried again, and in desperation he settled an arm around the damp chilled shoulders, tugging lightly. "Come," he said, rough with cold. And Mirain heard. He began to move. Swaying, staggering, but stubbornly afoot, he let his squire lead him away.

Vadin took him not to the king's chamber which was his now by right, but to his own familiar room. A fire was lit there, dispelling the rain's chill; a bath waited, and dry clothes, and wine and bread to break the death-fast. He

seemed hardly to see who ministered to him, although he
let himself be tended, fed, cajoled into bed.

When he lay wrapped in blankets, his eyes focused at
last. He saw who bent over him. Vadin he regarded without surprise, but the other made him start, half rising.
Ymin pushed him firmly back again and held him there.
"What is this?" he demanded. "Why are you here?"

She greeted his return to awareness with perfect calm.
"Tonight at least," she said, "you are entitled to your
solitude. I am seeing that you get it."

Vadin grimaced. "It hasn't been easy, either. And tomorrow it won't be possible. The king can't belong to
himself; he belongs to Ianon."

Mirain tried again to rise from his bed; they allied to
hold him down. He glared at them, struggling, but not
with any great force. "I have to go to the hall. The
feast—"

"No one looks for you tonight," Ymin said.

"But—"

"There is no need for the young king to drink the old
one into the god-country. Not when the god's own fire
has set the dead man upon his road."

"Is that what people are saying?"

"It happened," Vadin said. After a moment he added,
"Sire."

Mirain sat up, propping himself with shaking arms. "It
happened," he echoed. "You see how it's left me. I'm
hardly the god everyone must be thinking me."

"No; merely his son and our king." Calmly, matter-of-
factly, Ymin supported him. "If anyone has needed proof
of either, you have given it. Magnificently."

He tensed, drawing in upon himself. "I can never help
myself. Wherever I turn, whatever I do, the god is there,
waiting. Sometimes he takes me and wields me like a
sword; and when he lets me go I'm like a newborn child.
Strengthless, witless, and all but useless."

"Even gods have their limits."

"In Han-Gilen," he said, "they would call that a heresy."

"There are gods, and there is the High God. My doc-
trine is sound enough, my lord."

"In Ianon. Maybe." He glanced beyond her at Vadin. "I'm not a god. I'm scarcely yet a king. I don't know that I'll ever be one."

"Tomorrow you will be," Vadin said.

"In name. What if my grandfather was deceived? He was a great king. He thought he had found another like him. He paid for it with his life. What if he died for nothing?"

"He didn't," snapped Vadin with all the force he could muster, close as he was to tears. "And he knew it. Do you think Raban of Ianon would have let go the way he did if he wasn't leaving his kingdom in good hands?" Between them, he and Ymin eased Mirain down. "There now. Rest. You've a long day ahead of you."

"A long life." Mirain's burst of strength had faded; he labored even to speak. "I was so certain. That I had the right; that I was strong enough. That I could be king. I was an utter fool."

They said nothing. But Ymin smiled and gestured slightly, a flicker of dissent. He turned his face away from them both.

Vadin's eyes had overflowed again. They kept doing that; he had stopped trying to master them. But he was not weeping now for the king. The old man had gone in glory. It was the young one who made him want to lie down and howl.

A warm hand touched his arm. He met Ymin's gaze. "He has the strength," she said gently.

"Of course he does!" Vadin flared at her. "But—damn it, it's so soon!"

"It is never the proper time for a king to die." She sighed; her own eyes were suspiciously bright. "You too should rest, young lord. Have you even lain down since the Games?"

Vadin could not remember, and he did not care. "I'm not tired. I don't need to—"

Before he knew it he was in his cubicle, his pallet spread, her hand on his belt loosening the clasp. He slapped her away. She laughed, light and sweet as a girl, and stripped him with consummate neatness. Even as he

snatched at his kilt, she caught him off balance and tripped
him into his bed. She was amazingly strong. "Sleep," she
commanded.

"Or?"

"Or I sit on you until you do."

It was not an idle threat, nor entirely an unpleasant
one. For an older woman she had a fine figure. Thin, but
fine.

Her kiss was as chaste as his mother's, a brush of lips
upon his brow. Her tone was utterly maternal. "Sleep,
child. Dream well."

He growled, but he did not rise. With the last flicker of
a smile she left him.

VADIN COULD HAVE SLEPT THE MOON-CYCLE THROUGH AND
hardly noticed it, but Mirain woke renewed from his
brief night's sleep. He even smiled, rarity of rarities, until
darkness touched him. Memory, perhaps, of the king's
death; of his own kingship.

He rose and stretched and found his smile again, turning it on Vadin. It swelled into a grin; it swept away, left
him cold and shaking. "Avaryan," he said very low. "Oh,
Father. I don't think I can—"

"Sire."

They both whipped about. A servant faced them: an
elderly man of great dignity, dressed in the king's—in
Mirain's—scarlet livery. If he was in any way perturbed to
see his new lord reduced to a trembling child, he con-
cealed it well. "Sire," he said, "your bath awaits you."

In the bedchamber Ianon's king was served by men of
years and standing among their kind; in hall and about
his kingdom by pages and esquires, the sons of great
houses; and in the bath, which was a high service and
much honored, by the daughters of Ianon's highest lords.
Every one was a maiden, young and well-favored and clad
practically, if none too sufficiently, in a wisp of white
tunic.

Vadin went in with Mirain. He did not know that it was
allowed, but no one told him it was forbidden, or tried to
stop him.

He had fancied himself a man of the world. He was certainly no virgin. But he stopped short two paces past the door, ears afire, and could not move another step.

They did not even see him. They were waiting for Mirain. Modestly, with the dignity of their breeding, but their eyes were bright, their glances quick and eager. God or half-god or mortal man, he was young and well shaped and not at all ill to look on. After the aged Raban he must have been a delight.

Mirain too had stopped as if struck, but he was made of sterner stuff; he managed to drive himself forward. He even mustered something like nonchalance, although his back was stiff. His head turned, scanning downcast faces, pausing once or twice. One of the maidens had a marvelous tumble of curls. One had eyes like a doe's, melting upon him. And one was even smaller than himself, as delicate as a flower, with eyes as soft as sleep. She had Asanian blood: she was honey golden, with a hint of rose that deepened under his stare. But she smiled shyly. Mirain must have smiled back; her face lit like a lamp. Lightly then, with royal grace, Mirain gave himself into their hands.

When he was scoured clean, they did not dress him. There was nothing to dress him in. They shaved him; they combed his free hair and tamed it as much as they might; they anointed him with sweet oils, touching his brow, his lips, his heart and his hands, his genitals, his feet. Then they bowed one by one from least to greatest, and the greatest was the golden princess, and she kissed his torque and his golden palm.

The throne of Ianon stood no longer in the hall. Strong men had taken it in the night, brought it down through the Chain of Courts to the Court of the Gate, and there set it upon a high dais before the people. Spearmen in scarlet kept free a long aisle from the gate to the throne; lords and princes stood about it, surrounded by the king's own knights in all their panoply.

Between the royal bath and the outer court lay only empty halls. Mirain must pass them naked and alone, abandoned even by his squire. Who barely had time to bolt by side ways into the sun and the crowds and the place kept for him beside the high seat.

Yet it seemed a long wait, those slow moments under Avaryan. Vadin's breath eased; he settled himself into some semblance of calm, and tried not to think of assassins' knives, and ambushes, and one lone unarmed unclad not-quite-king. The clamor of gathered people stilled slowly. All eyes turned with his own toward the gate. It was open, empty.

A bell rang, far and sweet. Many glanced toward the sound of it. When they glanced back, he stood under the arch of the gate. Only a shadow from this distance, a shape that said *man* in the breadth of its shoulders and the narrowness of its hips. Then it began to move, and it became Mirain. No one else had quite that panther-stride, or that straightness of the shoulders, or that tilt of the head. Or ever that way of cutting the world to his measure. He walked Ianyn-tall among them, a man grown, wise beyond any count of years, and royally proud; yet he was also a youth just out of boyhood, alone and afraid, without even a rag to cover him. They could see everything in the pitiless light: the long seamed scar in his side where a boar had tusked him long ago and almost killed him; the thin grey lines of sword-scars and the pitted hollow where an arrow had taken him in battle; the raw new flesh on buttocks and thighs, mark of his wild ride to Umijan. They could see that he was mortal and that he was imperfect, smaller than any man of them, not remarkably fair of face; but he was male, whole and strong, without mark or blemish save what branded him a man and a warrior. No woman in disguise, no eunuch living a lie, no soft coward laying claim to the throne of fighting kings.

Pacing slowly, face set and stern, eyes fixed upon the throne, he drew near to the dais. The circle of knights closed. Before them stood the eldest priestess of Avaryan in Ianon, ancient yet vigorous, robed all in sun-gold. As Mirain approached, she spread her arms wide to bar his way. He halted; she raised her thin old voice, that was strong still, and penetrating. "Who approaches Ianon's throne?"

Mirain paused an eyeblink, as if he could not trust his voice. But when it came it was clear, steady, blessedly deep, the voice of a man who had never known doubt. "I," it said. "Ianon's king."

"King, say you? By what right?"

"By right of the king who is dead, may the gods rest his soul, who chose me to be his successor; and by that of my mother, who was his daughter and who once was heir of Ianon. In the gods' name, reverend priestess, and in the name of Avaryan my father, let me pass."

"So I would," she said, "but that power remains with the lords and the people of Ianon. It is they who must grant you leave, not I."

Mirain lifted his hands, turning slowly. "My lords. My people. Will you have me for your king?"

They let him turn full circle. When he faced the throne again, the high ones knelt. Behind and about him the people loosed their voices in the single word: "Aye!"

The priestess bowed low and stepped aside. The circle opened, letting pass a small company of squires. Vadin led them, trying for dignity, hoping for grace. He knelt with only the merest hint of wobble and signaled to the rest. Mirain stood still for a wonder, suffering them to adorn him like the image of a god. Kilt of white leather cured to the softness of velvet, and broad belt of gold set with plates of amber, and great golden pectoral, and rings and armlets and earrings all of the sun-metal, and ropes of golden beads worked into the intricacy of the royal braids—Vadin's task, that last, and he kept his curses to himself, only thanking the gods for once that Mirain had no beard to battle with. Even as he bound off the last rebellious plait, the others weighted Mirain's shoulders with the great cloak of leather dyed scarlet and lined with priceless fur, white, but each hair tipped with a golden glint.

Last of all Vadin bound white sandals on Mirain's feet, the thongs edged with gold. He looked up, still on one knee, to find Mirain's eyes upon him. They were warm, almost laughing, but distant too, with the light of the god waiting to fill them. Without thinking, Vadin caught the hand that was closer to his face and kissed the flaming palm. That was not part of the rite, but his words were. "Lord king, your throne is waiting. Will it please you to take it?"

The way was clear to it now. Mirain's eyes lifted, and the god came, turning him all royal. Slowly, in swelling tumult, he mounted the dais and turned to face his people. Their shouting rose to a crescendo. They cried his name, proclaiming him lord, king, Sunborn, god-begotten. Again he raised his hands. The roaring died. The people waited, willing him to take his throne.

In the almost-silence, a horn brayed. Hoofs clattered on stone. Mounted men burst through the open gate. People scattered before them, crying out in anger and in pain. The seneldi, war-trained, attacked with horns and teeth and sharpened hoofs; the riders broadened Mirain's erstwhile path with the flats of their swords.

The cries rose to shrieks. A chariot plunged through the riders: a scythed war-car, and in it a glittering figure, a warrior in full armor.

The charioteer brought his team to a foaming halt at the foot of the dais. Even the knights of Ianon dared not venture against the deadly blades. He laughed at them, hollow and booming within his helmet. "Cowards and children! Indeed you have the king you deserve. There he stands, exulting in his power, who murdered the king before him. Poisoned, was he not, your majesty? And quickly too, once he had disposed of your only rival."

A rumble ran through the crowd, a name they had forbidden themselves to speak. Moranden. *Moranden.* "Moranden!"

Mirain's voice lashed them into silence. "It is not he!" He addressed the armored man more quietly, but still with the crack of command. "Take off your helmet."

He obeyed willingly enough. He was a big man, and young, and a Marcher by his accent. He looked at Mirain with well-cultivated contempt. "I have a message for you, boy." Mirain waited. The warrior scowled but could not hold his gaze. "I come to you from Ianon's true king, who although he has been cast out unjustly, nevertheless bows to the will of the king who is gone. He bids me say to you: 'Not all in Ianon have been led astray by your sorceries. Those who know the truth will come to me; many indeed have come already and bowed before me. Acknowledge your lies, priestess' bastard, and surrender now while yet you may hope to find mercy.' "

"If my uncle accepts his exile, which was perpetual," Mirain said with no hint of anger, "how may he hope to hold Ianon's throne? How does he even dare to claim it?"

"He is the true king. When all Ianon bids him, he shall return."

"And if all Ianon does not?"

"The kingdom is blinded by its grief for its old king, whom in turn you blinded with your sorceries. Southerner, wizard's brat, not all fall into your snares. When the people pause to think, then where will you be?"

"On the throne which my grandfather left me." Mirain sat in it with dignity but without ceremony. His eyes never left the messenger's face. "My uncle said and did much that could be construed as bitter enmity, and somewhat that came close to treason. In my predecessor's mind he richly deserved his exile. And yet," he said, sitting straight, and although he did not raise his voice it penetrated to the edges of the wide court, "I am willing to recall him."

The man's lip curled. "At what price?"

"This," said Mirain. "That he present himself in true repentance; that he beg forgiveness of all Ianon for what has been done in his name; and that he swear fealty to me as his lord and king."

The envoy laughed. "Should he crawl at your feet, who are not worthy to stand in his shadow?" He spat in the dust. "You are no king of his or of ours."

As the echoes of his words died, the throng began to mutter. It was a low sound, barely audible, yet blood-chilling. Still no one dared the scythes, but the press of bodies had tightened about the mounted men, hampering the seneldi.

Mirain raised his hand. Instinctively the messenger flinched from it, hauling at the reins. The chariot backed half a length and stopped short. A solid wall of people barred his escape. His mares trembled and sweated with eyes rolling white.

Gently Mirain said, "Give my message to my uncle."

"He will destroy you."

"Tell him." Mirain's voice rose a very little, speaking now to his people. "It was my will that these men should come here unmolested, else the Towers of the Dawn would have forbidden them. Let them go now as they came, unharmed."

The mutter turned to a rumble. Anger hung thick in the air, gathering like a storm. A senel screamed, rearing. A hundred hands pulled it down before its rider could free his sword from its scabbard.

"Let them go." Mirain had not risen, nor had he shouted. Yet he was heard. The rumble faltered. For an eternal moment the envoys' fate hung in the balance.

Mirain lowered his hands and sat back as if at his ease. Slowly, with reluctance as palpable as their outrage, the crowd freed their prisoners. Equally slowly, the invaders backed away from them. The messenger turned his chariot, gentling his frightened mares. With a sudden shout he lashed them forward. His escort spurred behind him.

Even beyond the gate they could hear the full-throated roar, the acclamation of the king enthroned.

Seventeen

MIRAIN WOULD GLADLY HAVE FEASTED UNTIL DAWN, and his lords and his commons were minded to do just that, but it was hardly past sunset when Ymin gave the signal Vadin had been warned to expect. Although Mirain had been drinking considerably more than he ate, he was far from drunk; warm was the word, and joyous, and more prodigal than ever with the magic of his presence. His cloak was cast over the back of the high seat; he leaned across the table, watching a ring of fire-dancers and parrying the lethal wit of a lord who sat near the dais. Even as Vadin moved to touch his shoulder, he saluted a bold stroke and drank deep. He turned, laughing and glittering, and the simple nearness of him was enough to weaken Vadin's knees. "M—my lord," stammered Vadin, who had not stammered since he was weaned. "Sire, you must—"

The brilliance did not dim, but Mirain's eyes focused, touched with concern. "Trouble, Vadin?"

He laughed at that, shakily. "Gods, no! But it's time to go, my lord."

"Go!" Mirain frowned. "Am I a child, to be put to bed with the sun?"

Vadin had his self-possession back at last, and he grinned. "Of course not, my lord. You're the king, and there's one more thing you have to do to put the seal on it, and it's best you do it soon, before anyone catches on. Here, leave your cloak; they'll think you've just gone out to the privy."

For a moment Vadin knew Mirain would resist. But surely he knew what he was going to; he was the Sunborn, he knew everything. Except that he did not act as if he knew anything at all. Was it possible . . .?

He came slowly, but he came. Maybe he used magic; no one seemed to care that he was leaving. Vadin led him down the passage behind the throne, up to the hidden door and the chambers that were now Mirain's. Some of his belongings had appeared there, but the touch of his hand was very faint yet, hardly perceptible over the deep imprint of the one who was gone.

But Vadin had not brought Mirain here to brood on the dead. He turned toward the bedchamber, opened the door, and stood back. "My lord," he said.

If Mirain was beginning to understand, he was far enough gone in wine not to hesitate. He entered the great room, its austerity soft-lit now with lamps, scented with flowers.

Others were there before him. Nine, Vadin counted from the door. Ten with Ymin. Ten women sitting or standing or kneeling, waiting in a shimmer of jewels. One or two were familiar, maidens of the king's bath now adorned as befit their rank; Vadin recognized several more from court and castle, and one at least of the guests who had come for High Summer and lingered for a funeral and a kingmaking. There was even one in the collar of a slave, but she had a fine bold eye, and she was one of the fairest, a daughter of velvet night.

Mirain stood stock-still under their eyes, almost as he had stood in the gateway before he claimed his throne. Vadin heard the sharp intake of his breath, saw the tensing of his back.

Ymin smiled at him. "Yes, my lord. One last test remains in the making of the king. As sacred singer I have been given authority to free you from the vow that binds you; as the king's singer I am sworn to accept the testimony of the lady you choose. Or ladies," she added with a touch of wickedness.

Mirain's voice was flat. "I do not wish to partake of this rite."

"You must, my lord. It is prescribed. Ianon knows that you are a man and that you bear no blemish which will weaken the land. Now you must prove your strength. Time was when you would have done so in the fields under the stars, for any to watch who wished to; and you would have kept a share of your seed for the earth itself."

"And now?"

"You need only satisfy your chosen one. Who will satisfy me that you are fit, and I will bear witness before your people."

"And . . . if I fail?"

"You will not." She spoke with assurance, coming forward and bowing low and holding out her hands. "If you please, my lord. Your torque."

His hand went to it. "I may not—" He stopped; he stripped off all his jewels, flinging them at her feet. But not his robe, and almost not his torque. At last, with visible reluctance, he unclasped it, held it up on his flattened palms. The words he spoke were in a tongue Vadin did not know, chanted softly and swiftly, almost angrily.

Ymin raised her own hands, responding in the same mode, in the same sonorous tongue. With all reverence she took the torque, kissed it, bowed over it, and set it again upon him.

As simple as that? Vadin wondered.

It would seem so. Mirain drew a long breath, and the way he stood spoke of a little regret, and a great deal of fear, but a worldful of relief; though he would die before he acknowledged any but the first. When he spoke again he sounded more like himself. "Must I be given so difficult a set of choices? Nine ladies of such beauty—how can I choose?"

"A king must always choose," Ymin said with the barest hint of iron beneath the softness.

He was delaying, that was obvious. Nervous as a virgin, and probably he was not far from one; and now he had to prove himself for such a cause, after so long an abstinence, with bitter consequences if his body played him

false. Vadin wished desperately that there were something he could do. Anything.

He was not even supposed to be here. He bit his tongue
and knotted his fists and made himself stay out of it.
Mirain was Mirain, after all. And Ianon needed a strong
king.

Mirain gathered himself all at once, and laughed almost freely. "I shall choose, then; and may the god guide
my hand." He made a slow circuit, pausing before each
lady, taking her hand, saying a word or two. He lingered
longest for his golden princess of the bath, whose hands
he even kissed, and she looked at him with her heart in
her eyes. But he did not say the word that would seal the
choosing. He drew back, and they all waited, hardly breathing. He faced Ymin, held out his hand. "Come," he said.

There was a stunned silence. Even she had not looked
for this. Surely he was mocking her, taking his revenge
for the ordeal which she had forced upon him.

She said what they were all thinking. "I am more than
twice your age."

"And a head taller than I," he agreed willingly, "and no
tender maid, and my chosen. It is permitted that I choose
as I will." Again he held out his hand. "Come, singer."

If she shaped protests, she let them die before she
uttered them. Coolly and quietly she dismissed the ladies
who had been chosen with such care and to so little effect,
setting Vadin the task of looking after them. The last he
saw as he shut the door, they were facing one another,
king and singer, and it looked more like war than love.

"Why?" Ymin asked when the rest were gone. She
was still calm, but the mask was cracking.

Mirain's seemed the firmer for the weakness of hers.
He shrugged and smiled. "I want you."

"Not the Princess Shirani?"

"She's very lovely. She's also terrified of me, although
she calls it love. And tonight I'm not up to a maiden's
holy awe." His face darkened. "Is it that I repel you? I
know I have no beauty, and I'm too young to be a good
lover, and too small to look well beside you."

"*No!*" Her hands took it on themselves to seize his, to hold them fast. "Never say such things. Never even think them."

"I was taught to speak the truth."

"The truth, aye and well. But that is a lie. Mirain my dearest lord, do you not know that you are beautiful? You have that which makes even the lovely Shirani seem commonplace beside you. A brilliance; a splendor. A magic. And a very fine pair of eyes in a very striking face, and a body with which I can find no fault."

"What, none at all?"

"Perhaps," she mused, "if I might see the whole of it . . ."

"Have you not already?"

"Ah, but that was the kingmaking, and I was blinded by the god in your eyes. I should like to see the man, since he has persisted in choosing me."

He freed himself easily, dropped his robe, stood for her to look at. She looked long, and she looked with great pleasure, and she smiled, for he was rousing to her presence. "No flaw at all, my lord. Not one."

"Sweet-tongued singer." He unbound the cincture of her robe. His hands were not quite steady. "I hope, my lady, that your modesty is only for the world."

"My lord, I am a famous wanton." She cast aside the heavy garment, growing reckless now that she had no retreat, and shook down the masses of her hair. It tumbled from its woven braids, pouring like water to her feet; his gasp of wonder made her laugh. But when he touched her she gasped herself, and their eyes met, and she sank down in the pool of her hair. His arms closed about her; she trembled within them. "My lord, you should not have done this to me."

He stroked her hair with gentle hands. "My name is Mirain."

She raised her head in a flare of sudden heat. "My lord!"

"Mirain." Gentle, implacable. "The kingdom commands that I do this, and the god commands that you be my chosen, but I will not be *my lord*. Unless you honestly wish me to fail."

Her heart went cold. He had let slip the truth at last. The god had commanded it. Not his will. Not his desire, nor ever his love. That his body responded to her beauty, that was mere fleshly desire; it meant nothing.

She knew her face was calm, but he did not read faces. He stared stricken, and he cried, "No, Ymin. No! Oh, damn my tripping tongue! The god guided me, I admit it, but only because I would never have dared it alone. How much easier to take one of yon eager worshipful maids, to do my duty, to send her away. You came harder. Because you outshone them all, body and soul. Because— because with you I would have more than duty and ritual. With you I would have love."

She raised her hand, let it come to rest upon his cheek. "Curse you," she said very softly, "for a mage and a seer."

He kissed her palm.

"Child," she said. He smiled. "Insolent boy. I have a daughter only a little younger than you. I would spank her if she looked at me as you are looking now."

"It would be appalling if she did." His hand found her breast; he paid it the homage of a kiss. "How beautiful you are."

"How ancient."

"And how young I am, and how little it matters." He kissed her other breast, and the warm secret space between them, and the curve of her belly beneath. Her body sang where he touched it; keened when he withdrew; began to sing again as he led her to the bed. Her mind, letting go its resistance, took up the descant. Its refrain was perfect in its purity: simply and endlessly his name, with no *lord* or *king* to taint it. He saw; he knew. His fire flooded over her and drowned her.

VADIN YAWNED AND STRETCHED, AND GRINNED AT THE CEILing of his new chamber. Bold-eyed Jayida had gone back to her mistress, who had been one of the old king's ladies; but she had promised to visit him again. Nor had she seemed to find him a poor second to the king. After all, she had said, the king was half a god and all a priest, and that did not bode well for him as a lover. Whereas the king's squire . . .

Still grinning, he sat up, tossing back his loosened hair. No sound reached him from the king's bedchamber. He opened the door with great care and peered within. And jumped like a startled thief. Mirain stood in the opening and laughed, as bare and tousled as himself but somewhat wider awake. "Good morning, Vadin," he said. "Did she serve you well?"

Vadin flinched. It had occurred to him that he was usurping a woman chosen for the king. She had scoffed when he said it. But there were places where he would have paid in blood for his night's pleasure.

Mirain embraced him with unfeigned exuberance, dragged him to the bath that was blessedly empty of its maidens, pushed him in and leaped after him in a cloud of spray. Vadin came up spluttering, not ready yet to join in the game. "My lord, I—"

"My lord, you are forgiven, she is yours, you may have your joy of her. Shall I free her for you? I can do that."

Mirain was alight with it, knowing that he was king, that he was free, that he could do whatever he pleased. Vadin blinked water out of his eyes. "I don't think—she was just for a night. If I were asking for anyone I'd ask for Ledi. But—"

"But." Mirain had sobered. "You don't want gifts. When I hold Great Audience today I'll take the liege-oaths of all the lords who are here, and of the fighting men, and of the pages and the servants. And of the squires who served my grandfather. Would you like to go back to them? You no longer need look after me all alone; you can be a squire among the squires again, only taking your turn with me when it suits you. If it suits you at all."

Vadin stood very still in the warm ever-flowing water. Mirain waited without expression. Hoping, maybe, that Vadin would accept. Looking for an escape from his most reluctant servant.

Except that the reluctance had got itself lost somewhere, and the resistance had dwindled to a ritual, a saving of face. And the thought of going back to the

barracks, of being plain Vadin the squire again, held no
sweetness at all. Seeing someone else at Mirain's back—
knowing that someone else would stand here dripping,
enduring Mirain's gentle chaffing, sharing bath and
breakfast—

Vadin swallowed hard, half choking. "Do you want me
to go, my lord?"

"I don't want you to stay in a place that you dislike."

"What—" Vadin swallowed hard. "What if I don't dislike it?"

"Even though people call you my dog and my catamite?"

Vadin thought of the names they had called Mirain.
Which, if he could but hear them—

"I have."

"You're walking in my mind again. After all I've said.
You used my body when you sent me to that unspeakable
woman. Who knows what you'll do to me next? But I'm
getting used to you and your wizard's tricks. Life in the
barracks would bore me silly."

"It would win your wager for you."

"Sure it would. And who'd nursemaid you when you
got into one of your moods? No, my lord, you won't get
rid of me now. I said I'd stay with you, and I'm a man of
my word."

"Beware, Vadin; you'll be admitting to friendship next."

"Not likely," Vadin said, scooping up a handful of
cleansing-foam. "Turn around and I'll wash your back."

Mirain did as he was told, but first he said, "I know
exactly what I'm going to do with your soul when I win it.
I'll house it in crystal and net it in gold and hang it over
my bed."

"Fine sights it will see there," said Vadin unperturbed,
"now that you're allowed to live like a man."

Mirain laughed, and that was answer and to spare.

Eighteen

IN THE GREY LIGHT BEFORE SUNRISE, A LONE RIDER SENT his mount through its paces. He rode superbly well, wrapped with his stallion in a half-trance of leap and curvet and sudden swift gallop, challenging the targets set here and there on the practice ground of the castle: that art of princes called riding at the rings. Three circlets of copper glinted on his spearpoint; as Ymin watched, he turned his mount on its haunches, striking for a fourth.

"Well done!" she applauded him as he lowered his lance. Three rings rolled from it; the fourth spun through the air into her hand. She smiled and sank down in a low curtsey. "All thanks, my knight, for your tribute."

"It is given where it is due." Mirain doffed his helmet, shaking his braid free from its protective coil about his head. His face was damp; his eyes glittered. He slid smoothly from the Mad One's back and ran his hand down the sleek sweat-sheened neck; and turned more quickly than her eye could follow, and drew her head down, and kissed her.

"My lord," she protested, as she must. And when he glared: "Mirain, this is no fit place—"

"I have decreed that it is." But he stood a little apart, decorous, with glinting eyes. "Walk with me," he said.

They walked for a time in silence, he at the Mad One's shoulder, she at a cool and proper distance. At length she asked, "Would you ride to war as you do now, without a saddle?"

"That would be foolish even for a child king."

She glanced at him. "So bitter, my lord?"

He brushed a fly from the Mad One's ear, caressing the tender place beneath it. "In one thing," he said, "Moranden's man spoke the truth. The sheen has worn away. Ianon has the king it asked for, but now it has paused to think upon the asking."

"Wisely, for the most part. No one in town or castle seems to regret the choice."

"Ah," he said, "but Ianon is much more than a single city, or even a single mountain-guarded vale."

"True, my dear lord. But have you heard none of the old songs? Time was when a king had to fight his way to the throne, and fight to sit in it, and leave as soon as he had taken it to put down a dozen risings. The day after your grandsire claimed his kingship, the whole of eastern Ianon rose against him, led by two of his own brothers."

"And I should hold my peace, should I not? Central Ianon is firmly sworn to me, and I have no more to fear than a rumbling in the Marches. With, of course, enough slighting rumors to set my teeth on edge; but no open threat, as yet, of cold iron." He sighed. "I've waited so long to be king. Now I am, and the end is the merest beginning. I find myself wishing that I could live my life like a hero in a song, striding from peak to peak, paying no heed to the dull stretches between."

"Surely it would grow wearisome, always to be at the summit of one's attainments."

"You think so?" he asked. "How much simpler it would be if I didn't have to endure all this waiting, if I could pass from my enthronement straight to the heart of war and there find an end. Whether my enemy's or my own."

"That will come soon enough," she said levelly.

"None too soon for me. My nerves are raw, and people are whispering. Do you know that I'm supposed to have been the Red Prince's boy?"

"Were you?"

He stopped as if struck.

She laid a hand on his arm. "My lord. Mirain. They are only words."

"So are your songs."

"Certainly. And I sing the truth. What are all the lies and foul tales to that?"

"Moranden cursed us all." He began to walk again along the wall which bordered the field. "I can think of a worse curse than his. That he actually gain what he longs for."

"To be king?"

"It would be fitting. A throne, a title, a kingdom full of subjects all eager to serve him—those are only trappings. The truth is a wall and a cage and fetters of gold. My people are my jailers. They bind me; I can't escape them. Courts and councils and the cares of a kingdom . . . even in my bed I'm not free of them."

"Am I so much a burden?"

"You," he cried with sudden force, "no!"

"Ah," she said sagely. "Prince Mehtar's daughter."

He scowled; suddenly he laughed. "Just so. And Lord Anden's niece. And Baron Ushin's ward. Not to mention half my maidens of the bath. Young I may be, undersized and no beauty, certainly foreign born and arguably a bastard, but I have one asset that far outweighs the rest: Ianon's throne."

"I thought I had taught you not to underrate yourself."

Mirain smiled his swift smile. "Prince Mehtar was quite blunt," he said. "I'm no great marvel of manhood, or so he informed me, but I am royal. More than royal if my claims be true. House Mehtar would be quite pleased to ally itself with me. The girl, they tell me, is well worth the trouble."

"She is a beauty," Ymin agreed. "They call her the Jewel of the Hills." She paused, regarding him. "Will you consider the offer?"

"Should I?"

"Beauty, wealth, and breeding—she has all of those. And a father who can sway most of the eastern fiefdoms to his will."

"He would be pleased to add the whole of Ianon."

Their glances caught; his was bright and faintly mocking. "I pleaded extreme youth and the need to establish myself in my kingdom—and promised to have a look at the lady if I should happen to be in her vicinity."

Ymin laughed. "Spoken like a true king!"

"Or like a southerner born." He turned with his hand upon the Mad One's withers. "The sun is rising. Shall we sing him up together?"

THE SUN WAS FIERCE IN THE COURT OF JUDGMENT. Although the high seat rested in the shade of a canopy, there was no escape from the heat; even Vadin's light kilt weighed upon him. Yet Mirain sat apparently at his ease, cheek resting on palm, cool and unruffled and thoroughly alert.

"A dry spring," whined the man in front of him, "and a burning summer. My herd has overgrazed its pasture; my crops are withering in the heat. And now, sire—and now this young ingrate tells me he has bid for a girl in the next village, and I must give him the groom-price, and not a moment's thought to spare for the hardship."

The young ingrate was not so very young, Vadin judged, and looking older with hard work and poor feeding. He scowled at his feet and knotted his heavy hands, drawing up his shoulders as if against a blow. " 'S my right," he mumbled. "I waited. Every season I waited. 'S always too soon, or the weather's too bad, or the harvest's due in. No more, she said. Long enough is long enough. Bid for me like you've been promising to, or somebody else will get there first."

His father sputtered with fury.

"Are you the only son?" Mirain asked.

The young man looked up, a flash of sullen eyes that saw a throne and a blur of gold upon it, no more. "No," he said. "Sir. Got two brothers, sir."

"Older?"

"Yes, sir."

"Married?"

Again the eyes, more sullen still. "No, sir. Too soon, the weather's too bad, the harvest's due in . . ."

"So," Mirain said in his most neutral tone, but Vadin saw the glint in his eye. The son's hands twisted fiercely. "Go. Take your bride. Bid the groom-price, but see that your father adds to it another of equal worth, to begin your marriage properly." Mirain gestured to the scribe. "It is written. It shall be done."

There was no love in the young man's stare, and scarcely any gratitude. He bowed ungracefully, looked about for an exit, and departed, pursued by his father's howls of rage.

The next complainant had already begun. That was the king's justice: swift, thankless, and not to be opposed. Mirain shifted minutely in his seat. Vadin gestured where his eye could catch it, raising a cup of wine cooled with snow. He took the goblet and drank, a sip only, sighing just visibly. But his face was as calm as ever, intent. A perfect mask.

Vadin studied it and tried not to think of sleep. One of the older councillors was snoring on his feet. The voices droned on. So many matters of great moment to the people in the midst of them; so many tangled details flung down at the king's feet as if he and he alone could unravel them. "My lord," a scribe was saying in a bored monotone, "the titles to the property in question—"

Vadin did not know what roused him. Maybe it was only a precious whisper of breeze wandering lost in this sun-tortured place. Or maybe it was instinct honed by a season of serving a mage. But he was full awake and taut as a strung bow, his eyes sweeping the assembled faces. None rang the alarm in his brain. Good solid Ianyn faces with a sprinkling of foreigners: Asanian gold, southern brown, traders or sightseers; and there was the scholar from Anshan-i-Ormal, a wizened earth-colored creature with the merriest eyes Vadin had ever seen. They were almost quiet now, watching Mirain in tireless fascination. He was going to write a history, he had told Vadin only last night; he had been looking all his life for a fit subject, and now he thought he had found it in a young barbarian king. Mirain liked him, because he had no talent for flattery. He had a wicked tongue, which he tempered with laugh-

ter, and in his Ormalen custom he called even the king by
his given name.

Something caught Vadin's eye beyond the turbaned
head. A movement almost too quick to follow. A glint of
light on metal. A guard on the wall, surely, saluting the
king with his spear.

Spear. Vadin lunged, hurling Mirain away from the
throne. The world spun; fire pierced it, transfixed it.
Winds roared in Vadin's ears. The fire was pain, and it
pinned him. He could not move. "The wall," he tried to
cry out. "Damn you, the wall!"

The whirling stopped; the world came closer. Mirain
filled it. Vadin hit him. "Get down, you fool. Get—"

Mirain's hand descended like the night, vast and inescapable. But his face looked strange and small. Except for
the eyes. Such brilliant, bitter, ice-cold rage—

"Are you going to kill me?" Vadin's voice was faint,
weak as a child's. It seemed very far away. He was losing
his body. And yet how odd; how clear it all was. The
court; the people in their shock or their outrage or their
terror; the armed men hunting an assassin and finding
him dead upon the parapet with his own knife in his
throat. And the king on his knees in front of his throne,
gripping the haft of a spear that pierced a sprawled
ungainly body. Poor creature, he was done for, speared
just below the heart, beginning to struggle with blind
bodily panic. But he was brave; he was not screaming.

"No good," someone said. "The head's barbed. Poisoned too, I'll wager. Those are Marcher clan-marks on
the haft; and they don't take chances."

Someone else responded with doleful relish, "Poison or
not, they've won a life. That wound is mortal."

Gods rest him, Vadin thought. Whoever he was. Not that
it mattered. He was going away, winged like a bird. Court
and castle shrank beneath him. There was Ianon dwindling swiftly, a green jewel set in a ring of mountains,
glimmering in the center of an orb like a child's ball,
painted all in green and white and blue and brown. Why,
it was just like the world as it was painted over the altar in
Avaryan's temple. He traced the lands, naming them as

the priests had taught him years ago in Geitan. From western Asanion to the isles of the east that looked upon the open sea; from the great desert that bordered on the southern principates, across the Hundred Realms to Ianon again, and its mountains, and Death's Fells beyond, and the wastes of ice—all lay under his wondering eyes, perfect as a jewel on a lady's finger. And such a lady: deep-breasted Night herself in her robe of stars. She smiled; she drew him to her; she kissed him with a mother's gentleness but with a lover's warmth.

"Vadin." The voice was vaguely familiar. It was a beautiful voice for a man's, both sweet and deep. But it sounded impatient, even angry. "Vadin alVadin, for the love of Avaryan, listen to me!"

But it was so pleasant here. Dark and warm, and a beautiful lady smiling, and maybe later there would be loving.

"Vadin!"

Yes, he was angry. What was his name? Vadin had done nothing to earn his displeasure. Did he want the lady? There was enough of her for both.

"I want no lady. Come, Vadin."

Mirain. That was his name. It was very flattering that he wanted Vadin and not so lovely a lady, but alas, Vadin was not in the mood. Maybe later, if he should still be inclined . . .

"Vadin alVadin of Asan-Geitan, by Avaryan and Uveryen, by life and death, by the Light and by the Dark that embraces it, I summon you before me."

The lady's arms opened. Vadin was slipping away. He clutched, desperate. She was gone. It was dark. Wind howled, thin and bitter. It tore at him with teeth of iron. The voice rang through it. "By the oath of fealty you have sworn me, by the kingship I hold, come. Come or be forever lost."

The voice was warm, laden with power. Vadin yearned toward it. But the wind beat him back. It was dark still, darker than dark, yet he could see with more than eyes. He stood on a road in a country of night, and the road

ran but one way, and that was onward, away from that far
sweet calling.

It swelled in strength and sweetness. It sang like a harp,
it throbbed like drums. All words had forsaken it; it was
pure power. The night quailed before it. The wind faltered. Inch by tortured inch, Vadin dragged himself about.
There was no road behind. Only madness. Madness and
Mirain. Vadin stretched out his hands. He could not
reach—he could not—

He stretched impossibly, with every ounce of will and
pride and strength. He touched. Slipped. Mirain's fingers
clawed. Vadin clutched. They held.

The darkness burst in a storm of fire.

VADIN GASPED AS THE PAIN STRUCK HIM, GASPED AGAIN AS
it vanished beneath a warmth like the sun. He had his
body back again, and his wits, and a faint blur of sight.
He knew where he was: still in the Court of Judgment,
lying now on the dais in front of the throne, cradled in
Mirain's arms. The spear was gone. He could not see the
wound, and he did not want to. He knew that he was
dying. He had died already, and Mirain's power had
called him back. But it was not strong enough. It could
not hold him.

"No," Mirain said fiercely. His cheeks were wet. Weeping in front of his people—fool of a foreigner, did he
know what he was doing? "I know. I know to the last
breath. I'll hold you. I'll heal you. I won't let you die for
me."

As the old king had. And Mirain did not easily suffer
defeat. Vadin looked at the vivid furious eyes and thought
of reason and of sanity, but Mirain had never fallen prey
to either. The warmth that had been pain was rising into
heat. Sun's fire. Sun's child. It was something to be loved
by a mage of that rank, a master of power whose father
was a god. Maybe after all he could face death. Maybe,
with the god behind him, he could win.

"Help me," Mirain's face turned to the sun, his eyes
open to it, unblinded, unseeing. "Father, help me!" He

did not bargain, Vadin noticed. He simply pleaded, in a tone very close to command.

It was very quiet. People stood all about, staring, mute. Some had drawn close. White robes or kilts, golden torques. One or two in grey and silver. Ymin's eyes were fixed on Mirain, almost blazing. She was giving him what power she had, prodigal of the cost. Blessed madwoman.

The heat mounted. It was like agony, but it was exquisitely pleasant, like a scalding bath after the Great Race. Healing anguish, flooding his body, setting his bones afire. He felt it focus at his center. He *felt* the outraged flesh begin to knit, the great ragged wound to close from its depths to its topmost reaches. He saw the fire of power working in him, and he knew it, and he knew what it did, wise with the wisdom of the one who healed him, endowed with more than mortal sight.

Mirain drew a long shuddering breath. His face was drawn as it had been on the road to Umijan, but his eyes were clear and quiet, and he smiled. Without a sound he crumpled.

Vadin caught him before he struck the stone, moving without thought, without pain. Mirain was still conscious; he raised his hand to touch the deep scar beneath Vadin's breast. "I healed you," he whispered. "I promised."

Vadin rose. Mirain was a light weight and an indomitable will, giving his people a flash of golden hand before the darkness took him. Gently Vadin carried him down the steps through the murmurs of awe, the bodies crowding back to give him room, the eyes lowered and the heads bowed as before a god.

When this was over, Vadin was going to be amused. Whoever the assassin had been, whoever had sent him—whether Moranden or that unnatural mother of his—he had not only failed to fell his target. He had shown Ianon what in truth it had accepted as its king. Avaryan's temple would be full by evening, nor would it be Avaryan alone to whom the folk addressed their prayers. Mirain's legend would be all the stronger hereafter.

*   *   *

VADIN HAD EXPECTED PEOPLE TO LOOK ON MIRAIN WITH greater reverence now that he had shown them what power was in him. But the squire had not reckoned on the consequences to himself. He was a wonder and a strangeness, a man brought back from the dead. Even his friends walked shy of him, even Kav who had been known to doubt the gods. When he walked in the town, folk tried to touch him, to coax a blessing from him, or made signs of awe and would not look him in the face.

Ledi was the crowning blow. She who had shared her bed with him, called him by his love-name, faced him as an equal and slapped him when he got above himself— when he came into the alehouse she did not come running to wait on him, and when he called for her she bowed low and called him *lord*, and when he tried to embrace her she fled. And everyone in the drab familiar room was silent, staring, knowing who he was. The Reborn. The king's miracle.

He was on his feet. He had meant to go after Ledi, to beat her into her senses if need be. He turned slowly, with all the dignity he could muster, and began to walk. Swifter and swifter through the whispering streets in the hiss of the rain, running through the castle gate, winding among the courts and passages, coming up short in Mirain's chamber.

The king was there, alone for once, prowling like a caged panther. He had been in council with Ianon's elders; he was dressed for it still in a dazzle of gold and royal white, although his mantle lay on the floor where he had flung it. When Vadin halted, panting and almost sobbing, Mirain whipped about in a blind flare of temper. "Wait, they tell me. Wait, and wait, and wait. So wise, they are. So very wise." His lip curled; he began to pace again, hurling the words over his shoulder. "It will grow easier, they tell me. My people are testing me; they are proving my fitness. It is all a great testing. The judgments and the petitions; the lords with all their retinues, appearing unannounced with disputes which only the king can settle. The embassies from my royal and princely neighbors, demanding hospitality and courtesy, reminding me of alliances made and unmade and remade. The hordes of traders and mountebanks, each of whom must attract my august eye or spread abroad the tale of my niggardliness. And always—always that fire smoldering in the Marches. Wait, they tell me. Hold fast. Let my loyal lords and my own actions hold off the threat." He stopped, spun. "Actions! What actions? I've not even left this castle since I took the throne. And when I flung that in their faces, they bowed and scraped and prayed my majesty's pardon, but if an assassin could come to me here in my own stronghold, how much more perilous it would be for me to ride abroad. No, no, I am young, of course I chafe under the restraints of my rule, but only let me be patient and soon I will be strong upon my throne. Then I may do as I will. Yes, then, when Moranden is king of all but this castle."

Vadin started to turn away, sighed and stayed. Mirain still prowled, still muttered, still saw him only as a target for heated words. "Ah no, the exile will never come so far. Lord Yrian, Lord Cassin, Prince Kirlian, all the lords whose lands border on the Marches—they have sworn to bring him to me. Limb by limb. Surely I can trust them who always served King Raban well. Maybe I can even trust Moranden. But his mother—now there is an enemy to be afraid of. *She* would never have sent anyone as conspicuous as an assassin with a spear. She will have my life while I tarry, and never count the cost. And, *Wait*, my elders intone. *Wait, sire. Wait and see.*"

Vadin said nothing. What were his little troubles to this great matter of war and rebellion? One silly fool of a girl was afraid of him because he had been killed and had come to life again and had walked away with only a fading scar. Ianon was about to tear itself apart, and he cried over a tuppenny whore.

Mirain had come to his senses a little. He saw Vadin and knew him; his glare lightened to a scowl. "Your pardon, Vadin. I never meant to rage at you. But if I erupt in council, they all look gravely at one another and sigh, their wisdom sorely tried by my impetuous youth. I have to be cool, I have to be quiet, I have to try to reason

with minds set in stone. They know, surely and absolutely, that I must not risk my precious neck in a war. Not
even in a parley. Not even, gods forbid, in a royal prog-
ress. I must stay mewed up here while others do it all for
me."

"Isn't that what it is to be a king?"

"Not you too." But Mirain's rage had passed; he rubbed
his eyes with tired fingers. "I'm getting so I can't even
think. I need to do something. Would you—" He broke
off. "Aren't you supposed to be at liberty?"

"I . . . decided not to bother." Vadin picked up Mirain's
mantle and folded it, laying it carefully in its chest. "Shall
I fetch Ymin? Or would you prefer—"

Mirain stood in front of him, hands on his shoulders.
"Do I have to take the answer out of your mind?"

Vadin wrenched away. "Don't you—don't you ever—
Damn you, why didn't you let me die?"

"I couldn't." Mirain spoke very softly. "I *couldn't*, Vadin."

The squire choked on bile. Mirain's eyes were wide and
full of pain, and he could see into them. He could hear
the thoughts behind them. Love and grief, fear of loss,
regret that it had led to this. *"Regret!"* Vadin cried. "Oh
gods, you've even infected me with your magery. They
can all see it. They're terrified of me. I died. I died and I
came back, and I'm not Vadin anymore. Demons take
you, King of Ianon. May the goddess' birds peck your
bones."

There was a long throbbing silence. Vadin looked up
at last, and Mirain stood still. His hands were fists at his
sides. The god's brand rent him with its agony. Vadin
knew. He could feel it himself if he willed to.

"We are bound," Mirain said with perfect calm. "I went
very far to call you back. I cannot loose you, nor can I
alter what my people saw. But time can heal you somewhat. You died, you were healed, you have changed, but
you are still Vadin. Those who love you will learn to see
it, once their awe passes."

"You sound exactly like your council. *Wait. Wait and
see.*"

Mirain laughed, short and bitter. "Don't I? Unfortunately it's true."

"And what do I do while I wait? Study sorcery? It's all I seem to be fit for."

"You can go and show Ledi that you're still her favorite lover."

King or no king, Vadin would have struck him for that if he had been a shade less quick. "She hates me."

"She's crying now because she let herself listen to all the tales, and because she let them frighten her, and because you went away. Go to her, Vadin. She needs you."

"So do you, damn it."

"Not now. Go on."

"Come with me." Vadin's tongue had said that. Not his brain.

Mirain frowned, searching his mind, a touch like light fingers, or a warm breath, or a moth's wing in the dark. He thought of outrage, but he could not find it. Memory came between: the world floating in night, and a strong voice calling.

Between them they extricated Mirain from his state dress, unwound the king-braids and plaited his hair into the simplicity of priesthood, found a plain kilt and a plain dark mantle. Vadin wrapped himself in a dry cloak, swallowed the last of his regrets, and set his face toward the town.

This time no one seemed even to see Vadin, much less his companion. Ledi was not serving in the alehouse; the boy who waited on them did not know where she was, or care. They drank the ale he brought, Vadin tarrying out of fear, Mirain simply reveling in walls that were not the walls of his castle and in voices that were not the voices of his council. The taut lines of his face had begun to ease. He looked younger, less hagridden. Dear gods, Vadin thought, he could not remember when last he had seen Mirain smile.

He looked down into his dwindling ale, flushing a little with shame. He had been thinking that all this worship did not trouble Mirain; the Sunborn had been used to it from his birth. Maybe that made it worse. Vadin could go back in time to plain humanity, and he could hope that it would be soon. Mirain could never go back at all.

Vadin tossed a coin on the table and stood. Mirain followed him through the crowd to the curtain with its painted lovers. The old harridan who stood guard took Vadin's silver, tested it with her one remaining tooth, grinned and let them by.

It was not easy, climbing those steep fetid steps with the King of Ianon behind him and Ledi somewhere ahead. Maybe she had taken a man to console her. Or two; she liked two, especially if they were Kav and Vadin. The other girls were busy, raw night that it was, providing warmth and comfort for a handful of copper.

Ledi had one of the better rooms, the one at the top with a window which she kept open even in winter. It made the air sweet, she said. As if she needed anything but her own warm scent and the herbs she sprinkled on her pillow. Her door was shut, but no length of green ribbon hung from the latch; she was in but alone. Vadin's heart hammered. She was going to be afraid, and she was going to submit as any woman must to a great lord, and he was an idiot for tormenting himself like this. He turned to face the shadow that was Mirain. "You can have her," he said roughly. "I don't want her."

Mirain did not say it aloud, but the word hung in the air. *Coward.*

With a low growl Vadin spun back to the door. He raised his trembling fist, struck once and then twice and then once again.

Nothing moved within. She would be huddled in her bed, praying that he would go away. He stepped back, braced for flight.

The latch grated. The door eased open. Lamplight brightened the stair and its landing; Ledi's face peered out, all puffed with crying, and her hair was a tangle and she had on her worst rag of a dress, and she had never been less pretty or more beloved. "Ledi," he said stupidly. "Ledi, I—"

She drew herself up. "My lord."

"And what have I done," he snapped with desperate

temper, "to deserve that? Cold shoulder down below and cold words up here, and if it's that I haven't been coming so often lately, will you please remember that we've lost an old king and got a new one, and I've been caught in the middle?"

"That's not all you've been caught in," she said, unbending. She stood as straight and cold and haughty as a queen, and she would never bend now, since he had forced her to remember her pride.

"And can I help any of it?" he cried in a fine fire of rage. "Damn it, woman, don't you turn on me too!"

She looked at him with great care, squinting a little for her eyes were not of the best, frowning as if he were a stranger whose face she must remember. He was almost in tears, which was a great shame, but he did not care.

All at once she began to laugh, half weeping herself. She flung her arms about his neck and kissed him till he knew he would drown, and drew him through her door.

Then she saw who stood with him. She stiffened again. Only a little at first, with surprise. "You didn't say you'd brought a friend."

"He didn't," Mirain said. "I was only seeing to it that he didn't turn tail before he saw you."

"Then I owe you thanks," she said, letting Vadin go. It was a kiss she had in mind, with joy in it, and Mirain had both before she saw the light on his face and the sheen of his torque. She recoiled, dropping to her knees. "Majesty!"

Mirain did not raise her. "Madam." His voice was cold. "Since you know me, I trust that you will do as I command."

She bowed to the floor. "Yes, majesty."

"Very well. Get up and look at me, and do not bow to me again, nor ever call me by that unlovely title." She rose; she made herself look into his stern face. "Now, madam. Look after my squire, who stands in sore need of it, and consider well. When I was a prince you would speak to me without fear or fawning. Now that I am a king, I need that more than ever." The sternness softened; he held out his hands. "Can you forgive me, Ledi? I never meant to take your man away from you."

"Didn't you?" But she took his hands a little gingerly and mustered a smile. "Very well. I forgive you."

He bowed low, to her consternation and delight, and set a kiss in each palm as if she had been a great lady. "Look after my friend," he said.

Nineteen

VADIN ATE THORNFRUIT AND CREAM WITH NEW BREAD and honey and a mug of ale, and Ledi to sweeten it, combing and braiding his hair while he ate. Through the window he could hear the morning sounds of the town, feel the air cool on his face, bask in the fitful sunlight. It would rain again later, he suspected. The sky had that odd watery clarity it always had between storms, as if it had paused to rest before its new onslaught.

Ledi clasped her arms about his middle, resting warm and bare against his back. He half turned. She claimed a kiss that tasted of cream and honey, and said, "You should be going. Your king will be needing you."

He sighed a little. "Half a thousand people who live to wait on him, and I'm the one he always seems to be needing."

"You're his friend."

"I think I was born under a curse." He reached for his kilt but did not move to put it on. "I'm not his friend. I'm something fated. Like a shadow, or a second self, or a brother of the same birth. I used to think I hated him, till I realized that I didn't; I resented him. How dare he come out of nowhere and change the world?"

"Your world," she said. Very lightly, and for the first time, she touched the mark of the spear. "You're differ-

ent. You're more like him. Like . . . someone who knows
what the gods are."

"I don't know anything."

His sullenness made her smile. "Go on. He's waiting for
you."

Let him wait! he would have cried if he had had any
sense. He dressed instead, kissed her again, and then
again for good measure, and went lightly enough down
the stair.

There were one or two people in the common room
drinking their breakfast, and one who neither ate nor
drank but sat in a corner, unseen and unremarked by any
but Vadin, to whom his presence was like a fire on the
skin. "Have you been here all night?" Vadin demanded.

"No." Mirain rose. Under his cloak he was dressed for
riding: a short leather kilt over boots almost tall enough
to pass for leggings. "Rami is outside."

"Where are we going?"

Mirain did not answer. He walked ahead of Vadin into
the puddled courtyard. The Mad One was there, unsad-
dled, and Rami in saddle and bridle nibbling a bit of
weed. When Vadin had seen to her girth and mounted,
Mirain was already at the gate.

They rode in silence except for the thudding of hoofs
and the creaking of Vadin's saddle, winding through the
streets to the east gate, the Fieldgate that led to the open
Vale. It was open, its guard snapping to attention as he
recognized his king. Mirain laid him low with a smile and
clapped heels to the Mad One's sides. The stallion bucked
and belled and sprang into a gallop.

When at last they slowed, town and castle lay well
behind them. The Vale rolled ahead of them, its green
grass parched to gold with summer's heat, lapping at the
foot of the mountain wall.

The Mad One snorted and shied at a stone; Rami bent
a scornful ear at them both. She had no time to spare for
nonsense. Piqued but subdued, the stallion settled into a
swinging walk. His rider stroked his neck in wry sympathy. "Poor king. Neither of us has seen a sky without walls
about it in an eon and an age."

"You're not a prisoner, you know," Vadin said.

"Aren't I?"

"Only if you think you are. Yon old vultures of your council would have you locked in a single room, with servants to wipe your nose for you, and no sharp edges to threaten your priceless hide."

"And no common labor to sully my royal hands."

Vadin tried not to grin. "Went to fetch the seneldi yourself, did you?"

"I did," said Mirain, sharp with annoyance. "You'd have thought I was proposing to turn Avaryan's temple into a brothel. What, his majesty of Ianon in the muck of the stable, touching brush and bridle with his sacred fingers?"

"Appalling." Vadin breathed deep, letting his head fall back, opening his eyes to the tumbled sky. A gust of laughter escaped him, not at Mirain, simply for gladness that he was alive and whole and riding in the wind.

Rami halted and dropped her head to graze. After a moment the Mad One followed suit. "When your beauty comes into season," Mirain said, "I should like to see a mating. Would you be willing?"

"With the Mad One?" Vadin had been going to ask. To beg if need be. But he kept his voice cool and his eye critical. "He's close to perfect to look at, if a little smaller than he should be; but she's got height to spare. And the bloodlines on both sides are good. But aren't you concerned that he'll pass on his madness?"

"He is not mad. He is a king who demands his due."

"Same thing," Vadin said.

"So then, we pray the gods for a foal with Rami's good sense. And a little fire, Vadin. Surely you'll allow that."

Vadin met Mirain's mockery with a long stony stare; then he loosed a grin. "A *little* fire, my lord," he conceded. "Meanwhile you'd better settle your kingdom before winter."

Mirain's brow went up.

"Because," Vadin explained, "I won't ride Rami once she's in foal, and she'll die before she'll let anybody else carry me into battle."

"For Rami's sake, then, we must surely move soon."

Mirain was not laughing, not entirely. "This morning I sent out the hornsmen. I'm calling up my levies."

"You're joking." Mirain's gaze was unwavering. Vadin drew his breath in sharply. "All of them?"

"All within three days' ride."

"Your vul— Your elders will have a thing or two to say."

"Indeed."

Somewhere behind the royal mask was a wide and wicked smile. Vadin snorted at it. "When is the weapontake?"

"When Brightmoon comes to the full."

Vadin whooped, startling Rami into raising her head. Mirain's smile broke free, bloomed into a grin. The Mad One bucked and spun and danced, tossing his head like a half-broken colt. Rami observed him in queenly disdain; gathered herself together; bound him in a circle of flawless curvets and caracoles, and leaped from the last into flight, swift and weightless and breathless-beautiful as none but a seneldi mare could be. With a cry half of joy and half of royal outrage, the Mad One sprang in pursuit.

THEY CAME IN LATE AND WET WITH RAIN, THEIR BELLIES full of a farmwife's good solid provender. She had been generous with it, and bursting with pride that the king himself had chosen her house to shelter in.

Mirain left the farmstead even lighter of heart than he had entered it. Yet as he drew near to the castle his mood darkened. His face grew still, the youth frozen out of it, his eyes filling with strangeness. Vadin did not try to meet them.

The rain had driven the market under cover and confined the less hardy souls of the court to the hall. There should have been wine and dicing and a smuggled girl or two, and from behind the ladies' screens a whisper of harpsong. In its place was a low and steady murmur. People gathered in clusters in the corners of the hall as under the market awnings; the ladies' music was silent, their voices rippling high over the rumble of the men.

Under Mirain's darkly brilliant gaze the murmur faltered. Eyes dropped or shifted toward the door behind the throne. He strode past them, swift enough to swirl his sodden cloak behind him. No one ventured to stand in his way.

In the small solar behind the hall, the Council of Elders sat or stood in a rough circle. Vultures indeed, Vadin thought, hunched in their black robes, surrounding their prey: a thin and ragged figure spattered with mud, its hair a wild tangle. With a small shock Vadin realized that, although it wore armor and bore an empty scabbard at its side, the shape was a woman's.

She raised her head to the newcomers. A deep wound, half healed, scored her cheek from temple to chin. "More of us?" she muttered hoarsely. "They come in better state than I."

"Watch your tongue, woman!" snapped the steward of the council.

"Be silent," Mirain said mildly. He knelt in front of the woman and took her cold hands.

She stared at him, dull-witted with exhaustion. "Give it up, young sir. Whether the king be god or demon, his council is a pack of mumbling fools. There is no help here for the likes of us."

"Have you despaired then?" he asked her.

She laughed short and harsh. "You are young. You look highborn. I was both once. A ruling lady, I was, mistress of Asan-Abaidan, that I held in fief to the Lord Yrian. That was before the old king died. We had a new one, they told me, no more than a boy but a legend already: half a god or half a demon, and bred in the south. Well for him, we thought in Abaidan; if he left us alone, what cared we for his name or his pedigree?

"Abaidan is a small fief, but prosperous enough, close to the eastern edge of Lord Yrian's lands but not so close as to tempt his neighbors, and a hard day's ride from the Marches. We heard of raiding in the north and west, a common enough thing, no cause for alarm. For comfort more than for safety, we armed our farmfolk and doubled the guard on our castle, but we did not look for undue trouble.

"When last Brightmoon waned, the raiders grew bolder.

People began to appear on the roads, fleeing eastward. We took in such of those as asked for sanctuary. Our castle is fortunate; its wells are deep and never run dry, and we had laid in a good store of provisions. We had no need to turn suppliants away."

She stopped. She no longer saw Mirain, or anything about her. After a time she began again, speaking steadily, her tale worn smooth with much telling. "In the dark of Brightmoon, with Greatmoon three days from the full, a rider brought me my lord's summons. There was word that the raiding had ended. Many of our guests were glad, and made ready to return to their houses. But my lord Yrian was uneasy. He suspected that this was only a lull. He bade all his vassals gather to him, armed for battle.

"That was in the morning. By evening of the next day we were ready: myself; my son, who would not be left behind; my husband's old master-at-arms, and as many men as we could muster without leaving Abaidan defenseless.

"The eastward trickle had slowed. Yet as we marched toward the setting sun we met a great mass of folk, all in flight, all too wild with terror to heed us. Even as our lord's messengers set forth to summon the levies, an army had crossed the border. It was immense: all the tribes of the Marches had come together, laying aside their feuds and their quarrels. The border lords who ventured to resist had been overrun, yet those were terrifyingly few. The rest—all of them—had come to the enemy's heel.

"Some of my people would have turned back then and run with the tide. I lashed them forward with my tongue, and when that failed, with my scabbarded sword. Now more than ever our lord had need of us. Should we turn craven and betray him?"

Vadin set a cup in her hand. She drank blindly, without thought, tasting none of the honeyed wine. "We marched," she said. "Even after dark, with Greatmoon like a great swollen eye above us, we marched. I lost nine men out of my thirty. Maybe one or two of them indeed were too weak to keep the pace I set. By midnight five more were gone, lost in the dark, and we were close to the husting field. The roads had emptied. We were alone.

"And yet when we came in sight of the field we raised a shout. It was aglow with the fires of the army, and in its center they had raised our lord's standard. Surely all of Yrian's liege men had rallied to their lord.

"The closer we came, the greater grew our joy. For we saw other banners beside that of our lord. Lord Cassin was there, and Prince Kirlian, and more others than I could count. Looking to join a small but valiant company, we had come into a mighty army. Surely, I said to myself, however many the enemy might be, they could not hope to defeat such a force as this.

"Weary though I was, I held my head high. Perhaps even the king would come now and sweep his enemies away." She bent her head over the cup that lay half forgotten in her hand. "I instructed my sergeant to find a camping place for our men, and taking my son set off at once for my lord's tent. Late though it was, I knew he would wish to know that I had come. Lord Yrian pays heed to small things.

"As I had expected, he was awake still, and his tent was full to bursting with my fellow vassals. I saw Lord Cassin, and Prince Kirlian in his famous golden armor. And—" Her throat closed. She wrestled it open. "I saw the Prince Moranden."

The air rang into stillness as after the striking of a great bell. That was the tale that had struck to the heart both market and hall.

The woman tossed back her hair. "I saw the Prince Moranden. He sat as a king, and he wore a king's crowned helmet, and my lord Yrian bowed low at his feet.

"My eyes went blind. I had come to do battle with the rebel. Now, all too clearly, I was to follow him. Had not all the west already laid itself in his hand?

"I should have effaced myself, collected my men, and slipped away. But I have never been noted for my prudence. 'My lord,' I said to the one who held my oath, 'have we lost another king then?'

"Even then I might have escaped. I was close still to the

opening of the tent. But my son had gone to greet a
friend, a very young lord whose father, as fondly foolish
as I, had brought him to the war. Close by them was an
old enemy of mine. As soon as he heard my words, he
seized my son and held him, and thus held me.

"Lord Yrian had turned when I spoke. Strange, I
thought, he did not look like a traitor. 'Ah, Lady Alidan!'
he called. 'You come in a good hour. Behold, the king
himself is here to lead us.'

"It struck my heart to hear my words so twisted against
me, little though he knew it who did it. 'I had heard that
the king was a youth and a stranger,' I said. 'Is he dead?
Have we a new lord?'

" 'This is your only true king,' said my lord Yrian as
reverently as if he had never sworn his oath to the boy
in Han-Ianon.

"I looked at the one he bowed to. I knew the prince; we
all did. I had even sighed after him once, when I was a
new widow and he stood beside Yrian to hear my oath of
fealty. Yet now he was exiled by a king whose justice had
been famous, and he rebelled against the king's chosen
successor; and there was that in his eyes which I did not
like, even though he smiled at me. 'The true king,' I said,
to feel it on my tongue. 'Maybe. I have not seen the other.
Nor has he raised war against his own people.'

" 'Not war,' he said still smiling. Oh, he was a handsome man, and well he knew it. 'The claiming of my
right. You are beautiful, Lady Alidan. Will you ride beside me to take what is mine?'

"Now, mark you, even at my best, when I was a maid
adorned for my bridal, I was never more than passable to
look at. And that night I was clad as you see me now, and
glowering besides. I was anything but beautiful.

"Thinking on this and looking into his face, I knew that
he lied—if in this, then perhaps in everything. 'I think,' I
said, 'that I will pass by your offer. Surely there are
handsomer women to be found. Women who do not
object to treason.' I did not bow. 'Good night, Lord Yrian,
my lords. I wish you well of what you have chosen.'

"I turned to leave. But my way was barred. Even

hemmed in as I was, I tried to draw my sword. And I saw my enemy—may all the gods damn him to deepest hell!—I saw him draw his dagger across my son's throat.

"My blade was out. I think I made a mark or two before it was wrenched from my hand. A knife slashed my face; even as the blood began to flow, I grappled for the weapon. Perhaps I would have won it, or perhaps I would have died, had not the prince's bellow driven my assailants back. They were reluctant but obedient, as hounds must always be. 'Let her go,' he commanded them. And when they protested, he sneered at them. 'Do you fear her so much? She is but a woman. What can she do? Disarm her and let her go.'

"My sword of course was gone. They took my dagger from me. They would not let me near my son, nor would they suffer me to find my men or my mount. Alone and afoot, I turned my face eastward.

"I walked. Sometimes I slept. I drew level with the fugitives; I kept to their pace; I passed them. I took shelter where I might, when I must, speaking to no one. My only thought was to find the king.

"Once I found food and a bed in a barn. There was a senel there, old but sturdy. I stole her. She kept me ahead of pursuit and brought me here. At Han-Ianon's gate I remembered how to speak.

" 'Moranden has crossed the borders,' I said to the guards. 'All the west has risen to follow him,' I cried in the market. 'Soon he will advance into the east,' I said in the hall. 'Arm yourselves and fight, if you love your king!' " She turned her head from side to side, eyes glittering in the ruined face. "And here in the king's own council I hear naught but weaseling words stained with disbelief. Surely, I am told, my wits have deserted me. There is no army in the west. The lords have not turned against their king. I am deluded; I am lying; I am most presumptuous, and a scandal besides: a woman dressed as a man, riding a stolen senel with no more harness than a bit of rope. Only let me go and cease my ravings, that are not fit for royal ears to hear."

"Are they not?" asked Mirain softly. The elders, opening their mouths to protest this outrage, choked upon their words.

Her hands gripped his arm. "Maybe," she said with sudden fierce hope, "maybe they will listen to you. You are a man; you look sane. Make them listen, or all Ianon is lost!"

"I have no need to compel them." He met her eyes. "I am the king."

For a long moment her hands held. She had hardly seen him yet, had seen only her grief and her wrath and her terrible urgency. She strained to focus her weary eyes, to make him real, not only her listener and her source of strength, but the king for whom she had lost all she possessed. "I sought you. I sought you all across your kingdom. To see . . . if . . ." Her voice died.

"To see if I was worth the life of your son."

Her eyes closed in pain. Exhaustion held them so; she forced them to open. To her own dismay she began to laugh. Grimly she mastered herself. "Your majesty. I should have known." She would have knelt at his feet; he held her to her chair. His strength surprised her. "My lord—"

"You are my guest; you owe me no homage. Come. You need food, and healing, and sleep."

She braced her will against him. "I cannot. Until I know— Do you believe me?"

"I have called up my levies. When Brightmoon is full, we go to war."

The elders gasped. Neither Mirain nor Alidan heeded them. She clasped his hands and kissed them one by one, and slowly, very slowly, let her body give way to its weariness. "You are my king," she said, or thought, or wished to think.

Her last memory was of Mirain's face, and of his hand warm almost to burning on her torn cheek.

Twenty

EVEN BEFORE THE FULL OF BRIGHTMOON, THE LEVIES OF Ianon began to fill the castle and the town. "Three thousands," Mirain reckoned them, standing at his grandfather's old post upon the battlements. Brightmoon hung above the eastern mountains, its orb as yet two days from the full. There was a tang of frost in the air, harbinger of the long northern winter. He shivered slightly and drew his mantle about him.

Ymin sat on the parapet, shaping an odd winding melody upon her harp. Beyond her Vadin paced, restless with waiting. "Three thousands," he said, echoing the king. "A fine brave number to look at. But there should have been twice as many."

"Rumor gives Moranden more still," said Mirain, "and has him marching slowly eastward, pillaging and burning as he advances. I can't ask any lord to leave his lands unprotected."

Vadin laughed sharp and hard. "Can't you? They're holding back. Moranden they know; not everyone loves him, but he's famous for his strength. You may be the rightful king, but you're untried, and you weren't born here. This way, if you win, every petty baron can say he helped you; if you lose he can declare that you forced him, and point to all the men he kept home, and use them for a threat if anyone argues."

"I will force no one to follow me."

"When you use that tone," murmured Ymin, "I know you long to be contradicted."

Mirain laughed, but his words were somber. "I will not lead unwilling men to this battle. Better three thousand who are loyal than twenty who will turn against me at a word."

"You're a dreamer," growled Vadin.

"Surely. But I'm a mage; I dream true."

"A king can't rule a country full of friends."

"He can try. He can even be truly outrageous and dream of ruling a world of them."

"Can any man do that?" Ymin asked, soft beneath the ripple of harpsong.

Mirain's face was lost in shadow, but the moon caught the glitter of his eyes. "When I was begotten, my father laid a foretelling upon me. When I had won the throne ordained for me, I would come to a parting of my fate. Either I would die in early manhood and pass my throne to my slayer and be forgotten, or I would triumph over him and hold all the world in my hand."

"You are doing what you can to choose the first."

"I am doing what I can to be true to both my people and myself."

"Mostly the latter." She shrugged. "You are the king. You do as you will. The rest of us must live with it, or die trying."

"You sound like my council. They're horrified not simply that I should contemplate riding to war, but that I've called up my forces without consulting them. To silence them I had to invoke my kingship. Now they're convinced that I'm a tyrant in the making, and quite mad."

"I would not call you a tyrant. Nor would I call you mad. Not precisely."

"My thanks," he said dryly.

A fourth figure joined them. The moon limned the long pale scar upon one cheek.

"Alidan," said Mirain.

She bowed to him and moved toward the parapet, letting her cloak blow free about her. Given to choose, she had put on a woman's gown but belted it with sword and dagger. Both lords and commons looked askance at her; she had yet to acknowledge their existence, or indeed that of any but the three who stood with her now. "Look," she said, "Greatmoon is rising."

The Towers of the Dawn shimmered blue-pale as if through clear water; above them curved the great arc of the moon, a bow of ghostly blue, dimming the stars about it. At the full it was glorious; so close to its death it seemed a huge cancerous eye, glaring westward over the Vale of Ianon.

Alidan turned her back on it and her face to the wind. Mirain was close beside her. Without her willing it, her hand went to her cheek. "They say," she said slowly, "they say, my lord, that you have powers. A power. That you know all that is hidden. That you can bring down fire from heaven. Why do you not simply blast all your enemies now and have done?"

A gleam drew her eyes downward. Greatmoon shone in his palm, the Sun turned to blue-white fire. Darkness covered it: his fingers, closing into a fist. His voice came soft out of the night. Soft and strange, as if he were not truly there at all, but spoke from a great and dreaming distance. "What power I have, I have from my father, through his gift. Knowing and making and healing; ruling, perhaps. The fire is his own."

She hardly heard him. "If you smote them now, you would preserve your kingdom and the lives of your people. Ianon would be free again."

"Ianon would not be free. Ten thousand men would be dead, and I would still have lost."

Alidan strained to see his face. For all her efforts she gained only a blur of darker darkness, a suggestion of his profile. "It is a waste, all this war. You need not even destroy the enemy's army, only the leaders. Surely you would shed more blood than that if you rode into battle against them."

"I cannot use my power for destruction."

"Cannot or will not?"

For a long while he was silent. Surely he remembered

Umijan, and a man who had died, lured into the blade that had been meant for himself. At last he said, "It is an ancient war, this between my father and his sister. His victory is life. Hers is destruction. Were I to use his gifts to sweep away all my enemies, I would but serve his great enemy."

"Death by fire, death by the sword: what difference is there? It is all death."

"No," Mirain said. "Against the fire nothing mortal can stand. And I am half mortal. I would vanquish my enemies, but I myself would fall, crumbling into ash, and my soul would belong to the goddess." His voice turned wry, though still oddly remote. "So you see, beyond all the rest I think of my own safety. It's my father's law. For the works of light I may do whatever my will and my strength allow. But if I turn to the dark, I myself will be destroyed."

"And if that befalls—"

"If that befalls, the Sunborn will be no more, and the goddess will have won this battle in the long war. For I am not only the god's son whom he has made a king. I am also his weapon. The Sword of Avaryan, forged against the Dark."

She shivered. Quiet though his voice was, the voice of a young man, a boy scarcely older than the son she had lost, its very quietness was terrible. Her hand found his arm. Under the mantle it was rigid. "My lord. My poor king."

"Poor?" It came from the depths of his throat, yet it comforted her. For the growl in it was wholly human, drawn back entirely from whatever cold distances had held him. *"Poor,* say you? Dare you pity me?"

"It is not pity. It is compassion. To bear such a burden: so much fate, so much divinity. And for what? Why must it be you? Let your father fight his own battles."

She uttered heresy and certain blasphemy; and he was a priest. But the shadow of his head bent; his response was softer even than his words before. "I have asked him. Often. Too often. If he ever answers, it is in truth no answer at all: that it is his will, and that this is my world.

And that even gods must obey the laws which they have made."

"As must kings," said Ymin. It was not quite a question.

"As must kings." A sound escaped him. It might have been laughter; it might have been a sob. "And the first law of all is: Let nothing come easily. Let every man strive for what is his. Without transgressing any other of the laws."

"Which of course," she said, "by making the striving more difficult, strengthens the first law."

"The universe is perfect even in its imperfections." Mirain wrapped himself more tightly in his cloak. "It's cold on the heights."

"Even for you?" asked Alidan.

"Especially for me." He turned away from the battlements. "Shall we go down?"

TEN OF THE KING'S SQUIRES WOULD RIDE TO WAR WITH HIM, and Adjan at their head to see that they did not disgrace their training. The chosen few, still reeling with the honor and the terror of it, had won a night's escape. "Get out," Adjan had snarled at the pack of them, "and leave the others in peace. But mind you well, we ride at the stroke of sunup. Any man who comes late gets left behind."

They saw Vadin as he came to the alehouse in search of Ledi, and they were far enough gone in ale to forget that they were in awe of him. "Share a cup," begged Olvan, thrusting his own into Vadin's hand without heed for the great gout that leaped onto the table. "Just one. It's good for you. Warms up your blood." He winked broadly.

Vadin started to demur, but Ayan had his other hand and they were all crying for him to stay; and he could not see Ledi anywhere in the thronged and boisterous room. Someone pulled him down; he yielded to the inevitable and drained what little remained in the cup. They cheered. He found that he was grinning. He had Ledi back again, and in a little while he would go to her, and now his friends had remembered their friendship.

And yet it was not the same. With Ledi, it was better. Deeper, sweeter. Sometimes at the peak of loving he thought he could see her soul, and it was like a glass filled with light, inexpressibly beautiful. But crushed in with all these raucous young men, reeling in the fumes of wine and ale and dreamsmoke, he could think only of escape. Not that he disliked any of his companions. Some maybe he came close to loving. It was only . . . they seemed so foolish, like children playing at being men. Did it never occur to them that they would be utterly wretched when morning came?

He smiled and nursed a cup and waited for Ledi to find him. The others were growing uproarious. Nuran had begun a wardance on the table to a drumming of hilts and fists.

Suddenly Olvan loosed a shout. Nuran lost the rhythm and toppled laughing into half a dozen laps. Olvan sprang into his place. "Men!" he proclaimed. He had a strong voice and a gift for speechmaking; he won silence not only among the squires but for a fair distance round about. "Are we the king's men?"

"Yes!" they shouted back.

"Are we going to fight for him? Are we going to kill the traitor for him? Are we going to set him firm upon his throne?"

"Yes!"

"So then." He dropped to one knee and lowered his voice. "Listen to me. I say we should show him how loyal we are. Let's do something that brands us his in front of all Ianon."

Fists rocked the heavy table on its legs. *"All* Ianon!" the squires chorused joyfully.

But Ayan drew his brows together. "What should we do? We wear his colors. He's given us his new blazon, the Sun-badge that we all wear on our cloaks. We'll ride with him and we'll wait on him and we'll take care of his weapons. What else is there to do?"

"What else?" cried Olvan. "Why, my love, a thousand things. But one will do. Let's show him how we love him. Let's sacrifice our beards for him."

Jaws dropped. "Sacrifice our—" Ayan stopped. He caressed the wisps of down that he had struggled so long and so hard to grow. "Olvan, you're mad."

"I'm my king's man. Who's got courage? Who's with me?"

"All the girls will laugh at us," said Suvin.

"They don't laugh at the king." Nuran struck his hands together. "I'm with you! Here, whose knife is sharpest?"

Once one had fallen, the rest tumbled after, Ayan last and dubious and yielding only for love of Olvan. Vadin said nothing, and no one asked him to; when they poured into the courtyard to draw water, yelling for lamps and towels and cleansing-foam, he followed in silence, surrounded by clamorous onlookers.

Olvan went first, Ayan next with the air of a prisoner approaching the block. Kav whose hands were steadiest wielded the knife, transforming the lovers into strangers. Ayan was as pretty as a girl. Olvan, square and solid and bearded to the eyes, had a strong fine face beneath. Ayan looked at him and saw no one he knew, and fell promptly and utterly in love.

The rest crowded past them to the sacrifice. Kav yielded the blade to Nuran and gave himself up to water and foam. His beard was a man's already, full and thick and braided with copper; they roared as it fell away. He roared back. Nuran had nicked him. "Blood for the gods!" someone shrilled.

Vadin shuddered. They were turning toward him. "Ho, king's man! Come and join our brotherhood."

Others were doing it now, turning it into a high sacrifice, a hundred victims laid upon an altar none could see. Drunk as they were, it would be a miracle if the morning found no man dead with his throat slit.

Vadin stiffened against the hands that closed upon his arms. "No," he said. "Enough is enough. He knows my mind. I don't need to—"

They laughed, but their eyes glittered. They were many and they were strong; the ale was working in them, making them cruel. "Down with you, my lad. You'll be our captain. Aren't you the one he wept for? Aren't you the one he loves?"

He fought. They laughed. He cursed them. They pulled him down and sat on him. Kav had the knife again, newly honed, gleaming. Vadin lay still. "Kav," he said. "Don't."

His old friend looked at him out of an alien face. Kav had not profited from his sacrifice; without the beautiful beard he was even less lovely than before, a great brute of a man with a jaw like an outcropping of granite. He bent. He laid his blade against Vadin's cheek, and it was so cold that it burned. Vadin set his jaw against it.

With a bark of laughter Kav thrust the knife into his belt. "Let him go," he said. And kept saying it until they growled and obeyed.

Vadin got up stiffly, favoring a bruised knee. The squires had drawn back. Now they knew what he had known since he sat down with them. He was no longer one of them. They had chosen to be the king's men; he was Mirain's utterly, against his will and to his very soul. He dipped his head to Kav, even smiled a little, and walked away. They did not try to hold him back.

THE OLD WOMAN AT THE CURTAIN TOOK VADIN'S COIN, BUT she did not move to let him pass. She peered at him as if he had been a stranger. "Who'll it be?"

He scowled. Of all nights for Kondyi to turn senile, of course it had to be this one. "Who do you think? Ledi, of course."

"Can't have her."

"What do you mean, I can't have her? She promised me. Tonight she'd save for me."

"Can't have her," Kondyi repeated. "She went. Man came and bought her. Paid a gold sun for her."

Vadin could have howled aloud. He dragged the hag up by the neck, shaking her till she squealed in fear. "Who? *Who?* By the gods, I'll kill him!"

She would not tell him. Or could not. If she had been feigning witlessness before, his rage drove her within a whisper of the truth; she could only crouch and whimper and beg him to go away. At last the tavernkeeper came, and he had his man with him, and Vadin still had a few wits left. He spun away with a bitter curse and flung himself into the night.

Mirain's outer door was shut, his inner door barred. Happy man. He had his woman; she loved him and she belonged to him, and no one could buy her away from him. Vadin stalked from the mute mocking barrier into the dark of his own chamber, stripping off his finery as he went. He had put it on so joyfully only a little while ago, thinking of Ledi, of how she would look long at him and smile and declare him the handsomest of her lovers; and then they would make a game of taking it all off.

He stumbled. A sharp word escaped him. He had forgotten the baggage heaped by the door, awaiting the morning. He kicked it, and cursed again as his knee cried protest. He was perilously close to tears.

Something rustled in the dark. He froze, hand dropping to hilt, mind and body suddenly still. His sword hissed from its sheath.

A spark grew to a flame, settled into the lamp by his bed. Ledi blinked at the spectacle of him in a glittering trail of ornaments, sword in hand. She was as bare as she was born except for a string of beads as blue as heaven-flowers. She rose and came to him and embraced him, sword and all. "Poor love, were you looking for me? I tried to send you a message, but first there wasn't time, and then you were gone and they wouldn't let me go after you."

He buried his face in the sweetness of her hair. "Kondyi, damn her—Kondyi said you were sold."

"I was." He thrust free; she smiled, luminous with joy. "Yes, Vadin. A man came, and he had gold; Kondyi and Hodan dickered but they took it, though I fought and I damned them and I even cried. What say did I have in it, after all? I was only a slave. Then," she said, "then the man took me away, and he was very kind, and he didn't go far. Only to the castle. I was beginning to be afraid. The man handed me over to a roomful of very disdainful women; they all carried themselves like queens, though they said they were servants. They made me wash all

over, and they searched me for vermin and for worse
things, and I began to be angry."

Vadin let his sword slip into its scabbard, dropped
blade and belt atop his baggage, let Ledi draw him to the
bed and settle herself in his lap. She kissed his breast over
his heart and sighed. "Of course I knew what they took
me for. A common whore." Her hand on his lips silenced
the protest. "So I was, love, though I tried to be a clean
one and I wouldn't take every man who asked for me.
Now, the women said, I was to learn new ways. I'd not
been bought to ply my trade in the castle."

She was silent for a while. At last Vadin could not bear
it. "What were you bought for?"

"They wouldn't tell me," she said. "Not for a long time.
They showed me things. How to dress; and they gave me
fine clothes to learn in. How to do my hair. How to use
scents and paints. As if I didn't know all of that; but this
was different. They were showing me how to be a lady.
Or how to serve one. A very high one, Vadin. Do you
know the Princess Shirani?"

"Of course," he said. "She's one of the king's maidens."

"I know that. She loves him to distraction. Poor lady,
her father the Prince Kirlian is one of the rebels, and she
lives for a glance from the king, and she's sure she'll die
for being a traitor's daughter. I told her not to be afraid.
The king knows who's true and who's false."

"But how did Shirani happen to buy you? A man I
could understand; you're famous. But a maiden princess—"

Ledi laughed. "Of course she didn't buy me. I'm a gift.
That's what happened afterward, you see. A woman came
and asked the princess if I'd do, and she, sweet child, said
I was perfect. The woman wasn't amused. She told me I
was wanted elsewhere, and mind my manners. I wanted
sorely to act the way she was sure I would, perfectly
vulgar, but I wouldn't do that in front of my lady. I put
on my best new face and let the woman lead me out." She
laughed again. "Oh, it was wonderful, and I was terrified.
She took me to a man, and the man took me to a boy, and
the boy took me to the king. And he stood up in front of
a dozen lords, and he hugged me as if I'd been his kin,

and asked me if I was pleased with my new place. Then he told me—Vadin, he told me I was free. I could serve the princess if I liked, but if I'd rather go elsewhere I could, and he would give me whatever I needed. 'I mean that,' he said. 'Whatever you need.' So I said . . . I said I was happy, if only he would let me see you. He said I could see you whenever I wanted. Then he kissed me and sent me away."

Vadin could not breathe. Mirain had bought her. She was free. King's freedom, that could raise a woman from slave to queen. Not that Mirain had raised Ledi so high, but she could not have borne it; and Vadin was no prince. Only a king's servant, as she was servant to a princess.

His silence troubled her. She raised her head from his breast, and her face was still, braced for the worst. "You aren't glad. You have your women here. I was for your nights in the town, when you wanted a fresh face and a paid love: someone you could leave when you liked and forget when it suited you. I'll go away if you ask, my lord. I won't haunt you."

He tightened his grip on her and glared down into her eyes. They were wide, steady, steeled against tears. "Is that what you want? To go away?"

"I won't stay where I'm not wanted."

"He bought you for me, you know," Vadin said. "He knew I'd never take a gift from him. So he set you free and put you in Shirani's service and left it to you to decide if you wanted me. Sly little bastard."

"He is the king."

A queen could have said it with no more coolness and no more certainty. "He is that," Vadin agreed. "He's also a born conniver. And he thinks the world of you." That cast her into confusion; Vadin kissed her. "Ledi love, we'd best be careful, or he won't just see us bedded; he'll make sure we're wedded."

"Oh, no. We can't do that. You're a lord and a champion and a king's friend. While I—"

"While you are a lady and a wisewoman and a king's friend. Don't you see how he thinks? If I'd finally got together enough silver to buy your liberty, you'd only be a freedwoman. Since he bought you, you're of whatever rank the king decrees. And of free women, only the highest born may wait on a princess."

"Why," she said in wonder, "he is downright wicked." Her own smile was not a jot less. "Tell me, my lord. May a noblewoman disport herself with a man not her husband?"

"It's not widely approved, but it's done."

"I'm not widely approved, either. And I don't intend to be. That's fair warning, Vadin."

"Very fair." His eye was on her body, and half his mind with it. She pushed him down. He smiled; she played with the beard he had so nearly lost. "I suppose," he said, "I'll have to beggar myself to keep your favor."

"Maybe," she said, fitting her body to his. "Maybe not. I was not a good whore. I picked more favorites for love than for money, and many nights I wouldn't work at all."

"But when you did," he said, "ah!" His gasp drew itself out, catching as she did something exquisitely wanton. "Witch."

"Lovely boy," said she who was all of a season older than he. He bared his teeth; she laughed and wove another spell to tangle him in.

"MIRAIN!"

It kept them all warm in the chill of the dawn: the army drawing up on the Vale in an endless tangle of men and beasts and wagons and chariots; the people come to watch them go, women and children and old men, servants and caretakers and the elders who would ward the kingdom at Mirain's back. "Mirain!" they cried, now in snatches, now all together. And as chaos became an army, a new shout went up, rolling like a drumbeat. "An-Sh'Endor! An-Sh'Endor!"

From within the walls it was like the roaring of the sea. Vadin, dragged cold and surly from his warm bed, took a last unwarranted tug at Rami's girth. Her look of reproach made him feel like a monster. He mounted as gently as he could and looked about. Foolish; Ledi had not come to see him off. She had a princess to wait on, and she hated farewells. She would not even admit that he might not come back. But she had dressed him and armed him and braided his hair for war, and she had given him something to remember her by: a kiss ages long and far too short. His lips were still burning with it.

Grimly he turned his mind from her before he bolted back into her arms. The Mad One was being a fine hellion, taunting Adjan's sternly bitted charger with his own bridleless freedom. He had already kicked a groom for presuming to come after him with a halter.

At long last Mirain appeared, coming bright and exalted from solitary prayer in the temple. He was all scarlet and gold, aflame in the rising dawn; at the sight of him a shout went up among his escort and among the few townsfolk who had lingered inside the walls, dim echo of the crowds and clamor without. He flashed them a grin, striding swiftly to his waiting senel, catching himself in front of his squires. A poor hangdog few they looked, much the worse for their night's debauch, with every face scraped naked for the world to see. Vadin had heard the end of Adjan's peroration on their folly, and it had been scathing.

But under Mirain's eye they straightened. Their chins came up. Their eyes lifted and firmed and began to shine. When he saluted them, with a touch of irony it was true, but with more than a touch of respect, they looked as if they would burst with love and pride.

Mirain moved again in a flare of scarlet, springing into the Mad One's saddle. The gate rolled open; the morning wind cried through it, made potent with the roaring of the crowd. He rode down into it, and Vadin raised his new banner, Sun of gold on a blood-red field. The shouting rose to a fever pitch.

Where the ground leveled from the steep slope of the castle's rock, Mirain wheeled the Mad One on his haunches and swept out his sword, whirling it about his head. Along the column sparks leaped: swords and spears flung up in answer. A horn rang. With a clatter of hoofs and a rumbling of wagons and chariots, the army began to move.

*   *   *

"Now HE IS IN HIS ELEMENT," YMIN SAID. SHE RODE IN the van with Vadin and Alidan and the scholar from Anshan, with her harp upon her back and no weapon at her side. Her eyes were on Mirain, who was riding now far back among the footsoldiers. He had hung his helmet from his saddlebow; as she watched, his teeth flashed white in laughter at some jest.

"He's a born leader," said Vadin. "Whether he's a general too, we've yet to see."

"He will be." Alidan shifted in the saddle. Her stallion champed his bit; she let him dance a little until he settled again into his long-legged walk. "He can be anything he chooses to be."

"Remember," said Obri the chronicler, "he had his training in Han-Gilen. Soft the Hundred Realms may be in the reckoning of the north, but they breed famous commanders. A southern general, I've always thought, and an army from the north: the two together would be invincible."

"He is not a southerner!" Alidan cried.

"He is Sanelin's child and our king." Alidan's face did not soften; Ymin smiled at it. "And you, lady, are his most loyal worshipper."

Vadin's brows met. "It's talk like that, that he's desperate to get away from. Push him hard enough with it and he'll get himself killed, just to prove he's mortal."

"Or that he is not." Alidan left them, forging ahead upon the open road.

Twenty-One

THE ARMY ADVANCED AT A STEADY PACE PAST FIELDS RIPE with the harvest. Those who labored there were women and children, the old and the lame and a few—a very few—men of fighting strength who kept their weapons close to hand. They paused to watch the column pass, bowing low to the vivid figure of the king.

Yet even in Ianon's heart the poison had spread. Once from amid a field of bowing farmfolk a shout thrust forth like a spear: "Upstart! Priestess' bastard!"

With a snarl a full company burst from the line. Mirain clapped heels to the Mad One's sides, hurling him across their path, driving them back. He sat his stallion before them, eyes blazing. "Do we ride against farmers or fighters? The enemy lies yonder. Save your wrath for him." The Mad One bounded forward. "To the Marches!"

"To the Marches!" they thundered back.

The Towers of the Dawn rose before them, rose and loomed and passed. Some of them had come this way with Moranden as their commander, riding to a war that had been a lie; as this one was not. Beyond them rolled the green hills of Arkhan, and Medras fief, and the cold snow-waters of Ilien with its outstretched arms: Amilien that ran through the cleft of Sun's Pass into the eastern mountains, and Umilien flowing dark and deep into the labyrinths of Night's Pass in the south and east of Ianon.

But Mirain turned west past the branching of the waters and crossed the fords, entering into Yrios.

Here at last, terribly and inescapably, was the mark of the enemy. The fields were black and charred, the farmsteads crumbling in ruins. The villages were villages of the dead. It was as if a long line of fire had swept across the hills, sparing nothing made by man, stopping short where the level land began. Neither man nor beast remained, and of birds only the carrion creatures that feasted upon the fires' leavings.

"Days old," said Vadin through the bile of sickness, standing by a mound of ash that had been a byre. The stench of smoke was strong, catching at his throat, but stale; the ashes were cold.

Mirain trod through the ruins, heedless of the soot that blackened his cloak. His eyes were strange, blind. "Four days," he said. His foot brushed a grey-white shape: the arch of ribs, a small human skull. He lifted it tenderly, but it crumbled in his fingers. With a sound like a sob he let it fall. He wheeled. There were tears on his cheeks, white fury in his eyes. "All this land lies under a shadow. I find no sign in it of my enemy. But she is here. By her absence I shall find her."

"She?" wondered Kav who kept near to him, exchanging glances with Vadin.

Mirain heard. "The goddess," he said like a curse. "Come, up. Up, before more of my people die to feed her!"

Beyond the place of the skull he led his army north and west, following the wide swath of destruction. There seemed no end to it. The marauders had not always burned what they had taken; fields of grain lay low as if borne down by trampling feet, and amid them stood broken villages, and orchards hacked and hewn, the fruits taken or trodden into the ground.

"THIS IS NOT THE PASSAGE OF A KING COMING TO CLAIM HIS throne," said Alidan, her voice harsh with horror. "What can he hope to rule if he destroys all he passes? He must be mad."

It was evening, the sun new set; they had camped on

the east bank of Ilien, well outside of a village of corpses. Although Mirain had not summoned them, Alidan had come with Ymin and Obri to his tent, to find Vadin there as always, with Adjan and one or two other captains, and the burly form of that Prince Mehtar who had offered Mirain his daughter. Mirain himself sat well back among them, eyes closed, as if he would have preferred to be alone.

It was Prince Mehtar who responded to Alidan's words. "Not mad," he said. "Taunting. He tells us, 'Come, out, follow me; see what I'll do to you when I let you catch me.' "

"But to slaughter innocent people—his own people—"

"Now, lady," said Mehtar, "of course you find this hard to bear. War is no place for a woman."

She half rose; with an effort she controlled herself, but she could not keep her hand from her swordhilt. "A mountain bandit will take what he can and despoil the rest. A man who would be king would preserve all that he may and save his armed strength for his enemy."

Mirain stirred, drawing their eyes to him. "Moranden would be king. But you forget his mother and the one she serves. They have no care for common folk save as sacrifices. It is not he who commands this, but they."

"How do you know?" Mehtar demanded.

Mirain regarded him. He was a large man and overbearing, and though respectful of Mirain's rank and parentage, inclined to let the youth's body blind him to the king. Under that steady stare he subsided rapidly. "I know," Mirain said. "I think . . ." He spoke with care, as if the words tasted ill upon his tongue, yet he could not help but speak them. "I hate him for what he has done. Yet I think I pity him. To be condemned to this, to see his country laid waste and to have no power to prevent it— that is a suffering I would not wish on any man."

Soft, Mehtar's eyes said clearly, although his tongue was silent.

"Would it help any of us if I raged before you and howled for his blood?"

Still Mehtar said nothing.

Crowded though the tent was, Mirain rose and began
to prowl. He circled the silent staring company and left
them. After a moment Ymin followed.

He stood close by the tent, but the air was free upon his
face. She could see his guards, two of his proud shaven
squires, but they stood apart in shadow. Mirain was almost alone.

He drew a deep breath. His tent stood on a low hill; all
about it flickered the fires of the camp. The air was keen
with frost, Brightmoon waning but strong still. Greatmoon
would not rise until dawn, close as he was to his dark,
when was the goddess' greatest power. That was her holy
day, as Brightmoon's full marked Avaryan's rite.

He shivered. It was not a physical cold; his cloak was
lined with fleece and he was well clad beneath. Ymin
moved toward him, close but not touching, her face turned
to the stars. She was keenly aware of his eyes upon her;
she let him look his fill, knowing that he took comfort in
it.

He choked on laughter. She turned to him, thinking a
question. After a moment he answered it. "I stand here,
stark with the terror of my destiny, and lose all my fear in
a woman's face. It seems that I may be a man after all."

"Have you ever doubted it?"

"No," he said. "No. But it betrays a talent for distraction."

"Since you need it," she said, "shall we find a fire?
Then you may gaze to your heart's content, and I can
return the compliment."

"*I* am nothing to stare at." His finger brushed her
cheek. "They weave a cloth in Asanion, rich and soft, fit
for kings. Velvet, they call it. Your skin is dark velvet."

"And yours. You are far from ugly, my dear lord."

"But far from beautiful."

"Moranden has beauty. Has it saved him?"

"It may yet." The cold had come back into his voice.
"He's out there. I can't find him. But I feel him. Shadow
guards him."

"The goddess branded him. You healed the brand. You
are a part of him also, a little, although he has no knowledge of it."

"Not enough to help him. Far too much for my own peace."

"I think we had better look for that fire."

It was faint and feeble, but it was laughter. He took her hand and kissed it and held it a moment, head bowed. Before she could speak he was gone, back to the tent and the great ones huddled together like children afraid of the dark.

IT WAS VADIN WHO HALED THEM OUT, PRINCE AND ALL, and ordered the guards to see that no one else came to trouble the king's sleep.

"Sleep?" Mirain inquired with lifted brow.

"Sleep," said Vadin firmly. "You think I don't know how you've been spending your nights? Brooding doesn't make you any fitter for battle, and magic's not working, and you can't plot strategy till you know where your enemy is."

Mirain submitted to the stripping of his kilt and the freeing of his braid, but his brain was not so easily subdued. "We're being lured and we're being mocked. Odiya's revenge, long and deadly sweet. When it pleases her she'll slip her son's leash, and we'll lie neatly in the trap."

"For a mage whose enemy's spells are too strong to break, you know a great deal about her mind."

"She's not stronger than I. She's merely hiding. And I can use my wits as easily as anyone. I know what I would do if I were she."

"You wouldn't wreck your kingdom behind you."

"No?" Mirain lay where Vadin set him, on his stomach on the narrow cot, hands laced under his chin. As Vadin began to knead the tensed muscles of his shoulders, he sighed with the pure and unselfconscious pleasure of a cat. "I think," he mused, "if I were as bitter as she, and nursed so ancient a grudge, I might find no price too high to pay for my vengeance."

"That's your trouble. You persist in seeing all sides."

"So do you."

Vadin attacked a knot with such force that Mirain grunted. "I see them. I don't condone them. And I don't pity the man in whose name whole villages are burned to the ground. He's a man and a prince. He shouldn't suffer it."

"Ah well, you were raised a lord in Ianon. We foreign bastards are less implacable."

"Foreign," Vadin muttered. "Bastard." He glared at the smooth well-muscled back. Not a scar on it. Those were all in front, or below where a lord carried the brands of his life in the saddle. "You didn't lose your breakfast in the first village we came to."

"So then, Ianon breeds strong minds, the south strong stomachs. I saw as bad or worse in the war against the Nine Cities. They don't simply kill and burn the innocent. They make an art of torment."

"Did you pity them too?"

"I learned to. It was a hard lesson. I was very young then."

And what was he now?

Ageless, Vadin answered himself. And the more so the longer this march went on, with no enemy and no fighting and only a dead land before and behind. The army was losing its edge. Horror and outrage could only sustain them for so long; Mirain was holding them with his magic, spending himself with no certain hope of return.

Vadin's fingers lightened on the easing muscles, more caress now than compulsion. Mirain's eyes had fallen shut although his mind was still awake; his breathing eased, deepened. "Listen," he murmured. "Listen, Vadin."

Silence underlaid with the sounds of an army asleep. Far away a direwolf hymned the moon. Mirain's voice came soft and slow. "No, my brother. Listen within."

Nothing at all. Utter stillness.

"Yes. A fullness of silence. It will be soon now. Mark you. Mark . . ."

He was asleep, his last words surely part of a dream. Vadin drew up the rough blanket Mirain insisted on, no better than a common soldier's, and snuffed all the lamps but the one by the cot. In the dim flickering light he spread his own blanket and lay down. A grim smile had found its way to his face. He was fast going as mad as his master. Bidden to work magic, he had obeyed and not even thought to resist, let alone to be afraid.

When at last Vadin's mind let go, his dreams were of darkness and of silence and of nameless fear. But it was not he who was frightened. He lay cradled in Avaryan's hand upon the breast of his Lady Night.

Twenty-Two

A MIST CAME WITH THE DAWN. THE SUN TURNED it to gold and rolled it away, baring twin ranks of hills that marched from north to south. In the distance they curved together; here they bounded a level plain, all but treeless, with Ilien running narrow and swift down its center.

Across the western hills and spilling onto the level lay a darkness which did not lift. There were sparks in it. Swords' points, spearpoints, and the eyes of the enemy. Vadin's dream had taken shape in the living daylight.

Mirain stepped from his tent into the sun's warmth. He had taken time to dress, to plait his hair, to don his armor. At the sight of him a ragged cheer went up. But most eyes strained westward. "It's vast," someone whispered near Vadin. "Thousands—ten thousands—gods preserve us! They carry their own night."

"But we," said Mirain in a voice that carried, "bear light." He swept up his sword. "Avaryan is with us. No darkness shall conquer us. Swift now, to arms!"

His trumpeters took up the call. The enemy's spell broke; the army began to seethe.

"Well done, my lord," Adjan said, dry and cool. "Once they're armed, you'd best feed them and set the scouts to their work. Yonder horde doesn't have a feel of early battle."

"It does not," Mirain agreed. "Vadin, see to the feeding. The scouts, Captain, are yours to command."

Armed, fed, and drawn up in battle array on the western slope of the ridge, the king's men settled to wait. The enemy seemed motionless beneath their shroud. As the sun mounted and the stillness reigned unbroken, a horror crept through the ranks. Raid or skirmish, siege or open battle, all of those they could face. This half-seen enemy who had grown out of the night, who now showed no sign of attack or even of life, made them forget their courage. More and more their eyes sought the king.

At first he settled by his tent to break his fast and to speak with his commanders. Even from the edges of the camp his scarlet cloak was clear to see. As the morning advanced with no word from his scouts and no move from the enemy, he beckoned to Vadin, leaving the captains to debate battle now, battle later, battle never. The Mad One, whom no tether or hobble could hold, had freed Rami from her picket and led her up the hill. The grooms had brushed them both until they shone, and plaited their manes with scarlet battle-streamers.

King and squire descended to meet them. The Mad One lowered his head to blow into his comrade's hands, and pawed the ground. In an instant Mirain was on his back.

ADJAN FOUND THE KING AMONG THE CAVALRY OF ARKHAN, admiring the points of a trooper's dappled mare. His eyes flashed at once to the captain, but he brought his colloquy to a graceful and unhurried end, withdrawing easily, taking with him the men's goodwill. But once behind the lines, he loosed his hold on his patience. "Well? What news?"

"One scout has come back," Adjan answered. "The others he knows of are dead. He's not well off himself."

"Is he badly hurt?"

"Arrow in the shoulder. A flesh wound, no more; the doctors are taking care of it. But his mind . . ."

The Mad One was stretching already from canter into gallop.

It was as Adjan had said. The scout sat in the healers' tent, hale enough in body, while an apprentice bound his shoulder. But his eyes were too wide; a thin film of sweat gleamed on his brow. As Mirain approached he thrust himself to his feet, sending the healer sprawling. "Sire! Thank all the gods!" Under the terror he was a goodly enough man, square and solid though smaller than most men in Ianon, hardly taller than Mirain himself. He was no novice, nor was he the sort of man who was given to night terrors. Yet he fell at Mirain's feet, clutching them, weeping like a child.

Mirain dragged him erect. "Surian," he said sharply. At the sound of his name, the man quieted a little. "Surian, control yourself." With a visible effort the man obeyed. Mirain kept a grip on his good shoulder. "Soldier, you have a report to make."

He drew a shuddering breath. Under Mirain's hand and eye he found the words he needed. "I set out as commanded, to reconnoiter the southeastern edge of the enemy's army. There were six men with me. We kept to our places, each of us signaling his safety at intervals. We met no opposition. If the enemy had sent out scouts, they were better at their work than we.

"We advanced with all caution. A bowshot from the enemy we stopped. No; *were* stopped. It was an act of will to move forward. The enemy was still a shape in shadow; when I tried to reckon numbers my mind spun and went dark. I never called myself a coward, sire, but I swear, at that moment I could have bolted, honor and duty be damned.

"One of my men broke, left his cover and ran. An arrow caught him in the throat. An arrow out of the air, with no bowman to be seen behind it.

"That must have been a signal. Arrows swarmed over us. No matter where we were or what we did, we were hit. My lord, I swear by Avaryan's hand, I saw one *bend* around a rock and bury itself in a man's eye."

"Yes," Mirain said with flat and calming acceptance. "They all died, I was told. But you live."

Surian swallowed hard, trembling with shock and pain

and remembered horror. "I . . . I live. I think, sire, I was meant to. No, I know it. I'm meant for a message and a mockery."

"She knows us wholly," Mirain muttered, "and we grope for knowledge of her." Surian stared at him, afraid to understand him. He smiled faintly but truly. "You've done well. Rest now. While I live, no darkness shall harm you."

THE SUN PASSED ITS ZENITH AND BEGAN TO SINK INTO THE spell-wrought shadow. Still the enemy had not moved. Mirain's army, drawn taut too long, began to slacken.

"Imagine days of this," Vadin said.

"Our enemy is well capable of it." Mirain had bidden his men be fed again, for diversion as well as for strength, although Vadin had not been able to make him break his own fast. He paced instead with a bit of fruit forgotten in his hand. "But if we attack, we attack blind. Literally, maybe. I'm not yet as desperate as that."

"What do you counsel then?" demanded Prince Mehtar, doffing his helmet and handing it to his squire, biting into a half-loaf spread thick with softened cheese. "We can sit here until we starve, and then the enemy can roll over us."

"With all of us begging to be trampled." Alidan drained a cup of ale as handily as any man-at-arms. "My lord, we have to do better than that."

Mirain glared at the ground where already he had paced out a path in the sparse grass of the hilltop. "Yes, we must. But I dare not give in to my instincts and lead a full charge against the enemy. What they did to a dozen scouts, mountain tribesmen and hunters of Ianon, they can do to three thousand of my warriors."

"Die swift or die slow," Mehtar said, "die we will, if this army is as large as it looks."

"Ah, but is it?" Mirain ceased his pacing at the farthest extent of his path, eyes turned westward under his shading hand. "Think now. The Marchers have men in plenty, and my turncoat lords likewise. But not enough to fill yonder hills, or to stretch back as far as these seem to stretch."

"Yes," said Vadin, "and it's been making me wonder. These are men we know, men like us, some probably forced to fight at their lords' command, others following Moranden in good faith. If we can hardly endure the shadow at this distance, how can they march under it?"

"Illusion," Mirain answered him, "and delusion: the black heart of magic. They see no shadow; they think the sun is free and their minds likewise, even as they think only the thoughts the mages permit them to think. They dream that they have come to rid the throne of an impostor and the kingdom of a threat; commanded to slay and burn, they see in front of them not villages of women and children but camps of my soldiers. And the witch whose spells rule them—the witch laughs. Her laughter shudders in my bones."

He spun on his heel. They were all silent. Some of them thought he might be mad. "No," he said, "only god-ridden. My lords, my ladies, our enemy dares us to fight or fly. I've never had much skill in running. Shall we fight?"

"That will be a swift death," Mehtar said, approving.

"Maybe not, my lord. The witch taunts us with her strength. Let us prove to her that strength can matter little. The tactics of the wolf: strike, slash, leap away."

Adjan's eyes narrowed as he calculated. "We can do that. Wear down the enemy's men, who can't be so very many more than we are, and keep our own happy. But we can't stretch out our necks too far, or we'll lose too many and the other side not enough."

"Ten captains," said Mirain. "Ten men of proven courage with hand-picked troops. Adjan, my lord prince, will you command two of the companies?"

"Aye," Mehtar said for both. "Eight more to find, then. Shall I do it, sire?"

"Seven," Mirain corrected him. "I shall take a company. You may choose the rest as you will. We ride out within the hour. Choose well and choose swiftly."

Mehtar opened his mouth, shut it again carefully. With equal care he bowed. "As my king commands."

*   *   *

EACH CAPTAIN OF THE SORTIE LED TWICE NINE MEN. MIRAIN commanded nine men and five of his own guard, and Vadin, and Jeran and Tuan of the race to Umijan; and Alidan. They formed ranks quietly but without undue stealth behind the main line of forces, mounted on seneldi chosen for speed and courage.

Vadin glanced from side to side. Alidan was close on his right hand, anonymous in armor and helmet, wearing the scarlet cloak of the king's guard. She looked both capable and deadly, and she sat her fiery stallion better than most men. At his left rode Mirain, aglitter in his golden armor. Beyond them on either side he saw the other companies drawn up, mounted and ready.

It was like a melee at the Summer Games; and yet how unlike. This was real. Men would die here for the king who sat lightly in his tall saddle, toying with a wayward battle-streamer. By his word they stood; by his word they would fall.

Vadin's heart hammered. His nostrils twitched with the faint sharp tang of his own fear. Death he was not afraid of; he had lain in its arms. But he could fear pain, fear overlaid and underlaid and shot through with something light and fierce and salty-sweet. Something like gaiety, something like passion: the inimitable scent and sense of battle. Everything was sharper, clearer, more wonderful and more terrible. He laughed, and because people stared, laughed again in pure mirth. In the midst of it his eye caught a flame of gold. Mirain had raised his hand.

The lines opened, here, there. Rami gathered her haunches beneath her. The companies darted forth, no two at once, no two in the same direction. Mirain's force thundered straight to the center, over the plain, through the swift tumble of Ilien, up the slight slope beyond. There was no cover there; they were naked to the sky and to the waiting shadow.

Vadin settled himself more firmly in the saddle. Rami's gallop was smooth, effortless. The silver mane floated over his hand. One blood-red streamer whipped back to strike his wrist.

The enemy waited. He could see as one sees at dusk:

shapes, eyes, but no features. The eyes wore no more expression than the weapons bent against him.

He drew his sword. It was light in his hand, although the blade was strangely dark, its polished sheen lost in dimness.

The company rode together still, close at Mirain's back. But some did not ride easily; their mounts fretted, veering and shying. One man flogged his senel on with his scabbard, the face within the open helmet like a demon-mask, teeth bared, eyes white-rimmed. The horror touched Vadin as a wind will, brushing and chilling but going no deeper than the skin. Looking down, he saw with mild surprise that his body was clothed in a faint golden shimmer, a pale echo of the shining splendor that was Mirain.

Close now. No arrows hummed out of the massed ranks; no spear flew. There was a taste in his mouth as strong as fear. *Trap.* He set his teeth against it. Rami leaped the last yards, braced for battle. Vadin swung up his sword.

The enemy wavered like a mirage, melted and faded and vanished away. Vadin heard cries of anger or of terror. Seneldi screamed. The arrows began to fall.

The Mad One trumpeted, a great stallion-blast of rage and challenge. "On!" Mirain cried to him and to all who could hear. *"On!"*

Shadows, all shadows. Vadin's blade clove air again and again. Yet still he struck, still he pressed on. Bolts sang past him; one pierced his flying cloak. He laughed at them.

With a shock so powerful that it nearly flung him to the ground, his sword struck flesh. Blood fountained, red as Rami's streamers.

As if a spell had been broken, suddenly he could see. Though dim and shadowed still, an army spread before and about him, drawn up under banners he knew. They had few cavalry: the Marches were not known for their herds.

Those he could not face, even wild with battle as he was. Mirain had given them a wide berth, striking against knights and infantry; Vadin sent Rami after him. The enemy fought well and fiercely enough, but there was a strangeness in their eyes, as if they did not truly see him. They struck only when struck first; they did not attack. All along their lines, knots of combat alternated with unnatural stillness. Even the chariots did not roll forth to hew the attackers into bloody fragments, but stood where they were set, the charioteers' eyes fixed straight before them.

In Geitan they had told Vadin that he was rarely blessed, a warrior who could sing as he fought. But that was against men who were free to sing in turn, fight in turn, slay in turn. This was a travesty, a sorcerous horror. His lips drew back from his teeth in sudden, deadly rage. "Fight, damn you!" he howled. "Turn on us! Hammer us down!"

The eyes did not change. His sword turned in his hand; he began to lay about him with the flat of it, stunning but not wounding. He sensed Mirain close by him: a gathering of power, stronger, stronger, until surely he would burst with it.

Mirain let it go. The light upon him mounted to a blaze. Eyes woke to life, to fear, to battle-madness. With a shrill cry a charioteer lashed his team against the attackers.

Darkness roared down. Rami wheeled uncommanded, running as she had never run before, flat to the ground, ears pinned to her head. She burst from the shadow like a demon out of hell, eyes and nostrils fire-red. The stream flashed silver about her feet. Beyond it she slowed, became a seneldi mare again, breathing hard, with foam white on her neck.

Vadin blinked in the bright sunlight. His fingers were clamped about the hilt of his sword; painfully he loosed them, wiping his blade on his cloak. Blood faded into royal scarlet. With a convulsive movement he thrust the sword into its sheath.

Mirain's sortie had done what it intended. The enemy was in turmoil, too intent upon the spell's breaking to muster an assault. But the cost had been frighteningly high. Mirain's men milled here and there on the hither side of the water, with riderless seneldi running among them. They moved with order in their confusion, a swift and steady retreat with an eye constantly upon the enemy, and there were far fewer in the retreat than had ridden to the attack.

Mirain's own company gathered to him. Vadin counted and groaned aloud. Of eighteen, twelve were gone. The six who remained rode like wounded men, several on wounded beasts.

Alidan reached king and squire first, Alidan without her helmet, her hair escaped from its braids, her sword hand bloody to the wrist. But there was no wound on her. Mounted as they both were, Mirain pulled her into a tight embrace.

For each of the others he had the same. They all had the look of men who had passed through one of the thrice nine hells: grey and stunned, staring without comprehension at the plain daylight.

"We tried to follow you, my lords," Alidan said for them all. "The shadows turned into men and fought us; we fought back. But you were too fast for us. My lords, you shone like gods. You went deeper and deeper, and at last we could not force our mounts forward. We tried to hold the line behind you. It broke. Our seneldi carried us out. My lord king, any punishment you name—"

"Punishment?" Mirain laughed painfully. "I did exactly the same as you, and abandoned you to boot. No, my friends. You did what few other mortal men could have done." His eyes caught Alidan's; he laughed again with less pain and more mirth. "Mortal men, and one woman."

They rode back slowly. They were barely half of the way from the stream to the battle-lines—those lines bending outward against all discipline to receive their king—when a horn rang. The Mad One whipped about, Mirain's sword flashing from its scabbard.

The enemy's lines opened. Out of them came a single rider, a man on a smoke-grey senel, all in grey himself with a torque of grey iron about his neck. That and the grey banner without device proclaimed him a herald, sacred before men and gods, owing allegiance to one chosen lord. His eyes rested neutrally upon the army, but when they touched Mirain they narrowed and darkened.

"Men of Ianon," he said. He had a superb voice, rich

and deep, trained to carry without effort over a great distance. "Followers of the usurper, the one who calls himself Mirain, bastard child of a priestess and false claimant of the throne of the mountain kings, I bring you word from your true lord. Lay down your arms, he bids you. Yield up the boy and you shall go free."

"Never!" shouted Alidan, fierce and shrill. Deeper voices echoed her.

The herald waited patiently for silence. When he had it he spoke again. "You are loyal, if not wise. But your rightful king remembers what you choose to forget: that you are his people. He would not willingly send his army against you for a battle that would end only, and inevitably, in your destruction."

"What about the villages?" bawled a man with a voice of brass. "What about the children cut down and burned in their houses?"

The herald continued coolly, undismayed. "The king proposes a different course, one both ancient and honorable. Two men claim a throne which only one may hold. Let them contend for it, body to body and life to life: a single combat, with all spoils to the victor. Thus will none die but one man, and the division of Ianon be healed, and the throne secured. What say you, men of Ianon? Will you accept my lord's proposal?"

Mirain rode forward a senel-length. The movement silenced his army. He faced the herald, taking off his helmet and setting it on his pommel. "Will Moranden swear to that? That the victor take all, with no treachery and no further slaughter?"

The herald's nostrils flared. "Have I not said so?" *Upstart,* his eyes said. He was a man who believed in his commander.

Even from behind, Vadin heard the smile in Mirain's voice. "Will you condescend to take him my answer?"

"He gives you until sunset to make your choice."

"He is generous." The Mad One advanced another length. Mirain's words came bright and strong. "Tell him yes. Yes, I will do it."

The herald bowed: barest courtesy, no more. "It is the privilege of the challenger to choose time and place, of the challenged to choose the weapons and the mode of battle, whether single or seconded. My lord bids you to meet him here between the armies, tomorrow, at sunrise."

Mirain's bow was deeper, rebuking bare courtesy with true courtliness. "So shall I do. We shall fight singly, overseen by one judge and one witness of each side. As for weapons . . ." He paused. His army waited, drawn thin with tension. "Tell your commander that I choose *no* weapons. Bare hands and bare body: the most ancient way of all." He bowed again. "Tomorrow at sunrise. May the gods favor the truth."

Twenty-Three

"**U**NARMED!"

Even Adjan had taken up the cry, shocked out of all dignity. Mirain turned a deaf ear to him as to the rest, laboring first among the healers and then, and only then, returning to his tent. The protests had followed him; they continued as his squires disarmed him. Blood had soaked even to his undertunic, and dried there; there was a long breathless pause until his pursuers saw that none of it was his own. With sudden fierce revulsion he tore at the garment, stripping it off, flinging it as far from him as he might.

Which was, by design or chance, into Adjan's hands. "My lord," the arms master said with some remnant of his usual control, "single combat is an old and honored way of resolving conflicts. But unarmed combat—no weapon, no armor, no defense at all—"

Mirain looked at him. Simply looked, as a stranger might, a stranger who was a king. "If it would soothe your outraged modesty, I could wear a loinguard."

"The dark," someone muttered. "He rode into it and fought it. It's driven him mad."

Vadin stared the man down until he fled. That began an exodus. Vadin remained; and Adjan, and Obri the chronicler who was like a shadow on the wall, and Ymin with Alidan. Olvan and Ayan, moving with great care,

began to prepare the king's bath. They filled the broad
copper basin; Mirain let them wheedle him into the water, a letting that had no passivity in it. His eyes were still
upon Adjan. "Well, Captain, would a loinguard content
you?"

"Full armor would be no more than adequate. And
sword and spear and shield with it."

"And the body of one of your northern giants." Mirain
glanced down at himself. He had grown since he came to
Han-Ianon; he would not, after all, be so very small.
Middle height in the south, perhaps, but in Ianon, small
still; smoothly and compactly made, with the lithe strength
of a rider or a swordsman.

And ensorceled surely, to have bound himself to a
contest without weapons against the most formidable fighting man in Ianon.

"No," Mirain said with tight-reined impatience. *"No.*
Unbind your brains, my friends, and think. I'm skilled in
arms, I know it well enough; with the sword I may even
become a master. My charger has no peer in this kingdom. *But."* He stepped out of the bath, neither flaunting
his body nor belittling it. "Moranden is a man grown, in his
full prime, trained from earliest youth in the arts of war.
He can wield a larger sword, a longer spear; if he can't
out-ride me, he can hold his own against my Mad One.
While I flail uselessly at him, he can smite me at his
leisure, like a man beset by a little child."

"He can do the same without weapons," snapped Adjan.
"His arms are half again as long as yours; he stands head
and shoulders above you. And he's strong. The Python,
his enemies used to call him: he strikes like a snake, fast
and deadly, with all the force of his size."

"In the west," said Mirain, "there is a creature. She is
small, no larger than my two hands can hold, with a long
supple tail, and great soft eyes like a lovely woman's. She
sheathes her claws in velvet. They call her Dancer in the
Grasses, and Night Singer, and most often *Issan-ulin*,
Slayer of Serpents. There is no creature swifter or fiercer
or more cunning than she. Even the great serpent-lord,

the crested king, whose poison is most deadly of all—even he falls prey to this small hunter."

"She has claws and teeth," Adjan said, immovable. "What have you?"

"Hands," he answered, "and wits. Come, sir. You're a famous fighter; I've heard you called the best master-at-arms in the north of the world. See if you can strike me."

The old soldier looked hard at him. He stood loose, easy, smiling. But a keen eye could detect the tension in him.

Adjan was noted for his swift hand, whether or not it held a weapon. As the others drew back to the walls, he shifted slightly, almost invisibly; feinted right; lashed out with his left hand, too swift for the eye to follow.

Mirain seemed not to have moved. But Adjan's fist had struck only air.

Adjan's brows knit. He advanced a step or two. Mirain did not retreat. "Seriously now," he said, "strike me."

This time Mirain's movement was clearly visible, an effortless, sidewise bending. He laughed. "Seize me, Adjan. Surely you can do that. I'm in your arms already."

He was; he was not.

Adjan lowered his hands. His face was a study; he composed it. "So. You're uncatchable. What use is that in a duel, unless you can land a blow where it matters?"

Mirain stepped back with the supple grace of a cat. "You're angry. I've made you look like a fool. Attack me, Captain. Wrestle me down and teach me to listen to your wisdom."

There was nothing Adjan would have liked better. But he was wary, and well he might be. He had said it before when he faced Mirain at practice in front of the squires: In all his years of fighting and of training fighters, he had only once seen speed to equal Mirain's. In Moranden when the prince came into his manhood. Three years, four, five—let the king get his growth and hone his skill, and he would be a warrior to make songs of.

If he lived past the next sunrise.

Adjan attacked. Mirain let him come, shifting a little, poising upon the balls of his feet. Suddenly Adjan was in the air, whirling head over heels, sprawling amid the coverlets of Mirain's bed. And Mirain was kneeling by him, holding his reeling head, saying in a tone of deep contrition, "Adjan! Your pardon, I beg you. I never meant to throw you so far."

Adjan shut his mouth with a snap. A sound burst out of him, a harsh bark of laughter. "Throw me, boy? Throw me? I weigh enough for two of you!"

Mirain bit his lip. His eyes hovered between laughter and apology. "You do. And I used a good part of it against you. A little more and I could have killed you."

The arms master staggered to his feet. "Of course you could have. The more fool I. I should have known you'd have the western art."

"The gentle killing. Yes, I have it. I learned it of a master, by my mother's will. She knew I'd grow to be like her: western stature, northern face. And people in the west, being so small beside the rest of mankind, have learned to turn their smallness to advantage. Since they can't conquer by brute strength, they conquer by art. I've seen a child from Asanion, a maidchild mind you, younger and smaller than I, cast down a man nigh as big as Moranden, and kill him when he refused to yield."

"I've seen something like it. It's enough to make me believe the stories that Asanians have interbred with devils."

"Precisely the tale they tell of me." Mirain rose. "Now do you understand? With weapons I have no skill that Moranden cannot either equal or surpass. Without them I may be able to even the balance. He's a big man; he relies on his strength. So too shall I."

"I still think you're mad. If you would see sense, find another champion—" Adjan broke off. Abruptly and deeply he bowed, the full obeisance of a warrior to his king. "However it ends, my lord, it will be a battle to make songs of. There's no power of mine that will keep you from it."

Mirain bowed his head. Suddenly he seemed immeasurably weary. "Please go," he said. "All of you."

They obeyed, none willingly. Ymin hung back, but found

no yielding in him. Slowly she retreated, letting the tent flap fall behind her.

But Vadin did not go. He made himself invisible, withdrawing into the darkest corner, thinking not-thoughts. It had its effect. Mirain did not glance at him; did not order him out.

The tent seemed larger for the people who had left it, lit by a single lamp, warm and quiet in the heart of the night. The squires had taken the bath with them; Mirain sat where it had been, on carpets flattened by the weight of water and basin, and set himself to a task they had not come to: loosing and combing his hair. It was even less straight above the root of his braid than below; cut short, it would have sprung into a riot of curls.

A shield hung from the central pole, polished to mirror sheen. He met his reflected stare. Vadin, invisible, unable to help himself, slipped inch by inch into Mirain's mind, following his thoughts as if he had spoken them aloud. Quiet thoughts, a little wry, like the tilt of his head as he contemplated his face. Westerners had smooth oval faces and sleek rounded bodies and hair that curled with abandon; they were light-skinned, gold and sometimes ivory, and often their hair was straw-pale. Mirain had inherited none of that but the curling of his hair. He was all dark, indubitably of Ianon: high cheekbones, arched nose, proud thin-lipped mouth. "Imagine the alternative," he said aloud. "Western face, northern body. The strength to stand against Moranden as warrior to armed warrior, without art or trickery." He sighed. "And I would still be a boy half grown, with size and skill yet to gain."

He tied his hair back with a bit of cord and clasped his knees. There was the heart of it. Moranden was strong and skilled and implacable in his enmity; and he had strong sorcery behind him. What was to prevent his mother and her goddess from giving him art to equal Mirain's?

"Father," he whispered. "Father, I am afraid."

When he was very young, sometimes he had wept because his hand burned him so terribly, and because he had no father he could touch, or run to, or cry on. There was his mother, who was all the mother a child could wish

for, and Prince Orsan whom he called foster-father, and
the princess; and Halenan, and later Elian, brother and
sister in love if not in blood. But for father he had only
pain, and the distant fire of the sun, and the rites in the
temple.

When he was older, he taught himself not to weep. But
he faced his mother and demanded of her, "How can it
be true? I know how children are made; Hal told me.
How can my father be a spirit of fire?"

"He is a god," she had answered. "For a god, all things
are possible."

He set his chin, stubborn. "It takes a man, Mother. He
comes to a woman, and he—"

She laughed and laid a finger on his lips, silencing him.
"I know how it is done. But a god is not like a man. He
has no need to be. He can simply will a thing, and it is
so."

Mirain scowled. "That's horrible. To give you all the
pain and trouble of bearing me, without any pleasure at
all."

"Oh," she said, a breath of wonder and delight, "oh, no.
There was pleasure. More than pleasure. Ecstasy. He was
there, all about me; and I was his love, his bride, his
chosen one. I knew the very moment you began in me, a
joy so sweet that I wept. Oh, no, Mirain. How could I
wish for the feeble pleasures of the flesh when I have
known a god?"

"*I* don't know him," Mirain said sullenly, setting his will
against the strength of her joy.

She gathered him up, great lad that he was, seven
summers old and already making his mark among the
boys in training for war. "Of course you know him. This
very morning I saw him in you and you in him, riding
your pony down by the river."

"That was no god. That was—was—" Words failed him.
"I was happy, that's all."

"That was your father. Light and joy and a bright
strong presence. Did you not feel as if the world loved
you, and you loved it in return? As if there were someone

with you, taking joy in your joy, bearing you up when you faltered?"

"I'd rather have someone I can see."

"You have me. You have Prince Orsan, and Hal, and—"

"I don't want them. I want a father."

She laughed. She was full of laughter, was the Priestess of Han-Gilen. Some people frowned at her, thinking that the god's own bride should be grave and austere and visibly saintly; but Sanelin was a creature of light. And he, being her child, found to his dismay that he could not be sullen in front of her. Already the laughter was bubbling up in him. How absurd to cry for a father, when of course he had one already, more than anyone else had, present always in him and with him. And when he needed a physical presence he had no less than the Prince of Han-Gilen, that tall man with his stern face and his merry eyes and his hair like the sun's own fire.

Sanelin was dead, Prince Orsan long leagues away. But the god was there when Mirain looked for him, in the core of his own soul: a presence too intimate to bear either name or face. Nor did he offer comfort in words. It went far deeper than that.

Deeper still went the fear. "Father, I could die tomorrow. I probably will die. This is an enemy I am ill-equipped to face."

Should he be afraid of death? It was but a passage; and after it, joy unspeakable.

"But to die now with my destiny all unfulfilled—to know that by my death I leave my kingdom open to the servants of our Enemy—how can I endure it?"

Ah, then it was not death he feared. He feared that he would not live to hold back the goddess. He had a fine sense of his own worth.

"And who set it in me?"

To make him strong. Not to make him arrogant.

"It makes no difference, then. If Moranden kills me, the throne is safe; his mother will not rule through him with her wizards and her priests, turning all Ianon to the worship of the goddess."

It would make a difference. Perhaps, once Moranden

had his throne, he could hold against his mother; perhaps he would prove too feeble for her purposes. Or perhaps, and most likely, what Mirain foresaw would come to pass.

"*Perhaps* is an alarming word for a god to use."

A god might choose to think as a man, for his own ends. As he might choose to lend aid where aid was needed, if it were sought in the proper fashion.

"Father! You will be with me?"

The god was always with his son.

"You comfort me," said Mirain with a touch of irony.

But not completely.

"Of course not. I know what this battle is to you. Another stroke against your sister." Mirain tossed back his heavy mane, quivering with sudden, passionate anger. "But why? Why? You are a god. She is a goddess. Fight your own battles in your own realm. Let us be!"

The god's presence seemed to smile, a smile full of sadness; his thought took shape clearly as words in a voice soft and deep, like and yet unlike his son's. *Again I tell you, again I bid you remember: When we shaped your world, we swore a truce. War between us would destroy all we made together. Rather than chance that, we bound ourselves to this, that all our battles henceforth be waged through the creatures we had made.*

Mirain's lip curled. "Ah, Father, you are cruel. Say it clearly. Say that you toy with us as a cat toys with its prey."

No. We do not.

"If you do not, what of the other? It is annihilation she craves. Why should she not break the truce and conquer?"

She does not crave annihilation. No more than do I. She would destroy what is pleasing to me and cloak the world in the night she made, and rule it, sole queen and sole goddess.

"And you?"

I would have balance. Light and dark divided, each in its proper place.

"With you as sole king and sole god."

You say it. Not I.

"Yes," Mirain said bitterly. "It is always I who say it. I love you, I cannot help it. But, Father, I am mortal and I am young, and I do not have your wisdom to see always what I must do."

Win your battle. The rest will follow in its own time.

"Win my battle," Mirain repeated. "Win it." He flung himself on his bed. "Oh, dear gods, I am afraid!"

The lamp flickered; a thin cold wind skittered about the tent and fled. Vadin found himself standing over Mirain, and he could not stop shaking, and he could not name what shook him, whether it was terror of the god who burned and blazed in him, or terror of the king who huddled and trembled on the cot. A god without face or living voice, a king with the semblance of a frightened boy. Paradoxes. Vadin was a simple man, a mountain warrior. He was not made for this.

He had walked through death into the living light. He was marked with Mirain's power, that came from the god.

He lowered himself to one knee. Mirain's trembling had eased; he had drawn into a knot, almost pitifully small. Very lightly Vadin touched his shoulder.

"Get out," he said. His voice was still and cold.

Vadin did not move. The moment stretched, counted in slow breaths. Mirain drew tighter still.

Without warning he burst outward and upward, hurling Vadin onto his back. "Get out, damn you. Get out!"

Vadin found his wind where it had fled, blinked away the sparks of shock and mild pain. "Why?" he asked reasonably.

Mirain hauled him up. The king was stronger than he had any right to be, and fully as dangerous as a startled leopard; but Vadin could not remember to be afraid, even when the strong small hands shook him like a bundle of straw. He kept his body limp and his teeth together, and waited for the storm to pass.

Mirain let him go. He swayed, steadied. "Why should I get out?" he asked again. "Because I saw you acting human for once?"

"Have I no right to my solitude?"

Vadin drew a breath. His ribs ached, from the sortie, from Mirain's violence. He considered the vivid furious face. "Do you really want to be alone?"

"I—" It was a rarity indeed: Mirain at a loss for words.
"You were in my mind."

"Wasn't I?" And whose fault was it that Vadin could be?

Mirain heard all of it, spoken and unspoken. "You had
no right," he said.

"Not even the right of a friend?"

The silence sang on a high strange note. Vadin had
spoken without thought, through the fading brilliance of
the god. Mirain had heard at first only through the crackle
of his anger. As the crackle died, his eyes widened; Vadin
felt his own do the same. His heart began to hammer. His
fists clenched into pain.

Mirain spoke softly, with great care. "Say it again, Vadin.
Say it yourself, without my father to drive you."

Vadin's throat closed. He thought of cursing the god
and all his madness. He said, "A friend. A friend, may
your own father damn you, and if you're half the mage
you claim to be you'll know I lost my wager cycles ago.
And doesn't a friend have a right to stay where he's
needed? Especially," he added grimly, "when it's a god
who's possessed him to do it."

"I need no one."

Haughty words and most unwise, and a staring lie.
Vadin did not dignify them with his notice. "Friend," he
said. And more awkwardly: "Brother. I don't think less of
you because you're afraid. Only fools and infants, and
maybe gods, have never known fear."

"Gods—gods can be afraid." Mirain pricked his temper anew, reared up his pride and made a weapon of it.
"Do you think you can do anything to help me? You who
cannot even shape the letters of your name?"

Vadin burst out laughing. Mirain in the depths of terror was still worthy of all respect, because his fear was the
valiant fear of a strong man and a mage. But that he, so
wise, should insult Vadin for what any Ianyn lord was
more proud of than not . . . "What, my lord, have I had it
all wrong? Are you going to duel with pens and tablets?
It's true I can't write a word, but I can sharpen your pen
for you; shall I fletch it too and show you how to make a
dart of it?"

Mirain's chin came up. In spite of his reckless mood Vadin knew a moment's chill, a flicker of doubt lest he had gone too far. "You mock me," the king said, still and cold again.

"Listen to me," said Vadin in a flare of temper. "You have to go out there tomorrow and fight all alone, and no one's holding out much hope for you, and maybe you'll die; and you're so scared you can hardly see, but you'll do it because you have to. Because you can't do anything else. And you'd rather be eaten by demons than let anyone guess how close your bowels are to turning to water."

"They aren't," snapped Mirain. "They already have."

Vadin paused for a heartbeat. He was not sure he dared to smile. "So of course you wanted to be alone with your shame. You can't have the world finding out that you're a man and not the hero of a song." He struck his hands together. "Idiot! How do you think you'll be by morning if you spend the night brooding and shaking and hating yourself for being afraid? Do you *want* to lose this fight?"

"Vadin," Mirain said with elaborate patience, "Vadin my reluctant brother, I know as well as anyone what chance I have against Ianon's great champion. I also know how much brooding is good for me; and I have arts that will assure my rest. If," he added acidly, "you will let me practice them."

"You're playing with the truth again." Vadin eluded a blow without much force behind it, and seized Mirain. The king stiffened, but he did not struggle. "You've got my soul, Mirain. It's yours to do whatever you like with. Even to throw away, if that's your pleasure."

"That would be a dire waste." At half an arm's length Mirain had to tilt his head well back to see Vadin's face. The king did not smile, nor did his expression soften, but his eyes were clearer and steadier than they had been in a long while. "You called me by my name."

"I'm sorry, my lord."

"Sure you are." Vadin's own way of speaking, his very tone. A thin line grew between Mirain's brows, counter to the vanishingly faint upcurve of his lips. "You'll not 'my lord' me in private again, sir. It's bad enough that I have to suffer it from everyone else."

"You should have thought of that before you got yourself born a royal heir."

"Sweet hindsight." Mirain smiled at last, if somewhat thinly. "You're good for me, I think. Like one of Ivrin Healer's more potent doses."

"Gods! Am I that bad?"

"Worse." But Mirain's mood had shifted, turning from the old black madness to something almost light. "Bitter, I would say, but bracing. Will you be my witness tomorrow?"

"Is it politic? Prince Mehtar—"

"Damn Prince Mehtar," Mirain said in a voice so mild it was alarming. He took Vadin's hands, held them in a grip the other could not break. "If I live I'll be strong enough to deal with him. If I die, it won't matter. And," he said, "I'd much rather have you under my eye than trying to creep behind."

Vadin's ears were hot. "I wouldn't—"

"Now who's telling lies?" Mirain let go Vadin's hands. He moved closer yet, catching the squire in a sudden tight embrace. "Brother, I humble myself; I admit it. I need you. Will you be my witness?"

Yes, thought Vadin, knowing Mirain would hear. A little stiffly, a little shyly, he closed the embrace. He did not know why he thought of Ledi. She was his woman. Mirain was—was—

"Brother," Mirain said. He drew back, smiling a little. "Shall I bring her to you?"

Vadin did not doubt that Mirain could do it. But his hand rose in refusal. "Thank you, no. There's no need to tire yourself working magic. I'll be well enough for a little self-denial."

Mirain shrugged slightly, as if he would disagree, but he let Vadin go. "Good night, brother," he said.

"Good night," answered Vadin. "Brother."

YMIN SAT ON THE GROUND OUTSIDE OF MIRAIN'S TENT, A grey shadow on the edge of firelight. But Vadin, coming out under the sky, saw her as easily as she saw him. Their eyes met. His, she thought, were not the eyes of a boy, still less of a simple Ianyn warrior. She had to firm her will to face them.

He bowed his head a very little. Acknowledgment, encouragement, a sudden white smile. She rose. Her heart, foolish creature, was beating hard. When she glanced back, the squire had taken her place and her post.

Mirain lay on his bed, arms behind his head, eyes upon the lamp above him. She dropped her robe and lay beside him, folded about him, head pillowed on his breast. His arms came down to circle her; he kissed the smooth parting of her hair. His pulse had quickened, but he was cool yet, unready. She lay quietly, saying nothing, thinking of little but peace.

His voice came soft and deep yet very young. "Lady-love, do you know how alarmingly beautiful you are?"

"Alarming, my dear lord?"

"Terrifying. I'm an utter coward, my lady. Everything frightens me."

"Even battle?"

"That most of all. I have no courage, only its seeming. An instinct, blind and quite mad, which drives me full upon whatever I fear most."

"I think," she said, "that that is true courage. To know what horror one faces, and to dread it, yet to confront it with no appearance of flinching."

"Then is all bravery but cowardice turned upon itself?"

"Even so." She raised her head to look into his face. "I would not call you a coward, Mirain An-Sh'Endor."

"But I am!" He bit his lip. "I am," he said again. "I am also a madman, a fool, and all the rest of it. I know it all too well. And I want to forget it. For a while. Until I have to remember."

"In Ianon," she said, "in the old time before our people turned to the ways of the west and the soft south, when the king kept vigil before battle, there was a ritual. It gave strength to the king, and through him to his kingdom; often it brought him victory."

He sat motionless, his eyes wide, full of lamplight and of her face.

She continued softly, calmly. "After the sun had set, while his army kept the night watch, the king would sit in his tent, alone or perhaps with one other who was as close to him as a brother. There he would fight his secret battle against what fears he might have, for himself, for his people. But that battle is never wisely fought if fought too long. Near to its end, another would come, not only to fight beside him but to make him forget. This one was always a woman, neither maiden nor matron but one who by her vows and her will had chosen to set herself apart from the common lot of her sex, to be a thing far greater. The holy one, the king's strength."

"And his singer?"

"That too. Sometimes."

"Then it seems," he said, "that I chose wisely on the night of my kingmaking. One woman for all I might desire." His voice roughened. "But there's no need tonight to invent titles and rituals. Only say it. Say it plainly. You think I need a woman."

"Do you not?" she asked unruffled, even though she knew it maddened him.

Maddened, he struck to wound. "What makes you think it's you I need? Maybe it's time I chose one closer to my own size. One who is not old enough to be my mother."

She laughed on her inimitable, rippling scale, with no pain in it that she would let him perceive. "Perhaps it is time and perhaps it is wise, but I am here and I am quite comfortable; and you are much too fastidious to make do with a camp follower."

He gulped air and outrage. "How dare you—" It came as a half-shriek, so utterly disgraceful that it shattered all his anger. Laughter rose to fill the void: breathless, helpless laughter that loosened all his bones and left him hiccoughing in her arms.

Her own laughter died with his, but a smile lingered; her eyes danced. "There truly was a ritual," she said.

"And I truly ... seem to ... need ... Damn you, Ymin!" He was burning under her hands. Abruptly he pulled away, leaping to his feet. "Why do you keep coming back to me? What can you gain from it? Do you do it only because it is your office—your duty? Or . . . do you . . ."

"You have beauty. It is not a common beauty; it is stronger, stranger. It sings in the blood. You have strength, the strength of youth which will ripen into splendid manhood. You have that indefinable air which is royal. And," she said, taking both his hands and drawing them to her heart, "you have that which makes me love you."

He looked down at her. His face was cold, all at once, and very still.

"I am not your life's love," she said. "I do not ask to be. But what I can give you, what I have always given you, on this night of all nights I do give."

Almost he wept. Almost he laughed. In this she had succeeded magnificently: he had forgotten all his black dread. Yet he had given her a trouble of her own, albeit one as sweet as it was painful. She kept her face serene, her smile undimmed, her thoughts bright and strong and fearless. She did not think of what they both knew. They might never lie together again.

But he was too much the mage and too much the Sunborn. He saw; he knew. She had released his hands; he lifted one to stroke her cheek. "I would not give you grief," he said very gently.

"Then give me joy."

It flowered in him for all that he could do. Even without power she sensed it. Her arms enfolded him; she drew him down.

Twenty-Four

WITH THE SUN'S SINKING, THE SHADOW ABOUT THE enemy's camp seemed to melt away. By full dark the sentries upon the hilltops could discern a camp but little different from their own, an ordered pattern of watchfires gleaming in the night.

The level between the camps was dark even for one with night-eyes, the stream whispering in its passage. Alidan crept down the bank with a hunter's caution; she was clad in her own midnight skin, her hair braided and coiled tight about her head, a dagger bound to her thigh, hilt and sheath wrapped in black to hide the gleam of metal. So she had passed Mirain's sentries, as softly as a wind in the grass.

On Ilien's edge she paused. Briefly she looked back. Mirain's tent was invisible among the rest; he slept within it, safe in his singer's arms, his Geitani squire keeping watch without. She smiled, thinking of them, and sighed a little. She wished that she had been able to say farewell to the king at least; but he would have forbidden her, and this was a thing which she must do.

Ilien sang before her. The enemy's camp stretched beyond. Still she could detect no shadow but that of the night, no hint of vigilance other than the pacing of the guards. They moved easily in armor that glinted in the scattered firelight, some accoutered in the fashion of the

Marches, some clad as knights of western Ianon. One, close to the stream, wore on his cloak the badge of the Lord Cassin.

Alidan released her breath slowly and lowered herself into the water. It was bitter cold on her bare skin. She set her teeth and glided forward, shaping her movements to the rhythm of the stream upon its stones. More than once she froze, crouching, but no eyes turned toward her.

At last she lay upon the western bank. The sentries paced oblivious. They had the air of men who kept watch out of duty, but who feared no assault.

She gathered herself muscle by muscle. Silently but swiftly she ran up the slope. A guard paused, peering; she halted. He resumed his pacing.

The fires flickered before her; the sentries passed behind. She moved with somewhat less care, but cautious still, keeping to the shadows, edging toward the pavilion that stood in the center of the camp. A standard fluttered before it: Moranden's sign of the wolf's head, wearing now a crown.

LAMPLIGHT BLAZED WITHIN, CATCHING IN THE EYES OF THE two who confronted one another. Moranden stood as if drawn taut by a hidden hand. His mother sat enthroned upon a carven chair, clad with her perennial simplicity, starker still beside the prince's splendor. But her face was calm and unwearied, and his was worn to the bone as with a long and hopeless struggle.

"I let you play, child," she said. "I let your men call you king, while they shun me and call me witch and worse. I will let you finish your game of kings and warriors with yonder upstart. But I do not intend to give him the smallest chance of victory."

"How can he win? He's half my size. I can take him apart while he's still struggling to get close."

"The Sunchild is a fool, but he is not entirely mad. He sees some advantage in the mode of battle he has chosen. Very likely that advantage will partake of sorcery."

"I'll see that he swears to use none, and you can see

that he holds to the oath. But no more. None of your poisons and none of your spells. I'll kill him in fair fight."

"No," she said, flat and final. "You will know when I—"

He bent over her. So grim was his face that even she knew a moment's apprehension. He spoke very softly, very distinctly, with every vestige of his hoarded strength. "Woman, I have had enough. You thought you had my eyes well clouded, but I know what this army has been doing to my country. *My* country, woman. Ravaging it. Destroying it. Taking your revenge on an enemy cycles dead, who never did more to you than put down your viper of a father and set you as high as any traitor's spawn could be set. And love you, in his way. That was the unforgivable sin. He never condescended to hate you."

She struck him. Her long nails left weals above his beard; he made no move to touch them, although one begot a thin stream of blood. It seemed to spring from no new wound but from the old scar beneath his eye, remembrance of another battle in this same endless war. "Yes," he said, "when words fail, you always strike; and the truth drives you mad."

"Truth!" She laughed. "What do you know of truth? You whose claim to kingship is a lie. You were never a king's son, Moranden."

He drew back a step. The bile was thick in his throat, gnawing at his words. "That is vicious slander. He was my father. He acknowledged me."

She smiled, sure now that she had won, as she always had. "That was the bargain I struck. He could have me if he would give his name to my child. He was weak and I was very beautiful. He did as I bade him."

"Lies," gritted Moranden. "Or if they are the truth . . ." His teeth bared in a dire grin. "You've made a mistake, mother whore. By your testimony I have no legal claim to the throne of Ianon. I'll give it up; I'll go now, abandon this travesty of a war, and find my fortune somewhere far and safe. I'll no longer be your puppet."

He was stronger than she had thought, and saner. She

said it; and she said, "Certainly that must prove your parentage. Sanity does not run in the royal line."

"Neither does murder, which is unfortunate for me. My father should have strangled you the day he met you."

"No father of yours."

"He was all the father you ever let me have!" Moranden drew himself up, gathering both temper and courage. "I will fight my battle in my own way. The honorable way. If you make the slightest move toward my enemy, I will kill you with my own hands." His voice lashed her with sudden force. "Now get out!"

She rose, but she did not flee. "When he has his knee upon your throat, remember what you have said to me."

"When I cast him down and set my foot on him, take care, mother mine, that I don't throw you to his dogs. And the kingdom after it—the kingdom to which you tell me I have no right."

"You have the right of the king's acknowledged son." She drew her veil over her head above the glitter of her eyes. "I will rule Ianon with you or in spite of you. Perhaps after all it is time this land knew a ruling queen."

"You still need me to dispose of the ruling king."

"No," she said, "I need you not at all. But I too am weak. I suffer your folly because you are the child of my body. Because," she said with such raw outrage that he could not help but believe her, "because I love you."

ALIDAN CROUCHED IN DEEPEST SHADOW A PALM'S WIDTH from the tent wall, hardly breathing. But her dizziness came not only from the shortness of her breath, nor even from the terror of discovery. She had stopped thinking of revenge. There was only necessity; but what was that? The traitor prince would destroy Mirain's body. The sorceress would strike at his soul. And there would be no time to smite them both.

Which?

In the dark behind her eyes, she saw her son fall. And she saw Moranden's face in the moment after Shian died. It was stiff, stunned. She heard words through the roaring in her ears. "Have we fallen to the murder of children? Guards! Take that man!"

A king did as he must. Even the murder of children. And Ilien's course was one long bleak road of the dead.

And he had cried out against it.

But he would kill Mirain.

But the woman would steal the king's will, ensorcel his soul.

If she could.

If Moranden could—

Alidan crept through darkness. One hand closed about the hilt of the long thin dagger which she had meant for Moranden's heart. To save Mirain; to save his empire that would be.

Light flared. Alidan flattened herself into shadow. A tall dark shape held up the tent flap. Light from within struck fire in the silver at her throat.

Alidan's brain reeled. Betrayal upon betrayal. Treason upon treason. Hatred—

THE FLAP FELL. YMIN STOOD IN THE TENT, FACING MOTHER and son. They were astonished. She was cool, as if she had nothing to fear. "I give you greeting," she said. They did not speak. Perhaps they could not. She smiled and sat on a cushioned stool, arranging her robe with care, folding her hands in her lap.

Moranden broke the silence abruptly. "How did you get here? What do you want with us?"

"I walked," she answered. "Perhaps I sang a word or two. I wish to speak with you."

"Why? Can't he keep you satisfied?"

She smiled, rich with remembrance. "He is the king in all respects."

"So. You're making the best of it."

"I am more than content." She considered him. "You do not look well, my lord."

"War is hard on a man."

"Yes," she said. "And rebellion is cruel, is it not? One must destroy so much that one yearns to preserve."

He stiffened at the blow. His eyes flicked to his mother, hating, pleading. She watched without a word. Her startlement had given way to something less easily read; but it was not dismay. Not at all. Almost she might have been smiling.

She looked like Ymin. Serene, superior, secure in the certainty that the world was hers to shape as she willed.

Ymin met her gaze. "You know that if your son fails, you have no hope."

"My son will not fail."

"That is no child whom he faces. It is the son of a god. He is stronger by far than he seems; he is the fated king."

"My son shall be king in Ianon."

"So he may be," said Ymin. She turned back to Moranden. "So you can be. Do you think that Mirain will linger here? This is only his beginning. And when he rides to take his full inheritance, Ianon will need a man to rule her. What better man than his own kinsman?"

"His dear kinsman." Moranden bared his teeth. "I'm no sage and I'm no god's get, but I'm not an utter idiot. I know how much love I can expect from Mirain the priestess' bastard. He'd see me dead before he'd let me near his throne."

"Would he? You have begun all amiss, I grant you, but he has grown since he took the kingship. He can forgive you, if you will allow him. He can give you all you ever longed for."

Moranden's face contorted with sudden passion. He flung his hand toward his mother. "Even her head on a pike?"

"Even that," said Ymin steadily.

Odiya laughed, free and startlingly sweet. "Why, this is better than a troupe of mountebanks! Singer, have you lost your wits? Or is it merely the madness of desperation? Your lover has no hope in combat, you know as well as we. But you will not buy his life with empty promises."

"They are not empty," Ymin said.

Odiya merely smiled.

Ymin rose. She raised her chin; she pitched her voice to throb in Moranden's heart. "You are no fool, my lord; no woman's plaything. And yet your mother rules you. Without you she is nothing. Without her you are a man of strength and wisdom. Cast off your shackles. See the truth. Know that you can be king, if only you have patience."

He wavered. She tempted him. She lured him with a vision of splendors that would be. Freedom, joy, a throne at last. And no Odiya to make his life a misery.

He shook himself heavily, hands to head, breathing rough and hard. "No." His fingers clawed. He tore them away. The pain was less than the marks of his mother's hand, than the burning cold of her stare. "No. Too late. It was too late the day my father named Sanelin Amalin his heir. This is only the last movement of the long dance. I must finish it. I will be king."

"My lord," Ymin began.

"Madam," said Odiya, "the king has spoken."

"He has sealed his destruction." But Ymin's strength had faded into mere defiance. She was trapped here; her back knew that guards waited beyond the tent, armed and braced to take her. Moranden might have let her go. Odiya would never surrender so precious a captive. She glanced about, swift, desperate. She drew breath, mustering what magery she had, focusing it in her voice.

"Spare yourself," said Odiya. She spoke a Word. Ymin was mute, without even will to struggle. Odiya took her slack hand. "Come, child."

Ymin could not speak, nor could she resist, but she could smile. It was not the smile of one who had surrendered, nor was there any fear in it, although she saw her death in Odiya's eyes. She met them levelly. She made them fall. Her smile grew and steadied.

ALIDAN DREW HERSELF TOGETHER. HORROR, HAVING DARK-ened her mind, now swept it clear. She knew what she would do, and what she must. Captor and captive emerged from the tent. In their moment of blindness between light and night, Alidan sprang.

Demons and serpents, a body too sinuous-strong to be human, a gleam of deadly eyes. The knife pierced flesh, caught on bone, tore free. Breath broke off sharp in Alidan's ear. Iron fingers wrenched the hilt from her hand and locked about her throat. Too many fingers, too many hands beating her back and down. Firelight blinded her.

"By the gods!" a man burst out. "A woman."

"Ho there! The queen's hurt. Quick, you, fetch a blood-stancher!"

"Enough!" rapped the voice Alidan knew too well now, too strong by far for a woman sorely wounded. "She has but scratched me. Move back; let me see her."

The circle of shadows widened and fell away, but their eyes lingered on Alidan like burning hands. She thought of covering her nakedness; she thought of laughing, and she thought of weeping. She had failed. She had slain herself for nothing, not even for a savorless vengeance. They would die together, she and the mute motionless singer.

A new shadow loomed over her. A suggestion of great beauty, an aura of great terror, a tang of blood. "Goddess," whispered Alidan. "Goddess-bearer."

"Who are you?" The words boomed in her mind.

"Woman." She smiled. "Only woman."

"Who?" pressed the queen who was not. "Who are you?"

"Lost." Alidan's smile faded. The sorceress bent low, eyes armed to cleave her soul. The goddess dwelt in them, all dark. "But," protested Alidan, "she is not—she is not all—" No use; the sorceress could not know, would not. No more than she would know who, or why, or whence. There was blood bright and lurid upon her black gown, pain in the set of her face, wrath and power in her eyes. Great wrath, for with blood she lost strength, with strength the power to work her sorceries. Yet her power was great enough still to deal with this frail madwoman; and it promised torment.

Terror gibbered on the edges of Alidan's mind. Madness coiled at the center. Ymin's eyes burned between.

Words flamed in them. *Run. Run now.* Wise fool. There was no escape for either of them.

The singer stumbled. Her body lurched against Odiya's, striking the wounded side. The woman reeled, blind with pain. Ymin's eyes, Alidan's feet, met and clashed and chose. Alidan bolted into the night.

AS THE STARS WHEELED TOWARD MIDNIGHT, VADIN EASED himself into Mirain's tent. Ymin was gone. Mirain lay alone, sprawled like a child, smiling faintly in his sleep. Vadin settled beside him. It was not a thing of conscious thought. Mirain was warm and sated, fitting himself into the hollows of Vadin's body, sighing even deeper into sleep. But Vadin woke nightlong, guarding his dreams.

Mirain passed without transition from sleep into waking. One moment he was deep asleep; the next, he met Vadin's stare and smiled. That was unwonted enough to freeze Vadin where he lay. The king looked bright and clear-witted and almost happy, freed for once from his morning temper. Today, his eyes said, might be his death day; it might mark the first great victory of his kingship. Whatever the end, now that he came to it, he welcomed it.

Although it was barely dawn, most of the camp was up and about. None of them seemed to have had any more sleep than Vadin had. And all of them, soldiers, squires, lords and captains, were grim-faced, hollow-eyed, as if they and not Mirain would be dead by evening.

He was light and calm. He ate with good appetite; he smiled, he jested, he wrung laughter from them all. But it died as soon as he turned away.

Nuran and Kav took him in hand, bathed him and shaved him, plaited his hair and bound it about his head. While they were occupied, someone hissed from the door. Adjan caught Vadin's eye. The arms master's face was set in stone. Moving without haste but without tarrying, Vadin emerged into the cold dawn. "What—"

He stopped. Adjan supported a second figure, one to which, even cloaked and staggering, Vadin could set a name. "Alidan!" It was all he could do to keep his voice low. She was naked under the mantle, her hair straggling, matted with mud and blood. But her eyes were the worst of it. They were quiet, they were sane, and they had lost all hope.

He tried to be gentle. "Alidan, what's happened?"

"I left my mark on the western witch," she answered him, soft and calm. "She will have no power to betray my king."

Vadin's anxiety went cold. He could not even take refuge in incomprehension. He was too far gone in mage-craft. He knew what she was saying; he had begun to suspect what she had left unsaid. She rejoiced in what she had done: black treachery, betrayal of all honor, and perhaps the one hope of Mirain's salvation. But her joy was turned all to darkness.

Adjan said it, short and brutal. "They have the singer. If she's lucky, they'll have killed her quickly."

Vadin's feet carried him toward the ashes of the fire. He stood over them. There was no life left in them.

Adjan and Alidan were warm and painful presences at his back. His stomach wanted to empty itself. He exerted his will upon it; with dragging reluctance it yielded. "Why?" he demanded of Alidan. "Why did you do it?"

The woman closed her eyes. It was too dark to see her face; her shape in the gloom was stiff, her voice level. "We were not together. I was going to rid us of the rebel. I wounded his mother instead. The singer was going to persuade him to surrender. His mother overcame her. She was mad," said Alidan who for revenge had walked naked into the enemy's camp and blooded her blade in a witch's body. "She trusted in her singer's power, and in a few nights' loving long ago. He was her daughter's father, did you know that? He never did. Now he never will."

"Damn her," whispered Vadin. "Of all the people in Ianon—she knew what it would do to Mirain. She knew!"

"If she had succeeded—" Alidan began.

"If she had succeeded, she would have shamed him beyond retrieving: she would have proven that even his lover had no hope for his victory."

"It would have prevented bloodshed, and won him a mighty ally."

Vadin tossed his aching head. Women's logic. Damn honor, damn glory, damn manhood—nothing mattered but the winning. He flung up his fists. Alidan did not flinch. She said, "It was a sacrifice. Now the woman of Umijan must die. Now the old king shall be avenged. You speak of shame; what do you call my lord's folly in suffering his assassin to walk free?"

"She may not only walk free. She may rule us." Vadin knotted his hands behind his back, lest he strike the madwoman down. "Get out of sight and stay out of sight. I'll keep this from Mirain for as long as I can." He groaned aloud. *"Gods!* She was supposed to be one of his judges. Adjan, can we rescue her before the sun comes?"

"No." Adjan was quieter than Vadin, and much more deadly. "There's a solid wall of sentries around the camp. They let one woman go; they're keeping the other. She's their best weapon, and they know it."

"It may turn in their hands." Obri the chronicler stood at Vadin's elbow as if he had always been there, no more perturbed than ever by Ianyn size or Ianyn temper. "May I offer a thought?" Vadin snarled at him; he took it for assent. "The king has prepared his mind, no? It is all on the battle before him. Let it stay so. I will go in the judge's cloak, if someone will cut it in half for me." His teeth gleamed as he smiled. "After all, I need to see it to write of it. The singer is indisposed. Poor lady, she loves too much. She has broken, her friend is with her, they will not weaken the king's courage with their tears."

"Mirain will never believe it," Vadin said. "Another woman, maybe. Not Ymin. She's royal born; her heart is Ianyn iron."

"But," Obri persisted, "the king was born in the south, where both men and women are gentler. While he has the battle to think of, he will have less leisure for questions; I will see that he asks none." And when Vadin would not soften: "Trust me, young lord. I was hoodwinking princes when your father was in swaddling bands."

"What in all the hells are—" But Vadin was conquered.

Obri grinned, bowed his mocking bow, and melted into the night. In his wake he left a flicker of amusement, and an image of an infant wrapped from head to foot like a spider's prey. Vadin shuddered. "Go on," he snapped to Alidan. "Vanish. And you, Captain: stay as far from the king as you can. And pray that we carry it off, or we're all done for."

They obeyed him. He was rather surprised. He paused, steeling himself, and went to face Mirain.

He seemed not even to have noticed Vadin's absence. His squires were arranging the last fold of his scarlet cloak. Almost before they were done, he turned with that unmistakable grace of his, and paused. His armor lay all in its place, cleaned and burnished. He ran his finger along the edge of his shield, toyed for a moment with his helmet's scarlet plume.

Abruptly he turned away. They watched him, all of them. He lifted his chin and smiled at them, bright and strong. They parted to let him pass.

UPON THE EASTERNMOST HILL OF THE CAMP AN ALTAR HAD risen in the night: a hewn stone banked with earth and green turf. The sacred fire burned upon it, warded by the priests of the army, Avaryan's warriors armed and mantled in Sun-gold. Already before Mirain came to them they had begun the Rite of Battle. Ancient, half-pagan, its rhythms throbbed in the blood: blood and iron, earth and fire, interwoven with drums and the high eerie wailing of pipes. They set Mirain upon their altar, anointed him with earth and blood, hedged him with iron tempered in the god's fire.

Standing there on the height, with the rite weaving above him and his mind struggling to weave itself into Mirain's, Vadin gazed through the other's eyes across the dawn-dim hills. The enemy's fires flickered, growing pale as Avaryan drew nearer, but in the center near the great scarlet pavilion of the commander a torrent of flame roared up to heaven. Men massed about it. Nearest to it a lone shape, encircled by cowled figures, moved in what looked to be a strange wild dance. It was terrible to see,

black patched with scarlet, and its movements were jerky,
a parody of grace, like the dance of a cripple. Vadin did
not know it. Would not know it. Prayed with all his soul
that it was not what he feared.

Even as he watched, the flames leaped higher still. The
dancer whirled; music shrilled, high and maddening. The
fire writhed like hands clawing at the sky: hands of flame,
blood red, wine red, the black-red of flesh flayed from
bone. They reached. They enfolded the dancer. They
drew it keening into the fire's heart.

Sun's fire seared his face. Mirain's face. The priest
lowered the vessel of the sacred fire and turned the king
eastward toward the waxing flame of Avaryan. Mirain
raised his hands to it. The words of the rite flowed over
him and through him, and mingled there, shaping into a
single soul-deep cry of welcome, of panic-pleading, and at
the last, of acceptance.

"So be it," sang the priest. And in Mirain's heart, and in
Vadin's caught willy-nilly within: *So be it.*

BY THE LAW OF BATTLE THE CHAMPION MUST RIDE ALONE
to the place of combat, accompanied only by his judge
and his witness. They rode at Mirain's back, Obri's brown
robe and Vadin's lordly finery hidden beneath mantles of
white and ocher. White for victory, ocher for death. In
one hand Obri bore the staff of his office: a plain wooden
rod tipped at one end with ivory, at the other with amber.

They did not speak. Obri had been as good as his word.
Mirain accepted the chronicler's presence; he was not
fretting over the absence of his singer. All his mind fixed
firmly upon the battle before him.

The army had taken its ranks behind them, the foremost
marking the edge of the camp: near enough to see, too
far to help. The space between grew wider with each
stride, the sky brighter, the enemy closer.

Moranden's lines were free still of shadow or of illusion, as if the sorcery had failed or been abandoned. But
his following was very large for all that, the full strength
of western Ianon and the Marches. If Mirain had had a

second army, he could have overrun their lands behind them.

If he won this battle, he would rule them all unchallenged.

A small company left the ranks, approaching Ilien from the west. Vadin urged Rami forward between Mirain and the river, although what he could do without even a dagger, he did not know. Die again for Mirain, he supposed.

But he saw no weapons among the riders. The herald rode first, mantled in white and ocher, carrying the judge's wand. Directly behind him came Moranden on his black-barred stallion, riding straight and proud, cloaked as was Mirain in the scarlet of the king at war. And at Moranden's back rode his second witness, the Lady Odiya unmistakable even huddled and shrunken behind a swathing of veils; and her ancient eunuch leading a laden senel.

Vadin and the herald reached the water together, but neither ventured into it. "What is this?" Vadin called across the rush of Ilien. "Why do so many come to the field of combat?"

"We come who must," responded the herald, "and we bring your king what he appears to have mislaid."

The eunuch rode forward, dragging the reluctant packbeast down the bank and across the stream. Vadin knew the shape of the black-wrapped burden: long and narrow, stiff yet supple, with the shadow of death upon it. But he was like a man in a dream. He could do nothing but what he did: give the rider space to come up but none to approach Mirain, and wait for what inevitably must come. Without word or glance the eunuch tossed the leadrein into Vadin's hand, turned, spurred back toward his mistress.

Very slowly Vadin slid from Rami's saddle. He had not planned for this. He had not been thinking at all since he woke. He knew only that Mirain must not see. He had to fight. He could not be grieving for his lover. Or raging for the loss of her.

For a wild instant Vadin knew that he must bolt, he and this silent dead thing. Bolt far away and bury it deep, and Mirain would never know.

Someone moved past him, someone in royal scarlet, small enough to slip under his arm, swift enough to elude his snatching hand. Mirain reached for the bindings. Vadin tried again and desperately to pull him back. He was as immovable as a stone, his face set in stone. The cords gave way all at once, tumbling their contents into Mirain's arms.

She had not died easily, or prettily, or swiftly. Vadin knew. He had seen her die, driven into the goddess' fire. It had left only enough of her body that one could tell her sex, and one could tell that she had suffered before she died, beaten and flayed and perhaps worse still. But neither fire nor torturers had touched her face, save only her eyes. Beneath that twofold ruin her features were serene, free of either horror or pain.

"How she must have maddened them," Mirain said, "dying in peace in spite of them." His voice was mad, because it was so perfectly sane. Calm. Unmoved. He lowered her with all gentleness, drawing the black wrappings over her, as if she could wake and know pain. His hand lingered on her cheek. Vadin could not read his face; his mind was a fortress. Vadin's strongest assault could not break down its gate.

The herald's voice rang over the water. "So do we recompense all spies and assassins. Think well upon it, O king who would send a woman to slay his enemy. You see that she failed. You shall not escape this duel of honor."

Mirain stooped as if he had not heard, and kissed Ymin upon the lips. He said nothing to her that anyone could hear. He straightened, turned. Although he spoke softly, they heard him as if he had shouted every word. "You were not wise to do this, my lady Odiya. For even if I could forgive you the murder of my singer, you have shown Ianon once more what you would do to it and to its people. Ianon may endure your son hereafter, but you have lost all claim to its mercy."

She answered him with deadly quiet. Wounded though her body was, her voice was strong. "You are not the prophet your mother purported to be, nor the king you like to pretend. You are not even a lover. So much she confessed while still she had tongue to speak."

Mirain raised his head. He laughed, and it was terrible to hear, for even as he mocked her, he wept. "You are a poor liar, O servant of the Lie. I see your shame; I taste your thwarted wrath. She would not break. She died as she had lived, strong and valiant." His voice deepened. It had beauty still, but all its velvet had worn away. Iron lay beneath: iron and adamant. "I swear to you and to all the gods, she will have her vengeance."

Odiya would not be cowed. There was death between them; it bore witness to her power. It laid bare the truth: that he could not protect even where he loved. She met his mockery with bitter mockery. "Will you come to battle now, Mirain who had no father? Dare you?"

"I dare, O queen of vipers. And when I have done with your puppet, look well to yourself."

He turned the fire of his hand toward Obri. The chronicler urged his grey mare shying past the pool of black and scarlet, cloak and blood, into the swift bright water, halting in the center. "Here is the midpoint between our forces." He spoke evenly, with more strength than anyone might have believed possible, small and withered as he was. "But since no custom dictates that the champions engage in the midst of a river, and since the choice of ground rests with the challenger, let him choose where he will fight."

"My lord," answered the herald, "bids you engage upon the western bank."

"So shall we do," said Obri, riding forward.

Together with the herald in a barbed amity of duty, Obri dismounted and marked with his rod upon the ground the half of a circle: twenty paces from edge to edge, joined at its twin extremities to the half-circle of the other. When the battleground was made they left it. Moranden prepared to dismount; the herald took his bridle. Vadin stood at the Mad One's head.

Mirain sprang down lightly. His head did not even come to Vadin's shoulder. The squire's eyes pricked with tears; he blinked them away. By the gods' fortune Mirain had not seen. Eyes and mind bent upon the fastening of his cloak. Firmly, almost roughly, Vadin set his hands aside and loosed the clasp. Mirain smiled a very little. Vadin flung the cloak over the stallion's saddle; Mirain unwrapped his kilt, setting it atop the sweep of scarlet, running a hand down the Mad One's neck.

Moranden waited within the circle, arms folded. But Mirain paused. He caught Obri in a swift embrace, startling the scholar for once into speechlessness. And he reached for Vadin before the squire could escape, pulled his head down with effortless strength, and kissed him on the lips. The king's touch was like the lightning, swift and potent and burning-fierce.

Vadin drew a sharp and hurting breath. "Mirain," he said. "Mirain, try to hold on to your temper. You know what happens when you lose it."

"Be at ease, brother," Mirain said, light and calm: a royal calm. "I will mourn her when it is time to mourn. But now I have a battle to fight." He smiled his sudden smile, with a touch of wryness, a touch of something very like comfort. "May the god keep you," he said to them both.

He stepped into the circle. The herald stood in its center with rod uplifted. Obri raised his own rod and strode forward.

"Hold!"

Obri stopped.

Odiya would not enter the circle, but she stood at the witness' post on the western edge, leaning on her eunuch's shoulder. "One matter," she said, clear and cold, "is not yet settled. Yonder stands no simple warrior but a priest of demon Avaryan, mage-trained by masters. Shall he be left free to wield his power against one who cannot match it?"

"I will not," Mirain said with equal clarity, equal coldness.

"Swear," she commanded.

He raised his branded hand. For all her pride and power, she flinched. A small grim smile touched his mouth. He took off his torque and laid the golden weight of it in Vadin's unwilling hands, standing a little straighter for its passing, saying levelly, "I swear by the hand of my father, whose image I bear, whose torque I lay aside in token of my oath: This battle shall be a battle of bodies alone, without magecraft or deceit. Swear now in your turn, priestess of the goddess, mage-trained by masters. Swear as I have sworn."

"What need?" she countered haughtily. "It is not I whom you must fight."

"Swear." Moranden's voice, his face implacable. "Swear, my lady mother, or leave this field. Bound and gagged and sealed with my enemy's sorceries."

"Has he such strength?" *Have you?* her eyes demanded. But she yielded with all appearance of submission. She swore the solemn oath, lowering herself to the earth that was the breast of the goddess. "And may she cast me into her nethermost hell if I break this oath which I have sworn."

Before her servant had helped her to her feet, they had forgotten her. The judges stood back to back, each facing the other's champion, waiting. With infinite slowness Avaryan climbed above the eastern margin of the world. At last he poised upon the hills, his great disk swollen, the color of blood. As one, the rods swept down.

Twenty-Five

THE JUDGES WITHDREW FROM THE CENTER OF THE CIR-
cle to its edge; the champions advanced from edge to
center. From both armies a shout went up. That of
the west held a note of triumph; that of the east, of defiance.
For Moranden stood as tall as the mountains of his birth,
massive yet graceful, with a glitter of gold in his hair and
in the braids of his beard. Mirain beside him was no
larger than a child, slight and smooth-skinned, with weight
and inches yet to gain; and he would never equal his
enemy in either. And he had sacrificed his one advantage:
the sword and armor of his power. He had not even his
torque to defend his throat.

Vadin had slid from the verge of tears to the verge of
howling aloud. There was Mirain staring at his adversary
like a small cornered animal, but managing the shadow of
a smile. There was Moranden staring back and forbearing
to sneer. And yet how alike they were; how damnably
alike, two kinsmen matched in their pride, bristling and
baring their teeth and granting one another no quarter.
And for what? A word and a name and a piece of carven
wood.

They were slow to move, as if this battle must be one of
eyes alone. But after a while that stretched long and long,
Mirain said, "Greetings again at last, my uncle."

Moranden looked him up and down as he had on the

first day of Mirain's coming. If he knew any regret, he did not betray it. "Are you ready to die, boy?"

Mirain shrugged slightly. "I'm not afraid of it." His head tilted. "And you?"

"I'm not the one who'll fall here. Won't you reconsider, child? Take what I offered you once. Go back to your southlands and leave me what is mine."

"Bargains?" asked Mirain, amused. "Well then, let me cast my own counters into the cup. Recant and surrender your army. Swear fealty to me as your king. And when the time comes, if you prove yourself worthy, you will be king after all. King in Ianon as you always longed to be, subject only to me as emperor."

"There's the rub," Moranden said. "Under you. How have you managed on the throne of the mountain kings? Do you perch yourself on cushions like a child allowed to sit at table? With a footstool, of course, to keep your feet from dangling. I trust no one dares to laugh."

"Oh, no," said Mirain. "No one laughs at me."

As they spoke they crouched, circling slowly. Mirain wore a small tight smile. Moranden wore no expression at all. He was light on his feet for a big man, and fast; when he struck, he struck with the suddenness of a snake.

Mirain escaped the stroke, but only just. His smile slipped, shifted. Barred from Mirain's mind by the oath which the king had sworn—and dear gods, after all this time and in spite of all his resistance it had become second nature, so that its loss was cruel to endure—still Vadin could read Mirain's face and eyes and body as easily as that young scholar-king could read a book. His mind had narrowed and focused, doubt and grief and terror blurred into distance. There was no fear in him, only fierceness and the beginnings of delight. He was strong and he was swift, and ah, how he loved a battle.

Mirain poised, waiting. Moranden's hand came round: a long, lazy, contemptuous blow, as a man will cuff his hound. Mirain eluded it with a flicker of laughter.

He won no smile in return but a grin like a snarl. "Aha! They pit me against a dancing boy. Dance for me now, little priest. Awe me with your art."

"Better yet, uncle, let us dance together." Mirain moved close, tantalizing; and when Moranden made no move to strike or seize, closer still, deathly close, as if his daring had overwhelmed his prudence.

Moranden struck.

Mirain stood just out of his reach, hand on hip. "Adjan is faster than you," he said.

"Adjan stoops to dance with slaves and children. You can run, priestess' bastard. Can you fight?"

"If you like," said Mirain with the air of a king granting his vassal a favor.

Moranden straightened from his wrestler's crouch and stepped back. Mirain waited. The prince flexed his wide shoulders, filled his lungs, emptied them. Easily, fluidly, he settled into a stance that made Obri, close by Vadin, catch his breath. Vadin saw only that it was lethally graceful, like a cat before it springs. It had a look of—

"The gentle killing," Obri said. He was losing the coolness he was so proud of, the detachment of the scholar. He was like everyone but Moranden and the witch of Umijan. He had fallen in love with Mirain. "The rebel has it. Of course he has it. He is a Marcher and a westerner."

Mirain neither wavered nor retreated. If he saw that he faced a master of his own art, he was too much the warrior to show it. His body shifted toward its center and steadied, taking the posture of his defense.

"*Issan-ulin,*" Obri murmured. "The Serpent-slayer. Pray your gods, Vadin alVadin, that the tale your lord told Adjan was more than a vaunt. Pray your gods that it can save him."

Vadin's prayer was wordless, nor had he eye or mind for naming the movements of this subtle dance, but his will matched the foreigner's. Let Mirain be wise, let him be strong. Let him put up a good fight before he died.

Moranden stalked his prey in silence the more deadly for all his words before; Mirain watched him as the *issan-ulin* watches the serpent, both fierce and wary, striking no blow.

Moranden's hand lashed out and round; his foot followed it in a smooth concerted motion, as graceful as it was deadly. Mirain caught the hand upon his forearm, deflected it, swayed beneath and away from the striking foot.

There was a measured and measuring pause. Moranden feinted. Mirain slid away.

Moranden sprang. Mirain grasped his shoulder, then his surging thigh, and guided them up, back, headlong to the ground, whipping about even as Moranden left his hands.

The prince had spun in the air, coming to earth on one knee, bounding erect. Even as Mirain turned, Moranden seized him. One arm caught his middle in a grip of iron. One hand clamped upon his throat. Moranden laughed, little more than a gasp, and raised him higher, the better to break his body.

Mirain writhed, kicking, mouth gaping for air, eyes wide and blind. With all his failing strength, he drove his head into Moranden's jaw.

Moranden staggered. Mirain dropped. For a long count of breaths he lay utterly helpless.

His enemy loomed above him, foot raised and pointed for a bitter blow. Mirain snatched wildly at it. Held. Thrust it upward. Moranden went down like a mountain falling.

Mirain set his knee upon his kinsman's chest and closed his hands about the heavy neck, setting his thumbs over the windpipe. Moranden made no effort to cast him off. "Uncle," Mirain said, his voice a croak, coming hard from his bruised throat, "yield and I will pardon you."

Moranden's eyes opened wide. Mirain met them. He gasped and froze like a man under a spell, or like a boy who cannot make his kill. Vadin wanted to howl Ymin's name. But his throat had locked, and Mirain was lost. With a faint wordless protest, he hurled himself away.

His body struck the ground. Moranden's full weight plunged down upon it. Desperately Mirain scrambled sidewise. A hammer-blow smote him, driving his arm and shoulder deep into the yielding earth, wringing from him a short sharp cry. Moranden's hands tore cruelly at his hair, freeing the braid from its coil, twisting it,

dragging him to his feet. He looked into Moranden's face.
With brutal strength the prince wrenched his head back.

Mirain stood as one who waits to die. His left arm hung
useless; his body shook with tremors. He smiled.

Moranden thrust him away. He staggered and fell. Yet
he rose, although he bled from the stones that had stabbed
his cheek, although at first he could not stand. With
excruciating slowness he raised himself to his knees. More
slowly still, he stood. His lips were grey with pain.

Moranden watched him from a few strides' distance,
arms folded, lip curled. For yet a while longer he would
toy with his prey. Tease it; torment it; teach it all the
myriad degrees of pain. Then—only then—he would slay
it.

Mirain's head came up. His eyes glittered. He seemed
to grow, to swell with newborn strength. He raised his
hands, the left but little less easily than the right, and
glided forward. *Issan-ulin* once more, but *issan-ulin* pricked
to fury, closing in upon the Lord of Serpents.

Moranden's contempt wavered.

"Yes," Mirain said softly. "Yes, uncle. The game is past.
Now the battle begins in earnest."

Moranden spat at him. "Fool and braggart! God's son
or very god, you stand in a body reckoned puny even in
the south that bred you; and you have given up your
magic. You can do no more than your flesh allows. And
I," he said, spreading his arms wide, "am the Champion
of Ianon."

"Are you indeed?" Mirain beckoned. "Come, O champion. Conquer me."

Once and once again they circled. As smoothly as dancers in a king's hall, they closed. Moranden was strong, but
Mirain was swift to strike, swift to spring away. Moranden's
blow swung wide as he reeled.

Mirain struck again. Moranden staggered, flailing. One
fist brushed Mirain's brow, rocking but not felling him.
"Uncle, uncle," he chided, "where is your strength?"

Moranden hissed and began to sway, serpent-supple. It
was beautiful, it was horrible, to see that great-muscled

body turned suddenly boneless. The lips drew back; the eyes glittered, flat and cold. Death coiled within them.

For a bare instant Mirain faltered. His face twisted, as if all his hurts had burst free at once from their bonds. Moranden lashed out.

Mirain parried. Moranden advanced, hands a deadly blur, feet flying. This too had its name in the west: the Direwolf. Moranden was the great wolf-chieftain, Mirain the tender prey, fleeing round the circle of battle past the silent judges, the silent and helpless witnesses. Moranden passed his mother, who had let her veil fall. Her face was grey and old, furrowed deep with the pain of her wound. She smiled. He did not or would not see her. Full before her, Mirain turned at bay; the combatants closed, grappling near the circle's edge, almost upon it.

Metal flashed in Odiya's hand. She held that weapon which had dogged them all from Umijan: the black dagger of the goddess. It licked toward the struggling figures, hesitated. They were twined like lovers, flesh woven with flesh, no clear target for the blade. And the herald watched, making no move to prevent her.

"Foul!" cried Vadin. "Treason! Stop her!" He flung himself forward.

The dagger sang to its zenith. And fell. No will and no hand guided it. Odiya's eyes were very wide, very surprised, and very, very angry. Her eunuch stood beside her, still bearing her up with a hand on her arm. In his other hand, a blade ran red. "Treason indeed," he said with perfect calm, in part to Vadin, in part to her. "It is time the world was free of it."

Her lips drew back from her teeth. Her hands came up. Black fire filled them. She spoke a word; the fire leaped forth, caught the withered body, transfixed it. But the eunuch laughed. "See, mistress! I win the cast; revenge is mine. Do you not even know that you are dead?"

The fire leaped for his open mouth. Voice and laughter died. But even as he fell, Odiya convulsed. She reared up, and her face was the face of death, her power bleeding like black blood from her hands, hopeless, helpless, unstoppable. She clawed at the blind, uncaring sky. She raged at it. She cursed it and its deadly sun and the goddess whose realm lay beneath it. Her power poured away. The poison filled her body. Her life flamed and flared, guttered, rallied, and went out.

The eunuch was dead when he struck the ground. But Odiya was dead before she began to fall.

Mirain and Moranden were up, apart, staring appalled. Vadin, coming too late, dared the black mist of sorcery which hung even yet over the dead; he knelt beside them and closed the staring eyes of slayer and slain, each of whom was both. The woman's face raged even in death. The eunuch smiled with terrible sweetness.

Moranden stooped over them. One eye was swelling shut, but he bore no other wound. "Beautiful, treacherous bitch." He spat upon her, and he bent to kiss her brow. With a strangled roar he whirled.

Mirain, the madman, held out his hands. "Uncle." He might never have been wounded, never have come within a breath of dying with the goddess' blade in his back. "Uncle, it's over. The one who would have besmirched our honor is dead. Come. Swear peace. Rule with me."

Moranden's head sank between his shoulders. His fists clenched and unclenched. A shudder racked him; he nearly fell.

"Uncle," Mirain said, "it was she who drove you, she who made a bitter pawn of you. You yourself, you alone, I can forgive. Will you not share this kingdom with me?"

"Share! *Forgive!*" It was hardly human, that voice. Less human still was the laughter that came behind it. "I hated her, little bastard. I hated her and I loved her, and because of you she is dead. What have you left me but revenge?"

Moranden leaped. He took Mirain off guard. But not wholly. His assault drove the king back but not down. And Mirain, having offered peace at the utmost extremity, having shown Moranden the forbearance of a very saint, now had no mercy left. He had fought with passion and even with anger, in a red heat of battle. Now he advanced in white-cold rage.

Moranden looked into the other's eyes and saw his

death waiting there, as Mirain's waited in his own. He laughed at the paradox of it and made a hammer of his fist. Mirain caught it, set his weight against it, swung all that massive body about. Unbalancing it; wrenching the captive arm up and back. Moranden howled and flailed left-handed. Mirain rocked with the blows; his lip split and bled. He tightened his grip. His jaw set beneath dirt and blood. He twisted.

The bone snapped. Moranden bellowed like a bull. The force of his struggle flung Mirain's light weight away. But his arm was still prisoner, his pain a white agony. He hurled himself through it; his good hand clawed, raking breast and face, groping for eyes. He found the thick hair working free of its plait. With a snarl of triumph he wound his fingers into it.

Mirain let go the useless wrist. His face was a terrible thing, stretched out of all humanity by the grip on his hair, the bones thrusting fierce and sharp through the skin. Suddenly he went limp. Moranden loosened his hold a fraction, shifting to peer into the slack face. Two hands joined shot upward, smote his jaw with an audible crack. His head snapped back. His body arched.

Once more Mirain bestrode his chest. He struggled beneath as a fish struggles when hurled from water into the deadly air, and as vainly, and as mindlessly.

Mirain's cheeks were wet with more than blood, his breath sobbing with more than pain. Again he raised the club of his knotted hands. With all his strength he brought it down, full between the eyes.

There was a long silence. Ages long. Mirain stumbled up, away from the body that had stilled at last. His hands hung limp at his sides. His hair straggled about his face. He was crying like a child.

Vadin damned the circle, damned the Law of Battle. He crossed the line and reached for the trembling shoulders.

Mirain wheeled, poised to kill. But his strength was gone. He wavered; his hands dropped. Sanity dawned in his eyes. "Vadin?" He could hardly speak. "Vadin, I—"

"It's all right," Vadin said, rough with the effort of

keeping back his own tears. "It's all right. You're alive. You've won."

Mirain's head tossed from side to side. Vadin laid an arm about his shoulders, pulling him close, stroking away the dirt and blood and tears with a corner of the parti-colored cloak. Mirain neither resisted nor acknowledged his squire's ministrations. "I killed him. I didn't—I wanted—I killed him. Vadin, I killed him!"

His voice was shrill. Vadin nerved himself, and hit him.

Mirain gasped. His head rose. He opened his eyes to the sky, to Avaryan clear and strong and unsullied in a field of cloudless blue. "I killed him." But now he said it calmly, with sane and seemly grief. "He must go to his pyre with all honor. So must they all. Even—even she. She was my bitter enemy; she slew my grandfather, she destroyed my beloved, she would have shattered my king-dom. But she was a great queen."

Vadin could not speak. He was no godborn king. He had no power to forgive what was beyond forgiving.

Mirain's head bowed, raised again. He straightened. Vadin let him go. He faced his judges, standing erect and royal although the tears ran unchecked down his face. "Do your office," he commanded.

They woke as from a trance. The herald turned toward the west with his rod uplifted, its tip of amber catching the bitter light. But Obri faced the east, and ivory glowed with his own springing joy, proclaiming Mirain's victory.

They turned back to Mirain. Obri knelt and kissed his hand: homage as rare as it was heartfelt. Mirain found a smile for him, although it did not live long.

The herald stood stiff, fist clenched grey-knuckled upon his rod. Half of his anger was fear, and an awe for which he despised himself. He forced words through his clenched teeth. "You have won. You must put me to death. It is the law. I knew of the weapon which my lady turned against you."

Vadin could have struck the creature. Could he not see how utterly exhausted Mirain was? The king had spent all his strength; he had none left even for joy in his triumph. And he had so much yet to do. Ten thousand men wavered on the brink of battle, their commanders reeling still with the shock of Moranden's defeat. Only that, and the herald's stillness, held them back from a charge.

Mirain regarded the herald with eyes in which the god's fire burned ashen low. "You and all your people are bound to me now until death or I shall free you. That is a penalty more fitting than swift death, and perhaps more terrible."

For a long moment the herald did not stir. Then he bent down and down, even to the ground. His voice boomed forth as if from the earth itself. "Hail, Mirain, king in Ianon!"

Mirain's own men echoed him, clashing spear upon shield, shaking the sky with their jubilation.

The west was silent. Ominously silent.

Somewhere amid the ranks a great voice rang out. "Mirain!" Another joined it. Another. Another. Five, ten, a hundred, a thousand. It rose like a wave, and crested, and crashed down upon him. "Mirain! King in Ianon! Mirain!"

He moved away from his judges and his witness. The army of the west advanced with weapons reversed, chanting his name. But his eyes lifted, fixing beyond it where Ianon's mountains marched against the sky. Shadow lay coiled among them. He raised his golden hand. "Someday," he said, "I will chain you."

The Mad One burst free at last from the bonds of his will and plunged into the circle. Herald and squire and scholar parted before him. A hair's breadth from Mirain's body, the flying hoofs settled into stillness. The horned head bent, nostrils flaring at the scent of blood and battle. Softly Obri laid the scarlet cloak about Mirain's shoulders; Vadin set the torque about his throat. The Mad One knelt. Mirain settled in the saddle; smoothly the senel rose.

East and west and all about them, the armies came together, clashed, and mingled. One army, one kingdom. And above them all one banner: The Sun-standard of Ianon's king.

Mirain bowed under the weight of them all: grief and

joy and kingship, and triumph wrested from black defeat. But somewhere in the depths of his soul, he found a seed of strength. His eyes kindled. He drew himself erect, squared his shoulders, flung back his hair. The armies roared his name. He rode forth from the circle to claim his own.